Year's Best SF 4

Edited by David G. Hartwell

Year's Best SF
Year's Best SF 2
Year's Best SF 3
Year's Best SF 4

Published by HarperPrism

Year's Best SF 4

EDITED BY
David G. Hartwell

HarperPrism
A Division of HarperCollinsPublishers

🔥 **HarperPrism**
A Division of HarperCollins*Publishers*
10 East 53rd Street, New York, NY 10022-5299

These are works of fiction. The characters, incidents, and
dialogues are products of the authors' imaginations and are
not to be construed as real. Any resemblance to actual events
or persons, living or dead, is entirely coincidental.

Individual story copyrights appear on pages 483–84.

ISBN 0-06-105902-1

HarperCollins®, 🔥®, and HarperPrism® are trademarks of
HarperCollins Publishers Inc.

Cover illustration © 1999 by John Harris

First printing: June 1999

Printed in the United States of America

Visit HarperPrism on the World Wide Web at
http://www.harperprism.com

❖ 10 9 8 7 6 5 4 3 2 1

To Henry G. Hartwell (1907–1998), a good father, who died in 1998. He was an electrical engineer proud of his MIT degree, in his youth a passionate radio ham who never trusted Hugo Gernsback's magazines because some of the technology didn't work well. He did not often read fiction for pleasure until late in life. I got love of science and technology from him.

Acknowledgments

This part has not changed since last year. The existence of *Locus* and *Tangents* makes doing an annual anthology easier and I thank them both for their devotion to considering the short fiction published each year in the SF field. Secondly, I am grateful to the publishers of the SF magazines for continuing the uphill battle to stay in business and publish fiction in 1998.

Contents

Introduction

It has been another exciting year in the SF field for short fiction. In my survey of the works published, more good original collections cropped up from England and Australia and Canada than in any previous year. And the fiction magazines each had a bunch of good stories. So I must make my usual disclaimer, with perhaps more force than usual: this selection of science fiction stories *represents* the best that was published during the year 1998. In my opinion I could perhaps have filled two or three more volumes this size and then claimed to have nearly all of the best—though not all the best novellas.

Regular readers of this anthology will notice the absence of several familiar names, so let me point out that they have neither stopped writing nor is the quality of their work any less excellent than in other years. I believe that representing the best, while it is not physically possible to encompass it all in one even very large book, also implies presenting some substantial variety of excellences, and I left some writers out in order to include others in this limited space.

Next, my general principle for selection: this book is full of science fiction—every story in the book is clearly that and not something else. I have a high regard for horror, fantasy, speculative fiction, and slipstream and postmodern literature. But here, I chose science fiction. It is the intention of this year's best series to focus entirely on science fiction, and to provide readers who are looking especially for science fiction an annual home base.

After what I perceived as a mediocre year for novellas in 1997, 1998 was a strong year—there were fifteen or more good novellas—but '98 was at least as satisfying in all the shorter forms. *SF Age* had another strong year, as did *Asimov's*; they are unquestionably at the top of the field, and have quite similar tastes in the fiction they publish. There was less SF in *F&SF* and in *Interzone*, but some dynamite stuff in each, and some top-notch stories in the newly revived *Amazing*. *Analog* was uneven, publishing some of the best, and some of the worst stories. *On Spec*, from Canada, and *Eidolon*, from Australia, are generating some first-class writers with excellent stories, too, sometimes SF and sometimes horror or fantasy, as in *Interzone*.

Notable SF original anthologies include *Starlight 2*, edited by Patrick Nielsen Hayden (probably the single strongest fantasy and SF collection of the year); *Bending the Landscape: Science Fiction*, edited by Nicola Griffith and Stephen Pagel (another very strong collection, of stories billed as gay and lesbian writing); *Dreaming Down Under*, edited by Jack Dann and Janeen Webb (an impressive showcase of the best new Australian fantasy and SF writers, in time for this year's World SF convention in Melbourne); *Arrowdreams*, edited by John Dupuis and Mark Shainblum (devoted to alternate history SF about Canada); the latest volume in the *Man-Kzin Wars* series edited by Larry Niven; and the latest volume in the *Writers of the Future* series.

In summary, it was another year in which there were more than sixty or seventy, perhaps over a hundred, really good SF stories published, certainly enough to fill several year's best volumes, providing me with a rich diversity of selection for this one. For more information, including extensive monthly discussion of many fine individual stories, you are referred to Mark Kelly's excellent short fiction review columns in *Locus*.

Sadly, *Tangents*, the other main venue for short fiction reviews and commentary, was late and irregular in 1998, though a new online site has recently been established for the magazine where reviews may begin to be posted in a timely way.

I will make further observations on trends and themes in SF and remarks on the individual excellences of the contents of this book in the notes to the stories, that follow immediately. So here we go, into the best of the year. Follow me.

—David G. Hartwell

Market Report

ALEXANDER JABLOKOV

Alexander Jablokov published his first short story in 1985 and his first novel, *Carve the Sky*, in 1991. He is one of the most interesting SF writers to come to prominence in the 1990s. He has published five novels to date (his latest is *Deepdrive*, 1998), and occasional short stories. Some of his best work is collected in *The Breath of Suspension* (1994). He is part of the Boston-area SF writers workshop chaired by David Alexander Smith, the group that produced the collaborative original anthology, *Future Boston* (1994). The *Encyclopedia of Science Fiction* calls his work "both rounded and exploratory, and . . . generates the sense that an important SF career has gotten well underway." This story appeared in *Asimov's* and is the first of several in this book from that magazine, which seemed to me to publish a slightly higher percentage of SF, as opposed to fantasy of various sorts, again this past year. It was a particularly strong year for *Asimov's*. This was Jablokov's only short fiction this year.

I slid out of the rental car's AC, and the heat of the mid-western night wrapped itself around my face like a wet iguana. Lightning bugs blinked in the unmown grass of my parents' lawn, and cicadas rasped tenaciously at the subdivision's silence. Old Oak Orchard was so new it wasn't even on my most recent DeLorme map CD-ROM, and it had taken me a while to find the place.

My father pulled the door open before I could ring the bell.

"Bert." He peered past me. "Ah. And where is—"

"Stacy's not with me." I'd practiced what to say on the drive from the airport, but still hadn't come up with anything coherent. "We . . . well, let's just say there have been problems."

"So many marriages are ended in the passive voice." His voice was carefully neutral. "Come along back, then. I'll set you up a tent."

Dad wore a pair of once-fashionable pleated linen shorts and a floppy T-shirt with the name of an Internet provider on it. His skin was all dark and leathery, the color of retirement. He looked like he'd just woken up.

"I told Mom when I was coming. . . ."

"Sure." He grabbed my suitcase and wrestled it down the hall. "She must have nailed the note to a tree, and I didn't see it."

I didn't know why I always waited a moment for him to explain things. He never did. I was just sup-posed to catch on. I had spent my whole life trying to catch on.

"Lulu!" he called out the back slider. "Bert's home."

I winced as he dragged my leather suitcase over the sliding door tracks into the backyard. A glowing blue North Face tent sat on the grass. A Coleman lantern pooled yellow on a picnic table stolen from a roadside rest area. The snapped security chain dangled down underneath.

"Lulu!" he yelled, then managed a grin for me. "She must be checking the garden. We get . . . you know . . . slugs. Eat the tomatoes."

The yard didn't end in a garden. Beyond the grass was a dense growth of trees. Now and then headlights from the highway beyond paled the undersides of the maple leaves, but they didn't let me see anything.

"Sure." I sat down at the picnic table. "So how are you, Dad?"

He squinted at me, as if unsure whether I was joking. "Me? Oh, I'm fine. Never better. Life out here agrees with me. Should have done it a long time ago."

Clichés were my father's front defensive line. He was fortifying quickly, building walls in front of questions I hadn't even asked yet.

"Trouble?" I said. "With Mom?" Being subtle is a nonstarter in my family.

"And how is your fast-paced urban lifestyle?" he asked.

"We're working a few things out. A bit of a shakedown period, you might call it."

My parents' entire marriage had been a shakedown period. I was just an interim project that had somehow become permanent. I swear, all through my childhood, every morning they had been surprised to see me come downstairs to breakfast. Even now, my dad was looking at me as if he wasn't entirely sure who I was.

"Well, to start with, Dad, I guess the problems Stacy and I have been having stem from being in the same profession—"

"You know," Dad said, "your mother still has the darkest blue eyes I have ever seen."

"She does have lovely eyes."

"Cornflower blue, I always thought. Her eyes are cornflower blue."

Stacy's eyes were brown, but I guessed my father wasn't interested in hearing about that. "Cornflowers are not the flowers on corn." It had taken me years to figure that out.

"That's right."

"Someone once told me," I said, "that you can hear corn growing at night. It grows so fast on hot summer nights. A night like tonight."

"You need quiet to hear it," he said. "You don't like quiet, do you, Bert?" He was already looking for an argument. "You can't market quiet."

"That's where you're wrong," I said. "There's an ambient recording you can buy of corn growing. Cells dividing. Leaves rustling. Bugs, I don't know, eating the leaves. That little juicy crunch. Call it a grace note."

"And so you play it over your Home Theater system. With subwoofer, side speakers, the works? Pour yourself a single-malt, sit back, relax?"

"You don't *listen* to ambient, Dad. You let it wash over you. Through you. The whole point of modern life is never giving your full attention to any one thing. That gets boring. So you put the corn in the CD stack with the sound of windblown sand eroding the Sphinx, snow falling on the Ross Ice Shelf, the relaxing distant rattle of a horde of lemmings hitting the ocean, pop open your Powerbook to work some spreadsheets, and put a football game on the giant TV. You'll get the Oneness thing happening in no time."

"Are you getting it?" he asked softly. It wasn't like his regular voice at all.

"What?"

"The Oneness. Whatever it is you're looking for."

"There was a time when I was so close I could taste it. . . ."

"Bertram! There you are!" Had my mother just come out of the woods? She was knotting the sash of a fluffy white terrycloth robe, as if she'd just stepped from the bathroom. Her gray hair was cut close to her scalp. She looked great. She always had. Even rubbing sleep out of her eyes, her feet bare. She still painted her toenails, I noticed, and they weren't even chipped. "Franklin, weren't you going to go get him a tent?"

"I was," my dad said.

She hugged me, then tugged at the sleeve of my jacket. "Isn't it a little hot for wool?"

"It's tropic weight," I said. "Gabardine."

"The tropics have nothing on Illinois in August." With that last shot, my dad disappeared into the garage.

"Franklin's right. Here." An antique steamer trunk stood on end next to where the house's air-conditioning unit poked out of the rhododendrons.

Then my jacket was off, my tie was gone, and I was sitting at the picnic table with an iced glass of cranberry juice in my hand. Mothers do card tricks with comfort. All Dad had offered me was an argument—but then that was his way of letting me know I was home.

"Did the power go out, Mom?" I said.

She laughed. "Oh, no. How do you think I made the ice cubes? It's just the way we live now. Out here in the country."

Now that I had a chance to relax, I could see that the other backyards visible had encampments in them too: tents, tables, meat smokers, greenhouses, even a Port-O-Let or two. I could hear people talking quietly, even at this hour, and smell the smoke of banked cookfires. Something was wrong, seriously wrong, with this exclusive residential community. I should have known it as soon as my mom gave me the cranberry juice. Her comfort meant that something was not right.

There were times in my childhood when everything had been stable. For a couple of years, for example, my dad had worked in a regular pet store, selling neon tetras and spaniels to wide-eyed children who would lose interest in them as soon as they got them home. We'd lived in a suburban house with a yard, all that, and I'd been able to tell the other kids what my dad did for a living. The TV shows I watched seemed to be intended to be watched by people living the life I then lived.

But during that time my mother had barely paid attention to me. TV dinners had been the order of the day, and I remembered a lot of drive-thru eating. She thought I was safe, then, and could take care of myself.

It was times like when my dad tried to build a submerged house at the bottom of an abandoned water-filled quarry and stock the water with ornamental piranha that my mother would bake me apple cobbler and paint farm scenes with smiling cows on the riveted bulkhead in my room. She had always intervened to keep the panic in my memories on a perfectly even keel.

"I should have known," I said.

Ice cubes clinked in my empty glass and she refilled it. "Known what, Bertram?"

"That you and Dad could turn the most wholesome of carefully planned and secure communities into something disturbing. And here I thought, while driving around, that you two had finally settled down, so that I could visit you without fear. Nice neighborhood, Old Oak Orchard."

She looked off at the glowing tents of the neighbors. "It is a nice neighborhood. Do you smell roasting joints from oxen and goats hissing fat on ancient sacrificial stones? Hear the minor-key chants of the priests as they rip open the jugulars of bellowing kine with their bronze blades? Does that make you afraid?"

"Lulubelle." My father broke a branch on a forsythia as he wrestled a heavy bundle out of the garage. My mother winced. "You're frightening the boy with all this pseudo-biblical 'kine' stuff. That's cows, Bert, if you don't know. Herefords, Black Anguses. Besides, Lulu, you know our whole concept's not really about . . . that sort of thing. That's not the point."

"I thought we had agreed to disagree on the point, Franklin." I noticed that my mother had scratches up and down her arms, and that one of her little fingers was in a splint. Both Dad and I heard the danger in her tone.

He held up the tent. "It's canvas, Bert. White duck. Heavy as hell. You know, I saw some hunters out in the Gila with one of these once. They packed in on horses, and fried up a mess of potatoes in a cast-iron pan two feet across. My friend and I ate some kind of reconstituted gunk out of a plastic bowl. They were hunting elk with black-powder rifles. The things looked like cannon."

He'd told me the story before, but the actual physical tent was a new element. It was as if he now needed some real substance behind the memory. My father swore under his breath as he put the thing up. I knew better than to try and help him. It had all sorts of complicated ribs and locking joints. He pinched some skin and got real quiet. You could hear him breathing through his nostrils.

"Oh, come on, Bertram." My mother chuckled. "You won't see any animal-headed gods in the Lopezes' backyard, so quit staring. I was just . . . kidding."

She was really being hard on me. She'd noticed Stacy's absence, but wasn't going to ask about it. I was sure it pleased her, though.

"It's late, Lu." My father looked hungrily at my

mother. Men should not look at their own wives that way, and particularly not at the mothers of their sons.

"Yes," she said. "It's time for bed."

It was a peacemaking gesture of some sort. They'd been at war, but my arrival had brought them together. My mother smiled at me over her shoulder as she followed him into their dome tent. It was the same old story. My parents had always disappeared behind their locked bedroom door, sometimes in the middle of the day, sometimes when I was sitting down in the living room with uncomfortable shoes on, waiting to go to some relative's house, and I wasn't even allowed to turn the TV on.

I woke up. I hadn't really slept. It was quiet. Still dark. I was thirsty. I walked across the lawn to the back door. The cut ends of the grass tickled my bare feet. It was a great feeling, a suburban feeling. The stars were weirdly bright. The Milky Way was something you wanted to wipe off with a sponge.

The sliding glass door to the kitchen wasn't locked. As a child, I'd always asked for kitchen water rather than bathroom water. My mother would go downstairs for me. The stairs creaked and I would hear her and know that she loved me. My father would go into the bathroom, make a lot of noise so I knew he hadn't gone anywhere, even flush the toilet, and then come back and tell me that it was the finest kitchen water there was. If I was thirsty enough, I would believe him.

The kitchen was dark. I felt the edge of a Corian countertop. I worked my way toward the sink. I saw the high faucet silhouetted against the window. Wet on my fingers. Something was soaking in the full sink. The water did not feel soapy. The glasses would be in this cabinet over here.

Something hissed at me. For a second I thought it was air-conditioning after all, despite how hot it was in the kitchen. Then I saw the eyes.

"What is that thing he's got in his mouth?" my father said. He peered up above the cabinets, into the shadows cast by the lamp. "A vole? Do we have voles? Or is that a star-nosed mole? Native or . . . recreated?"

"Franklin," my mother said.

From a cookie jar shaped like a squat Chrysler Building she gave me a Tollhouse cookie. It couldn't have been baked more than a couple of hours before, probably about the time I was landing at O'Hare. The chocolate chips were still a little liquid. They unfurled themselves across my tongue. I lay on the textured floor. I didn't want to get up.

A magnet on the white dishwasher said CLEAN. The symbol for CLEAN was the smoking rubble of a city. I reached up and turned it over. DIRTY was that city whole, veiled in a haze of smog. A typical example of one of my father's deep ecology jokes. Smog is one of those antique sixties-type symbols he's always using as if they were arguments.

This time my father heard the warning in my mother's voice. He squatted down next to me. His knees cracked.

"Sorry, Bert," he said. "I guess I should have told you."

"Told me what? That you have animals in your sink?"

"It was a fisher."

I caught glimpses of the creature as it snaked its way across the tops of the cabinets, some kind of rodent limp in its mouth. It looked like a big weasel. Its eyes gleamed down at me in the lantern light. Its eyes . . .

"A fisher?" I didn't look at it. Frogs made a low thrumming noise in the sink. An owl hooted out in the living room. Things examined us from outside the circle of light. When I was little, and wouldn't go get a drink of water myself, this was what I had known it was really like out there.

"Actually, it's an extinct species of mustelid," he said. "This one vanished about the time the ice sheets left North America. It's part of a controlled breeding experiment, the reason we've moved here to Old Oak Orchard. We regress the DNA of animals that went extinct around the Pleistocene and implant it in related ova."

"Oh, God, Dad. Remember that time you raised insulated sea turtles to give rides at that Aleutian beach resort?"

The resort had been run as some government benefit for impoverished Aleuts. All I remembered of the experience was thick clouds, rocks, and giant lumbering shells covered with barnacles, all roughly the same shade of gray. I didn't remember the turtles having any heads. My only entertainment had been working on a seaweed collection. It had all climaxed in a riot by the disillusioned locals, who had invested heavily in beach-front cabanas and glitzy casinos, and blamed my father for the fact that sea turtle rides through choppy ice water failed to draw more tourists. Most of the turtles had been stewed in their own shells on the rocky beach in a drunken feast. Sea lions had barked their approval somewhere out in the mist, which glowed orange with the burning cabanas as we pulled away in our fiberglass *bidarka*. My mother had made my very favorite chili mac while we were there, and tucked me into bed every night with a sweet lullaby in a foreign language.

"We were undercapitalized, that's all." My dad was irritated at having it brought up. "The failure wasn't biological."

"No, they never are—"

"You're cranky, Bertram." My mother supported my shoulders, and I sat up. "Not enough sleep."

She had an almost suntan lotion smell, even though it was still dark. Some kind of collagen replacement cream. It was a comfort, to realize that my mother wanted to stay young. It was something to hold on to. The extinct mustelid slunk into shadows and did not come back out.

The lighter and fluffier my mom's scrambled eggs, the worse things were—a classic rule. This morning, with the innocent light streaming in through the kitchen windows, they were like clouds. I had looked around the house, but most of its nocturnal dwellers seemed to have hidden themselves in the cupboards and cabinets.

"Is Dad driving you crazy?" I asked. The orange juice was metallic, from concentrate, so maybe there was some hope.

"Since when hasn't he?" She smiled. "But this time I'm driving *him* crazy too. I came here under protest— who wants to move out to one of these bland compounds out in the middle of nowhere, even to raise extinct fauna? Really, that's no different than playing golf until you die, don't you think?"

I didn't tell her how happy I had been to see the place, to feel its stolid normality. Sodden, heavy scrambled eggs would have been a small price to pay to know that I was, at last, safe.

"But I've found things to do. I've found ways to enjoy this little place. And that, as you can guess, drives your dad bananas. I'm using it *wrong*, you see. I'm not enjoying it the proper way." She produced a day-labeled pillbox, and started filling it with red, yellow, and green pills. Sunday through Saturday. Her week was set up.

"And how are you enjoying it, Mother?"

She held up a deep-green lozenge. "Do you think my body used to produce this, and then stopped? What gland do you suppose made it?" The pill had a particularly hard gleam, like a liquid-oxygen tank on a Pixar-generated spacecraft in an SF movie.

"I don't know."

"You know how all these Pleisto-kooks got together? They all used to belong to the same Internet newsgroup. They'd trade breeding tips, give each other heads-up on available DNA sequencers and incubators. Then, a bunch of them decided to live together and work on a big project. They bought into Old Oak Orchard en masse. Some of these people were quite wealthy."

"It's the latest thing, you know," I said. "The transformation of virtual communities into real ones. One of those wonderful retrogressive steps that makes my job so much fun."

She sighed. "I know mothers can never explain their children's jobs right nowadays, and it always drives the kids crazy. But if you'd only have normal jobs, like, I don't know, accountant, or wrestler, or weatherman, or something . . ."

"Wrestler?"

"Then we could just *say* it, and people would know what we meant."

"I've *told* you what Stacy and I do. Call us experimental demographers. That's close enough."

There, I'd brought up the dread name. My mom pursed her lips, but maybe it was because she didn't like the OJ either. "That's not really what you are, is it?"

"No, Mom." I knew she could hear the sadness in my voice. "That's not really what I am. Not anymore."

"Oh, Bertram." Her eyes filled with tears. "I don't know who pushed whom, but she's gone, isn't she?"

"As gone as it gets. And my job along with her."

"She meant so much to you. . . ." She'd never liked Stacy, but she knew what hurt her son.

"The last job we did . . ." I said. "Stacy soloed, I only advised. She was good, real good. I'd taught her how to spot potentially self-defined groups . . . she found a little community of interest among teenagers. A disaffected layer in a lot of high schools, all across the country. People think it's all mass marketing, but that's not where the real value-added stuff comes in, not any more. These kids didn't identify themselves as any sort of group, but I could—Stacy could tell from what they bought, the kind of magazines they read, the web sites they hit, and music they listened to, and the street drugs they took, that they were looking for something. Something they hadn't found yet. So she gave it to them."

"What?" My mother was interested despite herself.

"The past. The real deep past. It just took a little marketing push, and they started mail-ordering flint blanks for spear points, birth-control dispensers in the shape of Paleolithic fertility figurines, ink-jet-sprayed wall paintings to conjure up mammoths. It was just this group, but they were really into it. Their rooms at home must have looked like Altamira or Lascaux. When the trend tanks you won't be able to *give* that Acheulean stuff away, but that's off in . . . the future."

My mother stood up and ran gnarled fingers through her short gray hair. She didn't look young. I wouldn't pretend that. She was old, she was my mother. But she had more light in her eyes than she'd had in years. She also had scratches on her hands, and calluses on her palms, like she'd been working hard somewhere outdoors for quite some time. My mother had never been a gardener and, in fact, there was no trace of any garden in the yard. I'd looked for it.

"You think you're so smart, don't you?" Her tone was bitter.

"Mom, I—"

"Talk to your dad. I mean, really talk to him. I think you still need a few lessons in what life is really like."

She walked out of the kitchen. A few minutes later I heard the door to the yard ease open. I craned my head out the kitchen window, but couldn't see where she went. I sat down to another cup of coffee. Something that looked a lot like a badger poked its head out from under the sink, saw me, and pulled back. The little door clicked back onto its magnet.

"Dad," I said. "I think you got some problems." Mom had gotten me thinking about the possible consequences of his new project. I felt like I was back on the job. It bugged me how much I liked that feeling.

"You're telling me?" He spent some time putting the ball on his tee. "I thought your mother and I could work together on this. Instead, she made a bunch of new girlfriends and now spends her time hunting ungulates in the woods with spears. Is that anything a woman her age should be doing?" He swung at the ball with his driver. It sliced viciously, off into the dark woods that bordered the course. In all our years together, this was the first time he'd ever taken me golfing. I already didn't like it.

"I . . . well, actually, you know, Dad, it's really about time. It's good for her to do something like that."

"God, I knew you'd take her side."

"I'm not taking her side!"

"Deer liver. I'm talking deer liver for supper, with forest mushrooms, fiddleheads, all sorts of sick hunter-gatherer crap. She just doesn't seem to get the *post*-technological nature of our enterprise. She's a woman who skulks with the foxes." He left the course and started hacking his way through the underbrush. I followed.

"Dad," I said. "Are we chasing after her? Bugging her?"

"Eh?" I'd caught him. He scratched the back of his head. "Not at all. A golf course is a good place to work out a few intellectual problems. That's all. Golf is the perfect combination of mathematics and frustration."

"Let her be, Dad. She has a right to do what she wants." Even if it was some up-market version of an old mid-teen trendlet. No wonder she'd gotten irritated with me. "You're doing what you want, aren't you?"

"I don't know. I don't know. I had a different idea when I came here . . . it doesn't work without Louise." He never called my mother Louise. Lulu, Lulubelle, Looly, all sorts of things. She never liked her given name. "You know, she spends all night out sometimes. Getting nocturnal on me. Pretty soon, her eyes will grow a tapetum and reflect in the headlights. And I'll never see her again."

"Dad, that's just not true, and you know it."

"I want you to help me talk to your mother." His voice was quiet now, matching the hush of the dense forest in which I was already completely lost. "That's all."

"Not here, Dad," I pleaded. "Don't try to talk to her here."

"I have to. I can't stand it anymore. Back me up, will you, son?"

They created me as a ref. Both of them. I might as well have been born with a black-and-white striped shirt on and a whistle in my mouth. I was the go-between in all their arguments.

"Dammit." He tripped over a thick tree root. "Where do you suppose that thing's gone? It was a good one, Titleist."

He was maintaining the imposture, even though we'd now been wandering in this thick jungle for a quarter of an hour. He'd occasionally brush some wild sarsaparilla or poison ivy aside with his iron, but he never actually looked at the ground underneath for his ball.

"Dad," I said. "Do you remember when you used to take me camping?"

"Eh?" That caught him by surprise. "Sure, of course I do."

"Why did you stop?"

"Stop?"

"Stop taking me!"

"You didn't like it."

"How did you know that?"

"Know what?"

That took a deep breath. "That I didn't like it."

"You just didn't, that's all. It was hard, you got blisters, we got rained on, the food was always kind of grainy or lumpy. Don't you remember? Those trails, mud where they weren't trippy rocks, bugs, and nothing, nothing to do except walk and look at stuff."

I didn't remember hating it. Oh, sure, I bet there were times when I had been a real pain in the butt, not wanting to poop in a trench, or unwilling to get out of a warm sleeping bag to greet the icy dawn, or whining over my blisters. But I remembered happiness when I would wake up in the middle of the night, moonlight streaming through the mosquito netting, trees rustling in the breeze, my father's heavy bulk snoring next to me. The mountains at sunrise had looked something like heaven.

"You shouldn't have stopped taking me, Dad," I said. "You love it." He still went every year, with his increasingly creaky friends he'd been going with since high school. "It's something to share."

"You can say that, but you didn't have to put up with you. All the questions, all the suggestions. Sometimes it was technical—ways of packing more efficiently, that sort of thing. But sometimes it was, I don't know, spiritual or something. How we could enjoy ourselves better. How we could be more ourselves. I tell you, Bert, that's a little hard to take when all you want to do is go on a hike."

He and his friends Bill and Frank had been the sort of limited demographic I later made my career out of satisfying. They weren't high-intensity rock-face-sleeping types. I did vaguely remember trying to figure out why they liked what they did, and how they could like it better. My dad's gear had even been pretty lame. For example, the waterproofing had come off the bottom of his tent and it always got a little wet.

I was starting to remember now. A fight. Not even on the trail, but before. I'd hauled his tent out of the garage, where he'd packed it up wet, cleaned all the dirt and grass off of it, and re-waterproofed the bottom. It had taken me all afternoon, patiently coating every square inch with the goo. While I was at it, I sealed all the seams. My father never really understood that they sold you the tent with the seams unsealed, so rain had always run down the stitching. When I was done you could have used that tent as a boat. I stood back, hands on my hips, and admired it as it stood in the backyard.

"What are you doing?" my father had said behind me, and I turned to explain.

I didn't remember the anger itself. All I remembered was his car driving away, his friends Bill and Frank sitting in it instead of me, both of them incredibly embarrassed. I had solved a problem for him, and that was something he just couldn't stand. All of my mother's entreaties had been useless. I had to stay behind. I was too young, he said. Too much trouble to take along. Maybe when I was older . . . That had been the last time.

"Maybe we can just go for a hike sometime," I said. "Let's count this as a start."

For a moment we moved in synch through the trees, as if we were together, heading for the same place.

"Let me take advantage of your expertise for a moment, Bert," he said. My dad had always known exactly what I did, though he had never approved of it. "Could you find us? I mean, if you were back in your office. Without knowing anything about us, would we pop up when you searched for unusual patterns in purchases?"

"Sure." I'd already been thinking about it. "This operation can't just bootstrap up from nothing. You had to have bought all sorts of things, gotten all sorts of technical information. All of that can be traced."

"But that's not so bad, is it? All you'd want to do is sell us more things. My dinner of antelope and tree bark will be interrupted by a call from someone trying to offer me a zone electrophoresis setup or a subscription to an Embryo of the Month club. Free samples of restriction enzymes and mammoth kibble in the mail. Right?"

He wanted me to reassure him. This was my territory.

I couldn't do it.

"You know, Dad, when I met Stacy, she was just a research assistant. Not mine, understand, just in the department. But she was eager to learn. She had a Ph.D. in sociology, but thought her whole life would be studying something like the distribution of ethnic first names in middle-class households. I showed her the ropes."

"She seemed . . . I don't know, Bert. She never seemed like your type. Dumb word, I know. Not clear at all. But what upset your mother was that, when you visited, you never seemed . . . yourself. Now, that's natural when you're starting out, I guess. . . ."

"I worked it, Dad. I mean, I really worked it. You have no idea how far I went. I wanted her . . . at first it was just sort of ambition. She was beautiful, right? But that wasn't all. She was so sharp, so crisp. So *focused*. For a while she focused on me. I melted. I resisted, that wasn't my plan, but it happened before I knew it. I don't know . . . I don't know if *she* ever did. There comes that moment, you know? Where the other person . . . melts. I always deluded myself into thinking it had happened. My game just wasn't good enough."

"Your mother, for example, was very resistant." Dad was reminiscent. "Somehow, my line of nonsense didn't particularly charm her. Imagine that! But one day, we went out canoeing. There were a lot of toppled cottonwoods in the river, and several times we had to pull the canoe over them. It was hot, and there were a lot of bugs. It should have made us cranky with each other, but instead, each drag across made us more of a team. I fell in the mud, more than once. Your mother wore white shorts and a light blue blouse with a collar. I remember her staying completely clean, she remembers herself getting covered with drying mud. That was all fine, it was a step forward. Mosquito bites and all, it was something we'd shared. Then, just as we were getting ready to turn around and go home, a water moccasin swam slowly out to us. Now, I knew a thing or two about poisonous snakes at the time—I had a Pentecostalist friend who made a great living at county fairs— and I was able to . . . hypnotize it, I guess you'd say. It fell asleep on my paddle, eyes still open, and your mother stroked its head. She wasn't afraid. She trusted me. Then she looked at me and . . . I knew it had happened. Nothing would ever be the same again. After that—"

"Dad—" He was pushing it.

"Oh, no details, no details. Not about the rest of that day, anyway. But after that, we got married and I started a viper ranch. I saw it as fate. Your mother helped raise the money to start it. After a year or two, it failed, and we had to let the snakes go. It still gives me a tear to remember the black mamba slithering across the parking lot toward the drainage ditch by the highway. . . . But, you know, your mom never faltered. She always stood by me. And she was already pregnant with you, by then. Given the amount of venom she encountered during her pregnancy, I'll bet you're immune to a wide range of toxins."

"I've never really had the chance to check that out. But Stacy . . . I suppose it was a cliché man/woman relationship, mentor and pupil. But she was so sharp! It was like no one had ever listened to me before—"

"You know, son, I've been meaning to work on that, really I have. . . ."

"That doesn't matter! For the first time, someone focused her full attention on me. It's an incredible rush. I never knew. . . . We fell in love. You know the rest. We became a team. I molded her, taught her everything."

My father cleared his throat. "For what it's worth, Bert, I think she really did . . . love you. That one time you visited . . . maybe she didn't melt. But you got her as close to it as anyone possibly could." He shook his head. "Your mother would kill me if she heard me telling you that."

I blinked my eyes and looked around. "Boy, this place really is a jungle."

"Yeah. They've gone too far, is all I can say. We get together, try to recreate a few species, just a gentle hobby, like miniature trains or building ships in bottles . . . and these guys go completely berserk. That's life in the exurbs for you. All sense of social control is lost. Your mom has to be somewhere around here. . . ."

My dad pulled a machete out of his golf bag and hacked at the trailing vines and lianas. Leaves flew around him, but he didn't make much headway. He'd had muscle once. I remembered him mowing the lawn with his shirt off. He'd insisted on a push mower. It was an old one he'd bought at a yard sale. Being my father, he'd never lubricated it right, and the blades were so dull they sort of folded the grass instead of cutting it. But I remembered his delts and back muscles gleaming with sweat as he struggled and swore and dug gouges in the lawn. In later years, Mom would have me borrow an incredibly noisy and smelly power mower from the Hendersons next door and cut the grass while he was away for the day. If my father ever noticed anything, he didn't think it worth mentioning, and eventually he stopped using the push mower. He left it outside by the side of the house and it rusted into a solid lump of metal.

But now his skin sagged down over slack muscle. I could tell his joints hurt by the clumsy way he swung the blade. Tomorrow he'd be awake before the first light of day with a rotator cuff on fire, slathering on the Ben-Gay. And he hadn't sharpened the damn blade. Some things never change.

"Dad."

"What?"

"Could I do that?"

He looked at me over his shoulder. "You ever handle a machete?"

"Just let me try it. Come on."

"It's not a toy, Bert. It's a very specialized tool, regardless of what you might have seen in some damn blowgun epic—ouch, dammit!"

The blade rebounded from a particularly resistant vine and the blunt trailing edge bounced off his forehead. I caught him under the arms as he fell backward. The machete embedded itself dramatically into a rotting tree stump and stood there, cracked Bakelite handle up.

He looked up at me. He'd have a bruise, but he hadn't broken the skin.

"Bert," he said. "What finally happened?"

"With Stacy?"

"With whatever."

I helped him to his feet. He'd lost a lot of muscle but he didn't feel any lighter. Without any objection from him, I pulled the machete out of its tree stump and started hacking at the vines. It was harder than it looked. A lot harder. Blowgun epics . . . I couldn't remember ever seeing any of those, no late-night TV viewings of *Yamomano!* or *Death on the Amazon*, but I suppose there could be such things, made on virtual soundstages in Malaysia.

"She was smarter even than I thought. Or maybe I was a better teacher than I ever imagined. You see, I'd marketed myself. I'd created an interest group for her, found what she'd secretly wanted, and gave it to her. Mom was right. I wasn't myself. I was an ad for myself. A good one, much better than the actual product. So she finally figured out. By then she was good, better than I was at what I do. We had our last fight when I said I could *become* my ad, really be what I had for so long pretended. She'd never know the truth, I told her. She would be living with the man she'd always thought I was. I was pathetic."

It was hard, remembering her contempt. I'd taught her to see clearly and here I was trying to get her to put blinders on again. I think it was that anger that drove her to what she did next. In the aftermath, I was forced to submit my resignation.

"She left the company when she left me and moved on to the *Interrogator On-Line* TV show. She uses what she learned for tabloid TV segments. She spots and exposes incipient cults, weird social groups, fads, that sort of thing. It's the coming thing. There are more bizarre groups all the time. And the first group she outed was us, my company. A bunch of paranoid megalomaniacs who think that they control the private interests and identities of millions of Americans."

"Us," he said. "Isn't that right? You're saying she's after *us*."

My old man wasn't so stupid after all. That was exactly what I was saying, I realized. I just hadn't known it myself. My dear Stacy could be floating above us right now in one of the media's black helicopters, scanning us, getting ready to drop a camera team down and expose this place on national TV. That fisher wouldn't make much of an image, but there had to be something more interesting around here. . . .

"Dad—"

"Look out!" He knocked me over.

I went down. The tawny shape of the springing animal blurred over us. It hit, turned quickly . . . but did not leap to finish us off. Instead, it sat back on its haunches.

It was a big cat, like a lion or a tiger. Except—I had to look again. I didn't know a lot of biology, but I did know that there wasn't anything in a zoo that looked like a tiger but had tusks like a walrus. It made a low rumble I could feel in my chest, and lashed its tail. In knocking me over, my father had twisted my ankle. All I could feel down there was that pressure that was the shadow of future pain.

"They're pretty near-sighted," my father said. "I don't think we should move."

"What the hell is that thing?"

"Eh? Oh. It's a smilodon. Call it a saber-toothed tiger, though that's not very accurate."

"Whatever it is, it's opening its mouth at us. I don't think I can move."

"If it's anything like a tiger, that's called flehmen. It's using its vomeronasal organ—trying to smell us. Which way is the wind blowing?"

I looked up at the leaves to see if I could tell, and found myself mesmerized by the sky. The trees stretched what seemed hundreds of feet up, and their gigantic crowns spread out against the placid blue. Birds flew back and forth up there. I could smell the thick loam under my head, and a single shaft of sunlight pierced through the upper stories and lay on the side of my face, as warm as a mother's kiss. Lacy-winged insects flickered through and were gone.

"Are you all right?" My father was so close I could feel his breath as he spoke.

"I don't know. My ankle . . ."

My father prodded at it, which actually did make it hurt.

"I have something to tell you," he said.

"What's that?"

"I have no idea whether it's broken or not. I don't know what to look for."

The saber-toothed tiger, as if puzzled by our incompetence, lay down completely and yawned again.

"I'm sorry, boy."

"That's okay, Dad."

"No it's not. I shouldn't have brought you here. It's between your mother and me."

"It's between all of us," I said.

"Will she . . . will Stacy find us, do you think?"

"If you've been buying the gear and subscribing to the magazines I think you have, yeah. I doubt the next development over buys as much as a single cloning setup a year, even as a gift."

"You got that right," he said. "The Menhir Manors people are mostly shamanistic fire worshippers. I think your mother has some bridge-playing friends over there. Buy briquettes by the truckload, but no restriction enzymes."

"Oh, God." I rubbed my forehead. "Another Internet newsgroup that decided to settle down in the exurbs?"

"Actually, I think most of them got a number to call off photocopied announcements on the walls of tattoo parlors. Traditionalists, the lot of them. But even they have to put gas-stack scrubbers on those big brazen idols of theirs, or they'll catch an EPA raid. But what can we do, Bert?"

Did the weight of his need make me feel lighter, or heavier? I wasn't sure.

"Franklin." My mother's voice, from somewhere off in the underbrush. "What are you doing here?"

"Lulu!" He shouted, even though she wasn't more than a few feet away. "It's important."

"Go away. I'll see you at dinner."

"Please! And Bert's twisted his ankle. That damn giant kitty . . ."

"Don't fuss about the smilodon. She doesn't hurt anyone. Besides, she hunts large game. Those teeth aren't any use against something as puny as a human being."

A rustle in the leaves, and five women appeared; my mother among them. There was nothing remarkable about them, really. They ranged in age from their midtwenties to at least their sixties, and my mother wasn't even the oldest. Several carried composite bows with pulleys on them. One had a dead rabbit hanging from her belt. They could have been students at some Adult Extension class.

A woman in her early thirties, with wild black hair, knelt down next to me. After silently examining my ankle, she pulled an instant-cold pack out of her bag and cracked the inside partition. Then she attached it to my ankle with an Ace bandage.

"RICE," she said. "Rest, ice, compression, elevation. Can you handle it?"

"Sure. Particularly the rest part."

I could smell the stink of her crudely cured buck-skins, but somehow that did not make her seem less attractive. Her face looked like she'd spent a lot of time squinting into the sun.

"Stacy!" My mother shrieked at what my dad told her. "I knew it." She knelt by me. "Oh, baby. I'm sorry. I know she meant a lot to you. You loved her."

"Don't embarrass him, Looly."

"I'm not . . . am I embarrassing you, Bert?"

"Yes, Mom, you are."

She sat back. "Well! Try to show a little maternal warmth—"

"He knows that, Lu. You know he does. But he has other things on his mind."

"What? He's a refugee, Franklin. When your marriage ends . . . you've lost your country. Your native language. Everything. And he's come here to us. . . ."

Was that what had happened? I wasn't sure any more. Sometimes what seems like free will is only the following of the deepest patterns, the ones you can no way resist. Stacy didn't need me, and in the aftermath of her departure, it seemed that no one did. Except here.

"Ladies!" I said. "Do you mind if I explain a few things to you?"

"Of course not." The black-haired woman patted my hand. "We know what helps a man relax."

"Don't patronize me. This is serious. I'll give you the information, and you can decide what you want to do with it. Now, imagine if Old Oak Orchard was on the cover of *Time*, the subject of three tabloid news shows, and had tiger-striped tour busses coming through to look at the fauna. What would that mean to your lives?"

That got their attention, big time. They sat around me in a circle and watched me closely.

"You've concealed yourselves pretty well. From

outside, you look just like any other exurban residential community centered on a golf course. Kudos for that. But, and this is even more important, all of your purchases can be tracked." I told them how they could be found, how, in fact, I would have found them a few months before, if that had been my job.

I felt a sudden surge of power as I spoke. I had no idea why changing from predator to prey felt so liberating, but it did.

"But there's one thing they aren't used to, those searchers after fads. They aren't prepared for a deliberate deception. They aren't ready for someone to be on to their game. Fake purchases, odd magazine subscriptions, anomalous hits on Internet sites. If we massage the statistics just right, we can send them baying off after entire demographic shoals of red herrings."

And a brilliantly specific deception came to me in a flash. A play with excavation equipment rental, freeze-dried food supply purchases, air recirculation systems, self-tanning gels . . . the works. It would show an incipient self-defining group. Call it Bomb Shelter Chic. Late-middle-age security-minded exurbanites moving into underground palaces. Stacy and her compadres would eat that up. The kitschy paranoia of the past made for the cool trends of the future. A few Morlock Madness Midnights at the local mall, and we'd have everyone from Malaysian marketeers to *Hardcopy* video journalists looking desperately for something that did not exist.

And that was only the beginning. Canned calves brains packed in caul fat on the Upper West Side of Manhattan, hyena-print sarongs in northern Minnesota, and sophisticated digital recording equipment in Shreveport would send the entire system wobbling on its axis. Old Oak Orchard would vanish into an Antarctica of white noise. We could survive.

The smilodon watched me carefully as I spoke. Did it know I was protecting it from exposure? Perhaps it would not have approved. Maybe it wanted to be in commercials. The woman with the buckskins and the bow—maybe she wanted to get the endorsements, like a beach volleyball star. But, no. The essence of the new marketing paradigm was that not everyone wants the same thing, no matter how much easier that made production.

Those women gave me a standing ovation. It felt good. I was here. I was at work. Then they picked up their bows and faded back into the woods.

I looked around for my father. He had passed the ball to me, and I wondered how he felt about it. At some level, of course, he had hoped, all the way along, that I would solve his problems for him. Still, it couldn't have been easy. I did remember that he had taken that damn waterproofed tent on that camping trip with his friends. I was sure he'd stayed dry.

He talked quietly with my mother. I wondered if either of them had paid any attention at all to my world-beater speech.

"Hey," I said. "Could I get a little help here?"

With their support, I managed to limp along, one arm on each of their shoulders.

"That woman," I said. "The one who fixed my ankle . . ."

"Jennifer?" my mother said.

"Her name is Jennifer?"

"Look, Bertram, having a popular first name is not the kiss of death. But you wouldn't be interested in her."

"Why not?"

"Well, she's really a bit of a tomboy."

"Mom, you run around the woods hunting deer with bow and arrow."

"Really, Bertram, as if that's relevant. Jennifer is not your type."

"Do we have any lasagna at home?" my father asked.

"Some of the spinach," my mother said.

"Spinach? None of the sausage?"

"We finished that on Tuesday. Is the spinach a problem?"

"No, of course not."

"I can make some sausage up fresh."

"Oh, no . . . no, don't take the trouble."

"It's no trouble." She shook her head. "Jennifer. Imagine."

"Give the boy a break."

"Please, Dad." I hated the way they talked about me right in front of me. "That's not important."

"That was quite a speech. Thanks for saving our saggy polyester-clad butts, son."

He made me laugh, even though my mom didn't seem to think it was funny.

"You're welcome, Dad."

Why was my mom working so hard at trying to make Jennifer seem interestingly forbidden? Was she really learning more about how her son's mind worked, even at this late date? That was a scary thought. I was more part of my family than I had thought.

"Your mother's lasagna will set you back on your feet in no time," my father said. "Even if it is spinach."

"I told you, I can *make* sausage. . . ."

Impossible creatures lurked in the underbrush, but I knew I was home.

A Dance to Strange Musics

GREGORY BENFORD

Gregory Benford is a plasma physicist and astrophysicist, and one of the leading SF writers of the last twenty-five years. He is a science columnist for *F&SF*, and in February 1999 published his first popular science book, *Deep Time*. In the last few years he has formed a group, with Greg Bear and David Brin, Reading for the Future, that advocates science fiction reading in junior and senior high schools. One of the chief spokesmen of hard SF of the last twenty years, Benford is articulate and contentious, and he has produced some of the best fiction of recent decades about scientists working, and about the riveting and astonishing concepts of cosmology and the nature of the universe. His most famous novel is *Timescape*, his most recent, *Cosm* (1998). In 1998 he published this story in two versions, in the small press magazine *Age of Wonders* and in *SF Age*. This text is the second, and longer, version. "A Dance to Strange Musics" is like a compressed Benford novel, with all the ideas, characters, speculations, and imaginative surprises packed into an episodic 8,500 words—much of the pleasure of a whole book in only a half an hour of reading.

Section 1

The first crewed starship, the *Adventurer*, hung like a gleaming metallic moon among the gyre of strange worlds. Alpha Centauri was a triple-star system. A tiny flare star dogged the two big suns. At this moment in its eternal dance, the brilliant mote swung slightly toward Sol. Even though it was far from the two bright stars it was the nearest star to Earth: Proxima.

The two rich, yellow stars defined the Centauri system. Still prosaically termed A and B, they swam about each other, ignoring far Proxima.

The *Adventurer*'s astronomer, John, dopplered in on both stars, refreshing memories that were lodged deep. The climax of his career loomed before him. He felt apprehension, excitement, and a thin note of something like fear.

Sun B had an orbital eccentricity of 0.52 about its near-twin, with the extended axis of its ellipse 23.2 astronomical units long. This meant that the closest approach between A and B was a bit farther than the distance of Saturn from Sol.

A was a hard yellow-white glare, a G star with 1.08 the Sun's mass. Its companion, B, was a K-class star that glowed a reddish yellow, since it had 0.88 times the Sun's mass. B orbited with a period of 80 years around A. These two were about 4.8 billion years of age, slightly older than Sol. Promising.

Sun A's planetary children had stirred *Adventurer*'s expedition forth from Earth. From Luna, the system's single Earth-class planet was a mere mote, first detected by an oxygen absorption line in its spectrum. Only a wobbly image could be resolved by Earth's kilometer-sized interferometric telescope, a long bar with mirror-eyes peering in the spaces between A and B. Just enough of an image to entice.

A new Earth? John peered at its shrouded majesty, feeling the slight hum and surge of their ship beneath him. They were steadily moving inward, exploring the Newtonian gavotte of worlds in this two-sunned ballroom of the skies. Proxima was so far away, it was not even a wallflower.

The Captain had named the fresh planet Shiva. It hung close to A, wreathed in water cirrus, a cloudball dazzling beneath A's simmering yellow-white glare. Shimmering with promise, it had beckoned to John for years during their approach.

Like Venus, but the gases don't match, he thought. The complex tides of the star system massaged Shiva's depths, releasing gases and rippling the crust. John's many-frequency probings had told him a lot, but how to stitch data into a weave of a world? He was the first astronomer to try out centuries of speculative thinking on a real planet.

Shiva was drier than Earth, oceans taking only 40 percent of the surface. Its air was heavy in nitrogen, with giveaway tags of 18 percent oxygen and traces of carbon dioxide; remarkably Earth-like. Shiva was too warm for comfort, in human terms, but not fatally so; no Venusian runaway greenhouse had developed here. How had Shiva escaped that fate?

Long before, the lunar telescopes had made one great fact clear: The atmosphere here was far, far out of chemical equilibrium. Biological theory held that this was inevitably the signature of life. And indeed, the expedition's first mapping had shown that green, abundant life clung to two well-separated habitable belts, each beginning about 30 degrees from the equator.

Apparently the weird tidal effects of the Centauri system had stolen Shiva's initial polar tilt. Such steady workings had now made its spin align to within a single degree with its orbital angular momentum, so that conditions were steady and calm. The equatorial belt was a pale, arid waste of perpetual tornadoes and blistering gales.

John close-upped in all available bands, peering at the planet's crescent. Large blue-green seas, but no great oceans. Particularly, no water links between the two milder zones, so no marine life could migrate between them. Land migrations, calculations showed, were effectively blocked by the great equatorial desert. Birds might make the long flight, John considered, but what evolutionary factor would condition them for such hardship? And what would be the reward? Why fight the jagged mountain chains? Better to lounge about in the many placid lakes.

A strange world, well worth the decades of grinding, slow, starship flight, John thought. He asked for the full display and the observing bowl opened like a flower around him. He swam above the entire disk of the Centauri system now, the images sharp and rich.

To be here at last! *Adventurer* was only a mote among many—yet *here*, in the lap of strangeness. Far Centauri.

It did not occur to him that humanity had anything truly vital to lose here. The doctrine of expansion and greater knowledge had begun seven centuries before, making European cultures the inheritors of Earth. Although science had found unsettling truths, even those revelations had not blunted the agenda of ever-greater knowledge. After all, what harm could come from merely looking?

▲   ▲   ▲

The truth about Shiva's elevated ocean only slowly emerged. Its very existence was plainly impossible, and therefore was not at first believed.

Odis was the first to notice the clues. Long days of sensory immersion in the data-streams repaid her. She was rather proud of having plucked such exotica from the bath of measurements their expedition got from their probes—the tiny, speeding, smart spindle-eyes that now cruised all over the double-stars' realm.

The Centauri system was odd, but even its strong tides could not explain this anomaly. Planets should be spherical, or nearly so; Earth bulged but a fraction of a percent at its equator, due to its spin. Not Shiva, though.

Odis found aberrations in this world's shape. The anomalies were far away from the equator, principally at the 1,694-kilometer-wide deep blue sea, immediately dubbed the Circular Ocean. It sat in the southern hemisphere, its nearly perfect ring hinting at an origin as a vast crater. Odis could not take her gaze from it, a blue eye peeking coyly at them through the clouds: a planet looking back.

Odis made her ranging measurements, gathering in her data like number-clouds, inhaling their cottony wealth. Beneath her, *Adventurer* prepared to go into orbit about Shiva.

She breathed in the banks of data-vapor, translated by her kinesthetic programming into intricate scent-inventories. Tangy, complex.

At first she did not believe the radar reflections. Contours leaped into view, artfully sketched by the mapping radars. Calibrations checked, though, so she tried other methods: slow, analytical, tedious, hard to do in her excitement. They gave the same result.

The Circular Ocean stood a full 10 kilometers higher than the continent upon which it rested.

No mountains surrounded it. It sat like some cosmic magic trick, insolently demanding an explanation.

Odis presented her discovery at the daily Oversight Group meeting. There was outright skepticism, even curled lips of derision, snorts of disbelief. "The range of methods is considerable," she said adamantly. "These results cannot be wrong."

"Only thing to resolve this," a lanky geologist said, "is get an edge-on view."

"I hoped someone would say that." Odis smiled. "Do I have the authorized observing time?"

They gave it reluctantly. *Adventurer* was orbiting in a severe ellipse about Shiva's cloud-wrack. Her long swing brought her into a side view of the target area two days later. Odis used the full panoply of optical, IR, UV, and microwave instruments to peer at the Circular Ocean's perimeter, probing for the basin that supported the round slab of azure water.

There was none. No land supported the hanging sea.

This result was utterly clear. The Circular Ocean was 1.36 kilometers thick and a brilliant blue. Spectral evidence suggested water rich in salt, veined by thick currents. It looked exactly like an enormous, troubled mountain lake, with the mountain subtracted.

Beneath that layer there was nothing but the thick atmosphere. No rocky mountain range to support the ocean-in-air. Just a many-kilometer gap.

All other observations halted. The incontrovertible pictures showed an immense layer of unimaginable weight, blissfully poised above mere thin gases, contradicting all known mechanics. Until this moment Odis had been a lesser figure in the expedition. Now her work captivated everyone and she was the center of every conversation. The concrete impossibility yawned like an inviting abyss.

Lissa found the answer to Shiva's mystery, but no one was happy with it.

An atmospheric chemist, Lissa's job was mostly done well before they achieved orbit around Shiva. She had already probed and labeled the gases, shown clearly that they implied a thriving biology below. After that, she had thought, the excitement would shift elsewhere, to the surface observers.

Not so. Lissa took a deep breath and began speaking to the Oversight Group. She had to show that she was not wasting their time. With all eyes on the Circular Ocean, few cared for mere air.

Yet it was the key, Lissa told them. The Circular Ocean had intrigued her, too: so she looked at the mixture of oxygen, nitrogen, and carbon dioxide that apparently supported the floating sea. These proved perfectly ordinary, almost Earth-standard, except for one oddity. Their spectral lines were slightly split, so that she found two small spikes to the right and left of where each line should be.

Lissa turned from the images she projected before the Oversight Group. "The only possible interpretation," she said crisply, "is that an immensely strong electric field is inducing the tiny electric dipoles of these molecules to move. That splits the lines."

"An *electric* shift?" a grizzled skeptic called. "In a charge-neutral atmosphere? Sure, maybe when lightning flashes you could get a momentary effect, but—"

"It is steady."

"You looked for lightning?" a shrewd woman demanded.

"It's there, sure. We see it forking between the

clouds below the Circular Ocean. But that's not what causes the electric fields."

"What does?" This from the grave captain, who never spoke in scientific disputes. All heads turned to him, then to Lissa.

She shrugged. "Nothing reasonable." It pained her to admit it, but ignorance was getting to be a common currency.

A voice called, "So there must be an impossibly strong electric field *everywhere* in that 10 kilometers of air below the ocean?" Murmurs of agreement. Worried frowns.

"Everywhere, yes." The bald truth of it stirred the audience. "Everywhere."

Tagore was in a hurry. Too much so.

He caromed off a stanchion but did not let that stop him from rebounding from the opposite wall, absorbing his momentum with his knees, and springing off with a full push. Rasters streaked his augmented vision, then flickered and faded.

He coasted by a full-view showing Shiva and the world below, a blazing crescent transcendent in its cloud-wrapped beauty. Tagore ignored the spectacle; marvels of the mind preoccupied him.

He was carrying the answer to it all, he was sure of that. In his haste he did not even glance at how blue-tinged sunlight glinted from the Circular Ocean. The thick disk of open air below it made a clear line under the blue wedge. At this angle the floating water refracted sunlight around the still-darkened limb of the planet. The glittering azure jewel heralded dawn, serene in its impudent impossibility.

The youngest of the entire expedition, Tagore was a mere theorist. He had specialized in planetary formation at university, but managed to snag a berth on this expedition by developing a ready, quick facility at explaining vexing problems the observers turned up. That, and a willingness to do scutwork.

"Cap'n, I've got it," he blurted as he came through the hatch. The captain greeted him, sitting at a small oak desk, the only wood on the whole ship—then got to business. Tagore had asked for this audience because he knew the effect his theory could have on the others; so the captain should see first.

"The Circular Ocean is held up by electric field pressure," he announced. The captain's reaction was less than he had hoped: unblinking calm, waiting for more information.

"See, electromagnetic fields exert forces on the electrons in atoms," Tagore persisted, going through the numbers, talking fast. "The fields down there are so strong—I got that measurement out of Lissa's data—they can act like a steady support."

He went on to make comparisons: the energy density of a hand grenade, contained in every suitcase-sized volume of air. Even though the fields could simply stand there, as trapped waves, they had to suffer some losses. The power demands were *huge*. Plus, how the hell did such a gargantuan construction *work*?

By now Tagore was thoroughly pumped, oblivious to his audience.

Finally the captain blinked and said, "Anything like this ever seen on Earth?"

"Nossir, not that I've ever heard."

"No natural process can do the stunt?"

"Nossir, not that I can imagine."

"Well, we came looking for something different."

Tagore did not know whether to laugh or not; the captain was unreadable. Was this what exploration was like—the slow anxiety of not knowing? On Earth such work had an abstract distance, but here . . .

He would rather have some other role. Bringing uncomfortable truths to those in power put him more in the spotlight than he wished.

Captain Badquor let the Tagore kid go on a bit longer before he said anything more. It was best to let these technical types sing their songs first. So few of them ever thought about anything beyond their own warblings.

He gave Tagore a captainly smile. Why did they all look so young? "So this whole big thing on Shiva is artificial."

"Well, yeah, I suppose so . . ."

Plainly Tagore hadn't actually thought about that part very much; the wonder of such strong fields had stunned him. Well, it was stunning. "And all that energy, just used to hold up a lake?"

"I'm sure of it, sir. The numbers work out, see? I equated the pressure exerted by those electric fields, assuming they're trapped in the volume under the Circular Ocean, the way waves can get caught if they're inside a conducting box—"

"You think that ocean's a conductor?" Might as well show the kid that even the captain knew a little physics. In fact, though he never mentioned it, he had a doctorate from MIT. Not that he had learned much about command there.

"Uh, well, no. I mean, it is a fairly good conductor, but for my model, it's only a way of speaking—"

"It has salt currents, true? They could carry electrical currents." The captain rubbed his chin, the machinery of his mind trying to grasp how such a thing could be. "Still, that doesn't explain why the thing doesn't evaporate away, at those altitudes."

"Uh, I really hadn't thought . . ."

The captain waved a hand. "Go on." *Sing for me.*

"Then the waves exert an upward force on the water every time they reflect from the underside of the ocean—"

"And transfer that weight down, on invisible waves, to the rock that's 10 kilometers below."

"Uh, yessir."

Tagore looked a bit constipated, bursting with enthusiasm, with the experience of the puzzle, but not knowing how to express it. The captain decided to have mercy on the kid. "Sounds good. Not anything impossible about it."

"Except the *size* of it, sir."

"That's one way to put it."

"Sir?"

A curious, powerful feeling washed over the captain. Long decades of anticipation had steeled him, made him steady in the presence of the crew. But now he felt his sense of the room tilt, as though he were losing control of his status-space. The mind could go whirling off, out here in the inky immensities between twin alien suns. He frowned. "This thing is bigger than anything humanity ever built. And there's not a clue what it's for. The majesty of it, son, that's what strikes me. Grandeur."

John slipped into his helmet and Shiva enclosed him. *To be wrapped in a world*—His pov shifted, strummed, arced with busy fretworks—then snapped into solidity, stabilized.

Astronomy had become intensely interactive in the past century, the spectral sensoria blanketing the viewer. Through *Adventurer*'s long voyage he had tuned the system to his every whim. Now it gave him a nuanced experience like a true, full-bodied immersion.

He was eager to immerse himself in the *feel* of Shiva, in full 3-D wraparound. Its crescent swelled below like a ripe, mottled fruit. He plunged toward it. A planet, fat in bandwidth.

For effect—decades before he had been a sky-diver—John had arranged the data-fields so that he accelerated into it. From their arcing orbit he shot directly toward Shiva's disk. Each mapping rushed toward him, exploding upward in finer detail. *There*—

The effect showed up first in the grasslands of the southern habitable belt. He slewed toward the plains, where patterns emerged in quilted confusions. After Tagore's astonishing theory about the Circular Ocean—odd, so audacious, and coming from a nonscientist—John had to be ready for anything. Somewhere in the data-fields must lurk the clue to who or what had made the ocean.

Below, the great grassy shelves swelled. But in places the grass was thin. Soon he saw why. The natural grass was only peeking out across plains covered with curious orderly patterns—hexagonals folding into triangles where necessary to cover hills and valleys, right up to the muddy banks of the slow-moving brown rivers.

Reflection in the UV showed that the tiles making this pattern were often small, but with some the size of houses, meters thick . . . and moving. They all jostled and worked with restless energy, to no obvious purpose.

Alive? The UV spectrum broke down into a description of a complex polymer. Cross-linked chains bonded at many oblique angles to each other, flexing like sleek micro-muscles.

John brought in chemists, biologists in an ensemble suite: Odis and Lissa chimed in the scientific choir. In the wraparound display he felt them by the shadings they gave the data.

The tiles, Lissa found, fed on their own sky. Simple sugars rained from the clotted air, the fruit of an atmosphere that resembled an airy chicken soup. *Atmospheric electro-chemistry seems responsible, somehow,* Lissa sent. Floating microbial nuggets moderated the process.

The tiles were prime eaters. Oxidizing radicals the size of golf balls patroled their sharp linear perimeters. These pack-like rollers attacked invader chemicals, ejecting most, harvesting those they could use.

Lissa brought in two more biologists, who of course had many questions. *Are these tiles like great turtles?* one ventured, then chuckled uneasily. They yearned to flip one over.

Diurnal or nocturnal? *Some are, most aren't.*

Are there any small ones? *A few.*

Do they divide by fission? *No, but . . .* Nobody understood the complicated process the biologists witnessed. Reproduction seems a tricky matter.

There is some periodicity to their movements, some slow rhythms, and particularly a fast Fourier-spectrum spike at 1.27 seconds—but again, no clear reason for it.

Could they be all one life form?—could that be?

A whole planet taken over by a tiling-thing that co-opts all resources?

The senior biologists scoffed. How could a species evolve to have only one member? And an ecosystem—a whole world!—with so few parts?

Evolution ruled that out. Bio-evolution, that is. But not social evolution.

John plunged further into the intricate matrices of analysis. The endless tile-seas cloaking mountains and valleys shifted and milled, fidgety, only occasionally leaving bare ground visible as a square fissioned into triangles. Oblongs met and butted with fevered energy.

Each hemisphere of the world was similar, though the tiles in the north had different shapes—pentagonals, mostly. Nowhere did the tiles cross rivers but they could ford streams. A Centauri variant of chlorophyll was everywhere, in the oceans and rivers, but not in the Circular Ocean.

The ground was covered with a thin grass, the sprigs living off the momentary sunlight that slipped between the edges in the jostling, jiggling, bumping, and shaking. Tiles that moved over the grass sometimes cropped it, sometimes not, leaving stubs that seemed to have been burned off.

The tiles' fevered dance ran incessantly, without sleep. Could these things be performing some agitated discourse, a lust-fest without end?

John slowed his descent. The tiles were a shock. Could these be the builders of the Circular Ocean? Time for the biologists to get to work.

The computer folk thought one way, the biologists— after an initial rout, when they rejected the very possibility of a single entity filling an entire biosphere—quite another.

After some friction, their views converged somewhat. A biologist remarked that the larger tiles came together like dwarf houses making love . . . gingerly, always presenting the same angles and edges.

Adventurer had scattered micro-landers all over the world. These showed only weak electromagnetic fringing fields among the tiles. Their deft collisions seemed almost like neurons in a two-dimensional plan.

The analogy stirred the theorists. Over the usual after-shift menu of beer, soy nuts, and friendly insults, one maven of the digital realm ventured an absurd idea: Could the planet have become a computer?

Everybody laughed. They kidded the advocate of this notion . . . and then lapsed into frowning silence.

Specialists find quite unsettling those ideas that cross disciplines.

Could a species turn itself into a biological computer? The tiles did rub and caress each other in systematic ways. Rather than carrying information in digital fashion, maybe they used a more complex language of position and angle, exploiting their planar geometry. If so, the information density flowing among them was immense. Every collision carried a sort of Euclidean talk, possibly rich in nuance.

The computer analogy brought up a next question— not that some big ones weren't left behind, perhaps lying in wait to bite them on their conceptual tail. Could the tiles know anything more than themselves? Or were they strange, geometroid solipsists? Should they call the tiles a single It?

Sealed inside a cosmos of Its own making, was It even in principle interested in the outside world? Alpha Centauri fed It gratuitous energy, the very soupy air fueled It: the last standing power on the globe. What reason did It have to converse with the great Outside?

Curiosity, perhaps? The biologists frowned at the prospect. Curiosity in early prehumans was rewarded in the environment. The evolving ape learned new tricks, found fresh water, killed a new kind of game, invented a better way to locate those delicious roots—and the world duly paid it back.

Apparently—*but don't ask us why just yet!* the biologists cried—the game was different here. What reward came from the tiles' endless smacking together?

So even if the visiting humans rang the conceptual doorbell on the tile-things, maybe nobody would answer. Maybe nobody was home.

Should they try?

John and Odis and Lissa, Tagore and the captain, over a hundred other crew—they all pondered.

Section 2

While they wrestled with the issue, exploration continued.

A flitter craft flew near the elevated ocean and inspected its supporting volume with distant sensors and probing telescopes. Even Shiva's weather patterns seemed wary of the Circular Ocean. Thunderclouds veered away from the gap between the ocean and the rugged land below. In the yawning height clouds formed but quickly dispersed, as if dissolved by unseen forces.

Birds flew through the space, birds like feathery kites.

Somehow they had missed noticing this class of life. Even the micro-landers had not had the speed to capture their darting lives. And while the kite-birds did seem to live mostly on tiny floating balloon-creatures that hovered in the murky air of the valleys, they were unusually common beneath the Circular Ocean.

John proposed that he send in a robo-craft of bird size, to measure physical parameters in the heart of the gap. Captain Badquor approved. The shops fabricated a convincing fake. Jet-powered and featuring fake feathers, it was reasonably convincing.

John flew escort in a rocket-plane. The bird-probe got 17 kilometers inside and then disappeared in a dazzling blue-white electrical discharge. Telemetry showed why: The Circular Ocean's support was a complex weave of electrical fields, supplying an upward pressure. These fields never exceeded the breakdown level of a megavolt per meter, above which Shiva's atmosphere would ionize. Field strength was about a million volts per meter.

The robo-craft had hit a critical peak in the field geometry. A conductor, it caused a flashover that dumped millions of watts into the bird within a millisecond.

As the cinder fell, John banked away from his monitoring position five kilometers beyond the gap perimeter. There was no particular reason to believe a discharge that deep within the gap would somehow spread, engulfing the region in a spontaneous discharge of the enormous stored energies. Surely whoever—no, whatever—had designed the Circular Ocean's supports would not allow the electromagnetic struts to collapse from the frying of a mere bird.

But something like that happened. The system responded.

The burned brown husk of the pseudo-bird turned lazily as it fell and sparks jumped from it. These formed a thin orange discharge that fed on the energy coursing through the now-atomized bird. The discharging line snaked away, following unerringly the bird's prior path. It raced at close to the speed of light back along the arc.

The system had *memory*, John realized. He saw a tendril of light at the corner of his vision as he turned his flitter craft. He had time only to think that it was like a huge, fast finger jabbing at him. An apt analogy, though he had no time to consider ironies. The orange discharge touched the flitter. John's hair stood on end as charge flooded into the interior.

Ideally, electrons move to the outer skin of a conductor. But when antennae connect deep into the interior, circuits can close.

Something had intended to dump an immense charge on the flitter, the origin of the pseudo-bird. Onboard instruments momentarily reported a charge exceeding 17 coulombs. By then John had, for all intents and purposes, ceased to exist as an organized bundle of electrical information.

▲   ▲   ▲

John's death did yield a harvest of data. Soon enough Lissa saw the true function of the Circular Ocean. It was but an ornament, perhaps an artwork.

Ozone fizzed all around it. Completely natural-seeming, the lake crowned a huge cavity that functioned like a steady, standing laser.

The electrical fields both supported the Ocean and primed the atoms of the entire atmosphere they permeated. Upon stimulus—from the same system that had fried John—the entire gap could release the stored energy into an outgoing electromagnetic wave. It was an optical bolt, powerful and complex in structure—triggered by John.

Twice more the ocean's gap discharged naturally as the humans orbited Shiva. The flash lasted but a second, not enough to rob the entire ocean structure of its stability. The emission sizzled out through the atmosphere and off into space.

Laser beams are tight, and this one gave away few of its secrets. The humans, viewing it from a wide angle, caught little of the complex structure and understood less.

Puzzled, mourning John, they returned to a careful study of the Shiva surface. Morale was low. The captain felt that a dramatic gesture could lift their spirits. He would have to do it himself.

To Captain Badquor fell the honor of the first landing. A show of bravery would overcome the crew's confusions, surely. He would direct the complex exploring machines in real-time, up close.

He left the landing craft fully suited up, impervious to the complex biochem mix of the atmosphere.

The tiles jostled downhill from him. Only in the steep flanks of this equatorial mountain range did the tiles not endlessly surge. Badquor's boots crunched on a dry, crusty soil. He took samples, sent them back by runner-robo.

A warning signal from orbit: The tiles in his area seemed more agitated than usual. A reaction to his landing?

The tile polygons were leathery, with no obvious way to sense him. No eyes or ears. They seemed to caress the ground lovingly, though Badquor knew that they tread upon big crabbed feet.

He went forward cautiously. Below, the valley seemed alive with rippling turf, long waves sweeping to the horizon in the twinkling of an instant. He got an impression of incessant pace, of enthusiasm unspoken but plainly endless.

His boots were well insulated thermally, but not electrically; thus, when his headphones crackled he thought he was receiving noise in his transmission lines. The dry sizzle began to make his skin tingle.

Only when the frying noise rose and buried all other signals did he blink, alarmed. By then it was too late.

Piezoelectric energy arises when mechanical stress massages rock. Pressure on an electrically neutral stone polarizes it at the lattice level by slightly separating the center of positive charge from the negative. The lattice moves, the shielding electron cloud does not. This happens whenever the rock crystal structure does not have a center of structural symmetry, and so occurs in nearly all bedrock.

The effect was well known on Earth, though weak. Stressed strata sometimes discharged, sending glow discharges into the air. Such plays of light were now a standard precursor warning of earthquakes. But Earth was a mild case.

Tides stressed the stony mantle of Shiva, driven by the eternal gravitational dance of both stars, A and B. Periodic alignments of the two stars stored enormous energy in the full body of the planet. Evolution favored life that could harness these electrical currents that rippled through the planetary crust. This, far more than the kilowatt per square meter of sunlight, drove the tile-forms.

All this explanation came after the fact, and seemed obvious in retrospect. The piezoelectric energy source was naturally dispersed and easily harvested. A sizzle of electric micro-fields fed the tiles' large, crusted footpads. After all, on Earth fish and eels routinely use electrical fields as both sensors and weapons.

This highly organized ecology sensed Badquor's intrusion immediately. To them, he probably had many of the signatures of a power-parasite. These were small creatures like stick insects that Badquor himself had noticed after landing; they lived by stealing electrical charge from the tile polygons.

Only later analysis made it clear what had happened. The interlinked commonality of piezo-driven life moved to expel the intruder by overpowering it—literally.

Badquor probably had no inkling of how strange a fate he had met, for the several hundreds of amperes caused his muscles to seize up, his heart to freeze in a clamped frenzy, and his synapses to discharge in a last vision that burned into his eyes a vision of an incandescent rainbow.

Lissa blinked. The spindly trees looked artificial, but weren't.

Groves of them spiraled around hills, zigzagged up razor-backed ridges and shot down the flanks of denuded rock piles. Hostile terrain for any sort of tree that earthly biologists understood. The trees, she noted, had growing patterns that bore no discernible relation to water flow, sunlight exposure, or wind patterns.

That was why Lissa went in to see. Her team of four had already sent the smart-eyes, rugged robots, and quasi-intelligent processors. Lightweight, patient, durable, these ambassadors had discovered little. Time for something a bit more interactive on the ground.

That is, a person. Captain Badquor's sacrifice had to mean something, and his death had strengthened his crew's resolve.

Lissa landed with electrically insulated boots. They now understood the piezoelectric ecology in broad outline, or thought they did. Courageous caution prevailed.

The odd beanpole trees made no sense. Their gnarled branches followed a fractal pattern and had no leaves. Still, there was ample fossil evidence—gathered by automatic prospectors sent down earlier—that the bristly trees had evolved from more traditional trees within the past few million years. But they had come so quickly into the geological record that Lissa suspected they were "driven" evolution—biological technology.

She carefully pressed her instruments against the sleek black sides of the trees. Their surfaces seethed with electric currents, but none strong enough to be a danger.

On Earth, the natural potential difference between the surface and the upper atmosphere provides a voltage drop of a hundred volts for each meter in height. A woman two meters tall could be at a significantly higher potential than her feet, especially if her feet had picked up extra electrons by walking across a thick carpet.

On Shiva this effect was much larger. The trees, Lissa realized, were harvesting the large potentials available between Shiva's rocky surface and the charged layers skating across the upper reaches of the atmosphere.

The "trees" were part of yet another way to reap the planetary energies—whose origin was ultimately the blunt forces of gravity, mass and torque—all for the use of life.

The potential-trees felt Lissa's presence quickly enough. They had evolved defenses against poachers who would garner stray voltages and currents from the unwary.

In concert—for the true living entity was the grove, comprising perhaps a million trees—they reacted.

Staggering back to her lander, pursued by vagrant electrical surges through both ground and the thick air, she shouted into her suit mike her conclusions. These proved useful in later analysis.

She survived, barely.

Section 3

When the sum of these incidents sank in, the full import become clear. The entire Shiva ecology was electrically driven. From the planet's rotation and strong magnetosphere, from the tidal stretching of the Centauri system, from geological rumblings and compressions, came far more energy than mere sunlight could ever provide.

Seen this way, all biology was an afterthought. The geologists, who had been feeling rather neglected lately, liked this turn of events quite a bit. They gave lectures on Shiva seismology which, for once, everybody attended.

To be sure, vestigial chemical processes still ran alongside the vastly larger stores of charges and potentials; these were important for understanding the ancient biosphere that had once governed here.

Much could be learned from classic, old-style biology: from samples of the bushes and wiry trees and leafy plants, from the small insect-like creatures of ten legs each, from the kite-birds, from the spiny, knife-like fish that prowled the lakes.

All these forms were ancient, unchanging. Something had fixed them in evolutionary amber. Their forms had not changed for many hundreds of millions of years.

There had once been higher forms, the fossil record showed. Something like mammals, even large tubular things that might have resembled reptiles.

But millions of years ago they had abruptly ceased. Not due to some trauma, either—they all ended together, but without the slightest sign of a shift in the biosphere, of disease or accident.

The suspicion arose that something had simply erased them, having no further need.

The highest form of life—defined as that with the highest brain/body volume ratio—had vanished slightly later than the others. It had begun as a predator wider than it was tall, and shaped like a turtle, though without a shell.

It had the leathery look of the tile-polygons, though.

Apparently it had not followed the classic mode of pursuit, but rather had outwitted its prey, boxing it in by pack-animal tactics. Later, it had arranged deadfalls and traps. Or so the sociobiologists suspected, from narrow evidence.

These later creatures had characteristic bony structures around the large, calculating brain. Subsequent forms were plainly intelligent, and had been engaged in a strange manipulation of their surroundings. Apparently without ever inventing cities or agriculture, they had domesticated many other species.

Then, the other high life forms vanished from the

fossil record. The scheme of the biosphere shifted. Electrical plant forms, like the spindly trees and those species that fed upon piezoelectric energy, came to the fore.

Next, the dominant, turtle-like predators vanished as well. Had they been dispatched?

On Shiva, all the forms humans thought of as life, plant and animal alike, were now in fact mere . . . well, maintenance workers. They served docilely in a far more complex ecology. They were as vital and as unnoticeable and as ignorable as the mitochondria in the stomach linings of *Adventurer*'s crew.

Of the immensely more complex electrical ecology, they were only beginning to learn even the rudiments. If Shiva was in a sense a single interdependent, colonial organism, what were its deep rules?

By focusing on the traditional elements of the organic biosphere they had quite missed the point.

Then the Circular Ocean's laser discharged again. The starship was nearer the lancing packet of emission, and picked up a side lobe. They learned more in a millisecond than they had in a month.

A human brain has about 10 billion neurons, each connected with about 100,000 of its neighbors. A firing neuron carries one bit of information. But the signal depends upon the path it follows, and in the labyrinth of the brain there are 1,015 pathways. This torrent of information flows through the brain in machine-gun packets of electrical impulses, coursing through myriad synapses. Since a single book has about a million bits in it, a single human carries the equivalent of a billion books of information—all riding around in a two-kilogram lump of electrically wired jelly.

Only 1 to 10 percent of a human brain's connections are firing at any one time. A neuron can charge and discharge at best a hundred times in a second. Human brains, then, can carry roughly 1,010 bits of information in a second.

Thus, to read out a brain containing 1,015 bits would take 100,000 seconds, or about a day.

The turtle-predators had approximately the same capacity. Indeed, there were theoretical arguments that a mobile, intelligent species would carry roughly the same load of stored information as a human could. For all its limitations, the human brain has an impressive data-store capability, even if, in many, it frequently went unused.

The Circular Ocean had sent discrete packets of information of about this size, 1,015 bits compressed into its powerful millisecond pulse. The packets within it were distinct, well bordered by banks of marker code. The representation was digital, an outcome mandated by the fact that any number enjoys a unique representation only in base 2.

Within the laser's millisecond burst were fully a thousand brain-equivalent transmissions. A trove. What the packets actually said was quite undecipherable.

The target was equally clear: a star 347 light years away. Targeting was precise; there could be no mistake. Far cheaper, if one knows the recipient, to send a focused message, rather than to broadcast wastefully in the low-grade, narrow bandwidth radio frequencies.

Earth had never heard such powerful signals, of course, not because humans were not straining to hear, but because Shiva was ignoring them.

After Badquor's death and Lissa's narrow escape, *Adventurer* studied the surface with elaborately planned robot expeditions. The machines skirted the edge of a vast tile-plain, observing the incessant jiggling, fed on the piezoelectric feast welling from the crusted rocks.

After some days, they came upon a small tile lying still. The others had forced it out of the eternal jostling jam. It lay stiff and discolored, baking in the double suns' glare. Scarcely a meter across and thin, it looked like construction material for a patio in Arizona.

The robots carried it off. Nothing pursued them. The tile-thing was dead, apparently left for mere chemical processes to harvest its body.

This bonanza kept the ship's biologists sleepless for weeks as they dissected it. Gray-green, hard of carapace, and extraordinarily complex in its nervous system—these they had expected. But the dead alien devoted fully a quarter of its body volume to a brain that was broken into compact, separate segments.

The tile-creatures were indeed part of an ecology driven by electrical harvesting of the planetary energies. The tiles alone used a far higher percentage of the total energetic wealth than did Earth's entire sluggish, chemically driven biosphere.

And deep within the tile-thing was the same bone structure as they had seen in the turtle-like predator. The dominant, apparently intelligent species had not gone to the stars. Instead, they had formed the basis of an intricate ecology of the mind.

Then the engineers had a chance to study the tile-thing, and found even more.

As a manifestation of their world, the tiles were impressive. Their neurological system fashioned a skein of interpretations, of lived scenarios, of expressive renderings—all apparently for communication outward in well-sculpted bunches of electrical information, intricately coded. They had large computing capacity and ceaselessly exchanged great gouts of information with each other. This explained their rough skins, which maximized piezo connections when they rubbed against each other. And they "spoke" to each other through the ground, as well, where their big, crabbed feet carried currents, too.

Slowly it dawned that Shiva was an unimaginably huge computational complex, operating in a state of information flux many orders of magnitude greater than the entire sum of human culture. Shiva was to Earth as humans are to beetles.

The first transmissions about Shiva's biosphere reached Earth four years later. Already, in a culture more than a century into the dual evolution of society and computers, there were disturbing parallels.

Some communities in the advanced regions of Earth felt that real-time itself was a pallid, ephemeral experience. After all, one could not archive it for replay, savor it, return until it became a true part of oneself. Real-time was for one time only, then lost.

So increasingly, some people lived instead in worlds made totally volitional—truncated, chopped, governed by technologies they could barely sense as ghostlike constraints on an otherwise wide compass.

"Disposable realities," some sneered—but the fascination of such lives was clear.

Shiva's implication was extreme: An entire world could give itself over to life-as-computation.

Could the intelligent species of Shiva have executed a huge fraction of their fellow inhabitants? And then themselves gone extinct? For what? Could they have fled—perhaps from the enormity of their own deeds?

Or had those original predators become the tile-polygons?

The *Adventurer* crew decided to return to Shiva's surface in force, to crack the puzzles. They notified Earth and descended.

▲   ▲   ▲

Shortly after, the Shiva teams ceased reporting back to Earth. Through the hiss of interstellar static there came no signal.

After years of anxious waiting, Earth launched the second expedition. They too survived the passage. Cautiously they approached Shiva.

Adventurer still orbited the planet, but was vacant.

This time they were wary. Further years of hard thinking and careful study passed before the truth began to come.

Section 4

> [—John/Odis/Lissa/Tagore/Cap'n—]
> —all assembled/congealed/thickened—
> —into a composite veneer persona—
> —on the central deck of their old starship,
> —to greet the second expedition.

Or so they seemed to intend.

They came up from the Shiva surface in a craft not of human construction. The sleek, webbed thing seemed to ride upon electromagnetic winds.

They entered through the main lock, after using proper hailing protocols.

But what came through the lock was an ordered array of people no one could recognize as being from the *Adventurer* crew.

They seemed younger, unworn. Smooth, bland features looked out at the bewildered second expedition. The party moved together, maintaining a hexagonal array with a constant spacing of four centimeters. Fifty-six pairs of eyes surveyed the new Earth ship, each momentarily gazing at a different portion of the field of view, as if to memorize only a portion, for later integration.

To convey a sentence, each person spoke a separate word. The effect was jarring, with no clue to how an individual knew what to say, or when, for the lines were not rehearsed. The group reacted to questions in a blur of scattershot talk, words like volleys.

Sentences ricocheted and bounced around the assembly deck where the survivors of the first expedition all stood, erect and clothed in a shapeless gray garment. Their phrases made sense when isolated, but the experience of hearing them was unsettling. Long minutes stretched out before the second expedition realized that these hexagonally spaced humans were trying to greet them, to induct them into something they termed the Being Suite.

This offer made, the faces within the hexagonal array began to show separate expressions. Tapes of this encounter show regular facial alterations with a fixed periodicity of 1.27 seconds. Each separate face racheted, jerking among a menu of finely graduated countenances—anger, sympathy, laughter, rage, curiosity, shock, puzzlement, ecstasy—flickering, flickering, endlessly flickering.

A witness later said that it was as if the hexagonals (as they came to be called) knew that human expressiveness centered on the face, and so had slipped into a kind of language of facial aspects. This seemed natural to them, and yet the 1.27 second pace quickly gave the witnesses a sense of creeping horror.

High-speed tapes of the event showed more. Beneath the 1.27 frequency there was a higher harmonic, barely perceptible to the human eye, in which other expressions shot across the hexagonals' faces. These were like waves, muscular twitches that washed over the skin like tidal pulls.

This periodicity was the same as the tile-polygons had displayed. The subliminal aspects were faster than the conscious human optical processor can manage, yet research showed that they were decipherable in the target audience.

Researchers later concluded that this rapid display was the origin of the growing unease felt by the second expedition. The hexagonals said nothing throughout all this.

The second expedition crew described the experience as uncanny, racking, unbearable. Their distinct impression was that the first expedition now manifested as like the *tile-things*. Such testimony was often followed by an involuntary twitch.

Tapes do not yield such an impression upon similar audiences: they have become the classic example of having to be in a place and time to sense the meaning of an event. Still, the tapes are disturbing, and access is controlled. Some Earth audiences experienced breakdowns after viewing them.

But the second expedition agreed even more strongly upon a second conclusion. Plainly, the *Adventurer* expedition had joined the computational labyrinth that was Shiva. How they were seduced was never clear; the second expedition feared finding out.

Indeed, their sole, momentary brush with [—John/ Odis/Lissa/Tagore/Cap'n . . . —] convinced the second expedition that there was no point in pursuing the maze of Shiva.

The hostility radiating from the second expedition soon drove the hexagonals back into their ship and away. The fresh humans from Earth felt something gut-level and instinctive, a reaction beyond words. The hexagonals retreated without showing a coherent reaction. They simply turned and walked away, holding to the four centimeter spacing. The 1.27-second flicker stopped and they returned to a bland expression, alert but giving nothing away.

The vision these hexagonals conveyed was austere, jarring . . . and yet, plainly intended to be inviting.

The magnitude of their failure was a measure of the abyss that separated the two parties. The hexagonals were now both more and less than human.

The hexagonals left recurrent patterns that told much, though only in retrospect. Behind the second expedition's revulsion lay a revelation: of a galaxy spanned by intelligences formal and remote, far developed beyond the organic stage. Such intelligences had been born variously, of early organic forms, or of later machine civilizations which had arisen upon the ashes of extinct organic societies. The gleam of the stars was in fact a metallic glitter.

This vision was daunting enough: of minds so distant and strange, hosted in bodies free of sinew and skin. But there was something more, an inexpressible repulsion in the manifestation of [—John/Odis/Lissa/Tagore/Cap'n . . . —].

A 19th-century philosopher, Goethe, had once remarked that if one stared into the abyss long enough, it stared back. This proved true. A mere moment's lingering look, quiet and almost casual, was enough. The second expedition panicked. It is not good to stare into a pit that has no bottom.

They had sensed the final implication of Shiva's evolution. To alight upon such interior worlds of deep, terrible exotica exacted a high cost: the body itself. Yet all those diverse people had joined the *syntony* of Shiva—an electrical harmony that danced to unheard musics. Whether they had been seduced, or even raped, would forever be unclear.

Out of the raw data-stream the second expedition could sample transmissions from the tile-things, as well.

The second expedition caught a link-locked sense of repulsive grandeur. Still organic in their basic organization, still tied to the eternal wheel of birth and death, the tiles had once been lords of their own world, holding dominion over all they knew.

Now they were patient, willing drones in a hive they could not comprehend. But—and here human terms undoubtedly fail—they loved their immersion.

Where was their consciousness housed? Partially in each, or in some displaced, additive sense? There was no clear way to test either idea.

The tile-things were like durable, patient machines that could best carry forward the first stages of a grand computation. Some biologists compared them with insects, but no evolutionary mechanism seemed capable of yielding a reason why a species would give itself over to computation. The insect analogy died, unable to predict the response of the polygons to stimulus, or even why they existed.

Or was their unending jostling only in the service of calculation? The tile-polygons would not say. They never responded to overtures.

The Circular Ocean's enormous atmospheric laser pulsed regularly, as the planet's orbit and rotation carried the laser's field of targeting onto a fresh partner-star system. Only then did the system send its rich messages out into the galaxy. The pulses carried mind-packets of unimaginable data, bound on expeditions of the intellect.

The second expedition reported, studied. Slowly at first, and then accelerating, the terror overcame them.

They could not fathom Shiva, and steadily they lost crew members to its clasp. Confronting the truly, irreducibly exotic, there is no end of ways to perish.

In the end they studied Shiva from a distance, no more. Try as they could, they always met a barrier in their understanding. Theories came and went, fruitlessly. Finally, they fled.

It is one thing to speak of embracing the new, the fresh, the strange. It is another to feel that one is an insect, crawling across a page of the *Encyclopedia Britannica*, knowing only that something vast is passing by beneath, all without your sensing more than a yawning vacancy. Worse, the lack was clearly in oneself, and was irredeemable.

This was the first contact humanity had with the true nature of the galaxy. It would not be the last. But the sense of utter and complete diminishment never left the species, in all the strange millennia that rolled on thereafter.

The Year of the Mouse

NORMAN SPINRAD

Norman Spinrad is one of the most interesting of all SF
writers, a major force in the field from the 1960s to the
present. He has lived in Paris, France, for the last ten
years or more. He grew up in New York, worked in high
school on the same literary magazine that Samuel R.
Delany did later, hung out in Greenwich Village with the
beatniks, then worked at the Scott Meredith literary
agency, sold fiction to John W. Campbell at *Analog*, but
also was a sparkling figure in the new wave and published his major, controversial novel, *Bug Jack Barron*,
in *New Worlds*, moved to California in the late '60s and
wrote a *Star Trek* script . . . you get the idea. He has
been a commentator on SF for decades, and a leading
critic in *Asimov's* in recent years. In 1998 *Asimov's*
finally got its own web site and is posting Spinrad's *On
Books* columns there after initial magazine publication.
He once told me an anecdote about being arrested in
Disneyland and taken to the Mickey Mouse jail. That
may or may not have something to do with the genesis
of this story, or with his feelings about the Disney organization. This work was originally commissioned and
published by the French national newspaper *Liberation*,
then published in *Asimov's*. It is Spinrad's only SF story
in the last couple of years. This is first-rate satire, extend-
ing that tradition that flowered in the 1950s, that was
perhaps the center of '50s SF, into the late '90s.

"**M**ess not with the Mouse."

"*Mess not with the Mouse?* We fly you to California *business* class and install you in a luxurious hotel in Anaheim and when you are summoned to give an account of the situation, you spout degenerate Taoist crypticisms?"

Xian Bai managed to resist the impulse to tug at the tight collar of his dress shirt, so uncomfortable after two weeks in Southern California, where even high level executives felt free to attend meetings in casual attire.

"This is not a Taoist epigram," he explained. "It is a precept common in high American corporate circles, where it is thought highly unwise to arouse the ire of the Disney Corporation."

Had the Deputy Minister for Overseas Cultural Relations been a Long Nose, his pale white skin would no doubt have turned crimson with rage. Despite the handicap of the lack of this Caucasian ability, he managed to make his displeasure clear enough by banging his hand on the desk with sufficient force to rattle the tea service.

"And what is the People's Republic of China, some Banana Republic owned by the United Fruit Corporation?" the Deputy Minister shouted. "We are a billion and a quarter people! We are the largest and fastest growing market in the world! We have the world's largest army! We have nuclear missiles! How dare the Mouse presume so outrageously to mess with *us*!"

He calmed himself with a sip of tea and regarded

Xian Bai with a colder species of outrage. "You *did* make this clear with sufficient force?"

"Indeed I did!" Xian Bai was constrained to reply firmly.

But he was dissembling. Two weeks in Anaheim to obtain a meeting with a Vice President in charge of overseas marketing and the results of that conversation had been enough to convince him that such force did not exist.

"Get real, Xian," that individual had advised him. "The idea that the Yellow Peril was gonna storm the beaches at Orlando went out with Ronald Reagan. What are you gonna do, nuke *Pirates of the Caribbean*?"

"But China is the largest consumer market in the world—"

"And you guys have been screwing us out of it since that Dalai Lama film dust-up that cost Ovitz his job and us a bundle for the golden parachute! You guys made a real bad career move."

The Disney Vice President glanced heavenward.

"You pissed Michael off."

"And this film is your vengeance?"

The Disney Vice President grinned like the Lion King.

"The bottom line," he said, "is always the best revenge."

The minions of the Mouse had not been reticent in allowing Xian Bai to attend a preview screening of *The Long March*, though at the reception afterward—white wine, simple dim sum, lo mein noodles, barbecued spare ribs—a disgruntled American reporter had complained that this was the "B-list" screening, those privileged to enjoy "A-list" prerogatives being treated to lobster, caviar, and champagne.

This mattered not to Xian Bai, since the film itself had quite destroyed his appetite—being an animated cartoon version of the heroic Long March of the Chinese Revolution, dripping with syrupy music, festooned with Busby Berkeley choreography, and featuring Chou En Lai as a fox, Chiang Kai Shek as a mongoose, the People's Army as happy ants, and starring *Chairman Mao* himself as a grinning and rather overweight panda.

"You *do* realize that the premiere of this atrocity in the United States will result in the immediate and permanent closure of the Chinese market to all your enterprises," Xian Bai informed the Disney Vice President as he was instructed to do.

"No problem, guy, you want us to premiere *The Long March* in China, you've got it."

"You cannot seriously expect to ever release this film in China!"

"Better inside the tent pissing out, than outside the tent pissing in, in the immortal words of Lyndon Johnson."

"This means what . . . ?"

"It means that one way or the other, we *will* crack open the Chinese market, but we don't need it to make the numbers golden. *The Long March* cost less than fifty million to make, negative and promo costs still keep the total under a hundred, and we've already laid off twice that on the merchandising rights! So the film's in the money before we even release it. We figure Mao the stuffed panda alone will gross enough this Christmas to cover the whole production budget!"

"You . . . you plan to market *Chairman Mao* as stuffed panda?" Xian Bai considered himself an apolitical modern Chinese pragmatist, but this was too much even for him.

"The kids we ran the marketing tests on *loved* it. Mao Tze Tung's gonna be ten times more popular as a panda doll than he ever was in the flesh."

The Disney Vice President leaned closer. "If I let you

in on something *really* hot, can you keep a secret?" he said conspiratorially.

"I can make no such commitment. . . ."

The Disney Vice President shrugged. "Well, what the hell, it's a fait accompli anyway. We've decided to stop renting out our characters to front other people's fast food franchises, and get into the business ourselves. Mickey and Donald and the old gang are tied up in long term contracts, but Mao the Panda—"

"You cannot be serious!"

"I *know* what you're thinking, dumb move, the market's oversaturated with hamburger and pizza and taco and fried chicken chains already. But . . . *nobody's doing Chinese!* Panda Pagodas in every shopping mall in the world! Fronted by Mao the Panda himself! We'll hang poor Ronald McDonald from his own Golden Arches!"

Even the edited and explicated version of this conversation was difficult for the Deputy Minister for Overseas Cultural Relations to comprehend.

"How can they expect to get away with this affront to the Middle Kingdom?" he demanded. "How can the American government permit this? You did make it clear that we may retaliate against other American corporations as well?"

Xian Bai nodded miserably.

"And?" demanded the Deputy Minister.

Xian Bai took a deep breath, fixed his gaze upon the desktop. "They . . . they issued their own ultimatum."

"*An ultimatum?*" whispered the Deputy Minister, clearly dumbfounded.

"The People's Republic of China must allow *The Long March* to open simultaneously in no less than one thousand theaters nationwide with Disney to retain sixty percent of the gross, must cede the necessary real estate for the establishment of no less than one thousand Panda Pagodas, plus Disneyworlds in Shanghai, Peking, and Hong Kong, and grant a one hundred percent tax abatement for a period of fifty years on these properties, or . . ."

"Or?"

"Or, I was told, the Mouse shall roar, Uncle Scrooge will dip into his money bin, Dumbo will fly, and the Big Bad Wolf will huff and puff and blow our house down!"

At first, it appeared that vast black storm-fronts were approaching China from several directions, then trepidation turned to bemused delight as the black clouds resolved into thousands upon untold thousands of kites.

Black kites. All identical.

All in the form of the happily grinning face of the world-famous Mouse.

No, not kites—

"Balloons!" shouted the Deputy Minister For Overseas Cultural Affairs. "Millions upon millions of them floating gently down from the skies all over China!"

"Amusing," said Xian Bai, "but I don't—"

"Amusing!" screamed the Deputy Minister, reaching into a pocket and extracting a deflated version of the apparently offending item. "They deflate in a moment to the size of a poor man's wallet! They reinflate with a few puffs of air!"

This ability he then proceeded to demonstrate, producing an example of the head of the famous Mouse somewhat larger than a soccer ball.

"Do you realize what this is, you imbecile?" he demanded.

Xian Bai regarded the grinning balloon face in perplexity. All seemed quite ordinary, except for the bulb at the end of the long white rodent's muzzle, which, instead of the traditional black ball, seemed to be a small silvery packet of some sort of electronic circuitry. . . .

"*This,*" said the Deputy Minister, poking Xian Bai's nose with that of Mickey, "is a satellite television antenna!"

If somewhere the spirit of Chairman Mao might be scowling down unhappily on this spectacle, surely that of Deng Shao Ping would approve, Xian Bai told himself, and at any rate Mao the Panda smiled down benignly on his enterprise from atop the steepled entrance as he cut the ribbon to open his fifth Panda Pagoda.

After all, as Lenin himself had pointed out, you can't make a revolution without breaking eggs, though in this case the standard recipes supplied in *Mao the Panda's Little Red Book* were admirably parsimonious with this relatively expensive ingredient.

Xian Bai, partly as punishment, and partly because there was no one more experienced to dispatch, had been sent back to Anaheim to confront the minions of the Mouse. This time, however, it was a cut-rate charter flight and a grim motel in Santa Ana, and when he finally penetrated the bureaucratic layers to the Vice Presidential level, he found himself dealing with the legal department, with what the natives called a "Suit," a hard-eyed fellow replete with tie and wire-rim glasses.

"No international laws, treaties, or conventions were violated," Xian Bai was told firmly. "The balloon antennas were released in international airspace."

"And just *happened* to drift en masse over China?"

The Suit shrugged. "An act of God," he said. "You could try suing the Pope, I suppose—I could give you my brother-in-law's card—but you'll get nowhere with us."

"Even though the only channel the balloon antennas will receive is the Disney Channel? Which just *hap-*

pens to have begun broadcasting in Mandarin and Cantonese?"

"The satellite is in geosynchronous orbit, which is international territory. We have a legal right to broadcast whatever we like in whatever languages we choose."

"But it's illegal for Chinese citizens to own satellite dishes. It's illegal for Chinese citizens to watch foreign broadcasts!"

The Suit displayed a porcelain crocodile grin that was a perfect example of the Beverly Hills dentist's art. "That's *your* problem," he said. "*Our* problem is your refusal to allow us to release *The Long March* in China and rake in the profits from the merchandising tie-ins and Panda Pagodas."

The grin vanished, but the crocodile remained.

"And unless *our* problem evaporates by the film's international release date," said the Suit, "*your* problem is going to get a lot worse."

"Worse . . . ?" stammered Xian Bai.

How could it get worse? There was no way to confiscate the millions of balloon antennas—at the approach of the police, they were just deflated and hidden away, to be redeployed the moment it was safe. Millions upon millions of Chinese were watching broadcasts from the Disneyworlds, cartoons and feature-length animated films, endless trailers for *The Long March*, endless commercials for the tie-in merchandising, endless promotions for the Panda Pagodas. The demand for the opening of China to the minions of the Mouse was building to a frenzy.

According to the latest public opinion polls, forty-one million Chinese people already believed that Mao Tze Tung had been born with black and white fur.

"*Much* worse," said the Suit. "We could give free air time to the Dalai Lama. We could broadcast clips of the Tien An Mien massacre with music by Nine Inch Nails. We could subject your people to reruns of old Charlie Chan movies. And if none of that worked, there's always the ultimate weapon . . ."

"The . . . ultimate weapon . . . ?"

"We broadcast the first twenty minutes of *The Long March* in clear, scramble the rest of it, force everyone in China to buy expensive decoders to see it, and blame the Communist Party."

The crocodile grin returned.

"Do you *really* believe any government could retain the Mandate of Heaven after that?"

"Mess not with the Mouse . . ." sighed Xian Bai.

"Not a good career move at all," agreed the Suit. "On the other hand, in return for say five percent of the gross, I could aid *you* in making a sweet one. In the words of Mao the Panda, one hand washes the other."

Well, the Chinese people had not survived several thousand years of turbulent history without paying due attention to the sacred bottom line. Indeed one might argue that the bottom line, like most else, had been a Chinese invention. Especially when there was rich profit to be made in convincing yourself that it was true.

And for those Panda Pagoda franchisees who had trouble swallowing that one, *Mao the Panda's Little Red Book*, in return for the Mouse's thirty percent of the gross, provided more than standard recipes and accounting procedures, it provided an ideological rationale.

Fast food was, after all, a Chinese invention itself. Dim sum, wonton soup, noodles, and stir-fried vegetables with a bit of meat, were quicker to make, tastier, ecologically more benign, and far more nutritious than hamburgers, pizzas, and greasy fried chicken parts.

And since the ingredients were much cheaper, the profit margin was higher too.

Today China, tomorrow the world, promised Chairman Mao the Panda.

And what did it matter if *Mao the Panda's Little Red Book* had appropriated the epigram from Confucius or Lao Tze or the Buddha himself if Chairman Mao the Panda's words had the ring of truth?

The wise man does well by doing good.

It was enough to keep Xian Bai smiling all the way on his frequent visits to the bank.

The Day Before
They Came

MARY SOON LEE

Mary Soon Lee grew up in London, got an MA in mathematics, and later an MS in astronautics and space engineering. "I have since lived in cleaner, safer, quieter cities," she says, "but London is the one that I miss." She moved to Cambridge, Massachusetts, in 1990 and then to Pittsburgh, Pennsylvania, where she splits her time between writing short stories and acting as a computer consultant to an artificial intelligence company. She has published more than thirty stories in the 1990s. She also runs a local writing workshop, the Pittsburgh Worldwrights. This story is from *Interzone*, a source for nearly a quarter of the stories in this book this year, and as this is written, the work is nominated for the British Science Fiction Association Award for best short SF story of 1998. It is a concise, effective piece of storytelling by misdirection, an evocation of the everyday anxiety of living in the future.

The morning before the aliens came, Molly Harris busied herself preparing her son's lunch-box. Since it was a Friday, Justin would be going to school in person for his social skills classes. Molly put a generous handful of cherries into the lunch-box. Even the vat-grown cherries cost more than she could really afford, but she wanted Justin to have a treat to swap with the other second-graders.

Most of the younger mothers Molly knew worried when their kids went to school, checking the germ count hourly, scared their children might come home with a bruise, or a scrape, or a runny nose. But Molly had been 53 when Justin was born, and she remembered when classroom violence meant knives and guns, the way her heart had thudded during the weekly bomb drill.

So instead of worrying about Justin on Fridays, Molly worried about him on Monday through Thursday. She would peek into his bedroom as she moved around the apartment. No matter how absorbed Justin looked, the tip of his tongue sticking out as the computer led him through a problem, Molly couldn't convince herself that it was right for a child to spend hours on end netted-in.

A terrible din erupted from Justin's bedroom: screeches and bleats, neighs and howls and squawks. Molly slapped her hands over her ears. She had bought Justin the Noah's Ark alarm clock for his sixth birthday, a year ago.

The din subsided for a moment, but Molly wasn't fooled. She kept her hands pressed to her ears as the alarm clock exploded into the deep bass trumpet of the elephants. In the silence that followed, Molly wiped her hands on her apron, then reached for the peanut butter jar.

Sounds of hasty splashing came from the bathroom, followed by bare feet running toward her. Two thin brown arms, somehow sticky despite the bathroom expedition, wrapped themselves around Molly's waist.

"Morning, Mom."

"Good morning, Justin." She stared down at the top of her son's head, pressed tight against her stomach, his fine black hair tousled.

"It's my birthday tomorrow."

"Really? I don't believe you."

Justin let go of her, and rolled his eyes exaggeratedly. "Yes, you do. You do, you do."

"I do," said Molly, wishing he had hugged her a little longer. "Tomorrow's your birthday and we're going to the water park. But today you have to go to school."

"Uh huh." Justin poured the milk onto his cereal, holding the milk carton with both hands, and managing not to spill any.

Breakfast took less than five minutes, and then Justin clattered down the staircase ahead of her, down the four flights to the porch to wait for the school bus.

The bus came early. One quick hug, and Justin scrambled on board.

The afternoon before the aliens came, Molly went birthday shopping. The city tax paid for glass roofs over the downtown streets. Molly told herself she approved of such a sensible precaution against the ultraviolet, but the enclosed air seemed stale despite the constant whir of fans, and the filtered sunlight seemed somehow flatter.

Molly spent half an hour choosing new swimming trunks for Justin. She couldn't decide between a pair covered with dapper penguins and another pair with plain blue and yellow stripes. Six months ago she would have bought the penguins without hesitation, but perhaps Justin would think them too childish now.

She tried to remember what his best friend, Adam, had worn the last time she took the two of them to the water park. Something simple she thought. She paid for the blue and yellow striped trunks, secretly yearning for the penguins.

Outside again, the air temperature fixed at the calculated summer optimum, warm but not hot. Perversely Molly wished the system would break down, even for an hour or two, just long enough for a mini heat wave. She paused for a minute, remembering playing on the beach one summer holiday. The sun had burnt the back of Molly's neck, too hot, too bright. Her face had stung from blowing sand. And yet everything sparkled, the very air buoyant, as if she breathed in tablespoons of undiluted joy.

People surged past Molly as she stood there on the downtown street. She pulled herself together with a shrug. She would have loved to take Justin to the beach, but no use dwelling on it now.

She set off again, heading for the AI store. She knew how much Justin wanted a pair of AI shoes, but even though most of his class had them by now, he had only asked for them once. When Molly had told him they cost too much for her to buy, he bit his lip and never asked again.

So two months ago, Molly had canceled her subscription to the interactives, making do with ordinary TV, and she thought she had saved enough to buy Justin his shoes.

Entering the AI store, Molly blinked. The floor, ceiling, and walls were velvet black. Glowing holograms danced to either side, marking the corridors. Molly took one cautious step forward.

"Can I be of assistance?" A caterpillar-shaped mechanical appeared in front of her. The mechanical raised the front of its long body until its head was level with her chest, its silvered skin gleaming.

"I'm looking for AI shoes."

"Please follow me." The mechanical started down a corridor, turning its head to check she was following. It stopped by a vast array of shoes. "First select a shoe style, and then I will demonstrate our selection of AI personalities."

Molly nodded, trying to look as if she came to shops like this every day. Sandals and ballet shoes, ice-skates and boots and babies' bootees stretched before her. After a long pause, she pointed at a pair of orange sneakers. "How much are those ones?"

"Eighty dollars, without any program installed. Did you have a particular AI personality in mind for the shoes?"

"No. They're for my son. He's turning seven."

"Perhaps an educational supplement?" The mechanical lifted its forelegs to a small keyboard, and typed in a command.

The left sneaker twitched. "What's two times twenty-six?" asked the orange shoe.

Molly said nothing. The mechanical made throat-clearing noise, though she knew it didn't really have a throat. "Fifty-two," said Molly.

"That's right!" said the shoe. "What a clever girl!"

The right shoe twitched beside it. "Two times twenty-six is fifty-two, and do you know how many states there are in America?"

"Fifty-two," said Molly. She looked at the mechanical. "I wanted something a little more fun."

The mechanical keyed in another command.

"Let's all sing to the sing-along-song," sang the two orange sneakers.

Molly shook her head. "Definitely not."

She declined the next dozen offerings. The cops and robbers program amused her, but she had overheard Justin and Adam discussing how old-fashioned police games were. Finally she settled on a program with no gimmicks at all. The left shoe and the right shoe just chatted away as if they were children; the left shoe, Bertie, was a little bossier, the right shoe, Alex, seeming shyer.

The mechanical wrapped up the shoes in orange tissue paper inside an orange box, explained how to switch off Alex and Bertie's voices, and assured her the program automatically deactivated during school hours.

Molly clutched the gift-wrapped shoe-box to her all the way home on the bus, picturing Justin's reaction the next morning.

The evening before the aliens came, Justin was hyperactive, overexcited about his coming birthday. Molly gave him a mug of hot milk, hoping it might calm him. But still Justin scaled Mount Everest (the sofa and the shelves beside it), using his scarf and six kitchen forks as equipment.

"But what if my birthday doesn't come?" demanded Justin, as he sat triumphantly atop the mountain peak, having retraced Sir Edmund Hillary and Tenzing Norgay's route along the Southeast Ridge.

"Of course your birthday will come, silly."

"What if there's a fire, and my presents are burned?"

"There won't be a fire," said Molly, lifting Justin up and sitting him on her lap, back down at first camp.

"But if there were a fire, I'd get you more presents. I promise. And now it really is time for bed."

"Just five more minutes, Mom. Please."

"Okay," said Molly, and watched him set off on a second ascent of Everest. She would have liked to have someone to share Justin with, to sit beside on the sofa while Justin played, to talk to when Justin fell asleep. Justin had aunts and uncles, but that wasn't the same.

Molly had waited till she was past 50 before she realized Mr. Right might never arrive. Her sister had accompanied her to the family planning clinic, waited patiently while the official checked that Molly hadn't already used up her one-child quota. Then Molly and her sister picked a father from the database, a gentle-eyed biochemist, with long fingers and a talent for playing the cello.

Molly knew it was silly, but from time to time she dreamed about Justin's father, wanting to tell him all about his son. She checked her watch. "Time to sleep."

She tucked Justin into bed, read him a chapter from *Watership Down*, kissed him once, trying to hold onto the moment as she had tried to hold onto every moment of his childhood, forcing herself to let go until the morning.

The night before the aliens came, Molly watched two mediocre comedy programs on TV, then got up to make a mug of cocoa as the late night news came on. She heard something about a group of meteors detected by the deep solar tracking system. Half-curious, thinking about the shooting stars she'd seen one night a decade ago, she wandered back to the living room.

A triangular formation of blue and green dots flickered on the TV screen, somewhere out past Saturn, according to the newscaster. *Past Saturn*. For a moment,

Molly rolled the words around in her mind; it sounded like the start of a fairy tale, "Far, far away . . ."

With a shake of her head, Molly turned off the TV. Time for bed. She knew Justin would be up early tomorrow. She paused by Justin's room, opened the door a crack for one last peek at her son, fast asleep. Silently she closed the door.

This Side of Independence

ROB CHILSON

Rob Chilson has been publishing SF for more than thirty years. He sold his first SF in 1968 to John W. Campbell at *Analog*, and has published seven SF novels, of which *The Shores of Kansas* (1976) is perhaps the best known. He is a knowledgeable and talented craftsman who writes thoroughly professional science fiction. This story first appeared in *F&SF*, which had a strong year as well (though much of the strongest fiction was fantasy), and provided three of our selections this year. It is a tale of the distant future, when humanity is no longer tied to the planet Earth. It is an interesting comparison, in respect to its vision of the distant future of humanity, to the Geston story, below.

They were taking up Kansas in big bites.

Geelie hovered above, detached, observing. Stark night cloaked the world under a shrunken sun, save for the pit, where hell glared. Magma glowed in the darkness where the rock, hectares wide, crumbled in the gravitor beam. Shards of the world upreared, uproared, black edged with glowing red, and lofted into the groaning air, pieces of a broken pot. The bloody light spattered on the swag-bellied ships that hung above—crows tearing at the carcass with a loud continuous clamor. Pieces of the planet fell back and splashed in thunder and liquid fire, yellow and scarlet. Old Earth shuddered for kilometers around.

The glare, the heat, the tumult filled the world. But from a distance, Geelie saw, it was reduced to a cheerful cherry glow and a murmur of sound, lost in the endless night. In her long view, Kansas was a vast sunken plain of contorted rock, dusted with silent snow under a shaded sun.

"Aung Charah in *Tigerclaw* to Goblong Seven," Geelie's speaker said.

"Goblong Seven to Aung Charah," she said.

"Geelie, take a swing around the south side of the working pit and look at the terraces there. I think the magma is flowing up on them."

"Hearing and obedience."

Kansas was a hole walled with stairsteps of cooled lava, terraced for kilometers down to the pit of hell. As fast as the rock froze, it was torn off in hectare-sized chips, to feed the hungry space colonies.

Geelie swung her goblong and swooped down and around the work site. She peered intently in dimness, blinded by the contrast. The magma was definitely crawling up on the lower terrace of cooled rock.

"It's slow as yet," she reported, sending the teleview to Aung Charah.

"We'll have to watch it, however, or we'll have another volcano. Check on it frequently," he told her.

"Hearing and obedience," Geelie said. She leaned forward to peer up through the windscreen.

The Sun was a flickering red candle, the cherry color of the magma. As she watched, it brightened; brightened; brightened again, to a dazzling orange. Then it faded, paused, recovered—briefly showed a gleam of brilliance that glimpsed the black rock below, streaked with snow. Then it faded, faded further, almost vanished.

The Sun was a candle seen through a haze of smoke. But each drifting mote was a space colony with solar panels extended, jostling in their billions jealously to seize the Sun. One by one, the planets of old Sol had been eaten by the colonies, till only Earth was left, passed into the shades of an eternal night.

And now the Old World's historical value had been overridden by the economic value of its water, air, and rock. Also, its vast gravity well was a major obstacle to space traffic.

Noon, planetary time, Geelie thought.

She took her goblong in a long sweep around the work site, occasionally touching the visual recorder's button. Her Colony, Kinabatangan, was a member of The Obstacle-Leaping Consortium; she was part of Kinabatangan's observer team.

A gleam of light caught her eye, and she looked sharply aside. East, she realized. Puzzled, she looped the goblong back again more slowly and sought for the gleam. She found it, but it immediately winked out.

That was odd, she thought. A bright light, yellow or even white—surely artificial—on the highlands to the east. That was disputed land, it was not yet being worked. Perhaps, she thought, observers had set up a camp on the planet.

She called Aung Charah and reported, got permission to check it out. "If I can find it," she said. "The light is gone again; door closed, perhaps."

"I'm having Communications call; I'll keep you informed," Aung Charah said.

She acknowledged and cruised as nearly straight as she could along the beam she'd seen. Presently the land mounted in broken scarps before her, vaguely seen in the wan bloody light of the Sun. Vast masses of shattered rock, covered with snow or capped with ice, tumbled down from the highlands. Missouri, that was what its uncouth name had been, Geelie saw, keying up her map.

At this point there'd been a great sprawling city, Kansas City by name, more populous than a dozen colonies. The parts which had straggled over the border had been mined and the once vertical scarp had collapsed. East of the line, everything this side of Independence on her map had fallen into the hole that was Kansas.

"Aung Charah in *Tigerclaw* to Geelie in Goblong Seven," said her speaker. "Communications reports no contact. We have no report of anyone in that area. Behinders?" Dubiously.

"Unlikely. However, I am checking. Goblong Seven out."

It was three hundred years since stay-behind planetarians had been found on the mother world. Considering how bleak it now was, Geelie considered them extremely unlikely, as by his tone did Aung Charah.

She cruised slowly over the tumbled mounds of snow-covered rubble that marked the old city. Kilometers it extended, and somehow Geelie found that more oppressive even than the vast expanse of riven rock behind her. She could not imagine the torrents of people who must have lived on this deck. The average Colony had only a hundred thousand.

She peered into the dimness. The rubble showed as black pocks in the blood-lit snow. Presently she came to hover and pondered.

Possibly she'd seen a transitory gleam off a sheet of transpex or polished rock or metal in the old city, she thought. But the color was wrong. No. She'd seen a light. Perhaps there were commercial observers here from a different consortium—not necessarily spying on The Obstacle-Leaping Consortium. There might be many reasons why commercial observers would want to keep secret.

Infrared, she thought. The goblong wasn't equipped with IR viewers, but Aung Charah had given her a pair of binox. She unharnessed and slipped into the back for them. And a few minutes later she saw a plume of light against the chill background.

It leaked in two dozen points from a hill of rubble a kilometer away. Geelie got its coordinates and called Aung Charah to report.

"I'm going to go down and request permission to land."

"Of course this 'Missouri' is not part of our grant," Aung Charah said. "They—whoever they are—will probably have a right to refuse. Do nothing to involve us legally."

"Hearing and obedience."

Geelie sloped the goblong down, circled the mound, presently found a trampled place in the thin snow and kicked on her lights. Aiming them down, she saw footprints and a door in an ancient wall made of clay brick, a wall patched with shards of concrete glued together.

The mound was a warren, a tumble of broken buildings run together, with forgotten doors and unlighted windows peering from odd angles under a lumpy, snow-covered roof.

She sent back a teleview, saying, "I wonder if this is an observers' nest after all."

"Any answer on the universal freqs?"

"One moment." She called, got no answer. "I'm going to land without formal permission and bang on the door."

"Very well."

Geelie landed the goblong, leaving its lights on, and slipped into the back. She pulled her parka hood forward, drew on her gloves, and opened the door. A breath of bitter cold air entered, making her gasp. Ducking out, she started for the door.

Movement caught her eye and she looked up, to see a heavily bundled figure standing atop a pile of rubble by the wall.

"Hello!" she called.

"Hello," came a man's voice. He was not twice as thick as a normal human, she saw—he was simply wearing many layers of cloth against the biting cold.

Geelie exhaled a cloud of vapor, calming herself. So crudely dressed a man had to be a behinder—and who knew how he would react?

"I-I am Geelie of Kinabatangan Colony, a member of The Obstacle-Leaping Consortium. Permission to land?"

"What? Oh, granted. That would be you, working over there in Kansas?" His tone was neutral, if guarded. His accent was harsh, rasping, but not unintelligible.

"Yes."

"What brings you here? Will you now begin on Missourah?"

"No," she said. "Missourah," carefully pronouncing it as he had, "is disputed by a number of consortiums and wrecking companies. It will be years before they have settled that dispute."

"That's good to hear," said the other, and moved. With a dangerous seeming scramble, he slid down from the rubble pile.

Confronting her, he was a head taller than she, and very pale, a pure caucasoid type, in the light from her goblong. He even had the deep blue eyes once confined to caucasoids, and his beard was yellow.

"Name's Clayborn," he said, proffering his hand. "Enos Clayborn."

She squeezed and shook it in the european fashion. "Pleased to meet you, U—er, Mr. Clayborn."

"Won't you come in out of the cold?" he asked, gesturing toward the door.

"Thank you." She followed him gratefully. The bleakness more than the cold chilled her.

The door opened, emitting a waft of warm air that condensed into fog. Geelie stepped in, inhaling humidity and the smell of many people, with an undertone of green plants. It was like, yet unlike, the air of a Colony; more people, less plants, she thought; not so pure an air. She was standing in a vestibule with wooden walls covered with peeling white paint; overhead a single square electrolumer gave a dim yellowish light.

Clayborn fastened the door behind her and stepped past her to open the other door, gesturing her through it. Pushing her hood back, Geelie opened her parka as she entered a room full of tubs of snow, slowly melting; piles of wooden boards; piles of scrap metal; shelves full of things obviously salvaged from the ruins; an assortment of tools. Beyond this was yet another door, opening into a large, brightly lit room full of furniture and people.

"Enos is ba—Enos has brought someone!" "Enos has brought a stranger!" "A strange woman!" The exclamations ran through the room quickly, and a couple of people slipped out. Moments later, they and several others returned.

"Folks, this is Geelie of—of—?" Clayborn turned to her.

"Kinabatangan Colony," Geelie said. Old people, she thought. "Observer of The Obstacle-Leaping Consortium."

"Those are the ones mining Kansas," Clayborn said. "Geelie tells me that they won't start mining Missouri" (pronouncing it differently, she noticed) "for quite a few years yet."

Clayborn in his mid-twenties was the youngest person in the room, she saw. The next youngest were four or five hale middle-aged sorts with gray in their hair, perhaps twice his age, and ranging up from there to a frail ancient on a couch, big pale eyes turned toward her and a thin wisp of cottony hair on a pillow. A dozen and a half at most.

"How long have you been here?" she asked, marveling.

"Forever," said one of the white-haired oldsters drily. "We never been anywheres else."

Geelie smiled back at their smiles. "I am awed that you have survived," she said simply, removing her parka and gloves.

"This is our leader, Alden," said Clayborn, pulling up a chair for her.

"The last hundred years was the worst," said Alden.

The behinders, having overcome their shyness, now crowded forward and Clayborn introduced them. Geelie bowed and spoke to all, shook with the bolder ones. When she seated herself, one of the women handed her a cup on a european saucer. She looked at them with awe, reflecting that they must be a thousand years old.

"Brown," she heard them murmur. "Brown. Beautiful—such a nice young woman. Such beautiful black hair."

She sipped a mild coffee brew and nodded her thanks. "The last hundred years?" she said to Alden. "Yes, it must have been."

For over nine hundred years Earth had been in partial shadow and permanent glaciation, but the Sun still shone. Then the greedy colonies broke their agreements and moved massively into the space between the Old World and the Sun. Earth passed into the shadows, and shortly thereafter they began to disassemble it.

"'Course, our ancestors laid in a good supply of power cells and everything else we'd need, way back when Earth was abandoned by everybody else," Alden said. "No problems there. But how much longer will the air last?"

"Oh, maybe another hundred years," she said, startled. "Freezing it for transport is a slow process."

"And the glaciers? They came down this way back when the Sun shone bright."

Geelie smiled, shook her head. "It's so cold now that even the oceans are freezing over, so the glaciers can't grow by snowfall. Also, frankly, the glaciers were the first to be mined; that much fresh water was worth plenty. Of course the oceans are valuable too, and they have been heavily mined also."

"The snowfall gets thinner every year," said Clayborn. "We have to go farther and farther to get enough. Soon we'll be reduced to thawing the soil for water."

Geelie's response was interrupted by the discreet beeping of her wrist radio. She keyed it on. "Aung Charah in *Tigerclaw* to Geelie in Goblong Seven," it said in a tiny voice, relayed from the goblong.

"Geelie to Aung Charah," she said into it. "I have received permission to land and am with a group of native Earthers."

"Behinders," said Alden drily.

She flashed him a smile and said, "Behinders, they call themselves."

"Er—yes," said Aung Charah, sounding startled. "Er—carry on. Aung Charah out."

"Hearing and obedience. Geelie out."

"Carry on?" Alden asked.

Geelie sobered. She had been excited and amazed at meeting these people and had not thought ahead. "Well," she said. "He represents the Consortium and dares not commit it. You are not his problem."

"We never thought of ourselves as anybody's problem," said Alden mildly. "More coffee?"

Geelie bowed to Lyou Ye, who stood to respond, then reseated herself behind her desk and frowned.

"Behinders," she said. "They must be the very last. It's been what, three hundred years since any have been found, that lot in Africa." She looked sharply at Geelie. "Aung Charah is right, they're not our problem. They live in 'Missouri,' however it's pronounced, outside our grant. They're the problem of the Missouri Compact."

"But those people won't settle their disputes for years, possibly decades," said Geelie. "We can't just let these behinders die."

Lyou Ye glanced aside, frowning, and tapped her finger. She'd come a long way, Geelie knew, in a short time. A very beautiful woman, ten years older than Geelie, with waving masses of dark red hair and the popular tiger-green eyes contributed by gene-splicing, she was commonly called Ma Kyaw, "Miss Smooth." But she was intelligent and fully aware of the power of public opinion.

"Very well, if you can find a Colony willing to sponsor them, I'll authorize shipping to lift them out," Lyou

Ye said abruptly. "It won't take much, fortunately, by your description. Declining population ever since the Sun was shaded, I take it, with only this 'Enosclayborn' in the last generation. They'd have ended soon enough. You found them just in time for him," she added. "He's probably still a virgin."

"I'd personally like to thank Geelie for all the time and trouble she's put in for us, her and all her folks," said Alden.

Geelie flushed with pleasure as they applauded her.

"Now, I'll just ask for a show of hands," Alden continued. "All them that's in favor of flyin' off into space to a colony, raise your hand."

Geelie leaned forward eagerly.

There was a long pause. The behinders turned their faces to each other, Geelie heard a whisper or two, someone cleared a throat. But no one looked at her.

Alden stood looking around, waited a bit, then finally said, "Don't look like there's anybody in favor of the city of Independence movin' into a colony. But that don't mean nobody can go. Anybody that wants to is naturally free to leave. Just speak to me, or to Miss Geelie here."

Shocked, horrified, Geelie looked at them. Someone coughed. Still no one looked at her. She turned a stricken gaze on Enos Clayborn. He looked thoughtful but unsurprised. And he had not raised his hand.

So silent was the room that the purring of a mother cat, entering at the far side with a squirming kitten in her mouth, seemed loud.

Alden turned to her. "New ideas, like flyin' space, sometimes is hard to take in," he said kindly. "We had since yesterday to talk it over, but still it's a new idea. Enos, you might take the little lady back to Gretchen's nest and give them kittens a little attention."

Enos smiled at her, and faces were turned from the cat to her, smiling in relief. "She's bringing her kittens out," Geelie heard them murmur. "They're old enough for her to introduce them around."

Numbly she followed the tall young man back through the warren of abandoned passages to the warm storage room where the cat had her nest.

When he evidently intended merely to play with the kittens, she said, "Enos, why—why didn't they vote to go?"

"Well, we're used to it here. As Alden said, it takes time to get used to new ideas." He handed her a kitten. "This is the runt—the last born of the litter. We named her Omega—we'll give them all shots in another month or two; she'll be the last cat born on Earth."

Absently she took the purring kitten, a tiny squirming handful of fur. "But you'll all die if you don't go!"

"Well, we'll all die anyway," he said mildly. "Ever notice most of us are old folks? A lot aren't so far from dying now. They'd just as soon die in a place they know. We've been here a long time, you know."

"But—but—*you're* not old! And your parents, and Alden's daughter Aina, and Camden—"

"I wouldn't know how to act, anywhere but here," he said mildly. He smiled down at the proudly purring mother cat.

Geelie, Lyou Ye, and Aung Charah sat in the small conference room.

Lyou Ye grimaced. "So that was their reaction? I'll admit it wasn't one I'd foreseen. All the other behinders in history agreed to go. Some of them signaled to us."

Geelie shifted her position uneasily, cross-legged on a pillow, and nodded unhappily. "I even offered to send them to a european Colony, so they'd be among familiar-seeming people, but that didn't help."

Aung Charah shook his head. "We're getting a lot of publicity on this," he said. "The newsmedia are not hostile yet. But what will they say when the behinders' refusal becomes known?"

Lyou Ye frowned. "They'll blame us, depend upon it. Have any of them interviewed the behinders?"

Aung Charah shook his head. "They have to get permission from the Missouri Compact, which is very cautious. These planetarians have rights too. Invasion of their privacy . . ." He shook his head again.

"If we leave them here to die, we'll certainly be blamed," said Lyou Ye. "I'm tempted to order Consortium Police in to evacuate them forcibly."

Geelie sipped her tea, looking at "Ma Kyaw." That's your sort of solution, she thought. Direct, uncompromising, get it done, get it over with. And somebody else can pick up the pieces, clean up the mess.

"Alden would certainly complain if that were done," she said, speaking up reluctantly. "The media attention would be far worse. Violation of planetary rights . . . they may even have some claim to the old city of Independence. The Missouri Compact may legally have to wait for them all to die to mine that part of its grant."

Lyou Ye grimaced again. "I suppose you're right."

Aung Charah set his cup down. "Media criticism won't hurt the Consortium if we leave them here. The criticism we'd get if we violate their rights might affect us adversely. Investors—"

Lyou Ye was a "careerman." She nodded, frowning, lips pursed.

Geelie looked around the room, so unlike the comfortably cluttered warren in which Enos lived. In one wall, a niche with an arrangement of flowers, signifying

This too shall pass; the woven screen against another wall, with its conventional pattern of crows over tiny fields curving up in the distance; the parquet floor with its fine rich grain; the subtle, not quite random leaf pattern of ivory and cream on the walls; the bronze samovar and the fantastically contorted porcelain dragon teapot, the only ornate thing in the room.

Enos was right, she thought. He would not know how to live in a place like this.

She thought of the world that was all he had ever known, a place of snow-powdered rock and brooding, perpetual night, a red-eyed Sun blown in the wind. A bare, harsh, bleak place without a future. For him in the end, it could only mean tending the old "folks" as one by one they died, and then the penultimate generation, the generation of his parents, as they also grew old. At last he would be left alone to struggle against the darkness and the cold until he too lay dying, years of solitude and then a lonely death.

"There's no help for it," said Lyou Ye broodingly. She looked at Geelie. "You'll have to seduce Enosclayborn."

Geelie swept snow from a rock onto a dustpan, dumped it into a bucket.

"Don't get it on your gloves," Enos said. "It's a lot colder than it looks."

"How much do you have to bring in each day?"

"Not much; I usually overdo it. I enjoy being outside. The air is clean and cold, and I can see so far."

Geelie shivered, looking around the lands of eternal night. "Doesn't the shaded sun bother you?"

"It's always been like that." He looked around at the dim, tumbled landscape, emptying his bucket into the tub. "It's always been like this. Okay, that should be enough. Take the other handle and we'll carry it in."

In the vestibule they put the tub of snow in the row of tubs, and shed their parkas. Despite the slowly melting snow here, it seemed warm and steamy after the sharp cold air outside. Still, remembering the bleak world without, Geelie shuddered. She would have moved close to Enos even if she had not planned to do so. He put an arm around her, not seeming particularly surprised.

"You'll soon get used to it yourself," he said tolerantly.

"Never," she said, meaning it, cuddling close, her arms around him. She lifted her face for a kiss, nuzzling her breasts against his chest.

Enos put his palm on her cheek and pushed her gently aside. "Let's not start something we can't finish," he said.

Geelie blinked up at him, uncomprehending. "In your room—or the kittens' room—out in the passages—" Independence was a maze of warm, unused, and private passages.

He cupped her face with both hands and looked fondly at her. "Thank you very much, Geelie, for your offer. I will treasure it all the days of my life. But your place is in Kinabatangan, and mine is here, and we should not start something we cannot finish."

The pain of rejection was like a child's pain—the heavy feeling in the chest, the sharp unshed tears. Then came a more poignant grief—grief for all that she could not give him, that he would not take from her.

"Enos!—Enos!" she said, and then her sobs stopped her speech.

"O Geelie, Geelie," he said, his voice trembling. He held her close and stroked her hair.

▲   ▲   ▲

Alden came and sat beside her in the cozy common room of Independence, where she sat watching Jackson Clayborn and Aina Alden play checkers.

"You look a little peaked," he said quietly.

She slid her chair back and spoke as quietly. "I suppose so."

"Enos will be back soon enough. He's lookin' through his things for something to fix that pump in the hydro room. Enos'd druther fix things and tinker around than play games like that." But he was looking inquiringly at her.

"Well, someone has to keep things going," she said wanly.

"Ye-ah." Alden drawled the word out, a skeptical affirmative. "Someone does, though we got a few hands here can still tend to things." Abruptly he said, "By your face and your attitudes, these last few days, I reckon you ain't persuaded Enos to go with you?"

Geelie looked sharply at him. "No," she said shortly.

"I was afraid of that," he said, low. Startled, Geelie leaned toward him. "Did you think I was fightin' you? No, I was hopin' you'd persuade him. God knows you got persuasions none of us can offer. *We* can't offer him nothing."

Passionately she whispered, "Then why won't he come with us? All he says is that his place is here—and after that he won't say anything! Why?"

Alden's response was slow in coming. "I suppose he can't say why because he don't know how. Why he should feel his place is here, I don't know. *My* place is here; I'm an old man. But he don't listen to me any more than he does to you."

He shook his head. "If he stays, what'll he have? All he'll have is Independence, as long as he lives—the man from the Missouri Compact explained that. That's all. I guess," slowly, "for him, that's enough."

▲   ▲   ▲

The kitten, Omega, jumped from Geelie's arms and began to investigate the room, not having sense enough to stay away from Lyou Ye. She was "Miss Smooth" no longer, stalking about the room and visibly trying to contain her anger.

"A flat refusal! I can't believe he refused you. Do you realize there've been over seven thousand Colonies offering them a place to live—over five thousand offering to take the whole group. And we can't get even the young one to leave Earth! What is wrong with him?"

"He says his place is there," said Geelie, nervously watching the kitten prowl.

"He's been brainwashed by those old people," Lyou Ye said.

"Not intentionally," Geelie said. "I discussed it with them, and they prefer to stay, but they would be happy to see Enos go. They know there's no future for him there."

"And for some uncommunicable reason, he thinks there's no future for him with us," said Lyou Ye, more calmly. She shook her head, ran her hands through her mass of auburn hair. "I suppose he's been unconsciously brainwashed from birth, knowing that he was the last one, that he was going to take care of them and die alone, and he's accepted that. It won't be easy to break that kind of life-long conditioning. Well." She shook Omega away from her ankle and turned to Geelie.

"Your tour as Observer is almost up. Would it be worthwhile to extend it and give you more time to work on him?"

Geelie put her hand to her chest. "No," she said, and cleared her throat. "No, it would not be worthwhile. I . . . can do nothing with him."

"We'll send somebody else, but I don't have much

hope. These cold-hearted euros can be so inscrutable."
Lyou Ye sat and examined Geelie. "You're right. It's
time we got you away from Earth," she said gently.

The weather in Kinabatangan was clear and calm when
Geelie returned from Earth. She pulled herself to the
bubble at the axis and looked down at the tiny, idyllic
fields and villages below, past the terraces climbing the
domed end of the vast cylinder. She could have walked
down the stairs, but took instead the elevator. At Deck
level she was met by her cousins and siblings, the
younger of whom rushed her and engulfed her in a mass
hug, all laughing and babbling at once, a torrent of
brown faces.

Half-floating in a golden mist of warmth, brilliant
sunshine from the Chandelier, and love, Geelie let them
lead her between the tiny fields and over the little
bridges. She breathed deep of her ancient home, air
redolent of the cycle of birth and death. They came
presently to her small house in the edges of Lahad Datu.
Frangipani grew by its door and squirrels ran nervously
across its roof. A flight of harsh black crows pounded
heavily up and away from the yard, where the tables
were.

They'd spread a feast for her, and she ate with them
and listened while they told her of the minute but important changes that had occurred in her absence. As she
floated in this supporting bubble of light and warmth,
Kinabatangan came back to her. All was as if she had
never been away.

Her lover had found another, in the easy way of
Kinabatangan, and that night Geelie slept alone. And in
sleep she remembered again the bleak black plains of
nighted Earth, and the man who inhabited them, who
had chosen to wander alone forever under a frozen Sun.

She awoke and had difficulty remembering whether she was in Kinabatangan, dreaming of Independence, the half-seen land of Missouri stretching stark around it—or in *Tigerclaw* dreaming of Kinabatangan. She looked around the tiny room with its paper walls, its mats, the scent of frangipani in the air—she was in Kinabatangan, in her own little house, on her own mattress on the floor, and it was over. All over.

Omega yawned, a tiny pink cavern floored with a delicately rough pink tongue. The kitten was curled on the other pillow. Geelie reached for her.

"Oh! You little devil," she cried, flinging the kitten aside.

Startled, Omega had bitten her hand, and now stood in the middle of the room, looking at her with slit eyes.

Furious, Geelie leaped from her bed. But she could not stand, all the strength went out of her legs and she sank to the floor, sobbing. "Omega, Omega, I'm sorry, s-sorry." Grief as great as for a planet tore at her.

Omega crept cautiously over and sat staring up at her, watching Geelie weep.

The Twelfth Album

STEPHEN BAXTER

Stephen Baxter is known as one best new hard SF writers of the '90s, the author of a number of highly-regarded novels (*The Time Ships* was a leading contender in 1996 for the Hugo Award for best novel, and he has won the Philip K. Dick Award, the John W. Campbell Memorial Award, the British SF Association Award, and others for his novels). At the same time he has in recent years managed to produce nearly ten short stories a year in fantasy, SF, and horror venues. Also in recent years, he has been attracted to the alternate history subgenre, a vein that has captured his serious interest, in a number of stories often involving the history of SF, or alternate versions of the space program of the sixties and seventies (see "Columbiad" in *Year's Best SF 3*). In 1998 he published a broad spectrum of works of SF and fantasy, not sticking to one subgenre. He appeared in most of the major magazines, sometimes twice. This is from *Interzone*, and if it is possible to say so about such a diverse writer, it is uncharacteristic of Baxter. It is pure alternate history, on the border of SF, in the tradition of Philip K. Dick's *The Man in the High Castle*.

In the bowels of a ship that would never sail again—mourning our friend Sick Note—Lightoller and I sat cross-legged on the carpet of a disused Turkish Bath, and listened to John Lennon.

"Fooking hell," said Lightoller. "That's 'Give Me Some Truth.' It was on the *Imagine* album. But—"

"But what?"

Lightoller, he says now, knew there was something different about the cut from the first chord. It might even be true. That's Lightoller for you.

"Typical Lennon," he said moodily. "He goes whole bars on a single note, a single fooking chord. Maneuvering around the harmonies like a crab. But—"

"But *what*?"

"Where's the fooking echo? Lennon solo always drowned his vocals. This is clean and hoarse. Sounds more like a George Martin production."

Not very interested, I was staring at the ceiling. Gilded beams in crimson.

We never knew how Sick Note had managed to blag himself quarters on the ship itself, let alone the Turkish Bath.

It was a whole set of rooms, with a mosaic floor, blue-green tiled walls, stanchions enclosed in carved teak. Queen Victoria's nightmare if she'd been goosed by Rudolph Valentino. As Lightoller said, Sick Note must have been the best fooking porter in this whole floating fooking hotel.

"Of course," Lightoller was saying, "it's plausible they'd have used this. Lennon offered it as a Beatles song during the *Let It Be* sessions in Feb '69. It was the way they worked. They were trying out songs that finished up on *Let It Be* and *Abbey Road*, even their solo albums, as far back as early 1968—"

"*Who* would have used the song for *what*?"

"The Beatles. On their next album. The twelfth."

Compared to Lightoller, and Sick Note, I'm a dilettante. But I'm enough of a Fabs fan to spot the problem with that.

I said, "The Beatles released eleven LPs, from *Please Please Me* through *Let It Be*."

"You're counting UK releases," said Lightoller.

"Of course."

"And you don't include, for instance, the *Yellow Submarine* album which was mostly a George Martin movie score, or the *Magical Mystery Tour* album they released in the US, or the EPs— "

"Of course not. So there was no twelfth Beatle album."

"Not in this fooking world," said Lightoller mysteriously.

John sang on, raw and powerful.

Oddly enough, Lightoller and I had been talking about other worlds even before we found the album, in Sick Note's abandoned quarters, deep inside the old ship.

You have to picture the scene.

I suppose you'd call it a wake: twenty, thirty blokes of indeterminate age standing around in the Cafe Parisien on B Deck—loaned by the floating hotel's owners for the occasion, all tumbling trellises and ivy pots and wicker chairs—drinking beer and wine we'd brought ourselves, and looking unsuccessfully for tortilla chips.

"Morgan Robertson," Lightoller had said around a mouthful of Monster Munches.

"Who?"

"Novelist. 1890s. Writes about a fooking big Atlantic liner, bigger than anything built before. Loads it with rich and complacent people, and wrecks it one cold April night on an iceberg. Called his ship the *Titan*—"

"Spooky," I said dryly.

"In another world—"

"Yeah."

Lightoller is full of crap like that, and not shy about sharing it.

But I welcomed Lightoller's bullshit, for once; we were, after all, just distracting ourselves from the fact that Sick Note was gone. What else are words for, at a time like that?

Bored, morbid, a little drunk, we had wandered off, through the ship, in search of Sick Note.

We had come through the foyer on A Deck, with its huge glass dome, the oak paneling, the balustrades with their wrought-iron scroll work, the gigantic wall clock with its two bronze nymphs. All faded and much scarred by restoration, of course. Like the ship. Like the city outside which we could glimpse through the windows: the shops and maritime museums of Albert Dock to which the ship was forevermore bolted, and the Liverpool waterfront beyond, all of it under a suitably gray sky.

I said something about it being as if they'd towed the Adelphi Hotel into Liverpool Bay. Lightoller made a ribald remark about Sick Note and the nymphs.

We had walked on, down the grand stairway from the boat deck, along the corridor where the valets and maids of the first-class passengers used to stay, past the second-class library and the third-class lounge, down the broad stairs towards steerage.

▲   ▲   ▲

The second track was, of all things, "It Don't Come Easy."

"Ringo," I said.

"Yeah. Solo single in April '71."

I strained to listen. I couldn't tell if it was different. Was the production a little sharper?

"Every Night," the next track, was Paul: just McCartney being McCartney, pretty much as he recorded it on his first solo album.

"Sentimental pap," I said.

Lightoller frowned. "Listen to it. The way he manages the shift from minor to major—"

"Oldest trick in the book."

"McCartney could make the sun come out, just by his fooking chromatic structure."

"I'll take your word for it."

"And it's another track they tried out for *Let It Be*. And—"

"What?"

"I think there are extra lyrics."

"Extra?"

The next track was quiet: Harrison's "All Things Must Pass."

Lightoller said sourly, "Another *Let It Be* demo. But they were still keeping George in his place. First track he's had."

The playing was simple and exquisite, little more than solo voice with acoustic guitar, closer to the demo George had made of the song in his Beatle days than his finished solo album version.

I didn't recognize the next song, a Lennon track. But it got Lightoller jumping up and down.

"It's 'Child of Nature,'" he kept saying. "Fooking hell. They tried it out for the *White Album*. But Lennon held it back and released it on *Imagine* after the split—"

Now I recognized it. It was "Jealous Guy." With different lyrics.

"Fooking hell," said Lightoller. "This has appeared nowhere, not even on a bootleg. And besides, this is no demo. It's a finished fooking production. *Listen* to it."

That's Lightoller for you. Excitable.

We had reached the alleyway on E Deck that Sick Note had always called Scottie Road. You could tell this was meant for steerage and crew: no carpet, low ceilings, naked light bulbs, plain white walls.

We worked our way towards the bow, where Sick Note had lived the last years of his life.

"Sick Note would never go down to the engine rooms," Lightoller reminisced.

"'Reciprocating engines,'" I said, imitating Sick Note. "'A revolutionary low-pressure turbine. Twenty-nine boilers.'"

"Yeah. All nailed down and painted in primary colors to show the kiddies how a steam ship used to work. Not that they care."

"No," I said. "But Sick Note did. He said it was humiliating to gut a working boat like that."

"That was Sick Note."

Away from Scottie Road the ship was a labyrinth of rooms and corridors and ducts.

"I never could figure out my way around here," I said.

Lightoller laughed. "Even Sick Note used to get lost. Especially after he'd had a few with the boys up in the Smoking Room. Do you remember that time he swore—"

"He found a rip in the hull?"

"Yeah. In a post room somewhere below. A rip, as

if the boat had collided with something. And he looked out—"

Sick Note had found Liverpool flattened. Like the Blitz but worse, he said. Mounds of rubble. Like the surface of the Moon.

". . . And he saw a sky glowing full of shooting stars," Lightoller said.

It was one of Sick Note's favorite drunken anecdotes.

"Of course," said Lightoller, "this old scow probably wouldn't have survived any sort of collision. The hull plates are made of brittle steel. And it was just too fooking big; it would have shaken itself to pieces as soon as a few rivets were popped—"

Lightoller can be an anorak sometimes. But he used to be an engineer, like me.

Correction. He is an engineer, like me.

At last, on F Deck, we found the Turkish Bath.

Sick Note had made this place his own: a few sticks of furniture, the walls lined with books, posters from rock concerts and Hammer horror movies and long-forgotten 1960s avant garde book stores plastered over the crimson ceiling. I found what looked like a complete run of the *International Times*. There was even a kitchen of sorts, equipped with antiques: a Hoover Keymatic washing machine and a Philco Marketer fridge-freezer and a General Electric cooker. Sick Note always did have an uncanny supply of artifacts from the '70s, or late '60s anyhow, in miraculously good condition, that the rest of us used to envy. But he'd never reveal his source.

And there were records here too: vinyl LPs, not CDs (of course), leaning up against each other all the way around the edge of the floor like toppling dominoes; the stack even curved a little to get around the corners. The odd thing was, if you looked all the way around the room, you couldn't see how they were being supported—or rather, they were all supporting each other. It was a record stack designed by Escher.

Lightoller bent to look at the albums. "Alphabetized."

"Of course." That was Sick Note.

"Let's find the Beatles. B for Beatles . . ." He grunted, sounding a little surprised. He pulled out an album with a jet-black sleeve. "Look at this fooking thing." He handed it to me.

The cover was elementally simple: just a black field, with a single word rendered in a white typewriter font in the lower left-hand corner.

God.

Just that, the word, and a full stop.

Nothing else. No image. Not even an artist name on the cover. Nothing on the spine or the back of the sleeve; no artist photos or track listings, or even a copyright mark or acknowledgment paragraph.

The record slid into my hand inside a plain black paper inner sleeve. And when I tried to pull out the record itself—reaching inside to rest my fingers on the center label—the sleeve static-clung to the vinyl, as if unwilling to let it go.

The vinyl was standard-issue oil black. The label was just the famous Apple logo—skin-side up on what was presumably Side One, the crisp white inner flesh on Side Two. Still no track listing—in fact, not even a title.

I held the album by its rim. I turned it this way and that; the tracks shone in the light.

Sometimes I forget how tactile the experience of owning an album used to be.

"Look at that fooking thing," breathed Lightoller.

"A couple of scratches at the rim. Otherwise perfect."

"Yeah." An album that had been played, but cared for. That was Sick Note for you.

We exchanged glances.

Lightoller lifted up the glass cover of Sick Note's deck, and I lifted on the album, settling it over the spindle delicately. Lightoller powered up the deck. It was a Quad stack Sick Note had been working on piece by piece since 1983. No CD player, of course.

When the needle touched the vinyl there was a moment of sharp crackle, then hissing expectancy.

The music came crashing out.

And that was how we found ourselves listening to a puzzlingly different John Lennon.

Side One's last track was the big song McCartney used to close *Ram*: "Back Seat of My Car."

"Another song they tried for *Let It Be*," Lightoller said. "And—"

"Shut up a minute," I said.

". . . What?"

"Listen to that."

In place of the multi-track of his own and Linda's voices that McCartney had plastered over his solo version, the song was laced with exquisite three-part harmonies.

Beatle harmonies.

"Lightoller," I said. "I'm starting to feel scared."

Lightoller let the stylus run off, reverently.

I got up from the carpeted floor and walked around the room. There were framed photos and news clippings here, showing scenes from the ship's long history.

I couldn't mistake the pounding piano and drum beat that started Side Two.

"'Instant Karma,'" I said.

"A single for Lennon in February 1970."

"In our world."

"Great fooking opener."

Then came a Harrison song, a wistful, slight thing called "Isn't It a Pity."

Lightoller nodded. "Another one they tried out in early 1969, but never used. It finished up on George's first solo album—"

The next track was "Junk," a short instrumental McCartney wrote when they were staying with the Maharishi in India. It sounded like the theme of a TV show about vets. But it was sweet and sad.

We just listened for a while.

With the gentle guitars playing, it was as if Sick Note was still there, in this cloud of possessions, the very air probably still full of a dusty haze of him.

. . . Here was the ship in dry dock in Belfast after her maiden voyage, with that famous big near-miss scar down her starboard flank. Here she was as a troop carrier in 1915, painted with gaudy geometric shapes that were supposed to fool German submarines. Here was a clipping about how she'd evaded a U-boat torpedo, and how she'd come about and rammed the damn thing.

"'Old Reliable,'" I said. "That was what Sick Note used to call her. The nickname given her by the troops she transported."

"He loved this old tub, in his way," said Lightoller.

"And he did love his Fabs."

That was Sick Note for you.

The fourth track was "Wah Wah," another Harrison song, a glittering, heavy-handed rocker with crystal-sharp three-part harmony.

Lightoller nodded. "Harrison wrote this when he stormed out during the *Let It Be* sessions. He kept it back for his solo album—"

"In our world."

"Yeah. I guess he brought it back to the group, in the God world . . ." Lightoller was sounding morbid. "But there was no fooking twelfth album, was there? This must be a fake. Or an import, or a compilation, or a bootleg. Once Allen Klein and Yoko got involved they were all too busy suing each other's fooking arses off."

I picked up the album sleeve. For a possession of Sick Note's, it was surprisingly grubby. Specked with some kind of ash. I felt obscurely disturbed by Lightoller's loss of faith in his own bullshit. "But all the Allen Klein stuff started in the spring of '69. Even after all that, they made another album together."

"*Abbey Road.*" Lightoller nodded, and I thought the spark was back in his eyes. "Yeah. They might have hung around for one more try. But something would have had to be different."

I kept roaming the room.

More clippings, of how White Star had merged with Cunard in 1934, and the old ship lost out to newer, faster, safer ships. She was almost sold for scrap—but then was put to work as a cargo scow in the southern Atlantic—and then, after Michael Heseltine parachuted into Merseyside after the 1981 riots, she was bought up and bolted to the dock, here at Liverpool, and refitted as a hotel, the center of what Heseltine hoped would become the regeneration of the city. Fat chance.

"So," I said, "your theory is that this album comes from an alternate world where somebody shot Allen Klein."

Lightoller shrugged. "It might have been something bigger."

"Like what?"

"I don't know. Like nuclear fooking war."

"Nuclear war?"

"Sure. If the world was going to fooking hell, it

would have touched everybody's lives, even before the Big One dropped. For the Beatles, it just kept them in the studio together a while longer."

"Their contribution to world peace," I said sourly.

"They used to think like that," he said defensively. "What was that story of Sick Note's? He found some way out the back of the boat—"

I tried to remember. "Liverpool was rubble."

The surface of the Moon. But Sick Note might have found some cellars, where things had survived—GE cookers and Philco fridges and Beatle albums—sheltered from the fire storms, preserved since 1971.

I felt scared again.

"We're running out of LP," said Lightoller.

"So what?"

"So there are a lot of great tracks not here," he said. "Like Lennon's 'Love.' Harrison's 'My Sweet Lord' and 'What Is Life.' 'Imagine,' for fook's sake."

"They must have been issuing singles."

"You're right." I could hear the pain in Lightoller's voice. "And we'll never get to hear them."

"But if we found the other world . . ."

We were silent for a while, just listening.

Lightoller said softly, "What if we couldn't find our way back?"

I shrugged. "Sick Note did."

He eyed me. "Are you sure?"

Neither of us tried it.

The fifth track was "God," in which Lennon, at great and obsessive length, discarded his childish idols, including Jesus, Elvis, Dylan, even the Beatles.

"Oh," said Lightoller. "There's the compromise. What McCartney agreed, to keep Lennon on board."

"That and not doing 'Teddy Boy.'"

"At least Lennon didn't push for 'Mother.'"

I tried to focus on the music. The production didn't

sound to me much different from the way I'd heard it on the *Plastic Ono Band* album.

But some unruly piece of my brain wasn't thinking about the Beatles.

Sick Note had said he saw shooting stars, everywhere, over ruined Liverpool. *Oh.*

"Comets," I said.

Lightoller said, "Comets?"

"Not nuclear war. Comets. That's it. If a comet hit the Earth, debris would be thrown up out of the atmosphere. Molten blobs of rock. They would re-enter the atmosphere as—"

"A skyful of shooting stars."

"Yes. They would reach low orbit, keep falling for years. The air would burn. Nitrous oxides, acid rain— the global temperatures would be raised all to hell."

"So in some alternate world a comet landed on Yoko, and the Beatles never broke up." Lightoller laughed. "Only a true Beatles fan would lay waste to the fooking Earth to get a new album."

"I don't think this is funny, Lightoller."

God wound to its leaden close. The stylus hissed on the spiraling intertrack, and Lightoller and I watched it. I knew what he was thinking, because I was thinking exactly the same.

This would be the ultimate track—the twelfth track on the twelfth album.

The last new Beatles song we would ever hear.

Because, of course, by now we both believed.

It was recognizable from the first, faded-in, descending piano chords. But then the vocals opened—and it was Lennon.

"It's 'Maybe I'm Amazed,'" I said, awed. "McCartney's greatest post-Beatles song—"

"Just listen to it," said Lightoller. "He gave it to Lennon. *Listen* to it."

It didn't sound like the version from our world, which McCartney, battered and bruised from the break-up, recorded in his kitchen.

Lennon's raw, majestic voice wrenched at the melody, while McCartney's melodic bass, Starr's powerful drumming, and Harrison's wailing guitar drove through the song's complex, compulsive chromatic structure. And then a long coda opened up, underpinned by clean, thrusting brass, obviously scored by George Martin.

At last the coda wound down to a final, almost whispered lament by Lennon, a final descending chord sequence, a last trickle of piano notes, as if the song itself couldn't bear to finish.

The stylus hissed briefly, reached the run-off groove, and lifted.

Lightoller and I just sat there, stunned.

Then the magic faded, and I got an unwelcome dose of reality: a sense of place, where we were and what we had become: two slightly sad, slightly overweight, forty-ish guys mourning the passing of a friend, and another little part of our own youth.

Lightoller put the album back in its sleeve, and slotted it carefully into its place.

We found our way outside, to the dock.

The old ship's stern towered over us. It was late by then, and the ship blazed with light from its big promenade decks and the long rows of portholes. Up top, I could see the four big funnels and the lacework of masts and rigging. People were crossing the permanent gangways that had been bolted to the side of the ship, like leashes to make sure she never shook loose again.

"She's an old relic," said Lightoller. "Just like Sick Note."

"Yeah."

"All fooking bullshit, of course," he said.

"Other worlds?"

"Yeah."

It was starting to rain, and I felt depressed, sour, mildly hung over. I looked up at the stern and saw how the post-Heseltine paint job had weathered. Even the lettering was running. You could still make out the registration, LIVERPOOL, but the ship's name was obscured, the I's and T's and the N streaking down over the hull, the A and C just blurred.

We turned our backs and started the walk to the bus stop.

Lightoller and I don't talk about it much.

I'd like to have heard those singles, though.

Story of Your Life

TED CHIANG

Ted Chiang has only published three SF stories prior to this one and his first, "Tower of Babylon" (1990), won the Nebula Award; another ("Understand") won the *Asimov's* Readers Award in 1991, and he won the John W. Campbell Award for Best New Writer in 1992. He is a careful and accomplished writer, and his work is distinguished by originality combined with the high quality of his re-imagining of old SF ideas. This is his fourth published story, his first in more than five years (he seems to have a satisfying life in the Seattle area that leaves him little time for SF writing). It is the longest story in this book and may well be the best. The theme of communicating with aliens was prominent in the SF fiction of 1998, but nowhere better done than here. It appeared in *Starlight 2*. In a year that was not notable for many strong original SF anthologies, this novella helped *Starlight 2* (which contained both fantasy and SF stories) stand out.

Your father is about to ask me the question. This is the most important moment in our lives, and I want to pay attention, note every detail. Your dad and I have just come back from an evening out, dinner and a show; it's after midnight. We came out onto the patio to look at the full moon; then I told your dad I wanted to dance, so he humors me and now we're slow-dancing, a pair of thirtysomethings swaying back and forth in the moonlight like kids. I don't feel the night chill at all. And then your dad says, "Do you want to make a baby?"

Right now your dad and I have been married for about two years, living on Ellis Avenue; when we move out you'll still be too young to remember the house, but we'll show you pictures of it, tell you stories about it. I'd love to tell you the story of this evening, the night you're conceived, but the right time to do that would be when you're ready to have children of your own, and we'll never get that chance.

Telling it to you any earlier wouldn't do any good; for most of your life you won't sit still to hear such a romantic—you'd say sappy—story. I remember the scenario of your origin you'll suggest when you're twelve.

"The only reason you had me was so you could get a maid you wouldn't have to pay," you'll say bitterly, dragging the vacuum cleaner out of the closet.

"That's right," I'll say. "Thirteen years ago I knew the carpets would need vacuuming around now, and having a baby seemed to be the cheapest and easiest way to get the job done. Now kindly get on with it."

"If you weren't my mother, this would be illegal,"

you'll say, seething as you unwind the power cord and plug it into the wall outlet.

That will be in the house on Belmont Street. I'll live to see strangers occupy both houses: the one you're conceived in and the one you grow up in. Your dad and I will sell the first a couple years after your arrival. I'll sell the second shortly after your departure. By then Nelson and I will have moved into our farmhouse, and your dad will be living with what's-her-name.

I know how this story ends; I think about it a lot. I also think a lot about how it began, just a few years ago, when ships appeared in orbit and artifacts appeared in meadows. The government said next to nothing about them, while the tabloids said every possible thing.

And then I got a phone call, a request for a meeting.

I spotted them waiting in the hallway, outside my office. They made an odd couple; one wore a military uniform and a crew cut, and carried an aluminum briefcase. He seemed to be assessing his surroundings with a critical eye. The other one was easily identifiable as an academic: full beard and mustache, wearing corduroy. He was browsing through the overlapping sheets stapled to a bulletin board nearby.

"Colonel Weber, I presume?" I shook hands with the soldier. "Louise Banks."

"Dr. Banks. Thank you for taking the time to speak with us," he said.

"Not at all; any excuse to avoid the faculty meeting."

Colonel Weber indicated his companion. "This is Dr. Gary Donnelly, the physicist I mentioned when we spoke on the phone."

"Call me Gary," he said as we shook hands. "I'm anxious to hear what you have to say."

We entered my office. I moved a couple of stacks of books off the second guest chair, and we all sat down. "You said you wanted me to listen to a recording. I presume this has something to do with the aliens?"

"All I can offer is the recording," said Colonel Weber.

"Okay, let's hear it."

Colonel Weber took a tape machine out of his briefcase and pressed PLAY. The recording sounded vaguely like that of a wet dog shaking the water out of its fur.

"What do you make of that?" he asked.

I withheld my comparison to a wet dog. "What was the context in which this recording was made?"

"I'm not at liberty to say."

"It would help me interpret those sounds. Could you see the alien while it was speaking? Was it doing anything at the time?"

"The recording is all I can offer."

"You won't be giving anything away if you tell me that you've seen the aliens; the public's assumed you have."

Colonel Weber wasn't budging. "Do you have any opinion about its linguistic properties?" he asked.

"Well, it's clear that their vocal tract is substantially different from a human vocal tract. I assume that these aliens don't look like humans?"

The colonel was about to say something noncommittal when Gary Donnelly asked, "Can you make any guesses based on the tape?"

"Not really. It doesn't sound like they're using a larynx to make those sounds, but that doesn't tell me what they look like."

"Anything—is there anything else you can tell us?" asked Colonel Weber.

I could see he wasn't accustomed to consulting a civilian. "Only that establishing communications is going to be really difficult because of the difference in anatomy. They're almost certainly using sounds that the human vocal tract can't reproduce, and maybe sounds that the human ear can't distinguish."

"You mean infra- or ultrasonic frequencies?" asked Gary Donnelly.

"Not specifically. I just mean that the human auditory system isn't an absolute acoustic instrument; it's optimized to recognize the sounds that a human larynx makes. With an alien vocal system, all bets are off." I shrugged. "*Maybe* we'll be able to hear the difference between alien phonemes, given enough practice, but it's possible our ears simply can't recognize the distinctions they consider meaningful. In that case we'd need a sound spectrograph to know what an alien is saying."

Colonel Weber asked, "Suppose I gave you an hour's worth of recordings; how long would it take you to determine if we need this sound spectrograph or not?"

"I couldn't determine that with just a recording no matter how much time I had. I'd need to talk with the aliens directly."

The colonel shook his head. "Not possible."

I tried to break it to him gently. "That's your call, of course. But the only way to learn an unknown language is to interact with a native speaker, and by that I mean asking questions, holding a conversation, that sort of thing. Without that, it's simply not possible. So if you want to learn the aliens' language, someone with training in field linguistics—whether it's me or someone else—will have to talk with an alien. Recordings alone aren't sufficient."

Colonel Weber frowned. "You seem to be implying that no alien could have learned human languages by monitoring our broadcasts."

"I doubt it. They'd need instructional material specifically designed to teach human languages to non-humans. Either that, or interaction with a human. If they had either of those, they could learn a lot from TV, but otherwise, they wouldn't have a starting point."

The colonel clearly found this interesting; evidently his philosophy was, the less the aliens knew, the better. Gary Donnelly read the colonel's expression too and rolled his eyes. I suppressed a smile.

Then Colonel Weber asked, "Suppose you were learning a new language by talking to its speakers; could you do it without teaching them English?"

"That would depend on how cooperative the native speakers were. They'd almost certainly pick up bits and pieces while I'm learning their language, but it wouldn't have to be much if they're willing to teach. On the other hand, if they'd rather learn English than teach us their language, that would make things far more difficult."

The colonel nodded. "I'll get back to you on this matter."

The request for that meeting was perhaps the second most momentous phone call in my life. The first, of course, will be the one from Mountain Rescue. At that point your dad and I will be speaking to each other maybe once a year, tops. After I get that phone call, though, the first thing I'll do will be to call your father.

He and I will drive out together to perform the identification, a long silent car ride. I remember the morgue, all tile and stainless steel, the hum of refrigeration and smell of antiseptic. An orderly will pull the sheet back to reveal your face. Your face will look wrong somehow, but I'll know it's you.

"Yes, that's her," I'll say. "She's mine."

You'll be twenty-five then.

▲   ▲   ▲

The MP checked my badge, made a notation on his clip-board, and opened the gate; I drove the off-road vehicle into the encampment, a small village of tents pitched by the Army in a farmer's sun-scorched pasture. At the cen-ter of the encampment was one of the alien devices, nicknamed "looking glasses."

According to the briefings I'd attended, there were nine of these in the United States, one hundred and twelve in the world. The looking glasses acted as two-way communication devices, presumably with the ships in orbit. No one knew why the aliens wouldn't talk to us in person; fear of cooties, maybe. A team of scientists, including a physicist and a linguist, was assigned to each looking glass; Gary Donnelly and I were on this one.

Gary was waiting for me in the parking area. We navigated a circular maze of concrete barricades until we reached the large tent that covered the looking glass itself. In front of the tent was an equipment cart loaded with goodies borrowed from the school's phonology lab; I had sent it ahead for inspection by the Army.

Also outside the tent were three tripod-mounted video cameras whose lenses peered, through windows in the fabric wall, into the main room. Everything Gary and I did would be reviewed by countless others, includ-ing military intelligence. In addition we would each send daily reports, of which mine had to include estimates on how much English I thought the aliens could under-stand.

Gary held open the tent flap and gestured for me to enter. "Step right up," he said, circus-barker-style. "Mar-vel at creatures the likes of which have never been seen on God's green earth."

"And all for one slim dime," I murmured, walking through the door. At the moment the looking glass was inactive, resembling a semicircular mirror over ten feet high and twenty feet across. On the brown grass in front of the looking glass, an arc of white spray paint outlined the activation area. Currently the area contained only a table, two folding chairs, and a power strip with a cord leading to a generator outside. The buzz of fluorescent lamps, hung from poles along the edge of the room, commingled with the buzz of flies in the sweltering heat.

Gary and I looked at each other, and then began pushing the cart of equipment up to the table. As we crossed the paint line, the looking glass appeared to grow transparent; it was as if someone was slowly raising the illumination behind tinted glass. The illusion of depth was uncanny; I felt I could walk right into it. Once the looking glass was fully lit it resembled a life-sized diorama of a semicircular room. The room contained a few large objects that might have been furniture, but no aliens. There was a door in the curved rear wall.

We busied ourselves connecting everything together: microphone, sound spectrograph, portable computer, and speaker. As we worked, I frequently glanced at the looking glass, anticipating the aliens' arrival. Even so I jumped when one of them entered.

It looked like a barrel suspended at the intersection of seven limbs. It was radially symmetric, and any of its limbs could serve as an arm or a leg. The one in front of me was walking around on four legs, three non-adjacent arms curled up at its sides. Gary called them "heptapods."

I'd been shown videotapes, but I still gawked. Its limbs had no distinct joints; anatomists guessed they might be supported by vertebral columns. Whatever their underlying structure, the heptapod's limbs conspired to move it in a disconcertingly fluid manner. Its "torso" rode atop the rippling limbs as smoothly as a hovercraft.

Seven lidless eyes ringed the top of the heptapod's body. It walked back to the doorway from which it entered, made a brief sputtering sound, and returned to the center of the room followed by another heptapod; at no point did it ever turn around. Eerie, but logical; with eyes on all sides, any direction might as well be "forward."

Gary had been watching my reaction. "Ready?" he asked.

I took a deep breath. "Ready enough." I'd done plenty of fieldwork before, in the Amazon, but it had always been a bilingual procedure: either my informants knew some Portuguese, which I could use, or I'd previously gotten an introduction to their language from the local missionaries. This would be my first attempt at conducting a true monolingual discovery procedure. It was straightforward enough in theory, though.

I walked up to the looking glass and a heptapod on the other side did the same. The image was so real that my skin crawled. I could see the texture of its gray skin, like corduroy ridges arranged in whorls and loops. There was no smell at all from the looking glass, which somehow made the situation stranger.

I pointed to myself and said slowly, "Human." Then I pointed to Gary. "Human." Then I pointed at each heptapod and said, "What are you?"

No reaction. I tried again, and then again.

One of the heptapods pointed to itself with one limb, the four terminal digits pressed together. That was lucky. In some cultures a person pointed with his chin; if the heptapod hadn't used one of its limbs, I wouldn't have known what gesture to look for. I heard a brief fluttering sound, and saw a puckered orifice at the top of its body vibrate; it was talking. Then it pointed to its companion and fluttered again.

I went back to my computer; on its screen were two

virtually identical spectrographs representing the flutter-ing sounds. I marked a sample for playback. I pointed to myself and said "Human" again, and did the same with Gary. Then I pointed to the heptapod, and played back the flutter on the speaker.

The heptapod fluttered some more. The second half of the spectrograph for this utterance looked like a rep-etition: call the previous utterances [flutter1], then this one was [flutter2flutter1].

I pointed at something that might have been a hep-tapod chair. "What is that?"

The heptapod paused, and then pointed at the "chair" and talked some more. The spectrograph for this differed distinctly from that of the earlier sounds: [flutter3]. Once again, I pointed to the "chair" while playing back [flutter3].

The heptapod replied; judging by the spectrograph, it looked like [flutter3flutter2]. Optimistic interpreta-tion: the heptapod was confirming my utterances as cor-rect, which implied compatibility between heptapod and human patterns of discourse. Pessimistic interpretation: it had a nagging cough.

At my computer I delimited certain sections of the spectrograph and typed in a tentative gloss for each: "heptapod" for [flutter1], "yes" for [flutter2], and "chair" for [flutter3]. Then I typed "Language: Hepta-pod A" as a heading for all the utterances.

Gary watched what I was typing. "What's the 'A' for?"

"It just distinguishes this language from any other ones the heptapods might use," I said. He nodded.

"Now let's try something, just for laughs." I pointed at each heptapod and tried to mimic the sound of [flutter1], "heptapod." After a long pause, the first heptapod said something and then the second one said something else, neither of whose spectrographs resembled anything said before. I couldn't tell if they were speaking to each other or to me since they had no faces to turn. I tried pronouncing [flutter1] again, but there was no reaction.

"Not even close," I grumbled.

"I'm impressed you can make sounds like that at all," said Gary.

"You should hear my moose call. Sends them running."

I tried again a few more times, but neither heptapod responded with anything I could recognize. Only when I replayed the recording of the heptapod's pronunciation did I get a confirmation; the heptapod replied with [flutter2], "yes."

"So we're stuck with using recordings?" asked Gary.

I nodded. "At least temporarily."

"So now what?"

"Now we make sure it hasn't actually been saying 'aren't they cute' or 'look what they're doing now.' Then we see if we can identify any of these words when that other heptapod pronounces them." I gestured for him to have a seat. "Get comfortable; this'll take a while."

In 1770, Captain Cook's ship *Endeavour* ran aground on the coast of Queensland, Australia. While some of his men made repairs, Cook led an exploration party and met the aboriginal people. One of the sailors pointed to the animals that hopped around with their young riding in pouches, and asked an aborigine what they were called. The aborigine replied, "Kanguru." From then on Cook and his sailors referred to the animals by this word. It wasn't until later that they learned it meant "What did you say?"

I tell that story in my introductory course every year.

It's almost certainly untrue, and I explain that afterwards, but it's a classic anecdote. Of course, the anecdotes my undergraduates will really want to hear are ones featuring the heptapods; for the rest of my teaching career, that'll be the reason many of them sign up for my courses. So I'll show them the old videotapes of my sessions at the looking glass, and the sessions that the other linguists conducted; the tapes are instructive, and they'll be useful if we're ever visited by aliens again, but they don't generate many good anecdotes.

When it comes to language-learning anecdotes, my favorite source is child language acquisition. I remember one afternoon when you are five years old, after you have come home from kindergarten. You'll be coloring with your crayons while I grade papers.

"Mom," you'll say, using the carefully casual tone reserved for requesting a favor, "can I ask you something?"

"Sure, sweetie. Go ahead."

"Can I be, um, honored?"

I'll look up from the paper I'm grading. "What do you mean?"

"At school Sharon said she got to be honored."

"Really? Did she tell you what for?"

"It was when her big sister got married. She said only one person could be, um, honored, and she was it."

"Ah, I see. You mean Sharon was maid of honor?"

"Yeah, that's it. Can I be made of honor?"

Gary and I entered the prefab building containing the center of operations for the looking glass site. Inside it looked like they were planning an invasion, or perhaps an evacuation: crew-cut soldiers worked around a large map of the area, or sat in front of burly electronic gear while speaking into headsets. We were shown into

Colonel Weber's office, a room in the back that was cool from air conditioning.

We briefed the colonel on our first day's results. "Doesn't sound like you got very far," he said.

"I have an idea as to how we can make faster progress," I said. "But you'll have to approve the use of more equipment."

"What more do you need?"

"A digital camera, and a big video screen." I showed him a drawing of the setup I imagined. "I want to try conducting the discovery procedure using writing; I'd display words on the screen, and use the camera to record the words they write. I'm hoping the heptapods will do the same."

Weber looked at the drawing dubiously. "What would be the advantage of that?"

"So far I've been proceeding the way I would with speakers of an unwritten language. Then it occurred to me that the heptapods must have writing, too."

"So?"

"If the heptapods have a mechanical way of producing writing, then their writing ought to be very regular, very consistent. That would make it easier for us to identify graphemes instead of phonemes. It's like picking out the letters in a printed sentence instead of trying to hear them when the sentence is spoken aloud."

"I take your point," he admitted. "And how would you respond to them? Show them the words they displayed to you?"

"Basically. And if they put spaces between words, any sentences we write would be a lot more intelligible than any spoken sentence we might splice together from recordings."

He leaned back in his chair. "You know we want to show as little of our technology as possible."

"I understand, but we're using machines as intermediaries already. If we can get them to use writing, I believe progress will go much faster than if we're restricted to the sound spectrographs."

The colonel turned to Gary. "Your opinion?"

"It sounds like a good idea to me. I'm curious whether the heptapods might have difficulty reading our monitors. Their looking glasses are based on a completely different technology than our video screens. As far as we can tell, they don't use pixels or scan lines, and they don't refresh on a frame-by-frame basis."

"You think the scan lines on our video screens might render them unreadable to the heptapods?"

"It's possible," said Gary. "We'll just have to try it and see."

Weber considered it. For me it wasn't even a question, but from his point of view it was a difficult one; like a soldier, though, he made it quickly. "Request granted. Talk to the sergeant outside about bringing in what you need. Have it ready for tomorrow."

I remember one day during the summer when you're sixteen. For once, the person waiting for her date to arrive is me. Of course, you'll be waiting around too, curious to see what he looks like. You'll have a friend of yours, a blond girl with the unlikely name of Roxie, hanging out with you, giggling.

"You may feel the urge to make comments about him," I'll say, checking myself in the hallway mirror. "Just restrain yourselves until we leave."

"Don't worry, Mom," you'll say. "We'll do it so that he won't know. Roxie, you ask me what I think the weather will be like tonight. Then I'll say what I think of Mom's date."

"Right," Roxie will say.

"No, you most definitely will not," I'll say.

"Relax, Mom. He'll never know; we do this all the time."

"What a comfort that is."

A little later on, Nelson will arrive to pick me up. I'll do the introductions, and we'll all engage in a little small talk on the front porch. Nelson is ruggedly handsome, to your evident approval. Just as we're about to leave, Roxie will say to you casually, "So what do you think the weather will be like tonight?"

"I think it's going to be really hot," you'll answer.

Roxie will nod in agreement. Nelson will say, "Really? I thought they said it was going to be cool."

"I have a sixth sense about these things," you'll say. Your face will give nothing away. "I get the feeling it's going to be a scorcher. Good thing you're dressed for it, Mom."

I'll glare at you, and say good night.

As I lead Nelson toward his car, he'll ask me, amused, "I'm missing something here, aren't I?"

"A private joke," I'll mutter. "Don't ask me to explain it."

At our next session at the looking glass, we repeated the procedure we had performed before, this time displaying a printed word on our computer screen at the same time we spoke: showing HUMAN while saying "Human," and so forth. Eventually, the heptapods understood what we wanted, and set up a flat circular screen mounted on a small pedestal. One heptapod spoke, and then inserted a limb into a large socket in the pedestal; a doodle of script, vaguely cursive, popped onto the screen.

We soon settled into a routine, and I compiled two parallel corpora: one of spoken utterances, one of writing samples. Based on first impressions, their writing appeared to be logographic, which was disappointing; I'd been hoping for an alphabetic script to help us learn their speech. Their logograms might include some phonetic information, but finding it would be a lot harder than with an alphabetic script.

By getting up close to the looking glass, I was able to point to various heptapod body parts, such as limbs, digits, and eyes, and elicit terms for each. It turned out that they had an orifice on the underside of their body, lined with articulated bony ridges: probably used for eating, while the one at the top was for respiration and speech. There were no other conspicuous orifices; perhaps their mouth was their anus too. Those sorts of questions would have to wait.

I also tried asking our two informants for terms for addressing each individually; personal names, if they had such things. Their answers were of course unpronounceable, so for Gary's and my purposes, I dubbed them Flapper and Raspberry. I hoped I'd be able to tell them apart.

The next day I conferred with Gary before we entered the looking-glass tent. "I'll need your help with this session," I told him.

"Sure. What do you want me to do?"

"We need to elicit some verbs, and it's easiest with third-person forms. Would you act out a few verbs while I type the written form on the computer? If we're lucky, the heptapods will figure out what we're doing and do the same. I've brought a bunch of props for you to use."

"No problem," said Gary, cracking his knuckles. "Ready when you are."

We began with some simple intransitive verbs: walking, jumping, speaking, writing. Gary demonstrated each one with a charming lack of self-consciousness; the presence of the video cameras didn't inhibit him at all. For the first few actions he performed, I asked the heptapods, "What do you call that?" Before long, the heptapods caught on to what we were trying to do; Raspberry began mimicking Gary, or at least performing the equivalent heptapod action, while Flapper worked their computer, displaying a written description and pronouncing it aloud.

In the spectrographs of their spoken utterances, I could recognize their word I had glossed as "heptapod." The rest of each utterance was presumably the verb phrase; it looked like they had analogs of nouns and verbs, thank goodness.

In their writing, however, things weren't as clear-cut. For each action, they had displayed a single logogram instead of two separate ones. At first I thought they had written something like "walks," with the subject implied. But why would Flapper say "the heptapod walks" while writing "walks," instead of maintaining parallelism? Then I noticed that some of the logograms looked like the logogram for "heptapod" with some extra strokes added to one side or another. Perhaps their verbs could be written as affixes to a noun. If so, why was Flapper writing the noun in some instances but not in others?

I decided to try a transitive verb; substituting object words might clarify things. Among the props I'd brought were an apple and a slice of bread. "Okay," I said to Gary, "show them the food, and then eat some. First the apple, then the bread."

Gary pointed at the Golden Delicious and then he took a bite out of it, while I displayed the "what do you call that?" expression. Then we repeated it with the slice of whole wheat.

Raspberry left the room and returned with some kind of giant nut or gourd and a gelatinous ellipsoid.

Raspberry pointed at the gourd while Flapper said a word and displayed a logogram. Then Raspberry brought the gourd down between its legs, a crunching sound resulted, and the gourd reemerged minus a bite; there were corn-like kernels beneath the shell. Flapper talked and displayed a large logogram on their screen. The sound spectrograph for "gourd" changed when it was used in the sentence; possibly a case marker. The logogram was odd: after some study, I could identify graphic elements that resembled the individual logograms for "heptapod" and "gourd." They looked as if they had been melted together, with several extra strokes in the mix that presumably meant "eat." Was it a multiword ligature?

Next we got spoken and written names for the gelatin egg, and descriptions of the act of eating it. The sound spectrograph for "heptapod eats gelatin egg" was analyzable; "gelatin egg" bore a case marker, as expected, though the sentence's word order differed from last time. The written form, another large logogram, was another matter. This time it took much longer for me to recognize anything in it; not only were the individual logograms melted together again, it looked as if the one for "heptapod" was laid on its back, while on top of it the logogram for "gelatin egg" was standing on its head.

"Uh-oh." I took another look at the writing for the simple noun-verb examples, the ones that had seemed inconsistent before. Now I realized all of them actually did contain the logogram for "heptapod"; some were rotated and distorted by being combined with the various verbs, so I hadn't recognized them at first. "You guys have got to be kidding," I muttered.

"What's wrong?" asked Gary.

"Their script isn't word-divided; a sentence is written by joining the logograms for the constituent words. They join the logograms by rotating and modifying them. Take a look." I showed him how the logograms were rotated.

"So they can read a word with equal ease no matter how it's rotated," Gary said. He turned to look at the heptapods, impressed. "I wonder if it's a consequence of their bodies' radial symmetry: their bodies have no 'forward' direction, so maybe their writing doesn't either. Highly neat."

I couldn't believe it; I was working with someone who modified the word "neat" with "highly." "It certainly is interesting," I said, "but it also means there's no easy way for us to write our own sentences in their language. We can't simply cut their sentences into individual words and recombine them; we'll have to learn the rules of their script before we can write anything legible. It's the same continuity problem we'd have had splicing together speech fragments, except applied to writing."

I looked at Flapper and Raspberry in the looking glass, who were waiting for us to continue, and sighed. "You aren't going to make this easy for us, are you?"

To be fair, the heptapods were completely cooperative. In the days that followed, they readily taught us their language without requiring us to teach them any more English. Colonel Weber and his cohorts pondered the implications of that, while I and the linguists at the other looking glasses met via video conferencing to share what we had learned about the heptapod language. The videoconferencing made for an incongruous working environment: our video screens were primitive compared to the heptapods' looking glasses, so that my colleagues seemed more remote than the aliens. The familiar was far away, while the bizarre was close at hand.

It would be a while before we'd be ready to ask the heptapods why they had come, or to discuss physics well enough to ask them about their technology. For the time being, we worked on the basics: phonemics/graphemics, vocabulary, syntax. The heptapods at every looking glass were using the same language, so we were able to pool our data and coordinate our efforts.

Our biggest source of confusion was the heptapods' "writing." It didn't appear to be writing at all; it looked more like a bunch of intricate graphic designs. The logograms weren't arranged in rows, or a spiral, or any linear fashion. Instead, Flapper or Raspberry would write a sentence by sticking together as many logograms as needed into a giant conglomeration.

This form of writing was reminiscent of primitive sign systems, which required a reader to know a message's context in order to understand it. Such systems were considered too limited for systematic recording of information. Yet it was unlikely that the heptapods developed their level of technology with only an oral tradition. That implied one of three possibilities: the first was that the heptapods had a true writing system, but they didn't want to use it in front of us; Colonel Weber would identify with that one. The second was that the heptapods hadn't originated the technology they were using; they were illiterates using someone else's technology. The third, and most interesting to me, was that the heptapods were using a nonlinear system of orthography that qualified as true writing.

I remember a conversation we'll have when you're in your junior year of high school. It'll be Sunday morning, and I'll be scrambling some eggs while you set the table for brunch. You'll laugh as you tell me about the party you went to last night.

"Oh man," you'll say, "they're not kidding when they say that body weight makes a difference. I didn't drink any more than the guys did, but I got so much *drunk*er."

I'll try to maintain a neutral, pleasant expression. I'll really try. Then you'll say, "Oh, come on, Mom."

"What?"

"You know you did the exact same things when you were my age."

I did nothing of the sort, but I know that if I were to admit that, you'd lose respect for me completely. "You know never to drive, or get into a car if—"

"God, of course I know that. Do you think I'm an idiot?"

"No, of course not."

What I'll think is that you are clearly, maddeningly not me. It will remind me, again, that you won't be a clone of me; you can be wonderful, a daily delight, but you won't be someone I could have created by myself.

The military had set up a trailer containing our offices at the looking glass site. I saw Gary walking toward the trailer, and ran to catch up with him. "It's a semasiographic writing system," I said when I reached him.

"Excuse me?" said Gary.

"Here, let me show you." I directed Gary into my office. Once we were inside, I went to the chalkboard and drew a circle with a diagonal line bisecting it. "What does this mean?"

"'Not allowed'?"

"Right." Next I printed the words NOT ALLOWED on the chalkboard. "And so does this. But only one is a representation of speech."

Gary nodded. "Okay."

"Linguists describe writing like this—" I indicated the printed words "—as 'glottographic,' because it represents speech. Every human written language is in this category. However, this symbol—" I indicated the circle and diagonal line "—is 'semasiographic' writing, because it conveys meaning without reference to speech. There's no correspondence between its components and any particular sounds."

"And you think all of heptapod writing is like this?"

"From what I've seen so far, yes. It's not picture writing, it's far more complex. It has its own system of rules for constructing sentences, like a visual syntax that's unrelated to the syntax for their spoken language."

"A visual syntax? Can you show me an example?"

"Coming right up." I sat down at my desk and, using the computer, pulled up a frame from the recording of yesterday's conversation with Raspberry. I turned the monitor so he could see it. "In their spoken language, a noun has a case marker indicating whether it's a subject or object. In their written language, however, a noun is identified as subject or object based on the orientation of its logogram relative to that of the verb. Here, take a look." I pointed at one of the figures. "For instance, when 'heptapod' is integrated with 'hears' this way, with these strokes parallel, it means that the heptapod is doing the hearing." I showed him a different one. "When they're combined this way, with the strokes perpendicular, it means that the heptapod is being heard. This morphology applies to several verbs.

"Another example is the inflection system." I called up another frame from the recording. "In their written language, this logogram means roughly 'hear easily' or 'hear clearly.' See the elements it has in common with the logogram for 'hear'? You can still combine it with 'heptapod' in the same ways as before, to indicate that the heptapod can hear something clearly or that the heptapod is clearly heard. But what's really interesting is that the modulation of 'hear' into 'hear clearly' isn't a special case; you see the transformation they applied?"

Gary nodded, pointing. "It's like they express the idea of 'clearly' by changing the curve of those strokes in the middle."

"Right. That modulation is applicable to lots of verbs. The logogram for 'see' can be modulated in the same way to form 'see clearly,' and so can the logogram for 'read' and others. And changing the curve of those strokes has no parallel in their speech; with the spoken version of these verbs, they add a prefix to the verb to express ease of manner, and the prefixes for 'see' and 'hear' are different.

"There are other examples, but you get the idea. It's essentially a grammar in two dimensions."

He began pacing thoughtfully. "Is there anything like this in human writing systems?"

"Mathematical equations, notations for music and dance. But those are all very specialized; we couldn't record this conversation using them. But I suspect, if we knew it well enough, we could record this conversation in the heptapod writing system. I think it's a full-fledged, general-purpose graphical language."

Gary frowned. "So their writing constitutes a completely separate language from their speech, right?"

"Right. In fact, it'd be more accurate to refer to the writing system as 'Heptapod B,' and use 'Heptapod A' strictly for referring to the spoken language."

"Hold on a second. Why use two languages when one would suffice? That seems unnecessarily hard to learn."

"Like English spelling?" I said. "Ease of learning isn't the primary force in language evolution. For the heptapods, writing and speech may play such different cultural or cognitive roles that using separate languages makes more sense than using different forms of the same one."

He considered it. "I see what you mean. Maybe they

think our form of writing is redundant, like we're wasting a second communications channel."

"That's entirely possible. Finding out why they use a second language for writing will tell us a lot about them."

"So I take it this means we won't be able to use their writing to help us learn their spoken language."

I sighed. "Yeah, that's the most immediate implication. But I don't think we should ignore either Heptapod A or B; we need a two-pronged approach." I pointed at the screen. "I'll bet you that learning their two-dimensional grammar will help you when it comes time to learn their mathematical notation."

"You've got a point there. So are we ready to start asking about their mathematics?"

"Not yet. We need a better grasp on this writing system before we begin anything else," I said, and then smiled when he mimed frustration. "Patience, good sir. Patience is a virtue."

You'll be six when your father has a conference to attend in Hawaii, and we'll accompany him. You'll be so excited that you'll make preparations for weeks beforehand. You'll ask me about coconuts and volcanoes and surfing, and practice hula dancing in the mirror. You'll pack a suitcase with the clothes and toys you want to bring, and you'll drag it around the house to see how long you can carry it. You'll ask me if I can carry your Etch-a-Sketch in my bag, since there won't be any more room for it in yours and you simply can't leave without it.

"You won't need all of these," I'll say. "There'll be so many fun things to do there, you won't have time to play with so many toys."

You'll consider that; dimples will appear above your eyebrows when you think hard. Eventually you'll agree to pack fewer toys, but your expectations will, if anything, increase.

"I wanna be in Hawaii now," you'll whine.

"Sometimes it's good to wait," I'll say. "The anticipation makes it more fun when you get there."

You'll just pout.

In the next report I submitted, I suggested that the term "logogram" was a misnomer because it implied that each graph represented a spoken word, when in fact the graphs didn't correspond to our notion of spoken words at all. I didn't want to use the term "ideogram" either because of how it had been used in the past; I suggested the term "semagram" instead.

It appeared that a semagram corresponded roughly to a written word in human languages: it was meaningful on its own, and in combination with other semagrams could form endless statements. We couldn't define it precisely, but then no one had ever satisfactorily defined "word" for human languages either. When it came to sentences in Heptapod B, though, things became much more confusing. The language had no written punctuation: its syntax was indicated in the way the semagrams were combined, and there was no need to indicate the cadence of speech. There was certainly no way to slice out subject-predicate pairings neatly to make sentences. A "sentence" seemed to be whatever number of semagrams a heptapod wanted to join together; the only difference between a sentence and a paragraph, or a page, was size.

When a Heptapod B sentence grew fairly sizable, its visual impact was remarkable. If I wasn't trying to decipher it, the writing looked like fanciful praying mantids drawn in a cursive style, all clinging to each other to form an Escheresque lattice, each slightly dif-

ferent in its stance. And the biggest sentences had an
effect similar to that of psychedelic posters: sometimes
eye-watering, sometimes hypnotic.

I remember a picture of you taken at your college graduation. In the photo you're striking a pose for the camera, mortarboard stylishly tilted on your head, one hand
touching your sunglasses, the other hand on your hip,
holding open your gown to reveal the tank top and
shorts you're wearing underneath.

I remember your graduation. There will be the distraction of having Nelson and your father and what's-
her-name there all at the same time, but that will be
minor. That entire weekend, while you're introducing me
to your classmates and hugging everyone incessantly, I'll
be all but mute with amazement. I can't believe that you,
a grown woman taller than me and beautiful enough to
make my heart ache, will be the same girl I used to lift off
the ground so you could reach the drinking fountain, the
same girl who used to trundle out of my bedroom draped
in a dress and hat and four scarves from my closet.

And after graduation, you'll be heading for a job as
a financial analyst. I won't understand what you do
there, I won't even understand your fascination with
money, the preeminence you gave to salary when negotiating job offers. I would prefer it if you'd pursue something without regard for its monetary rewards, but I'll
have no complaints. My own mother could never understand why I couldn't just be a high school English
teacher. You'll do what makes you happy, and that'll be
all I ask for.

As time went on, the teams at each looking glass began
working in earnest on learning heptapod terminology

for elementary mathematics and physics. We worked together on presentations, with the linguists focusing on procedure and the physicists focusing on subject matter. The physicists showed us previously devised systems for communicating with aliens, based on mathematics, but those were intended for use over a radio telescope. We reworked them for face-to-face communication.

Our teams were successful with basic arithmetic, but we hit a road block with geometry and algebra. We tried using a spherical coordinate system instead of a rectangular one, thinking it might be more natural to the heptapods given their anatomy, but that approach wasn't any more fruitful. The heptapods didn't seem to understand what we were getting at.

Likewise, the physics discussions went poorly. Only with the most concrete terms, like the names of the elements, did we have any success; after several attempts at representing the periodic table, the heptapods got the idea. For anything remotely abstract, we might as well have been gibbering. We tried to demonstrate basic physical attributes like mass and acceleration so we could elicit their terms for them, but the heptapods simply responded with requests for clarification. To avoid perceptual problems that might be associated with any particular medium, we tried physical demonstrations as well as line drawings, photos, and animations; none were effective. Days with no progress became weeks, and the physicists were becoming disillusioned.

By contrast, the linguists were having much more success. We made steady progress decoding the grammar of the spoken language, Heptapod A. It didn't follow the pattern of human languages, as expected, but it was comprehensible so far: free word order, even to the extent that there was no preferred order for the clauses in a conditional statement, in defiance of a human language "universal." It also appeared that the heptapods had no objection to many levels of center-embedding of clauses, something that quickly defeated humans. Peculiar, but not impenetrable.

Much more interesting were the newly discovered morphological and grammatical processes in Heptapod B that were uniquely two-dimensional. Depending on a semagram's declension, inflections could be indicated by varying a certain stroke's curvature, or its thickness, or its manner of undulation; or by varying the relative sizes of two radicals, or their relative distance to another radical, or their orientations; or various other means. These were non-segmental graphemes; they couldn't be isolated from the rest of a semagram. And despite how such traits behaved in human writing, these had nothing to do with calligraphic style; their meanings were defined according to a consistent and unambiguous grammar.

We regularly asked the heptapods why they had come. Each time, they answered "to see," or "to observe." Indeed, sometimes they preferred to watch us silently rather than answer our questions. Perhaps they were scientists, perhaps they were tourists. The State Department instructed us to reveal as little as possible about humanity, in case that information could be used as a bargaining chip in subsequent negotiations. We obliged, though it didn't require much effort: the heptapods never asked questions about anything. Whether scientists or tourists, they were an awfully incurious bunch.

I remember once when we'll be driving to the mall to buy some new clothes for you. You'll be thirteen. One moment you'll be sprawled in your seat, completely un-self-conscious, all child; the next, you'll toss your hair with a practiced casualness, like a fashion model in training.

You'll give me some instructions as I'm parking the

car. "Okay, Mom, give me one of the credit cards, and we can meet back at the entrance here in two hours."

I'll laugh. "Not a chance. All the credit cards stay with me."

"You're kidding." You'll become the embodiment of exasperation. We'll get out of the car and I will start walking to the mall entrance. After seeing that I won't budge on the matter, you'll quickly reformulate your plans.

"Okay Mom, okay. You can come with me, just walk a little ways behind me, so it doesn't look like we're together. If I see any friends of mine, I'm gonna stop and talk to them, but you just keep walking, okay? I'll come find you later."

I'll stop in my tracks. "Excuse me? I am not the hired help, nor am I some mutant relative for you to be ashamed of."

"But Mom, I can't let anyone see you with me."

"What are you talking about? I've already met your friends; they've been to the house."

"That was different," you'll say, incredulous that you have to explain it. "This is shopping."

"Too bad."

Then the explosion: "You won't do the least thing to make me happy! You don't care about me at all!"

It won't have been that long since you enjoyed going shopping with me; it will forever astonish me how quickly you grow out of one phase and enter another. Living with you will be like aiming for a moving target; you'll always be further along than I expect.

I looked at the sentence in Heptapod B that I had just written, using simple pen and paper. Like all the sentences I generated myself, this one looked misshapen, like a heptapod-written sentence that had been smashed with a hammer and then inexpertly taped back together. I had sheets of such inelegant semagrams covering my desk, fluttering occasionally when the oscillating fan swung past.

It was strange trying to learn a language that had no spoken form. Instead of practicing my pronunciation, I had taken to squeezing my eyes shut and trying to paint semagrams on the insides of my eyelids.

There was a knock at the door and before I could answer Gary came in looking jubilant. "Illinois got a repetition in physics."

"Really? That's great; when did it happen?"

"It happened a few hours ago; we just had the videoconference. Let me show you what it is." He started erasing my blackboard.

"Don't worry, I didn't need any of that."

"Good." He picked up a nub of chalk and drew a diagram:

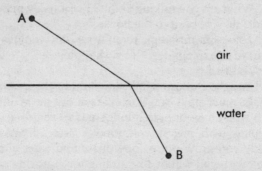

"Okay, here's the path a ray of light takes when crossing from air to water. The light ray travels in a straight line until it hits the water; the water has a different index of refraction, so the light changes direction. You've heard of this before, right?"

I nodded. "Sure."

"Now here's an interesting property about the path

the light takes. The path is the fastest possible route
between these two points."

"Come again?"

"Imagine, just for grins, that the ray of light traveled
along this path." He added a dotted line to his diagram:

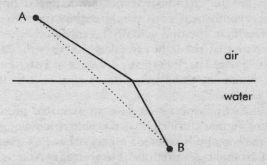

"This hypothetical path is shorter than the path
the light actually takes. But light travels more slowly in
water than it does in air, and a greater percentage of
this path is underwater. So it would take longer for
light to travel along this path than it does along the real
path."

"Okay, I get it."

"Now imagine if light were to travel along this
other path." He drew a second dotted path:

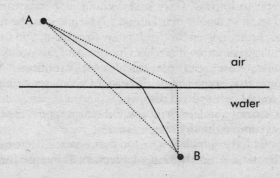

"This path reduces the percentage that's underwater, but the total length is larger. It would also take longer for light to travel along this path than along the actual one."

Gary put down the chalk and gestured at the diagram on the chalkboard with white-tipped fingers. "Any hypothetical path would require more time to traverse than the one actually taken. In other words, the route that the light ray takes is always the fastest possible one. That's Fermat's Principle of Least Time."

"Hmm, interesting. And this is what the heptapods responded to?"

"Exactly. Moorehead gave an animated presentation of Fermat's Principle at the Illinois looking glass, and the heptapods repeated it back. Now he's trying to get a symbolic description." He grinned. "Now is that highly neat, or what?"

"It's neat all right, but how come I haven't heard of Fermat's Principle before?" I picked up a binder and waved it at him; it was a primer on the physics topics suggested for use in communication with the heptapods. "This thing goes on forever about Planck masses and the spin-flip of atomic hydrogen, and not a word about the refraction of light."

"We guessed wrong about what'd be most useful for you to know," Gary said without embarrassment. "In fact, it's curious that Fermat's Principle was the first breakthrough; even though it's easy to explain, you need calculus to describe it mathematically. And not ordinary calculus; you need the calculus of variations. We thought that some simple theorem of geometry or algebra would be the breakthrough."

"Curious indeed. You think the heptapods' idea of what's simple doesn't match ours?"

"Exactly, which is why I'm *dying* to see what their mathematical description of Fermat's Principle looks like." He paced as he talked. "If their version of the calculus of variations is simpler to them than their equivalent of algebra, that might explain why we've had so much trouble talking about physics; their entire system of mathematics may be topsy-turvy compared to ours." He pointed to the physics primer. "You can be sure that we're going to revise that."

"So can you build from Fermat's Principle to other areas of physics?"

"Probably. There are lots of physical principles just like Fermat's."

"What, like Louise's principle of least closet space? When did physics become so minimalist?"

"Well, the word 'least' is misleading. You see, Fermat's Principle of Least Time is incomplete; in certain situations light follows a path that takes *more* time than any of the other possibilities. It's more accurate to say that light always follows an *extreme* path, either one that minimizes the time taken or one that maximizes it. A minimum and a maximum share certain mathematical properties, so both situations can be described with one equation. So to be precise, Fermat's Principle isn't a minimal principle; instead it's what's known as a 'variational' principle."

"And there are more of these variational principles?"

He nodded. "In all branches of physics. Almost every physical law can be restated as a variational principle. The only difference between these principles is in which attribute is minimized or maximized." He gestured as if the different branches of physics were arrayed before him on a table. "In optics, where Fermat's Principle applies, time is the attribute that has to be an extreme. In mechanics, it's a different attribute. In electromagnetism, it's something else again. But all these principles are similar mathematically."

"So once you get their mathematical description of Fermat's Principle, you should be able to decode the other ones."

"God, I hope so. I think this is the wedge that we've been looking for, the one that cracks open their formulation of physics. This calls for a celebration." He stopped his pacing and turned to me. "Hey Louise, want to go out for dinner? My treat."

I was mildly surprised. "Sure," I said.

It'll be when you first learn to walk that I get daily demonstrations of the asymmetry in our relationship. You'll be incessantly running off somewhere, and each time you walk into a door frame or scrape your knee, the pain feels like it's my own. It'll be like growing an errant limb, an extension of myself whose sensory nerves report pain just fine, but whose motor nerves don't convey my commands at all. It's so unfair: I'm going to give birth to an animated voodoo doll of myself. I didn't see this in the contract when I signed up. Was this part of the deal?

And then there will be the times when I see you laughing. Like the time you'll be playing with the neighbor's puppy, poking your hands through the chain-link fence separating our back yards, and you'll be laughing so hard you'll start hiccuping. The puppy will run inside the neighbor's house, and your laughter will gradually subside, letting you catch your breath. Then the puppy will come back to the fence to lick your fingers again, and you'll shriek and start laughing again. It will be the most wonderful sound I could ever imagine, a sound that makes me feel like a fountain, or a wellspring.

Now if only I can remember that sound the next time your blithe disregard for self-preservation gives me a heart attack.

▲   ▲   ▲

After the breakthrough with Fermat's Principle, discussions of scientific concepts became more fruitful. It wasn't as if all of heptapod physics was suddenly rendered transparent, but progress was steady. According to Gary, the heptapods' formulation of physics was indeed topsy-turvy relative to ours. Physical attributes that humans defined using integral calculus were seen as fundamental by the heptapods. As an example, Gary described an attribute that, in physics jargon, bore the deceptively simple name "action," which represented "the difference between kinetic and potential energy, integrated over time," whatever that meant. Calculus for us; elementary to them.

Conversely, to define attributes that humans thought of as fundamental, like velocity, the heptapods employed mathematics that were, Gary assured me, "highly weird." The physicists were ultimately able to prove the equivalence of heptapod mathematics and human mathematics; even though their approaches were almost the reverse of one another, both were systems of describing the same physical universe.

I tried following some of the equations that the physicists were coming up with, but it was no use. I couldn't really grasp the significance of physical attributes like "action"; I couldn't, with any confidence, ponder the significance of treating such an attribute as fundamental. Still, I tried to ponder questions formulated in terms more familiar to me: what kind of worldview did the heptapods have, that they would consider Fermat's Principle the simplest explanation of light refraction? What kind of perception made a minimum or maximum readily apparent to them?

▲   ▲   ▲

Your eyes will be blue like your dad's, not mud brown like mine. Boys will stare into those eyes the way I did, and do, into your dad's, surprised and enchanted, as I was and am, to find them in combination with black hair. You will have many suitors.

I remember when you are fifteen, coming home after a weekend at your dad's, incredulous over the interrogation he'll have put you through regarding the boy you're currently dating. You'll sprawl on the sofa, recounting your dad's latest breach of common sense: "You know what he said? He said, 'I know what teenage boys are like.'" Roll of the eyes. "Like I don't?"

"Don't hold it against him," I'll say. "He's a father; he can't help it." Having seen you interact with your friends, I won't worry much about a boy taking advantage of you; if anything, the opposite will be more likely. I'll worry about that.

"He wishes I were still a kid. He hasn't known how to act toward me since I grew breasts."

"Well, that development was a shock for him. Give him time to recover."

"It's been *years*, Mom. How long is it gonna take?"

"I'll let you know when my father has come to terms with mine."

During one of the videoconferences for the linguists, Cisneros from the Massachusetts looking glass had raised an interesting question: was there a particular order in which semagrams were written in a Heptapod B sentence? It was clear that word order meant next to nothing when speaking in Heptapod A; when asked to repeat what it had just said, a heptapod would likely as not use a different word order unless we specifically asked them not to. Was word order similarly unimportant when writing in Heptapod B?

Previously, we had only focused our attention on how a sentence in Heptapod B looked once it was complete. As far as anyone could tell, there was no preferred order when reading the semagrams in a sentence; you could start almost anywhere in the nest, then follow the branching clauses until you'd read the whole thing. But that was reading; was the same true about writing?

. During my most recent session with Flapper and Raspberry I had asked them if, instead of displaying a semagram only after it was completed, they could show it to us while it was being written. They had agreed. I inserted the videotape of the session into the VCR, and on my computer I consulted the session transcript.

I picked one of the longer utterances from the conversation. What Flapper had said was that the heptapods' planet had two moons, one significantly larger than the other; the three primary constituents of the planet's atmosphere were nitrogen, argon, and oxygen; and fifteen twenty-eighths of the planet's surface was covered by water. The first words of the spoken utterance translated literally as "inequality-of-size rocky-orbiter rocky-orbiters related-as-primary-to-secondary."

Then I rewound the videotape until the time signature matched the one in the transcription. I started playing the tape, and watched the web of semagrams being spun out of inky spider's silk. I rewound it and played it several times. Finally I froze the video right after the first stroke was completed and before the second one was begun; all that was visible onscreen was a single sinuous line.

Comparing that initial stroke with the completed sentence, I realized that the stroke participated in several different clauses of the message. It began in the semagram for 'oxygen,' as the determinant that distinguished it from certain other elements; then it slid down to become the morpheme of comparison in the description of the two moons' sizes; and lastly it flared out as the arched backbone of the semagram for 'ocean.' Yet this stroke was a single continuous line, and it was the first one that Flapper wrote. That meant the heptapod had to know how the entire sentence would be laid out before it could write the very first stroke.

The other strokes in the sentence also traversed several clauses, making them so interconnected that none could be removed without redesigning the entire sentence. The heptapods didn't write a sentence one semagram at a time; they built it out of strokes irrespective of individual semagrams. I had seen a similarly high degree of integration before in calligraphic designs, particularly those employing the Arabic alphabet. But those designs had required careful planning by expert calligraphers. No one could lay out such an intricate design at the speed needed for holding a conversation. At least, no human could.

There's a joke that I once heard a comedienne tell. It goes like this: "I'm not sure if I'm ready to have children. I asked a friend of mine who has children, 'Suppose I do have kids. What if when they grow up, they blame me for everything that's wrong with their lives?' She laughed and said, 'What do you mean, if?'"

That's my favorite joke.

Gary and I were at a little Chinese restaurant, one of the local places we had taken to patronizing to get away from the encampment. We sat eating the appetizers: potstickers, redolent of pork and sesame oil. My favorite.

I dipped one in soy sauce and vinegar. "So how are

you doing with your Heptapod B practice?" I asked.

Gary looked obliquely at the ceiling. I tried to meet his gaze, but he kept shifting it.

"You've given up, haven't you?" I said. "You're not even trying any more."

He did a wonderful hangdog expression. "I'm just no good at languages," he confessed. "I thought learning Heptapod B might be more like learning mathematics than trying to speak another language, but it's not. It's too foreign for me."

"It would help you discuss physics with them."

"Probably, but since we had our breakthrough, I can get by with just a few phrases."

I sighed. "I suppose that's fair; I have to admit, I've given up on trying to learn the mathematics."

"So we're even?"

"We're even." I sipped my tea. "Though I did want to ask you about Fermat's Principle. Something about it feels odd to me, but I can't put my finger on it. It just doesn't sound like a law of physics."

A twinkle appeared in Gary's eyes. "I'll bet I know what you're talking about." He snipped a potsticker in half with his chopsticks. "You're used to thinking of refraction in terms of cause and effect: reaching the water's surface is the cause, and the change in direction is the effect. But Fermat's Principle sounds weird because it describes light's behavior in goal-oriented terms. It sounds like a commandment to a light beam: 'Thou shalt minimize or maximize the time taken to reach thy destination.'"

I considered it. "Go on."

"It's an old question in the philosophy of physics. People have been talking about it since Fermat first formulated it in the 1600s; Planck wrote volumes about it. The thing is, while the common formulation of physical laws is causal, a variational principle like

Fermat's is purposive, almost teleological."

"Hmm, that's an interesting way to put it. Let me think about that for a minute." I pulled out a felt-tip pen and, on my paper napkin, drew a copy of the diagram that Gary had drawn on my blackboard. "Okay," I said, thinking aloud, "so let's say the goal of a ray of light is to take the fastest path. How does the light go about doing that?"

"Well, if I can speak anthropomorphic-projectionally, the light has to examine the possible paths and compute how long each one would take." He plucked the last potsticker from the serving dish.

"And to do that," I continued, "the ray of light has to know just where its destination is. If the destination were somewhere else, the fastest path would be different."

Gary nodded again. "That's right; the notion of a 'fastest path' is meaningless unless there's a destination specified. And computing how long a given path takes also requires information about what lies along that path, like where the water's surface is."

I kept staring at the diagram on the napkin. "And the light ray has to know all that ahead of time, before it starts moving, right?"

"So to speak," said Gary. "The light can't start traveling in any old direction and make course corrections later on, because the path resulting from such behavior wouldn't be the fastest possible one. The light has to do all its computations at the very beginning."

I thought to myself, *The ray of light has to know where it will ultimately end up before it can choose the direction to begin moving in.* I knew what that reminded me of. I looked up at Gary. "That's what was bugging me."

▲   ▲   ▲

I remember when you're fourteen. You'll come out of your bedroom, a graffiti-covered notebook computer in hand, working on a report for school.

"Mom, what do you call it when both sides can win?"

I'll look up from my computer and the paper I'll be writing. "What, you mean a win-win situation?"

"There's some technical name for it, some math word. Remember that time Dad was here, and he was talking about the stock market? He used it then."

"Hmm, that sounds familiar, but I can't remember what he called it."

"I need to know. I want to use that phrase in my social studies report. I can't even search for information on it unless I know what it's called."

"I'm sorry, I don't know it either. Why don't you call your dad?"

Judging from your expression, that will be more effort than you want to make. At this point, you and your father won't be getting along well. "Can you call Dad and ask him? But don't tell him it's for me."

"I think you can call him yourself."

You'll fume, "Jesus, Mom, I can never get help with my homework since you and Dad split up."

It's amazing the diverse situations in which you can bring up the divorce. "I've helped you with your homework."

"Like a million years ago, Mom."

I'll let that pass. "I'd help you with this if I could, but I don't remember what it's called."

You'll head back to your bedroom in a huff.

I practiced Heptapod B at every opportunity, both with the other linguists and by myself. The novelty of reading a semasiographic language made it compelling in a way that Heptapod A wasn't, and my improvement in writing it excited me. Over time, the sentences I wrote grew shapelier, more cohesive. I had reached the point where it worked better when I didn't think about it too much. Instead of carefully trying to design a sentence before writing, I could simply begin putting down strokes immediately; my initial strokes almost always turned out to be compatible with an elegant rendition of what I was trying to say. I was developing a faculty like that of the heptapods.

More interesting was the fact that Heptapod B was changing the way I thought. For me, thinking typically meant speaking in an internal voice; as we say in the trade, my thoughts were phonologically coded. My internal voice normally spoke in English, but that wasn't a requirement. The summer after my senior year in high school, I attended a total immersion program for learning Russian; by the end of the summer, I was thinking and even dreaming in Russian. But it was always *spoken* Russian. Different language, same mode: a voice speaking silently aloud.

The idea of thinking in a linguistic yet non-phonological mode always intrigued me. I had a friend born of deaf parents; he grew up using American Sign Language, and he told me that he often thought in ASL instead of English. I used to wonder what it was like to have one's thoughts be manually coded, to reason using an inner pair of hands instead of an inner voice.

With Heptapod B, I was experiencing something just as foreign: my thoughts were becoming graphically coded. There were trance-like moments during the day when my thoughts weren't expressed with my internal voice; instead, I saw semagrams with my mind's eye, sprouting like frost on a windowpane.

As I grew more fluent, semagraphic designs would appear fully-formed, articulating even complex ideas all at once. My thought processes weren't moving any faster as a result, though. Instead of racing forward, my mind hung balanced on the symmetry underlying the semagrams. The semagrams seemed to be something more than language; they were almost like mandalas. I found myself in a meditative state, contemplating the way in which premises and conclusions were interchangeable. There was no direction inherent in the way propositions were connected, no "train of thought" moving along a particular route; all the components in an act of reasoning were equally powerful, all having identical precedence.

A representative from the State Department named Hossner had the job of briefing the U.S. scientists on our agenda with the heptapods. We sat in the videoconference room, listening to him lecture. Our microphone was turned off, so Gary and I could exchange comments without interrupting Hossner. As we listened, I worried that Gary might harm his vision, rolling his eyes so often.

"They must have had some reason for coming all this way," said the diplomat, his voice tinny through the speakers. "It does not look like their reason was conquest, thank God. But if that's not the reason, what is? Are they prospectors? Anthropologists? Missionaries? Whatever their motives, there must be something we can offer them. Maybe it's mineral rights to our solar system. Maybe it's information about ourselves. Maybe it's the right to deliver sermons to our populations. But we can be sure that there's something.

"My point is this: their motive might not be to trade, but that doesn't mean that we cannot conduct trade. We simply need to know why they're here, and what we have that they want. Once we have that information, we can begin trade negotiations.

"I should emphasize that our relationship with the heptapods need not be adversarial. This is not a situation where every gain on their part is a loss on ours, or vice versa. If we handle ourselves correctly, both we and the heptapods can come out winners."

"You mean it's a non-zero-sum game?" Gary said in mock incredulity. "Oh my gosh."

"A non-zero-sum game."

"What?" You'll reverse course, heading back from your bedroom.

"When both sides can win: I just remembered, it's called a non-zero-sum game."

"That's it!" you'll say, writing it down on your notebook. "Thanks, Mom!"

"I guess I knew it after all," I'll say. "All those years with your father, some of it must have rubbed off."

"I knew you'd know it," you'll say. You'll give me a sudden, brief hug, and your hair will smell of apples. "You're the best."

"Louise?"

"Hmm? Sorry, I was distracted. What did you say?"

"I said, what do you think about our Mr. Hossner here?"

"I prefer not to."

"I've tried that myself: ignoring the government, seeing if it would go away. It hasn't."

As evidence of Gary's assertion, Hossner kept blathering: "Your immediate task is to think back on what you've learned. Look for anything that might help us. Has there been any indication of what the heptapods want? Of what they value?"

"Gee, it never occurred to us to look for things like that," I said. "We'll get right on it, sir."

"The sad thing is, that's just what we'll have to do," said Gary.

"Are there any questions?" asked Hossner.

Burghart, the linguist at the Fort Worth looking glass, spoke up. "We've been through this with the heptapods many times. They maintain that they're here to observe, and they maintain that information is not tradable."

"So they would have us believe," said Hossner. "But consider: how could that be true? I know that the heptapods have occasionally stopped talking to us for brief periods. That may be a tactical maneuver on their part. If we were to stop talking to them tomorrow—"

"Wake me up if he says something interesting," said Gary.

"I was just going to ask you to do the same for me."

That day when Gary first explained Fermat's Principle to me, he had mentioned that almost every physical law could be stated as a variational principle. Yet when humans thought about physical laws, they preferred to work with them in their causal formulation. I could understand that: the physical attributes that humans found intuitive, like kinetic energy or acceleration, were all properties of an object at a given moment in time. And these were conducive to a chronological, causal interpretation of events: one moment growing out of another, causes and effects created a chain reaction that grew from past to future.

In contrast, the physical attributes that the heptapods found intuitive, like "action" or those other things defined by integrals, were meaningful only over a period of time. And these were conducive to a teleological interpretation of events: by viewing events over a period of time, one recognized that there was a requirement that had to be satisfied, a goal of minimizing or maximizing. And one had to know the initial and final states to meet that goal; one needed knowledge of the effects before the causes could be initiated.

I was growing to understand that, too.

"Why?" you'll ask again. You'll be three.

"Because it's your bedtime," I'll say again. We'll have gotten as far as getting you bathed and into your jammies, but no further than that.

"But I'm not sleepy," you'll whine. You'll be standing at the bookshelf, pulling down a video to watch: your latest diversionary tactic to keep away from your bedroom.

"It doesn't matter: you still have to go to bed."

"But why?"

"Because I'm the mom and I said so."

I'm actually going to say that, aren't I? God, somebody please shoot me.

I'll pick you up and carry you under my arm to your bed, you wailing piteously all the while, but my sole concern will be my own distress. All those vows made in childhood that I would give reasonable answers when I became a parent, that I would treat my own child as an intelligent, thinking individual, all for naught: I'm going to turn into my mother. I can fight it as much as I want, but there'll be no stopping my slide down that long, dreadful slope.

Was it actually possible to know the future? Not simply to guess at it; was it possible to *know* what was going to happen, with absolute certainty and in specific detail? Gary once told me that the fundamental laws of physics were time-symmetric, that there was no physical difference between past and future. Given that, some might say, "yes, theoretically." But speaking more concretely, most would answer "no," because of free will.

I liked to imagine the objection as a Borgesian fabulation: consider a person standing before the *Book of Ages*, the chronicle that records every event, past and future. Even though the text has been photoreduced from the full-sized edition, the volume is enormous. With magnifier in hand, she flips through the tissue-thin leaves until she locates the story of her life. She finds the passage that describes her flipping through the *Book of Ages*, and she skips to the next column, where it details what she'll be doing later in the day: acting on information she's read in the *Book*, she'll bet one hundred dollars on the racehorse Devil May Care and win twenty times that much.

The thought of doing just that had crossed her mind, but being a contrary sort, she now resolves to refrain from betting on the ponies altogether.

There's the rub. The *Book of Ages* cannot be wrong; this scenario is based on the premise that a person is given knowledge of the actual future, not of some possible future. If this were Greek myth, circumstances would conspire to make her enact her fate despite her best efforts, but prophecies in myth are notoriously vague; the *Book of Ages* is quite specific, and there's no way she can be forced to bet on a racehorse in the manner specified. The result is a contradiction: the *Book of Ages* must be right, by definition; yet no matter what the *Book* says she'll do, she can choose to do otherwise. How can these two facts be reconciled?

They can't be, was the common answer. A volume like the *Book of Ages* is a logical impossibility, for the precise reason that its existence would result in the above contradiction. Or, to be generous, some might say that the *Book of Ages* could exist, as long as it wasn't accessible to readers: that volume is housed in a special collection, and no one has viewing privileges.

The existence of free will meant that we couldn't know the future. And we knew free will existed because we had direct experience of it. Volition was an intrinsic part of consciousness.

Or was it? What if the experience of knowing the future changed a person? What if it evoked a sense of urgency, a sense of obligation to act precisely as she knew she would?

I stopped by Gary's office before leaving for the day. "I'm calling it quits. Did you want to grab something to eat?"

"Sure, just wait a second," he said. He shut down his computer and gathered some papers together. Then he looked up at me. "Hey, want to come to my place for dinner tonight? I'll cook."

I looked at him dubiously. "You can cook?"

"Just one dish," he admitted. "But it's a good one."

"Sure," I said. "I'm game."

"Great. We just need to go shopping for the ingredients."

"Don't go to any trouble—"

"There's a market on the way to my house. It won't take a minute."

We took separate cars, me following him. I almost lost him when he abruptly turned in to a parking lot. It was a gourmet market, not large, but fancy; tall glass jars stuffed with imported foods sat next to specialty utensils on the store's stainless-steel shelves.

I accompanied Gary as he collected fresh basil,

tomatoes, garlic, linguini. "There's a fish market next door; we can get fresh clams there," he said.

"Sounds good." We walked past the section of kitchen utensils. My gaze wandered over the shelves— peppermills, garlic presses, salad tongs—and stopped on a wooden salad bowl.

When you are three, you'll pull a dishtowel off the kitchen counter and bring that salad bowl down on top of you. I'll make a grab for it, but I'll miss. The edge of the bowl will leave you with a cut, on the upper edge of your forehead, that will require a single stitch. Your father and I will hold you, sobbing and stained with Caesar Salad dressing, as we wait in the emergency room for hours.

I reached out and took the bowl from the shelf. The motion didn't feel like something I was forced to do. Instead it seemed just as urgent as my rushing to catch the bowl when it falls on you: an instinct that I felt right in following.

"I could use a salad bowl like this."

Gary looked at the bowl and nodded approvingly. "See, wasn't it a good thing that I had to stop at the market?"

"Yes it was." We got in line to pay for our purchases.

Consider the sentence "The rabbit is ready to eat." Interpret "rabbit" to be the object of "eat," and the sentence was an announcement that dinner would be served shortly. Interpret "rabbit" to be the subject of "eat," and it was a hint, such as a young girl might give her mother so she'll open a bag of Purina Bunny Chow. Two very different utterances; in fact, they were probably mutually exclusive within a single household. Yet either was a valid interpretation; only context could determine what the sentence meant.

Consider the phenomenon of light hitting water at one angle, and traveling through it at a different angle. Explain it by saying that a difference in the index of refraction caused the light to change direction, and one saw the world as humans saw it. Explain it by saying that light minimized the time needed to travel to its destination, and one saw the world as the heptapods saw it. Two very different interpretations.

The physical universe was a language with a perfectly ambiguous grammar. Every physical event was an utterance that could be parsed in two entirely different ways, one causal and the other teleological, both valid, neither one disqualifiable no matter how much context was available.

When the ancestors of humans and heptapods first acquired the spark of consciousness, they both perceived the same physical world, but they parsed their perceptions differently; the world-views that ultimately arose were the end result of that divergence. Humans had developed a sequential mode of awareness, while heptapods had developed a simultaneous mode of awareness. We experienced events in an order, and perceived their relationship as cause and effect. They experienced all events at once, and perceived a purpose underlying them all. A minimizing, maximizing purpose.

I have a recurring dream about your death. In the dream, I'm the one who's rock climbing—me, can you imagine it?—and you're three years old, riding in some kind of backpack I'm wearing. We're just a few feet below a ledge where we can rest, and you won't wait until I've climbed up to it. You start pulling yourself out of the pack; I order you to stop, but of course you ignore me. I feel your weight alternating from one side of the pack to the other as you climb out; then I feel your left foot on my shoulder, and then your right. I'm screaming at you, but I can't get a hand free to grab you. I can see the wavy design on the soles of your sneakers as you climb, and then I see a flake of stone give way beneath one of them. You slide right past me, and I can't move a muscle. I look down and see you shrink into the distance below me.

Then, all of a sudden, I'm at the morgue. An orderly lifts the sheet from your face, and I see that you're twenty-five.

"You okay?"

I was sitting upright in bed; I'd woken Gary with my movements. "I'm fine. I was just startled; I didn't recognize where I was for a moment."

Sleepily, he said, "We can stay at your place next time."

I kissed him. "Don't worry; your place is fine." We curled up, my back against his chest, and went back to sleep.

When you're three and we're climbing a steep, spiral flight of stairs, I'll hold your hand extra tightly. You'll pull your hand away from me. "I can do it by myself," you'll insist, and then move away from me to prove it, and I'll remember that dream. We'll repeat that scene countless times during your childhood. I can almost believe that, given your contrary nature, my attempts to protect you will be what create your love of climbing: first the jungle gym at the playground, then trees out in the green belt around our neighborhood, the rock walls at the climbing club, and ultimately cliff faces in national parks.

▲   ▲   ▲

I finished the last radical in the sentence, put down the chalk, and sat down in my desk chair. I leaned back and surveyed the giant Heptapod B sentence I'd written that covered the entire blackboard in my office. It included several complex clauses, and I had managed to integrate all of them rather nicely.

Looking at a sentence like this one, I understood why the heptapods had evolved a semasiographic writing system like Heptapod B; it was better suited for a species with a simultaneous mode of consciousness. For them, speech was a bottleneck because it required that one word follow another sequentially. With writing, on the other hand, every mark on a page was visible simultaneously. Why constrain writing with a glottographic straitjacket, demanding that it be just as sequential as speech? It would never occur to them. Semasiographic writing naturally took advantage of the page's two-dimensionality; instead of doling out morphemes one at a time, it offered an entire page full of them all at once.

And now that Heptapod B had introduced me to a simultaneous mode of consciousness, I understood the rationale behind Heptapod A's grammar: what my sequential mind had perceived as unnecessarily convoluted, I now recognized as an attempt to provide flexibility within the confines of sequential speech. I could use Heptapod A more easily as a result, though it was still a poor substitute for Heptapod B.

There was a knock at the door and then Gary poked his head in. "Colonel Weber'll be here any minute."

I grimaced. "Right." Weber was coming to participate in a session with Flapper and Raspberry; I was to act as translator, a job I wasn't trained for and that I detested.

Gary stepped inside and closed the door. He pulled me out of my chair and kissed me.

I smiled. "You trying to cheer me up before he gets here?"

"No, I'm trying to cheer me up."

"You weren't interested in talking to the heptapods at all, were you? You worked on this project just to get me into bed."

"Ah, you see right through me."

I looked into his eyes. "You better believe it," I said.

I remember when you'll be a month old, and I'll stumble out of bed to give you your 2:00 A.M. feeding. Your nursery will have that "baby smell" of diaper rash cream and talcum powder, with a faint ammoniac whiff coming from the diaper pail in the corner. I'll lean over your crib, lift your squalling form out, and sit in the rocking chair to nurse you.

The word "infant" is derived from the Latin word for "unable to speak," but you'll be perfectly capable of saying one thing: "I suffer," and you'll do it tirelessly and without hesitation. I have to admire your utter commitment to that statement; when you cry, you'll become outrage incarnate, every fiber of your body employed in expressing that emotion. It's funny: when you're tranquil, you will seem to radiate light, and if someone were to paint a portrait of you like that, I'd insist that they include the halo. But when you're unhappy, you will become a klaxon, built for radiating sound; a portrait of you then could simply be a fire alarm bell.

At that stage of your life, there'll be no past or future for you; until I give you my breast, you'll have no memory of contentment in the past nor expectation of relief in the future. Once you begin nursing, everything will reverse, and all will be right with the world. NOW is the only moment you'll perceive; you'll live in the present tense. In many ways, it's an enviable state.

▲   ▲   ▲

The heptapods are neither free nor bound as we understand those concepts; they don't act according to their will, nor are they helpless automatons. What distinguishes the heptapods' mode of awareness is not just that their actions coincide with history's events; it is also that their motives coincide with history's purposes. They act to create the future, to enact chronology.

Freedom isn't an illusion; it's perfectly real in the context of sequential consciousness. Within the context of simultaneous consciousness, freedom is not meaningful, but neither is coercion; it's simply a different context, no more or less valid than the other. It's like that famous optical illusion, the drawing of either an elegant young woman, face turned away from the viewer, or a wart-nosed crone, chin tucked down on her chest. There's no "correct" interpretation; both are equally valid. But you can't see both at the same time.

Similarly, knowledge of the future was incompatible with free will. What made it possible for me to exercise freedom of choice also made it impossible for me to know the future. Conversely, now that I know the future, I would never act contrary to that future, including telling others what I know: those who know the future don't talk about it. Those who've read the *Book of Ages* never admit to it.

I turned on the VCR and slotted a cassette of a session from the Fort Worth looking glass. A diplomatic negotiator was having a discussion with the heptapods there, with Burghart acting as translator.

The negotiator was describing humans' moral beliefs, trying to lay some groundwork for the concept of altruism. I knew the heptapods were familiar with the conversation's eventual outcome, but they still participated enthusiastically.

If I could have described this to someone who didn't already know, she might ask, if the heptapods already knew everything that they would ever say or hear, what was the point of their using language at all? A reasonable question. But language wasn't only for communication: it was also a form of action. According to speech act theory, statements like "You're under arrest," "I christen this vessel," or "I promise" were all performative: a speaker could perform the action only by uttering the words. For such acts, knowing what would be said didn't change anything. Everyone at a wedding anticipated the words "I now pronounce you husband and wife," but until the minister actually said them, the ceremony didn't count. With performative language, saying equaled doing.

For the heptapods, all language was performative. Instead of using language to inform, they used language to actualize. Sure, heptapods already knew what would be said in any conversation; but in order for their knowledge to be true, the conversation would have to take place.

"First Goldilocks tried the papa bear's bowl of porridge, but it was full of brussels sprouts, which she hated."

You'll laugh. "No, that's wrong!" We'll be sitting side by side on the sofa, the skinny, overpriced hardcover spread open on our laps.

I'll keep reading. "Then Goldilocks tried the mama bear's bowl of porridge, but it was full of spinach, which she also hated."

You'll put your hand on the page of the book to stop me. "You have to read it the right way!"

"I'm reading just what it says here," I'll say, all innocence.

"No you're not. That's not how the story goes."

"Well if you already know how the story goes, why do you need me to read it to you?"

"Cause I wanna hear it!"

.

The air conditioning in Weber's office almost compensated for having to talk to the man.

"They're willing to engage in a type of exchange," I explained, "but it's not trade. We simply give them something, and they give us something in return. Neither party tells the other what they're giving beforehand."

Colonel Weber's brow furrowed just slightly. "You mean they're willing to exchange gifts?"

I knew what I had to say. "We shouldn't think of it as 'gift-giving.' We don't know if this transaction has the same associations for the heptapods that gift-giving has for us."

"Can we—" he searched for the right wording "—drop hints about the kind of gift we want?"

"They don't do that themselves for this type of transaction. I asked them if we could make a request, and they said we could, but it won't make them tell us what they're giving." I suddenly remembered that a morphological relative of "performative" was "performance," which could describe the sensation of conversing when you knew what would be said: it was like performing in a play.

"But would it make them more likely to give us what we asked for?" Colonel Weber asked. He was perfectly oblivious of the script, yet his responses matched his assigned lines exactly.

"No way of knowing," I said. "I doubt it, given that it's not a custom they engage in."

"If we give our gift first, will the value of our gift influence the value of theirs?" He was improvising, while I had carefully rehearsed for this one and only show.

"No," I said. "As far as we can tell, the value of the exchanged items is irrelevant."

"If only my relatives felt that way," murmured Gary wryly.

I watched Colonel Weber turn to Gary. "Have you discovered anything new in the physics discussions?" he asked, right on cue.

"If you mean, any information new to mankind, no," said Gary. "The heptapods haven't varied from the routine. If we demonstrate something to them, they'll show us their formulation of it, but they won't volunteer anything and they won't answer our questions about what they know."

An utterance that was spontaneous and communicative in the context of human discourse became a ritual recitation when viewed by the light of Heptapod B.

Weber scowled. "All right then, we'll see how the State Department feels about this. Maybe we can arrange some kind of gift-giving ceremony."

Like physical events, with their causal and teleological interpretations, every linguistic event had two possible interpretations: as a transmission of information and as the realization of a plan.

"I think that's a good idea, Colonel," I said.

It was an ambiguity invisible to most. A private joke; don't ask me to explain it.

Even though I'm proficient with Heptapod B, I know I don't experience reality the way a heptapod does. My mind was cast in the mold of human, sequential languages, and no amount of immersion in an alien language can completely reshape it. My world-view is an amalgam of human and heptapod.

Before I learned how to think in Heptapod B, my memories grew like a column of cigarette ash, laid down by the infinitesimal sliver of combustion that was my consciousness, marking the sequential present. After I learned Heptapod B, new memories fell into place like gigantic blocks, each one measuring years in duration, and though they didn't arrive in order or land contiguously, they soon composed a period of five decades. It is the period during which I know Heptapod B well enough to think in it, starting during my interviews with Flapper and Raspberry and ending with my death.

Usually, Heptapod B affects just my memory: my consciousness crawls along as it did before, a glowing sliver crawling forward in time, the difference being that the ash of memory lies ahead as well as behind: there is no real combustion. But occasionally I have glimpses when Heptapod B truly reigns, and I experience past and future all at once; my consciousness becomes a half-century-long ember burning outside time. I perceive—during those glimpses—that entire epoch as a simultaneity. It's a period encompassing the rest of my life, and the entirety of yours.

I wrote out the semagrams for "process create-endpoint inclusive-we," meaning "let's start." Raspberry replied in the affirmative, and the slide shows began. The second display screen that the heptapods had provided began presenting a series of images, composed of semagrams and equations, while one of our video screens did the same.

This was the second "gift exchange" I had been present for, the eighth one overall, and I knew it would be the last. The looking glass tent was crowded with people; Burghart from Fort Worth was here, as were Gary and a nuclear physicist, assorted biologists, anthropologists, military brass, and diplomats. Thankfully they had set up an air conditioner to cool the place off. We would review the tapes of the images later to figure out just what the heptapods' "gift" was. Our own "gift" was a presentation on the Lascaux cave paintings.

We all crowded around the heptapods' second screen, trying to glean some idea of the images' content as they went by. "Preliminary assessments?" asked Colonel Weber.

"It's not a return," said Burghart. In a previous exchange, the heptapods had given us information about ourselves that we had previously told them. This had infuriated the State Department, but we had no reason to think of it as an insult: it probably indicated that trade value really didn't play a role in these exchanges. It didn't exclude the possibility that the heptapods might yet offer us a space drive, or cold fusion, or some other wish-fulfilling miracle.

"That looks like inorganic chemistry," said the nuclear physicist, pointing at an equation before the image was replaced.

Gary nodded. "It could be materials technology," he said.

"Maybe we're finally getting somewhere," said Colonel Weber.

"I wanna see more animal pictures," I whispered, quietly so that only Gary could hear me, and pouted like a child. He smiled and poked me. Truthfully, I wished the heptapods had given another xenobiology lecture, as they had on two previous exchanges; judging from those, humans were more similar to the heptapods than any other species they'd ever encountered. Or another lecture on heptapod history; those had been filled with apparent non-sequiturs, but were interesting nonetheless. I didn't want the heptapods to give us new technology, because I didn't want to see what our governments might do with it.

I watched Raspberry while the information was being exchanged, looking for any anomalous behavior. It stood barely moving as usual; I saw no indications of what would happen shortly.

After a minute, the heptapod's screen went blank, and a minute after that, ours did too. Gary and most of the other scientists clustered around a tiny video screen that was replaying the heptapods' presentation. I could hear them talk about the need to call in a solid-state physicist.

Colonel Weber turned. "You two," he said, pointing to me and then to Burghart, "schedule the time and location for the next exchange." Then he followed the others to the playback screen.

"Coming right up," I said. To Burghart, I asked, "Would you care to do the honors, or shall I?"

I knew Burghart had gained a proficiency in Heptapod B similar to mine. "It's your looking glass," he said. "You drive."

I sat down again at the transmitting computer. "Bet you never figured you'd wind up working as an Army translator back when you were a grad student."

"That's for goddamn sure," he said. "Even now I can hardly believe it." Everything we said to each other felt like the carefully bland exchanges of spies who meet in public, but never break cover.

I wrote out the semagrams for "locus exchange-transaction converse inclusive-we" with the projective aspect modulation.

Raspberry wrote its reply. That was my cue to frown, and for Burghart to ask, "What does it mean by that?" His delivery was perfect.

I wrote a request for clarification; Raspberry's reply

was the same as before. Then I watched it glide out of the room. The curtain was about to fall on this act of our performance.

Colonel Weber stepped forward. "What's going on? Where did it go?"

"It said that the heptapods are leaving now," I said. "Not just itself; all of them."

"Call it back here now. Ask it what it means."

"Um, I don't think Raspberry's wearing a pager," I said.

The image of the room in the looking glass disappeared so abruptly that it took a moment for my eyes to register what I was seeing instead: it was the other side of the looking-glass tent. The looking glass had become completely transparent. The conversation around the playback screen fell silent.

"What the hell is going on here?" said Colonel Weber.

Gary walked up to the looking glass, and then around it to the other side. He touched the rear surface with one hand; I could see the pale ovals where his fingertips made contact with the looking glass. "I think," he said, "we just saw a demonstration of transmutation at a distance."

I heard the sounds of heavy footfalls on dry grass. A soldier came in through the tent door, short of breath from sprinting, holding an oversize walkie-talkie. "Colonel, message from—"

Weber grabbed the walkie-talkie from him.

I remember what it'll be like watching you when you are a day old. Your father will have gone for a quick visit to the hospital cafeteria, and you'll be lying in your bassinet, and I'll be leaning over you.

So soon after the delivery, I will still be feeling like a

wrung-out towel. You will seem incongruously tiny, given how enormous I felt during the pregnancy; I could swear there was room for someone much larger and more robust than you in there. Your hands and feet will be long and thin, not chubby yet. Your face will still be all red and pinched, puffy eyelids squeezed shut, the gnome-like phase that precedes the cherubic.

I'll run a finger over your belly, marveling at the uncanny softness of your skin, wondering if silk would abrade your body like burlap. Then you'll writhe, twisting your body while poking out your legs one at a time, and I'll recognize the gesture as one I had felt you do inside me, many times. So *that's* what it looks like.

I'll feel elated at this evidence of a unique mother-child bond, this certitude that you're the one I carried. Even if I had never laid eyes on you before, I'd be able to pick you out from a sea of babies: Not that one. No, not her either. Wait, that one over there.

Yes, that's her. She's mine.

That final "gift exchange" was the last we ever saw of the heptapods. All at once, all over the world, their looking glasses became transparent and their ships left orbit. Subsequent analysis of the looking glasses revealed them to be nothing more than sheets of fused silica, completely inert. The information from the final exchange session described a new class of superconducting materials, but it later proved to duplicate the results of research just completed in Japan: nothing that humans didn't already know.

We never did learn why the heptapods left, any more than we learned what brought them here, or why they acted the way they did. My own new awareness didn't provide that type of knowledge; the heptapods' behavior was presumably explicable from a sequential point of view, but we never found that explanation.

I would have liked to experience more of the heptapods' world-view, to feel the way they feel. Then, perhaps I could immerse myself fully in the necessity of events, as they must, instead of merely wading in its surf for the rest of my life. But that will never come to pass. I will continue to practice the heptapod languages, as will the other linguists on the looking glass teams, but none of us will ever progress any further than we did when the heptapods were here.

Working with the heptapods changed my life. I met your father and learned Heptapod B, both of which make it possible for me to know you now, here on the patio in the moonlight. Eventually, many years from now, I'll be without your father, and without you. All I will have left from this moment is the heptapod language. So I pay close attention, and note every detail.

From the beginning I knew my destination, and I chose my route accordingly. But am I working toward an extreme of joy, or of pain? Will I achieve a minimum, or a maximum?

These questions are in my mind when your father asks me, "Do you want to make a baby?" And I smile and answer, "Yes," and I unwrap his arms from around me, and we hold hands as we walk inside to make love, to make you.

Whiptail

ROBERT REED

Robert Reed is one of the finest and most prolific writers of short fiction in SF and fantasy. His stories appear in amazing profusion, six to ten or more of them a year, and at least five or six of them worthy of consideration for a year's best volume. What is particularly impressive is his range, which approaches such masters as Ray Bradbury or Gene Wolfe. And he writes about a novel a year as well (his first, *The Leeshore*, appeared in 1987). He has been publishing SF since 1986, when he won the grand prize in the annual Writers of the Future contest, but has only reached his present level of achievement in the mid-'90s. To date, his novels, though favorably reviewed, have not unfortunately lived up to the achievement of his short fiction, and so he is not as highly ranked nor as popular in the field as he deserves. This story is from *Asimov's*. Sex and gender roles were a concern to many writers in SF in 1998, but nowhere with more wit than here.

"**W**hat a beautiful morning," I was singing. "And so strange! Isn't it? This incredible, wonderful fog, and how the frost clings everywhere. Lovely, lovely, just lovely. Is this how it always is, Chrome . . . ?"

"Always," she joked, laughing quietly. Patiently. "All year long, practically."

She was teasing. I knew that, and I didn't care. A river of words just kept pouring out of me: I was talking about the scenery and the hour, and goodness, we were late and her poor mother would be waiting, and God on her throne, I was hungry. Sometimes I told my Chrome to drive faster, and she would, and then I would find myself worrying, and I'd tell her, "Slow down a little." I'd say, "This road doesn't look all that dry."

Chrome smiled the whole time, not minding my prattle.

At least I hoped she didn't.

I can't help what I am. Dunlins, by nature, are small and electric. Nervous energy always bubbling. Particularly when they're trying not to be nervous. Particularly when their lover is taking them to meet her family for the first time.

"Have you ever seen a more magical morning, Chrome?"

"Never," she promised, her handsome face smiling at me.

It was the morning of the Solstice, which helped that sense of magic. But mostly it was because of the weather. A powerful cold front had fallen south from the chilly Arctic Sea, smashing into the normally warm winter air. The resulting fog was luscious thick, except in sudden little patches where it was thin enough to give us a glimpse of the pale northern sun. Wherever the fog touched a cold surface, it froze, leaving every tree limb and bush branch and tall blade of grass coated with a glittering hard frost. Whiteness lay over everything. Everything wore a delicate, perishable whiteness born of degrees. A touch colder, and there wouldn't have been any fog. Warmed slightly, and everything white would have turned to vapor and an afternoon's penetrating dampness.

The road had its own magic. A weathered charm, I'd call it. Old and narrow, its pavement was rutted by tires and cracked in places, and the potholes were marked with splashes of fading yellow paint. Chrome explained that it had been thirty years since the highway association had touched it. "Not enough traffic to bother with," she said. We were climbing up a long hillside, and at the top, where the road flattened, there was a corner and a weedy graveled road that went due south.

"Our temple's down there," she told me.

I looked and looked, but all I saw was the little road flanked by the white farm fields, both vanishing into the thickest fog yet.

For maybe the fiftieth time, I asked, "How do I look?"

"Awful," she joked.

Then she grabbed my knee, and with a laughing voice, Chrome said, "No, you look gorgeous, darling. Just perfect."

I just hoped that I wasn't too ugly. That's all.

We started down a long hillside, passing a small weathered sign that quietly announced that we were entering Chromatella. I read the name aloud, twice. Then came the first of the empty buildings, set on both sides of the little highway. My Chrome had warned me, but it was still a sad shock. There were groceries and hardware stores and clothing stores and gas stations, and all of them were slowly collapsing into their basements, old roofs pitched this way and that. One block of buildings had been burned down. A pair of Chrome's near-daughters had been cooking opossum in one of the abandoned kitchens. At least that was the official story. But my Chrome gave me this look, confessing, "When I was their age, I wanted to burn all of this. Every night I fought the urge. It wasn't until I was grown up that I understood why Mother left these buildings alone."

I didn't understand why, I thought. But I managed not to admit it.

A big old mothering house halfway filled the next block. Its roof was in good repair, and its white walls looked like they'd been painted this year. Yet the house itself seemed dark and drab compared to the whiteness of the frost. Even with the OPEN sign flashing in the window, it looked abandoned. Forgotten. And awfully lonely.

"Finally," my Chrome purred. "She's run out of things to say."

Was I that bad? I wondered.

We pulled up to the front of the house, up under the verandah, and I used the mirror, checking my little Dunlin face before climbing out.

There was an old dog and what looked like her puppies waiting for us. They had long wolfish faces and big bodies, and each of them wore a heavy collar, each collar with a different colored tag. "Red Guard!" Chrome shouted at the mother dog. Then she said, "Gold. Green. Pink. Blue. Hello, ladies. Hello!"

The animals were bouncing, and sniffing. And I stood like a statue, trying to forget how much dogs scare me.

Just then the front door crashed open, and a solid old voice was shouting, "Get away from her, you bitches! Get!"

Every dog bolted.

Thankfully.

I looked up at my savior, then gushed, "Mother Chromatella. I'm *so* glad to meet you, finally!"

"A sweet Dunlin," she said. "And my first daughter, too."

I shook the offered hand, trying to smile as much as she smiled. Then we pulled our hands apart, and I found myself staring, looking at the bent nose and the rounded face and the gray spreading through her short black hair. That nose was shattered long ago by a pony, my Chrome had told me. Otherwise the face was the same, except for its age. And for the eyes, I noticed. They were the same brown as my Chrome's, but when I looked deep, I saw something very sad lurking in them.

Both of them shivered at the same moment, saying, "Let's go inside."

I said, "Fine."

I grabbed my suitcase, even though Mother Chromatella offered to carry it. Then I followed her through the old door with its cut-glass and its brass knob and an ancient yellow sign telling me, "Welcome."

The air inside was warm, smelling of bacon and books. There was a long bar and maybe six tables in a huge room that could have held twenty tables. Bookshelves covered two entire walls. Music was flowing from a radio, a thousand voices singing about the Solstice. I asked where I should put my things, and my Chrome said, "Here," and wrestled the bag from me, carrying it and hers somewhere upstairs.

Mother Chrome asked if it was a comfortable trip.

"Very," I said. "And I adore your fog!"

"My fog." That made her laugh. She set a single

plate into the sink, then ran the tap until the water was hot. "Are you hungry, Dunlin?"

I said, "A little, yes," when I could have said, "I'm starving."

My Chrome came downstairs again. Without looking her way, Mother Chrome said, "Daughter, we've got plenty of eggs here."

My Chrome pulled down a clean skillet and spatula, then asked, "The others?"

Her sisters and near-daughters, she meant.

"They're walking up. Now, or soon."

To the Temple, I assumed. For their Solstice service.

"I don't need to eat now," I lied, not wanting to be a burden.

But Mother Chrome said, "Nonsense," while smiling at me. "My daughter's hungry, too. Have a bite to carry you over to the feast."

I found myself dancing around the main room, looking at the old neon beer signs and the newly made bookshelves. Like before, I couldn't stop talking. Jabbering. I asked every question that came to me, and sometimes I interrupted Mother Chrome's patient answers.

"Have you ever met a Dunlin before?"

She admitted, "Never, no."

"My Chrome says that this is the oldest mothering house in the district? Is that so?"

"As far as I know—"

"Neat old signs. I bet they're worth something, if you're a collector."

"I'm not, but I believe you're right."

"Are these shelves walnut?"

"Yes."

"They're beautiful," I said, knowing that I sounded like a brain-damaged fool. "How many books do you have here?"

"Several thousand, I imagine."

"And you've read all of them?"

"Once, or more."

"Which doesn't surprise me," I blurted. "Your daughter's a huge reader, too. In fact, she makes me feel a little stupid sometimes."

From behind the bar, over the sounds of cooking eggs, my Chrome asked, "Do I?"

"Nonsense," said Mother Chrome. But I could hear the pride in her voice. She was standing next to me, making me feel small—in so many ways, Chromatellas are big strong people—and she started to say something else. Something else kind, probably. But her voice got cut off by the soft *bing-bing-bing* of the telephone.

"Excuse me," she said, picking up the receiver.

I looked at my Chrome, then said, "It's one of your sisters. She's wondering what's keeping us."

"It's not." My Chrome shook her head, saying, "That's the out-of-town ring." And she looked from the eggs to her mother and back again, her brown eyes curious but not particularly excited.

Not then, at least.

The eggs got cooked and put on plates, and I helped pour apple juice into two clean glasses. I was setting the glasses on one of the empty tables when Mother Chrome said, "Good-bye. And thank you." Then she set down the receiver and leaned forward, resting for a minute. And her daughter approached her, touching her on the shoulder, asking, "Who was it? Is something wrong?"

"Corvus," she said.

I recognized that family name. Even then.

She said, "My old instructor. She was calling from the Institute . . . to warn me. . . ."

"About what?" my Chrome asked. Then her face changed, as if she realized it for herself. "Is it done?" she asked. "Is it?"

"And it's been done for a long time, apparently. In secret." Mother Chrome looked at the phone again, as if she still didn't believe what she had just heard. That it was a mistake, or someone's silly joke.

I said nothing, watching them.

My Chrome asked, "When?"

"Years ago, apparently."

Mine asked, "And they kept it a secret?"

Mother Chrome nodded and halfway smiled. Then she said, "Today," and took a huge breath. "Dr. Corvus and her staff are going to hold a press conference at noon. She wanted me to be warned. And thank me, I guess."

My Chrome said, "Oh, my."

I finally asked, "What is it? What's happening?"

They didn't hear me.

I got the two plates from the bar and announced, "These eggs smell *gorgeous*."

The Chromatellas were trading looks, saying everything with their eyes.

Just hoping to be noticed, I said, "I'm awfully hungry, really. May I start?"

With the same voice, together, they told me, "Go on."

But I couldn't eat alone. Not like that. So I walked up to my Chrome and put an arm up around her, saying, "Join me, darling."

She said, "No."

Smiling and crying at the same time, she confessed, "I'm not hungry anymore."

She was the first new face in an entire week.

Even in Boreal City, with its millions from everywhere, there are only so many families and so many faces. So when I saw the doctor at the clinic, I was a little startled. And interested, of course. Dunlins are very social people. We love diversity in our friends and lovers, and everywhere in our daily lives.

"Dunlins have weak lungs," I warned her.

She said, "Quiet," as she listened to my breathing. Then she said, "I know about you. Your lungs are usually fine. But your immune system has a few holes in it."

I was looking at her face. Staring, probably.

She asked if I was from the Great Delta. A substantial colony of Dunlins had built that port city in that southern district, its hot climate reminding us of our homeland back on Mother's Land.

"But I live here now," I volunteered. "My sisters and I have a trade shop in the new mall. Have you been there?" Then I glanced at the name on her tag, blurting out, "I've never heard of the Chromatellas before."

"That's because there aren't many of us," she admitted.

"In Borcal?"

"Anywhere," she said. Then she didn't mention it again.

In what for me was a rare show of self-restraint, I said nothing. For as long as we were just doctor and patient, I managed to keep my little teeth firmly planted on my babbling tongue. But I made a point of researching her name, and after screwing up my courage and asking her to dinner, I confessed what I knew and told her that I was sorry. "It's just so tragic," I told her, as if she didn't know. Then desperate to say anything that might help, I said, "In this day and age, you just don't think it could ever happen anywhere."

Which was, I learned, a mistake.

My Chrome regarded me over her sweet cream dessert, her beautiful eyes dry and her strong jaw pushed a little forward. Then she set down her spoon and calmly, quietly told me all of those dark things that doctors know, and every Chromatella feels in her blood:

Inoculations and antibiotics have put an end to the old plagues. Families don't have to live in isolated communities, in relative quarantine, fearing any stranger because she might bring a new flu bug, or worse. People today can travel far, and if they wish, they can live and work in the new cosmopolitan cities, surrounded by an array of faces and voices and countless new ideas.

But the modern world only seems stable and healthy.

Diseases mutate. And worse, new diseases emerge every year. As the population soars, the margin for error diminishes. "Something horrible will finally get loose," Dr. Chromatella promised me. "And when it does, it'll move fast and it'll go everywhere, and the carnage is going to dwarf all of the famous old epidemics. There's absolutely no doubt in my mind."

I am such a weakling. I couldn't help but cry into my sweet cream.

A strong hand reached across and wiped away my tears. But instead of apologizing, she said, "Vulnerability," and smiled in a knowing way.

"What do you mean?" I sniffled.

"I want my daughters to experience it. If only through their mother's lover."

How could I think of love just then?

I didn't even try.

Then with the softest voice she could muster, my Chrome told me, "But even if the worst does happen, you know what we'll do. We'll pick ourselves up again. We always do."

I nodded, then whispered, "We do, don't we?"

"And I'll be there with you, my Dunnie."

I smiled at her, surprising myself.

"Say that again," I told her.

"I'll be with you. If you'll have me, of course."

"No, that other part—"

"My Dunnie?"

I felt my smile growing and growing.

"Call up to the temple," my Chrome suggested.

"Can't," her mother replied. "The line blew down this summer, and nobody's felt inspired to put it up again."

Both of them stared at the nearest clock.

I stared at my cooling eggs, waiting for someone to explain this to me.

Then Mother Chrome said, "There's that old television in the temple basement. We have to walk there and set it up."

"Or we could eat," I suggested. "Then drive."

My Chrome shook her head, saying, "I feel like walking."

"So do I," said her mother. And with that both of them were laughing, their faces happier than even a giddy Dunlin's.

"Get your coat, darling," said my Chrome.

I gave up looking at my breakfast.

Stepping out the back door, out into the chill wet air, I realized that the fog had somehow grown thicker. I saw nothing of the world but a brown yard with an old bird feeder set out on a tree stump, spilling over with grain, dozens of brown sparrows and brown-green finches eating and talking in soft cackles. From above, I could hear the ringing of the temple bells. They sounded soft and pretty, and suddenly I remembered how it felt to be a little girl walking between my big sisters, knowing that the Solstice ceremony would take forever, but afterward, if I was patient, there would come the feast and the fun of opening gifts.

Mother Chrome set the pace. She was quick for a woman of her years, her eyes flipping one way, then another. I knew that expression from my Chrome. She was obviously thinking hard about her phone call.

We were heading south, following an empty concrete road. The next house was long and built of wood, three stories tall and wearing a steeply pitched roof. People lived there. I could tell by the roof and the fresh coat of white paint, and when we were close, I saw little tractors for children to ride and old dolls dressed in farmer clothes, plus an antique dollhouse that was the same shape and color as the big house.

I couldn't keep myself from talking anymore.

I admitted, "I don't understand. What was that call about?"

Neither spoke, at first.

On the frosty sidewalk I could see the little shoeprints of children, and in the grass, their mothers' prints. I found myself listening for voices up ahead, and giggles. Yet I heard nothing but the bells. Suddenly I wanted to be with those children, sitting in the temple, nothing to do but sing for summer's return.

As if reading my mind, Mother Chrome said, "We have a beautiful temple. Did you see it in all *my* fog?"

I shook my head. "No."

"Beautiful," she repeated. "We built it from the local sandstone. More than a hundred and fifty years ago."

"Yes, ma'am," I muttered.

Past the long house, tucked inside a grove of little trees, was a pig pen. There was a strong high fence, electrified and barbed. The shaggy brown adults glared at us, while their newest daughters, striped and halfway cute, came closer, begging for scraps and careless fingers.

I asked again, "What about that call? What's so important?"

"We were always a successful family," said Mother Chrome. "My daughter's told you, I'm sure."

"Yes, ma'am."

"Mostly we were farmers, but in the last few centuries, our real talents emerged. We like science and the healing arts most of all."

My Chrome had told me the same thing. In the same words and tone.

We turned to the west, climbing up the hill toward the temple. Empty homes left empty for too long lined both sides of the little street. They were sad and sloppy, surrounded by thick stands of brown weeds. Up ahead of us, running from thicket to thicket, was a flock of wild pheasants, dark brown against the swirling fog.

"Chromatellas were a successful family," she told me, "and relatively rich, too."

Just before I made a fool of myself, I realized that Mother Chrome was trying to answer my questions.

"Nearly forty years ago, I was awarded a student slot at the Great Western Institute." She looked back at me, then past me. "It was such a wonderful honor and a great opportunity. And of course my family threw a party for me. Complete with a parade. With my mother and my grand, I walked this route. This ground. My gown was new, and it was decorated with ribbons and flower blossoms. Everyone in Chromatella stood in two long lines, holding hands and singing to me. My sisters. My near-sisters. Plus travelers at the mother house, and various lovers, too."

I was listening, trying hard to picture the day.

"A special feast was held in the temple. A hundred fat pigs were served. People got drunk and stood up on their chairs and told the same embarrassing stories about me, again and again. I was drunk for the first time. Badly. And when I finished throwing up, my mother and sisters bundled me up, made certain that my inoculation records were in my pocket, then they put me on the express train racing south."

We were past the abandoned homes, and the bells were louder. Closer.

"When I woke, I had a premonition. I realized that I would never come home again. Which is a common enough premonition. And silly. Of course your family will always be there. Always, always. Where else can they be?"

Mother Chrome said those last words with a flat voice and strange eyes.

She was walking slower now, and I was beside her, the air tingling with old fears and angers. And that's when the first of the tombstones appeared: Coming out of the cold fog, they were simple chunks of fieldstone set on end and crudely engraved.

They looked unreal at first.

Ready to dissolve back into the fog.

But with a few more steps, they turned as real as any of us, and a breath of wind began blowing away the worst of the fog, the long hillside suddenly visible, covered with hundreds and thousands of crude markers, the ground in front of each slumping and every grave decorated with wild flowers: Easy to seed, eager to grow, requiring no care and perfectly happy in this city of ghosts.

When my great was alive, she loved to talk about her voyage from Mother's Land. She would describe the food she ate, the fleas in her clothes, the hurricane that tore the sails from the ship's masts, and finally the extraordinary hope she felt when the New Lands finally passed into view.

None of it ever happened to her, of course.

The truth is that she was born on the Great Delta. It

was her grand who had ridden on the immigrant boat, and what she remembered were her grand's old stories. But isn't that the way with families? Surrounded by people who are so much like you, you can't help but have their large lives bleed into yours, and yours, you can only hope, into theirs.

Now the Chromatellas told the story together.

The older one would talk until she couldn't anymore, then her daughter would effortlessly pick up the threads, barely a breath separating their two voices.

Like our great cities, they said, the Institutes are recent inventions.

Even four decades ago, the old precautions remained in effect. Students and professors had to keep their inoculation records on hand. No one could travel without a doctor's certificate and forms to the Plague Bureau. To be given the chance to actually live with hundreds and thousands of people who didn't share your blood—who didn't even know you a little bit—was an honor and an astonishment for the young Chromatella.

After two years, she earned honors and new opportunities. One of her professors hired her as a research assistant, and after passing a battery of immunological tests, the two of them were allowed up into the wild mountain country. Aboriginals still lived the old ways. Most kept their distance. But a brave young person came forward, offering to be their guide and provider and very best friend. Assuming, of course, that they would pay her and pay her well.

She was a wild creature, said Mother Chrome.

She hunted deer for food and made what little clothing she needed from their skins. And to make herself more beautiful to her sister-lover, she would rub her body and hair with the fresh fat of a bear.

In those days, those mountains were barely mapped. Only a handful of biologists had even walked that ground, much less made a thorough listing of its species.

As an assistant, Mother Chrome was given the simple jobs: She captured every kind of animal possible, by whatever means, measuring them and marking their location on the professor's maps, then killing them and putting them away for future studies. To catch lizards, she used a string noose. Nooses worked well enough with the broad-headed, slow-witted fence lizards. But not with the swift, narrow-headed whiptails. They drove her crazy. She found herself screaming and chasing after them, which was how she slipped on rocks and tumbled to the rocky ground below.

The guide came running.

Her knee was bleeding and a thumb was jammed. But the Chromatella was mostly angry, reporting what had happened, cursing the idiot lizards until she realized that her hired friend and protector was laughing wildly.

"All right," said Mother Chrome. "You do it better!"

The guide rose and strolled over to the nearest rock pile, and after waiting forever with a rock's patience, she easily snatched up the first whiptail that crawled out of its crevice.

A deal was soon struck: One copper for each whiptail captured.

The guide brought her dozens of specimens, and whenever there was a backlog, she would sit in the shade and watch Mother Chrome at work. After a while, with genuine curiosity, the guide asked, "Why?" She held up a dull brown lizard, then asked, "Why do you put this one on that page, while the one in your hand goes on that other page?"

"Because they're different species," Mother Chrome explained. Then she flipped it on its back, pointing and saying, "The orange neck is the difference. And if you look carefully, you can tell that they're not quite the same size."

But the guide remained stubbornly puzzled. She shook her head and blew out her cheeks as if she was inflating a balloon.

Mother Chrome opened up her field guide. She found the right page and pointed. "There!" At least one field biologist had come to the same easy conclusion: Two whiptails, two species. Sister species, obviously. Probably separated by one or two million years of evolution, from the looks of it.

The guide gave a big snort.

Then she calmly put the orange neck into her mouth and bit off the lizard's head, and with a small steel blade, she opened up its belly and groin, telling Mother Chrome, "Look until you see it. Until you can."

Chromatellas have a taste for details. With a field lens and the last of her patience, she examined the animal's internal organs. Most were in their proper places, but a few were misplaced, or they were badly deformed.

The guide had a ready explanation:

"The colorful ones are lazy ladies," she claimed. "They lure in the drab ones with their colors, and they're the aggressors in love. But they never lay any eggs. What they do, I think, is slip their eggs inside their lovers. Then their lovers have to lay both hers and the mate's together, in a common nest."

It was an imaginative story, and wrong.

But it took the professor and her assistant another month to be sure it was wrong, and then another few months at the Institute to realize what was really happening.

And at that point in the story, suddenly, the two Chromatellas stopped talking. They were staring at each other, talking again with their eyes.

We were in the oldest, uppermost end of the cemetery. The tombstones there were older and better made, polished and pink and carefully engraved with nicknames and birthdates and deathdates. The temple bells were no longer ringing. But we were close now. I saw the big building looming over us for a moment, then it vanished as the fog thickened again. And that's when I admitted, "I don't understand." I asked my Chrome, "If the guide was wrong, then what's the right explanation?"

"The lizard is one species. But it exists in two forms." She sighed and showed an odd little smile. "One form lays eggs. While the other one does nothing. Nothing but donate half of its genetic information, that is."

I was lost.

I felt strange and alone, and lost, and now I wanted to cry, only I didn't know why. How could I know?

"As it happens," said Mother Chrome, "a team of biologists working near the south pole were first to report a similar species. A strange bird that comes in two forms. It's the eggless form that wears the pretty colors."

Something tugged at my memory.

Had my Chrome told me something about this, or did I read about it myself? Maybe from my days in school . . . maybe . . . ?

"Biologists have found several hundred species like that," said my Chrome. "Some are snakes. Some are mice. Most of them are insects." She looked in my direction, almost smiling. "Of course flowering plants do this trick, too. Pollen is made by the stamen, and the genetics in the seeds are constantly mixing and remixing their genes. Which can be helpful. If your conditions are changing, you need to make new models to keep current. To evolve."

Again, the temple appeared from the fog.

I had been promised something beautiful, but the building only looked tall and cold to me. The stone was dull and simple and sad, and I hated it. I had to chew on my tongue just to keep myself from saying what I was thinking.

What was I thinking?

Finally, needing to break up all this deep thinking, I turned to Mother Chrome and said, "It must have been exciting, anyway. Being one of the first to learn something like that."

Her eyes went blind, and she turned and walked away.

I stopped, and my Chrome stopped. We watched the old woman marching toward the big doors of the temple, and when she was out of earshot, I heard my lover say, "She wasn't there when Dr. Corvus made the breakthrough."

I swallowed and said, "No?"

"She was called home suddenly. In the middle of the term." My Chrome took me by the shoulder and squeezed too hard, telling me, "Her family here, and everywhere else . . . all the Chromatellas in the world were just beginning to die. . . ."

.

A stupid pesticide was to blame.

It was sold for the first time just after Mother Chrome left for school. It was too new and expensive for most farmers, but the Chromatellas loved it. I can never remember its name: Some clumsy thing full of ethanes and chlorines and phenyl-somethings. Her sisters sprayed it on their fields and their animals, and they ate traces of it on their favorite foods, and after the first summer, a few of the oldest Chromes complained of headaches that began to turn into brain tumors, which is how the plague showed itself.

At first, people considered the tumors to be bad luck.

When Mother Chrome's great and grand died in the

same winter, it was called a coincidence, and it was sad. Nothing more.

Not until the next summer did the Plague Bureau realize what was happening. Something in the Chromatella blood wasn't right. The pesticide sneaked into their bodies and brains, and fast-growing tumors would flare up. First in the old, then the very young. The Bureau banned the poison immediately. Whatever was left unused was buried or destroyed. But almost every Chromatella had already eaten and breathed too much of it. When Mother Chrome finally came home, her mother met her at the train station, weeping uncontrollably. Babies were sick, she reported, and all the old people were dying. Even healthy adults were beginning to suffer headaches and tremors, which meant it would all be over by spring. Her mother said that several times. "Over by spring," she said. Then she wiped at her tears and put on a brave Chromatella face, telling her daughter, "Dig your grave now. That's my advice. And find a headstone you like, before they're all gone."

But Mother Chrome never got ill.

"The Institute grew their own food," my Chrome told me.

We were in bed together, warm and happy and in love, and she told the story because it was important for me to know what had happened, and because she thought that I was curious. Even though I wasn't. I knew enough already, I was telling myself.

"They grew their own food," she repeated, "and they used different kinds of pesticides. Safer ones, it turns out."

I nodded, saying nothing.

"Besides," she told me, "Mother spent that summer in the wilderness. She ate clean deer and berries and the like."

"That helped too?" I asked.

"She's never had a sick day in her life," my Chrome assured me. "But after she came home, and for those next few months, she watched everyone else get sicker and weaker. Neighbor communities sent help when they could, but it was never enough. Mother took care of her dying sisters and her mother, then she buried them. And by spring, as promised, it was over. The plague had burnt itself out. But instead of being like the old plagues, where a dozen or fifty of us would survive . . . instead of a nucleus of a town, there was one of us left. In the entire world, there was no one exactly like my mother."

I was crying. I couldn't help but sob and sniffle.

"Mother has lived at home ever since." My Chrome was answering the question that she only imagined I would ask. "Mother felt it was her duty. To make a living, she reopened the old mothering house. A traveler was her lover, for a few nights, and that helped her conceive. Which was me. Until my twin sisters were born, I was the only other Chromatella in the world."

And she was my Chrome.

Unimaginably rare, and because of it, precious.

Five sisters and better than a dozen children were waiting inside the temple, sitting together up front, singing loudly for the Solstice.

But the place felt empty nonetheless.

We walked up the long, long center aisle. After a few steps, Mother Chrome was pulling away from us. She was halfway running, while I found myself moving slower. And between us was my Chrome. She looked ahead, then turned and stared at me. I could see her being patient. I could hear her patience. She asked, "What?" Then she drifted back to me, asking again, "What?"

I felt out of place.

Lonely, and lost.

But instead of confessing it, I said, "I'm stupid. I know."

"You are not stupid," she told me. Her patience was fraying away. Too quietly, she said, "What don't you understand? Tell me."

"How can those lizards survive? If half of them are like you say, how do they ever lay enough eggs?"

"Because the eggs they lay have remixed genes," she told me, as if nothing could be simpler. "Every whiptail born is different from every other one. Each is unique. A lot of them are weaker than their parents, sure. But if their world decides to change around them—which can happen in the mountains—then a few of them will thrive."

But the earth is a mild place, mostly. Our sun has always been steady, and our axis tilts only a few degrees. Which was why I had to point out, "God knew what she was doing, making us the way we are. Why would anyone need to change?"

My Chrome almost spoke. Her mouth came open, then her face tilted, and she slowly turned away from me, saying nothing.

The singing had stopped.

Mother Chrome was speaking with a quick quiet voice, telling everyone about the telephone call. She didn't need to explain it to her daughters for them to understand. Even the children seemed captivated, or maybe they were just bored with singing and wanted to play a new game.

My Chrome took one of her sisters downstairs to retrieve the old television.

I sat next to one of the twins, waiting.

There was no confusing her for my Chrome. She had a farmer's hands and solid shoulders, and she was six months pregnant. With those scarred hands on her belly, she made small talk about the fog and the frost. But I could tell that her mind was elsewhere, and after a few moments, our conversation came to a halt.

The television was set up high on the wooden altar, between Winter's haggard face and Spring's swollen belly.

My Chrome found an electrical cord and a channel, then fought with the antenna until we had a clear picture and sound. The broadcast was from Boreal City, from one of the giant All-Family temples. For a moment, I thought there was a mistake. My Chrome was walking toward me, finally ready to sit, and I was thinking that nothing would happen. We would watch the service from Boreal, then have our feast, and everyone would laugh about this very strange misunderstanding.

Then the temple vanished.

Suddenly I was looking at an old person standing behind a forest of microphones, and beside her, looking young and strange, was a very homely girl.

Huge, she was.

She had a heavy skull, and thick hair sprouted from both her head and her face.

But I didn't say one word about her appearance. I sat motionless, feeling more lost than ever, and my Chrome slid in beside me, and her mother sat beside her.

Everyone in the temple said, "Oh my!" when they saw that ugly girl.

They sounded very impressed and very silly, and I started laughing, then bit down on my tongue.

To the world, the old woman announced, "My name is Corvus. This is my child. Today is her sixteenth birthday."

The pregnant sister leaned and asked her mother, "How soon till we get ours?"

Mother Chrome leaned, and loud enough for everyone to hear, she said, "Very soon. It's already sent."

I asked my Chrome, "What's sent?"

"The pollen," she whispered. "We're supposed to get one of the very first shipments. Corvus promised it to Mother years ago."

What pollen? I wondered.

"I'll need help with the fertilizations," said her mother. "And a physician's hands would be most appreciated."

She was speaking to my Chrome.

On television, the woman was saying, "My child represents a breakthrough. By unlocking ancient, unused genes, then modifying one of her nuclear bodies, we have produced the first of what should be hundreds, perhaps thousands of special children whose duty and honor it will be to prepare us for our future!"

"I'll stay here with you," I promised my Chrome. "As long as necessary."

Then the hairy girl was asked to say something. Anything. So she stepped up to the microphones, gave the world this long, strange smile, then with the deepest, slowest voice that I had ever heard, she said, "Bless us all. I am pleased to serve."

I had to laugh.

Finally.

My Chrome's eyes stabbed at me.

"I'm sorry," I said, not really meaning it. Then I was laughing harder, admitting, "I expected *it* to look prettier. You know? With a nice orange neck, or some brightly colored hair."

My Chrome was staring.

Like never before, she was studying me.

"What's wrong?" I finally asked.

Then I wasn't laughing. I sat up straight, and because I couldn't help myself, I told all the Chromatellas, "I don't care how smart you know you are. What you're talking about here is just plain stupid!"

I said, "Insane."

Then I said, "It's my world, too. Or did you forget that?"

And that's when my Chrome finally told me, "Shut up," with the voice that ended everything. "Will you please, for once, you idiot-bitch, think and *shut up*!"

The Eye of God

MARY ROSENBLUM

Mary Rosenblum grew up near Pittsburgh and has lived in Oregon for years. The Clarion West workshop was a turning point for her. "At Clarion I discovered I had wings and could fly." She has published SF stories throughout the early 1990s (her first story was in *Asimov's* in 1990) and three SF novels (her first, *The Drylands*, won the Compton Crook Award for Best First Novel in 1994), but is moving into the mystery genre in recent years so her SF stories are now infrequent. *The Encyclopedia of Science Fiction* says her "strengths are in the vigorous realism of her rendering of human relationships as they evolve under the stresses of the new worlds to come." The best of her early work is collected in *Synthesis and Other Virtual Realities*, from Arkham House. This story is from *Asimov's* and is as impressive an example of her strengths as one might wish.

The coral-reeds' agitation alerted her. Etienne came out onto the porch of her cottage to watch three Rethe wade through the thick blue-green stems. From this distance, they could have been three tall women, as human as herself. The coral-reeds stirred at their passage, the anxious rasp of their stems like distant whispering—words at the bare edge of comprehension.

She had never expected to see Rethe here. Etienne swallowed, fighting back memories that she had banished years ago. For a moment she entertained the hope that this visit was a mistake, or some kind of minor bureaucratic ritual.

She knew better.

Abruptly, she turned on her heel, and went inside to make tea. The Rethe would drink tea. That much at least humanity knew about them.

Etienne filled the teapot and arranged fruit-flavored gels on a plate. She had bought them in the shabby squatter village that had grown up around the Gate. Vat-grown in someone's back yard as masses of amorphous cells, the orange and ruby cubes bore no resemblance to apricot or cherries except taste. The plants on this world—or sessile animals that photosynthesized—did not bear fruit. She missed apples the most—crisp and tart after a frost. Vilya had bought her a miniature apple tree in a pot. For their balcony. It was a winesap—a true genetic antique. She had never gone back for it.

Etienne realized that she was arranging and rearranging the gels on their plate, and took her hand away. Outside, the reeds rustled softly. The squatters ate them—cracked their silicaceous stems and sucked out the flesh inside. They turned your urine orange, but they didn't make you sick.

She had never eaten one. Sometimes Etienne entertained the fantasy that that was the reason for the whispering meadow of the creatures that had formed around her cottage. Anthropomorphism, she thought. A seductive danger, in her profession as interpreter of aliens.

Her former profession.

Angry at herself for this lapse into yesterday, Etienne picked up the tray of tea, gels, and utensils. The Rethe were waiting for her on the shaded porch. Politely. Patiently. They nodded in unison as she came through the door, and Etienne froze. Memory was optional. Life went on for a long time, and yesterdays gathered like dust in the cramped vault of the human skull. You could go to a reputable body shop and have a well-trained tech in sterile greens sweep it all away. Or, for more money, you could have them sweep out only selected bits. Memory could be tucked, tightened, and tailored, as easily as any other part of the body.

She had never chosen to excise Vilya from her memory. Etienne set the tray down on the small table so hard that tea slopped over beneath the pot's lid. Staring at the smallest of the Rethe—the one who stood at the rear, right on the boundary between shade and searing sun—Etienne wished suddenly that she had done so.

First real contact with an alien species, the Rethe disturbed humanity. Not because they were creepy nightmares or incomprehensible monsters. That might have been easier to take. But they looked utterly human. And utterly female, although each individual possessed three X and three Y chromosomes. Gender was one of the many things about themselves that the Rethe refused to discuss. All humans and Rethe were referred to as "it" in translated conversation.

The small Rethe whose wide face was slashed by sun and shadow looked utterly like Vilya.

Etienne looked down at the amber puddle soaking into the napkins she had laid out on the tray. "Would you care for tea?"

The oldest of the Rethe—at least her . . . his? . . . face looked oldest—extended a hand, palm up. A small iridescent vial lay on her . . . his? . . . palm.

She, Etienne decided as she scowled at the vial. They were all *she*, and to hell with their chromosomal makeup. The vial contained a fungus that would infiltrate her ear canal, growing mycocelia through her skull within minutes to interface directly with her brain. A translator, it was a bit of Rethe bio-tech, and as yet incomprehensible. But necessary. Because the Rethe weren't about to share their language, or waste their time learning humanity's dialects. The Rethe was waiting silently, *her* eyes on Etienne's face, smiling.

Impatient behind that smile. "No need." Etienne arched an eyebrow. "I was infected nearly two decades ago. As you must surely know, if you checked me out at all."

The eldest Rethe bowed, still smiling. Dropped the vial into a pocket in her loose robe. "I hope you will pardon our intrusion."

"You're pardoned." Etienne began to fill mugs. "So why are you here?"

"Retirement from public service must provide many benefits." The Rethe lifted her steaming mug in a small salute. "Not the least of which is the privilege to be rude."

"I didn't retire. I quit. Yes, I'm rude." Etienne sat down in the only chair and smiled up at the Rethe. Waiting.

For several minutes the Rethe sipped their tea, their expressions relaxed and appreciative, as if they had come all this way in the hot sun to savor her cheap tea, bought from the squatters. But their impatience hummed in the air and made the nearest coral-reeds shiver.

At last, the eldest Rethe sank gracefully to the fabbed-wood planks of the porch and folded her legs into lotus position. "I am Grik." She nodded at the two Rethe behind her. "Rnn and Zynth."

Zynth was the one who might have been Vilya's twin. Etienne turned her eyes away as that one sat down. The loose garments that the Rethe wore hinted at solid bone and sleek, thickly muscled bodies. Peasant body, Vilya used to say of her stocky form. Etienne clenched her teeth and made a show of arranging her caftan. "Since I am entitled to be rude, why *are* you here?"

"To hire you." Grik reached for a cherry gel. "It is a matter of rescue."

"I . . . am no longer a registered empath. As you obviously know. And I retired from Search and Rescue last year." Etienne offered the plate of gels to the other two Rethe. The one called Rynn declined with a smile and nod. Zynth gave her boss a quick apprehensive look and took an orange cube.

"And I'm not for hire in any case." Etienne put the plate down on the table with a decisive thump. The girl's diffident air annoyed her. "I'm sorry you wasted your time coming here."

Grik lifted her left hand, palm up, tilted it in a pouring gesture.

Etienne interpreted a shrug from the emotional context. As she reached for her mug of tea, she noticed that Zynth had closed her hand into a fist. Orange gel leaked between her white-knuckled fingers, and the reeds rustled at her anguish.

Basic emotion seemed to be such a universal language, Etienne thought bitterly. Pleasure, anger, pain, and fear. Reeds, and humans, and Rethe. Etienne looked at Grik, who was smiling gently.

"Your superior at the Interface Center referred us to you," she said. "It told us that you were the best empath it had worked with."

"That was long ago." It jolted her that he would remember. He had been angry when she had quit to work for Search and Rescue.

"It said it was time someone reminded you." She shrugged. "I do not understand what it meant."

Anton. Colonel Xyrus Anton, chief of the Interface Team—the euphemism for the human negotiators with the aloof Rethe. Etienne looked out at the reeds bathing and feeding in the planet's young hot sun. *We need you,* he had yelled at her when she had turned in her resignation. *We need every edge we can get against the Rethe. We never really believed that we'd meet a species more advanced than us. Not in our gut. Look what it's doing to us. Our morale as a race is eroding all over the planet. This is a war, and we need to win.* "I don't understand either," she murmured. "But it doesn't matter."

"One of your . . . creators of art became a friend to one of our people." Grik went on as if Etienne hadn't spoken. "Its sincerity was apparently impressive. So that one offered it access to a world we have not opened to your species."

"You haven't opened many worlds to us."

The Rethe did the pouring-gesture again. "The art-creator was lost there in a tragic accident."

"There are several registered empaths working for Search and Rescue." Etienne watched the Rethe narrowly. "Why *me?* We are back to that question."

"According to your datafile, you are a very intelligent human." Grik placed her hands palm up on her thighs, her eyes shifting very slightly toward the young Zynth. "Do I truly need to answer this question for you?"

Zynth sat with her head bowed, pale, her anguish an almost palpable mist. The reeds had inched away from her, leaving a semicircle of clear soil beyond her. Etienne knew suddenly who had invited the artist onto a forbidden world.

"You closely control the Gates—allow us onto only a few poor planets. Like this one. Only the culls for us humans, eh? And you won't transport extraction technology for us—in the name of environmental concern." Etienne turned back to Grik, teeth bared. "We accept that limitation because you awed us. And because we can't operate the Gates without you." She smiled. "If you go to a registered empath, the media will surely find out about this . . . art-creator. And interview him or her. The grass is always greener in someone else's pasture, and now you've let one of us through the fence. We're quite an envious bunch, and we don't stay awed very long." She grinned and reached for a cherry gel. "A species trait, I'm afraid. People will begin to clamor for admittance to these wonderful forbidden worlds and there will be friction. Since our treaty with you is up for renewal this year, friction could be . . . a problem. Thus, you come to an unregistered empath, hoping to keep the media out of it."

The Rethe turned her hands palm down. "We will pay you well," she said. "Ending a life—even accidentally—is no trivial matter to us."

Etienne stole a glance at Zynth. She was looking at Etienne now, fear and desperate hope like a violin note humming on the hot, dusty air. The reeds quivered to its song, and Etienne sighed. "I will not take any money," she said, and wondered how much she was going to regret this.

▲   ▲   ▲

A synskin habitat had been anchored to a wide terrace cut into a cliff. Below, dark water lapped at the roots of worn ancient mountains. They were capped and streaked with a white deposit that looked more like guano than snow. But it wasn't the severely beautiful landscape that held Etienne's attention. It was the moon. Huge, bloated, haloed by a pink mist, it floated above the horizon. An irregular brown blotch in the center of the blue and white orb gave it the appearance of a giant, unwinking eye. Beautiful, she thought. Unforgiving. And she shivered, although her light thermal suit kept her warm enough. The habitat shivered too, straining against its anchors.

Behind her, invisible and undetectable to any human tech, lay a Rethe Gateway. Zynth had brought them through. A dozen steps could take Etienne back to summer heat and whispering coral-reeds. But only if Zynth escorted her. The bio-engineering of the Gates didn't work for humans.

This was humanity's humiliation. That the Rethe could walk across the galaxy unhindered and in moments. Human technology didn't so much lag behind—it was as extinct as the dinosaurs. And it left humanity obedient to the Rethe—for the price of the Gateways that the Rethe opened for them. Once, she had been one of the negotiators. They had staffed the Interface Team with empaths, hoping for an edge, a clue as to how the Rethe could be met as equals. It hadn't yet happened. With each renewed Treaty, humanity lost a little more ground, granted a few more concessions. Eventually, they'll own us, Etienne thought cynically. For the price of a few mediocre planets.

Vilya had been fascinated by the Rethe. She had understood them far better than Etienne ever would.

A sudden gust of wind shoved Etienne so that she staggered. That invisible doorway behind her seemed less than real beneath the inhuman scrutiny of that planetary eye. I do not want to be here, she thought.

"The Eye of God." Zynth's voice was clear and high.

She would sing mezzo. Like Vilya. "I wish it would close." Etienne tensed as Zynth laid a gentle hand on her arm. "Please don't touch me." She shook her off.

"Are you well?" Zynth's dark eyes were full of concern.

"Yes, yes, I'm fine." Etienne let her breath out in a rush. "Why couldn't we have come here at the beginning of the day?" She glowered at the girl, needing to be angry at her, because no emotion except anger was safe. "It's too dark to search. Why spend the night here?"

"I . . . am required to be here." Zynth's eyes evaded hers. "Until the artist is found. All life is sacred, and I permitted it to be put at risk. This is a place of truth. Beneath the Eye of God, I must face my failure. Can you understand?" She spread her fingers wide. "But I can open the Gateway for you. You may go back to your home and return in fifteen hours. It will be dawn then. I am thoughtless." She raised her face to the bloated moon. "There is no need for you to be here."

"I'll stay." Etienne turned her back on that unsettling orb, realizing that she had offered to stay because Zynth was afraid. "Who named that thing, anyway? I'd call it the Dead Eye, myself." Etienne stomped over to their habitat, ignoring Zynth's shocked silence. "Why don't you tell me how this person got lost—and where?" She knelt and shoved her way into the sphinctered opening. The transparent smart-plastic squeezed her body gently as she crawled through, blocking out the wind, but not the judgmental stare of the Eye. It's a *moon*, she told herself. A planetoid with weird coloring. But she couldn't deny her relief as she touched the light strip and warm yellow light subdued its glare. "We need to plan our search for the morning," she said as Zynth crawled through the sphincter after her.

As the Rethe began to take off her thermal suit, Etienne pulled a sleeping bag over against the wall and wrapped it around her. Like armor. The sculpted curves of Zynth's muscled arms and shoulders showed through her undershirt. It was warm in here. Thermal fibers were woven into the shell, and Etienne was sweating in her own suit. But she was damned if she'd strip, too.

"I will tell you," Zynth said in a low voice. "It is my shame." She flung herself onto her own bag with a grace so much like Vilya's that Etienne's throat closed.

"So I guessed," she managed, felt immediately guilty as Zynth flinched.

"I met him at our embassy in New Amsterdam." Propped on her elbows, she kept her eyes on the floor. "He had been hired to create several visual environments for the conference center there. The environments . . . moved me. We talked a lot. And one evening I told him about the Eye of Truth, and the song of this place. He . . . asked me to bring him here. The seeing mattered to his soul, so I did." She clenched one fist slowly. "I returned to find this camp empty. Duran was gone. I do not know. . . ."

"Shit!" Etienne slammed her fist down on the synskin floor.

Zynth's eyes widened. "I . . . I am sorry," she stammered, her cheeks flaming. "Grik said that you were . . . friends."

This was *Duran's* bloody camp! He had slept here, breathed the air in here. Etienne got abruptly to her feet, afraid she might catch his scent, some trace of his physical presence. I hope he fell over the damn cliff! she thought savagely. She lifted her head to face the bloated eye staring at her through the shuddering walls of the habitat. That's the truth, she told it silently.

"Etienne, please. I apologize." The anguish in Zynth's voice pierced her.

"Apologize?" Etienne laughed, winced at the cracked sound, and stared down at the kneeling Rethe. "What for?"

Tears streaked Zynth's face and she looked frightened. "For referring to its ... status," she whispered. "He ... it ... told me that it had been the *giver* for a child. And I thought that because you were its friend, you must know." She bowed from the waist until her forehead rested on the floor at Etienne's feet. "I was wrong to be so familiar."

"Sit up. I knew *he* ... fathered a child." Tight-lipped, Etienne turned away, met the Eye's stare. "I knew very well, thank you. You can call *him* he, or it, or whatever you want. It was his name that startled me. That's all."

"But he is a friend?" Zynth asked eagerly. "That will make it easier for you to find him, perhaps?"

The Eye's stare prodded her and Etienne licked her lips. "I didn't expect to run into him again," she said shortly. Not if she could help it anyway. Interesting that Grik hadn't mentioned his name, since she obviously knew of Etienne's connection to Duran. "So Duran talked you into bringing him here, and you got in trouble for it. That sounds like Duran. Always the opportunist."

"It wasn't ... like that." Zynth stared at the floor between her knees, her face stricken.

Almost without volition, Etienne reached across the space between them to brush wisps of dark hair from her face. "I'm not angry at you." She let her breath out in a slow sigh. "Really."

"I should never have told it about . . . the Eye."

"Him." Etienne's lips were tight. "Say *him*."

"Him." Head bowed, Zynth spoke so softly that Etienne could barely make out her words. "He . . . said that he would translate the Eye into sound and vision . . . so that you might know it, too. And . . . I could see the light of the Eye shining in his face as he spoke. So I . . . opened the door for him, even though it is forbidden. And then I came back for him and . . . he was no longer here." She raised her head at last, and her face was composed now. "He could not have passed the Gateway, so he must have fallen. I told Grik."

"Because the Eye was watching?"

"Because life is sacred." Zynth drew herself up straight, then hesitated. "And yes." She bowed her head. "Because the Eye watches."

Etienne sighed. "Will you be punished?"

"This *is* my punishment."

She was afraid. Fear was such a universal. Even the coral-reeds felt fear. "It's just a moon." Etienne put her arm around Zynth's shoulders. "Duran is careless." Careless enough to have cost Vilya her life. "If he fell, it's his own fault."

Zynth flinched at her tone. "I just . . . I have never been . . . in danger." She began to tremble. "That is one of the things I like most about your race. There are so *many* of you," she said in a nearly inaudible voice. "Is that why you can all walk down the street, have jobs, *do* things? It . . . he . . . Duran told me how he climbed up the sides of mountains. He *risked* himself!"

"Huh?" I should have a recorder, Etienne thought dizzily. We don't know any of this. "I don't understand," she said.

"He is a . . . giver." She blushed. "A breeder? Is that your word? Grik said that because so many of you can create life, none of you really matter to each other." She

eyed Etienne apprehensively. "But you can go with anyone you wish, do anything you want, even risk yourself—just like any it of our people. True?"

"We matter to each other. Some of us matter a lot."
Was love a universal, like fear? Etienne touched Zynth's
cheek lightly. "Can't your people go with anyone they
wish?"

"The ones who are *it* can." She hunched her shoulders. "The . . . few who are *he* or *she* . . ." She blushed.
". . . We love. But we can love only one of the cooperative expression. It can be no other way. We . . . are the
jewels of our people, treasured by all. We are tomorrow."

We. Etienne was beginning to understand. "What
you're saying is that very few of you can breed?" Secre-
tive as they were about their culture, the Rethe were
more than open about their physical attributes. They
seemed to be potentially hermaphroditic for all their
feminine form. Which troubled humanity even more
than their female appearance, Etienne thought cynically.
Zynth's blush had deepened. Obviously, reproduction
was not a topic of casual conversation.

"I'm sorry. I don't mean to embarrass you." Etienne
ruffled her hair lightly, then took her hand quickly away.
That was how she had touched Vilya when she needed
to be teased from one of her dark moods. Beyond the
flimsy wall, the Eye glared, reminding her that Duran
was here and that this was not Vilya. Did *she* know
that he was lost? Etienne wondered suddenly. Duran's
daughter?

Vilya's daughter, too.

As if that thought had conjured Duran, she felt him.
Or someone. The jagged note of human pain and
despair pierced her briefly, then faded, dissipating like
smoke in a breeze. Etienne turned, automatically groping to pinpoint the source, responding with years of

search and rescue practice. But it had been too brief, too weak, for her to be sure of more than a vague direction.

"What is it? Do you sense him?" Zynth's hands came up, fingers stiffly together. "He is alive? Oh please, he is still alive?"

"Yes." Etienne looked up to meet the Eye's stark gaze. "He's alive. And injured. I don't know how badly."

"He must live." Zynth leaned forward to clutch Etienne's hand. "Your biotechnology is quite good, really. We will find him, and your people will heal him. Where is he?"

"Out there." Etienne nodded at the cliff edge. "I couldn't get an accurate position," she said stiffly. Zynth smelled of cinnamon, with a musky undertone that was unfamiliar, but not repulsive. Not like Vilya at all.

"We will climb down, and then you can hear him better." Zynth began to rummage urgently in the pack she had brought through the Gateway. "Here." She handed Etienne a tangle of neon blue webbing. "You know how to put this on, yes?"

A climbing harness. "You've pried into my entire damn life, haven't you?" Etienne clenched her fingers around the supple webbing, wanting to throw it across the chamber. "I don't climb any more," she said between clenched teeth.

"Grik did the research." Zynth put on her thermal suit, and began to don a second harness. She moved clumsily. "You know *how*. I do not. We cannot use a floater because of the wind."

"If you don't know how to climb, then no way you go over that edge." Etienne crossed her arms.

"It will be safe." Zynth reached for the pack. "We will anchor the line to the top of the cliff. And you will be with me. So I am not afraid at all." Her smile filled her face with beauty. Vilya's face had been filled with the same beauty on that long ago morning when she had propped herself on one elbow in Etienne's bed and whispered *I think I love you*. They had both been so young. So sure.

"No." Etienne swallowed, fighting the images. "Open the Gate for me. I'm leaving. I won't be responsible for your death. Life is sacred to me, too, damn it!"

For a moment, Zynth faced her, head thrown back, face burning with defiance and Vilya's beauty. Then her shoulders slumped, and she turned away. "All right, I'll stay," she whispered, and her hands quivered with defeat. "I am afraid to go without you. Will you go down?"

Etienne nodded and crawled out of the habitat, with Zynth on her heels. Bending into the gusty wind, she snapped the clasps on her harness. Her fingers were trembling. I will get you for this night, she promised Grik silently. Somehow, some day, I will pay you back for doing this to me. Lips tight, she took the anchor drill that Zynth handed her.

"Can you hear him?" Zynth peered over her shoulder as Etienne drilled the anchor into the gray stone well back from the cliff edge.

The rock wanted to fracture. Bad stone for an anchor point, but there wasn't anything better. "I'll listen when I can concentrate." Satisfied at last that the anchor would hold, she threaded the tough thin rope through it and tied it off to her harness.

It moved in her hands and she almost dropped it. Bio-fibers, she realized. Another bit of Rethe biotechnology. The rope was woven of thousands of living fibers that could heal minor injuries and responded to direct stimuli such as stress. She tugged once on the rope, then stepped deliberately to the lip of the chasm. For a heartbeat she hesitated, reluctant to trust herself to this alien rope. Then the wind gusted fiercely, and she swayed with it, leaning outward, with her feet planted firmly on the lip of stone. The rope tensed in her fingers. And held her.

Your small-act-of-defiance ritual, Vilya had dubbed this preliminary testing. Couldn't she have found a better climbing partner? Etienne asked the staring orb of the Eye. Why *Duran?* Just because he had provided chromosomes for her daughter? Or had she been trying to wound Etienne—replacing the expert partner with the novice?

It had cost her her life.

There are a hundred labs that can put a kid together for you, she had yelled during their last fight. They could recombine your own gametes. They could use my DNA and . . . fix what's wrong. Her voice hadn't given her away when she had said that. *Wrong,* because that was how Vilya thought of her empathic talent. As a burden—too much for a child to have to bear.

Vilya had refused to get angry. If we create her, she had said implacably, if some technician snips out sections of your code and replaces them, then what is she? Not you—not me—but our *construct.* I don't want that. I want her to be her own person—not our creation.

You're in love with this Duran, aren't you? Etienne's angry words had scalded her throat. Don't give me that artificial insemination song again either. Maybe I'm a failure, a genetic mutation, but that's not really the issue, is it? You just want to fuck him!

Vilya had walked out of their condo and closed the door gently behind her. That had hurt the worst—that she hadn't even slammed the damn door. Etienne had packed and left that afternoon. She didn't know if Vilya had ever come back to the apartment.

Far below, still water filled the fjord-like channel between this cliff and the rounded mountains beyond.

Their blue-white images reflected in water that gleamed purple beneath the baleful glare of the Eye. No wind down there? Maybe the Eye was just trying to blow them off the cliff, she thought bitterly.

She turned around in time to see Zynth lift her face to the Eye, hands weaving a graceful pattern in the air.

Acceptance? Reverence? Worship?

A human empath could read only a few universal emotions. Beyond that, you guessed what the Rethe were really feeling. Zynth's head was bowed now, and Etienne caught the gleam of tears on her face, within the shadow of her thermal suit's hood. Her grief she could be sure of. Without another word, Etienne began to rappel cautiously down the cliff. When you trust your rope, your life seeps into it and it becomes part of you. You feel the solid mass of the anchoring stone, feel the quivering strain in the rope as if it is your own tendon and ligament straining, your fingers wrapped around that ring of steel far above. The biofiber rope tensed like muscle in her gloved hands.

The wind snatched at her, trying to smash her against the wall. Teeth clenched, Etienne fought it. The cliff face was sheer, polished to a smoothness that was eerie. It made her wonder if the damned wind blew forever up here. Grit stung her face and she regretted that she hadn't asked for goggles. The only holds were tiny cracks and uneven protrusions. It would be a bad climb back up.

And he was down there. Duran. She had picked the wrong place to go over—he was off to the right. She wondered if he had tried to climb down—if he was that stupid. From above, Zynth's flash beam probed the darkness, a weak finger of light that didn't penetrate much below Etienne's position.

An eye for an eye. The words shivered through her and Etienne paused for a moment, looked up to meet the

Eye's stare. She remembered those words most clearly from her childhood brush with religion: An eye for an eye. A life for a life.

Duran's consciousness was like a whisper in the darkness. His lack of skill had cost Vilya her life. It had cost Vilya's infant daughter a mother. Etienne's groping foot came down hard on a ledge and the shock jarred up through the top of her skull. Standing on the bare meter of polished stone, Etienne listened to the wind and the faint murmur of Duran's dying. Maybe Zynth's flash beam would find him. Maybe not. He wouldn't live much longer. Until daylight?

"Zynth?" She raised her voice. "I hear only wind." Only truth beneath the Eye's stare. She met it, cold inside, maybe cold forever—but everything has a price. "I'm coming back up."

"No." The determination in Zynth's voice pierced Etienne with memory.

You can't quit the team, Vilya had said, again and again, when Etienne got tired of the endless meetings, the familiar boring dance of diplomat circling diplomat. We need to understand the Rethe, we need to learn that we are their equals. If we don't, our spirit will die.

Throat tight, she threaded the loose end of the rope through the autobrake, and searched the rock face in front of her for a toehold. The living rope quivered and she looked upward. "Stop!" she cried as the dark shape of Zynth backed out over the cliff edge. "Zynth, go back up!"

"I cannot." Zynth's voice was calm. "This is my punishment—that I should risk my life."

"That anchor won't hold us both!" Etienne's fingers clenched uselessly around her own rope. "Zynth! Stop!"

Zynth's foot slipped on the polished stone face. Etienne sucked in a gasping breath as the Rethe skidded downward, but the rope jerked her to a bouncing stop before she had fallen more than three meters. Either she had managed to use the auto-brake but not properly, or this living rope had the ability to stop a fall. "Climb back up," she croaked. "Before the anchor goes. If you have to come down here, I'll put in another anchor. Do it *now*."

Too late. A gust of wind slammed along the cliff face, striking Etienne like a giant fist. Staggering, gasping for breath, Etienne skidded across the narrow ledge. The rope was stretching, thinning as it took up the strain. Then stone crumbled beneath her, and she dangled briefly over the void. The rope gave. Etienne threw her weight forward, clawing her way onto the ledge.

The anchor was breaking loose. "Climb up!" she screamed into the howling wind. "Damn it, Zynth, climb *up*."

Another hammering fist struck them. A vague shape flapped along the edge of the cliff, stooping like an alien bird of prey. The habitat had torn loose from its anchors. For a moment Zynth was obscured by the twisting folds of plastic. Then the rope convulsed in Etienne's hands and went slack. Zynth's scream echoed from the walls as Etienne flung herself against the face of the cliff. Zynth's falling body was directly above her—seeming to drift downward in slow motion. In another moment, she would hit, would smash her downward and outward, and they would both fall into that dark void beneath the Eye's mocking stare.

Because I lied, Etienne thought.

Zynth's wide eyes met hers for a second, sharing fear, sharing death. Then her body twisted convulsively, and she hit the wall, rebounding as she clawed for a hold.

She missed Etienne, hit the widest part of the narrow ledge. Etienne threw herself on top of her, knowing that it was a stupid thing to do, that they would both go over. Her toes dug into the slippery stone as Zynth's momentum torqued them both toward the lip of darkness.

They stopped, poised on the brink, still alive. Etienne inched her way backward, arms around Zynth, pulling her away from that dark drop. "Zynth?" she breathed, her heart pounding in her chest. "Are you hurt?"

Zynth sobbed once deep in her throat, burrowed her face against Etienne's shoulder. "Yes." The whisper was a breath of terror. "It hurts so bad. Inside." Her body tensed convulsively within Etienne's arms. "What if I'm damaged? Etienne? I . . . I can't be damaged."

She was so young—perhaps too young yet to have learned she was mortal. It could come as such a shock to you to realize that you could really die. "It's all right. It's going to be all right." She stroked Zynth's hair, holding her close, smothering her own fear. "I'm going to climb up," she murmured. "I'll get Grik. She'll bring help." Oh God. The Gateway. The Rethe could come and go, but not humans. Not without a Rethe.

"I'm afraid," Zynth whispered. "Don't leave me?"

Don't leave me. The words echoed through the black tunnel of the past, and Etienne raised her face to the Eye, remembering the image of Vilya's pale face on her e-mail screen. Don't leave me, Etienne. I love you. Why can't you understand? When Etienne hadn't answered, she had sent no more mail. "I may not be able to leave you." The words caught in her throat, choking her. "The Gate . . ."

"It's all right." Zynth drew back a little, her face clearing, pain lines smoothing into an expression of peace. "Etienne . . . I need to tell you . . ." She lifted her hand, fingers opening like the petals of a flower. Gently she touched Etienne's face. "I wish . . . you could have been . . . other than what you are." She closed her eyes, her fingers exploring the planes of Etienne's face as if to commit it to memory. "You can go and I won't be afraid." She opened her eyes, her smile making her beautiful. "You will need to take the key. It's just below my collarbone. On the left."

"Key?"

"To the Gate. You will have to take it out." She shuddered. "But it is just beneath the skin, so it should not hurt much."

So, the Rethe's ability to manipulate the Gateways was *not* an inborn psychic ability, as they had claimed! They used tech after all! Even as these thoughts were running through her head, Etienne had clicked on her flash and was opening the neck of Zynth's suit, feeling beneath her shirt. Her skin was clammy and her skin had gone pale. Shock? Internal bleeding? Her pain was seeping shrilly into Etienne's head, as she found a tiny subdermal lump just below the knob of Zynth's left collarbone. She looked into Zynth's wide eyes, brushed sweaty hair back from her forehead. "I'll be quick," she said softly.

"Thank you." Zynth swallowed. Her eyes followed Etienne's hand as it slid into the pocket of her suit to retrieve her laser blade. As Etienne thumbed it on, Zynth shuddered and closed her eyes.

Etienne placed a restraining hand on her shoulder, but Zynth lay utterly still as the tiny beam of energy sliced neatly through the skin just above the sphere. She caught her breath as Etienne pinched the embedded sphere free of the surrounding tissue, but made no other sound. "Press." Etienne placed Zynth's fingers over the gash. "It's not bleeding much." Fingers red with Zynth's blood, she studied the sphere. It was made of a matte black material, was about the size of a garden pea. Carefully, Etienne slipped it into an inside pocket on her suit, sealed the pocket closed. "I'm going to climb up. It shouldn't take me too long. We'll be back soon." She leaned down to kiss Zynth gently on the forehead. "I promise."

Zynth's eyes opened and she reached up to cup Etienne's face between her palms. "I know you'll come back." She kissed Etienne slowly, sensuously, on the lips. "Be careful."

"I will." Etienne got stiffly to her feet. The damned wind had died, as if the Eye had accomplished what it had wanted to accomplish. Or maybe it thought that they were trapped. You've never watched me climb, Etienne told it silently. When I come back, I will come back for them both. She bowed slowly, formally to the Eye, then turned and searched for the first holds.

You never look down. You look up, to the sides, focus on that next crevice or ledge where you might jam fingers or toes. You don't think about wind or the seconds ticking by as a girl dies.

And a man, too. She caught a whisper of Duran's delirium, pressed her lips together, and eased her weight upward.

You don't look at the top, either. Not after your muscles start to shake and your fingers are numb and you know that you can't do this a whole lot longer. So when she reached up, groping blindly, and her hand slapped down on level ground, she almost lost her grip and fell. With a final spasm of exhausted muscles, she shoved herself upward, lunging over the edge to flop belly-down onto the blessed stone. For a while she simply lay there, panting and shaking. Then she forced herself to her feet.

It was still dark—didn't dawn ever come here?—and the habitat was gone, of course. Etienne staggered to her feet and stumbled away from the cliff edge. Clutching the tiny key, she headed for the place where the Gate had been. For a moment she thought that it wasn't going to work—there was still nothing to see. Then, in an eyeblink of time, she stepped through into the dusty square near the squatter village. The shacks and pre-fab cottages drowsed in the hot afternoon sun, and Grik sat beneath a tower of branching turquoise silicate that housed a native hive creature.

Asleep, her head leaning back against the stem of the structure, Grik's face was carved into gaunt lines of worry, or exhaustion. She jerked awake as Etienne approached.

"Where is . . . it." She bolted to her feet.

"Hurt." Etienne took a single step toward her, fists clenching. "Are you satisfied? Has she been punished enough, or does she have to die there?"

"You mean . . . injured?" Grik's face had gone pinched and white. "She needed to risk herself, yes . . . but to be *injured* . . ." Outrage filled her voice. "How could you let that happen? Impossible!"

"I was right," Etienne said coldly. "About why you hired me."

"Enough." Grik was already striding toward the gate. "How badly is she injured?"

"I don't know." Etienne had to trot to keep pace with her. "She said it hurt inside."

Grik made a short ugly chopping gesture with both hands. "Remain here."

She took a single long stride into the air and vanished.

How the hell did they know where the damn Gates *were*? Etienne wondered. More buried hardware? She wasn't buying the "higher evolution" explanation any more. She looked toward the cottages. A girl peeped at her from the sparse reed bed that grew along the south side of the square. She ducked out of sight when she saw Etienne looking. Her excited curiosity came to Etienne like the bright smell of rain on summer dust. Etienne smiled at her, closed her fist around the black sphere, and stepped through the Gateway.

A dozen Rethe clustered at the top of the cliff. Light globes mounted on long poles flooded the area with blue-white radiance and four of the Rethe lowered a stretcher. Another Rethe was just clipping herself to an anchor. Fast response time, Etienne thought cynically. They must have been waiting at another Gate for just such an emergency. This whole escapade felt more and more orchestrated. She didn't see Grik, but another anchor and rope suggested that she might be below. Etienne walked over to the small red-haired Rethe who was about to climb over the edge and put a hand on her shoulder. The Rethe recoiled with a sharp clap of her cupped palms, but Etienne ignored her as she unclipped the rope from her harness.

They had researched her well enough to give Zynth a rope without a clip, knowing that Etienne always tied off. With an angry snap, she secured the clip to the harness she still wore. The Rethe was saying something, but Etienne ignored her. Grabbing the ropes, she stepped over the edge. No time for small defiances now. She was going for a big one. The Eye stared down impassively as she bounced fast down the wall, ignoring caution, eyes fixed on the single figure crouched beside Zynth's curled body.

"What are you doing here?" Grik barely looked up as Etienne knelt beside her.

Zynth's eyes were closed. Fine blue veins webbed the pale skin of her eyelids, and for a terrible instant, Etienne thought she wasn't breathing. She touched her throat, felt the reassuring twitch of a pulse before Grik shoved her hand away.

"Don't touch me again," Etienne said carefully. "Or I will throw you off this ledge." Only truth beneath the

Eye of God. She smiled thinly as Grik recoiled. "You have used me very thoroughly." She kept her eyes on Grik's face. "What did you do? Review the personal profiles of every empath on the planet? Until you found someone who would be highly motivated to keep your breeder safe? She *is* fertile, isn't she? One of your national treasures?" Her lips drew back from her teeth. "And you needed to punish her properly so as to satisfy your evolved sense of *ethics*." She spat the word. "But you didn't really want to *risk* her, eh? An eye for an eye? You haven't really evolved beyond us, have you? You've just learned how to cheat." She looked down at Zynth. "Well, I took care of her—for her own sake," she said softly.

"I thank you for the risk you assumed." Grik's nostrils flared slightly, but whatever her emotions were, they were too complex for Etienne to read. "That is a difficult climb." She inclined her head at the sheer cliff face behind her.

"Why did you make her do this?" Etienne asked softly.

"Your race is sated with fertility. The creation of new life has little value to you." Her face looked as smooth and hard as marble in the Eye's cold glare. "For us . . . there are very few who can rightfully claim the pronouns you so casually toss around. We have avoided the internal strife that has weakened you as a race, but everything has its price. Continuation of our species is a privilege and an obligation that involves the species— above and beyond the individual. You cannot comprehend." She made a chopping gesture. "The rule that Zynth broke was not a minor infraction. In our society, the failure of the individual is the failure of us all. The punishment—the risk of her loss—was inflicted upon us all." She stood and looked beyond Etienne. Two more Rethe were descending, guiding the stretcher downward. In a moment, it was going to get very crowded on the ledge.

"The creation of new life isn't always a casual thing for us, either." Etienne looked down at Zynth, remembering the trust in her voice. She didn't look so much like Vilya now. "I care about her," she said softly. "For herself, not for her face."

"Do not fantasize, Empath." Grik's tone was icy. "Love is only possible with another . . . appropriate Rethe. That is the way it is."

Etienne smiled at her. "What is the penalty for lying beneath the Eye?"

Grik turned abruptly away to speak to the descending Rethe. Etienne moved back as far as she could along the diminishing ledge. Duran's dying whispered in her mind. It strengthened suddenly, and a murky image formed in her head—a girl with dark hair, pale, with a spare, elegant face. Etienne felt a piercing grief. Duran's vision, Duran's grief. For a rending moment, she thought he was remembering Vilya, but he hadn't known Vilya when she was that young. And then she realized . . .

His daughter. Terane.

His daughter. That was how she had thought of the child. She had been a baby when Vilya had died, and Duran had laid legal claim to her. So Etienne had never seen her. Not because Duran had forbidden it. She herself had forbidden it. *His* daughter. She closed her eyes, but his love and grief beat in her head, filling her brain with the merciless image of the girl who was Vilya's daughter, too.

Grik believed that Zynth could not love anyone who couldn't father a child for her. Etienne looked up into the Eye, met its cold stare. "So did I," she murmured. "Grik!" She raised her voice and the Rethe paused as she was about to begin her climb to the top of the cliff. "Send the stretcher back down," she called.

"Why?"

"For Duran," she said shortly. "You sent me here to find him, didn't you?"

The two Rethe with the stretcher paused and looked down, too, and for a moment there was only the sound of wind across the ledge. "You are correct." Grik sounded reluctant. "I will . . . send the stretcher down."

"How is she doing?" Etienne forced out the question. Brown and green blobs like fat slugs clung to Zynth's forehead, chest, arms, and belly. More Rethe biotech? "Grik?"

"She may live." Grik shrugged and began to climb. After a second, the two other Rethe continued to ease the stretcher up the cliff face.

Go to hell, Etienne thought, but she was too weary to say it aloud. Taking a deep breath, she leaned out over the void. One more small defiance. The living rope quivered in her hands as she turned around, found a toe hold, and began to follow Duran's grief for his daughter, crevice by crevice, across the face of polished stone.

He lay on another ledge, similar to the one Zynth had landed on. It occurred to Etienne, as she pulled some slack into the rope and knelt beside his huddled body, that they were remarkably regular. Perhaps too regular to be natural, but she was too exhausted to worry about it. In the light of her flash, she saw that Duran's hair was beginning to go gray, and his face had thinned a bit in twenty years. He was no youth any more, but he looked pretty much as she remembered him. Blood stained the fabric of his thermal suit, red and fresh in one place. That arm was crooked, and a touch confirmed her diagnosis. Compound fracture, and he had bled a lot. Broken leg, too, and probably more damage that wasn't so obvious. There was no sign of a climbing harness.

His eyelids fluttered as she started to get up. "Wh . . . who?" he mumbled, squinting up at her. "E . . . tienne?" Dried blood crusted his lips, and one side of his face was scraped and bruised from the fall. *"You?"*

She was surprised that he recognized her. She had been older than Duran, when he and Vilya had first been friends. Older, verging on old. Twenty years of search and rescue work had changed her a lot. "It's me, Duran. Help is on the way." Maybe. She looked up at the cliff top, yanked on the rope. A part of her half expected it to come loose and fall around her in writhing living coils. Who would know if the Rethe left both of them to die here?

"Hang on," she said to him. Conscious, his pain beat at her, bad enough to get in past her barriers. She fumbled in her belt pack, took out a couple of pain patches. Two would put him out, or nearly so. She peeled the protective backing from the first patch, smoothed it onto his throat.

She didn't want any more of his grieving images. But he fumbled a hand up to stop her before she could apply the second patch. "Etienne?"

"Yes, it's me. Help is on the way."

"Can you hear it?" His eyes were ringed with white, mundane gray turned to a clear blue by the Eye's glare. "The voice of God, of *their* God. It shaped them, hear it? The wind is its breath. It sings to them, Etienne. This is their soul. Zynth told me, and it's true. This is where they . . . were born."

Their soul? Their God? Etienne remembered Zynth, her hands weaving worship on the lip of the cliff. *The* Eye of God. Not just a casual name dubbed onto an alien landmark then. Their God. Their . . . homeworld. She looked out into the purple darkness and shivered. No wonder Grik had spoken of Zynth's transgression as a sin. And it occurred to her suddenly that perhaps Grik *hadn't* been searching for an empath who would protect a precious breeder.

Perhaps she had been searching for an empath who would kill.

"I wanted . . . to tell you . . . how she died." Duran was losing consciousness as the drugs hit him. "It was my fault. I . . . tried to stop her fall, but she . . . had too much rope. She . . . cut it. So I wouldn't fall, too. I . . . tried to tell you. I'm . . . so sorry, Etienne. I should have stopped her fall. So . . . sorry . . ." His eyes closed and his hand fell away from her wrist.

So Vilya had fallen, not he. And she had relinquished her last chance of life, in order to save Duran. So that her daughter would have a parent?

And if *you* had been there, Etienne? To be a parent? That was what Vilya wanted.

The whisper in her head was in her own voice, but she looked up at the Eye. Slowly, she got to her feet. The accident report was public record. She could have looked it up any time in the last twenty years. If she had wanted to know.

Only truth beneath the Eye of God?

Something scraped loudly behind her and she started. It was the stretcher bumping down the face, followed closely by the two Rethe. "He has a broken arm and leg," she called up to them. "Maybe internal injuries. I'll help you move him."

She wasn't sure how flexible Rethe ethics might be, after all.

But the team was efficient and careful. They helped her strap Duran into the stretcher, and guided him silently up the face of the cliff. The wind eased off again, as if this god was willing to let them depart in peace now. At the top of the cliff, the remaining two Rethe unhooked the stretcher from the ropes, and carried it silently through the Gateway. Grik and Zynth had disappeared.

Etienne trudged after them, exhaustion dragging at her. The two Rethe who had climbed with her flanked her. Oh yeah. Operating the Gateway, because she was a mere human. They didn't realize yet that she had a key. Etienne blinked as they emerged from night into bright day. The same girl was still at the edge of the plaza, playing some game with a ball and bits of empty reed shell.

The girl leaped to her feet as the Rethe set the stretcher down in the dust and went running barefoot across the dusty ground, her shift flapping around her thighs. She was heading for the small medical clinic.

Etienne sighed as her Rethe escort made identical wiping motions with their left hands. Good riddance? Farewell? Still silent, they walked back through the Gateway and vanished. Wanting only to drag herself home and climb into bed, Etienne squatted beside the stretcher. She was already sweating in her thermal suit, and she unsealed it. Duran was still alive. She held his wrist, his pulse faltering beneath her fingertips. "I don't like you," she said softly. "I don't think I can change that." Three of the squatters came running toward her, dust rising from their feet. "But I don't blame you anymore," Etienne said. And she looked up automatically, as if the Eye would be there in the off-blue sky.

It wasn't, of course. The squatters—two men and a woman in cut-offs and grimy shirts—arrived. "I'm the med-tech," said one of the women. "Pick up an end and give us a hand," she snapped at Etienne. "Then you can tell me what's going on here."

The reeds swayed and rattled, happy in the morning sun. Etienne kneaded bread dough in her small hands-on kitchen, listening to the familiar susurration. The reed-song soothed her as the dough stretched and flattened beneath her palms. But as she shaped a round loaf, the reeds' song changed to a scattered rattle. A visitor? Etienne wiped her hands on a towel, scrubbing briefly and vainly at the drying dough on her fingers.

She hoped it wasn't Duran, come to thank her for saving his life. But it had only been three days since the accident. The med-tech at the squatters' clinic had told her it would be at least a week before Duran could be released. Medical technology was less than cutting-edge out here.

Tossing the towel onto the counter, she crossed the small living room in three strides and flung the door open. She had tried to hide it from herself—how much she wanted it to be Zynth waiting on the porch. The sight of her actually standing there took Etienne's breath away, and made her blush, because she felt about as transparent as a teenager in the throes of true love.

"May I come in?" Zynth sounded as uncertain as Etienne felt. Her hand lifted in the direction of her shoulder, and Etienne followed its movement. Ah yes. Grik was hovering. Of course.

"Please do." Etienne was impressed with the cool graciousness of her tone. What a lie! She backed, held the door open as Zynth walked through, then closed it firmly, before Grik could follow. "Would you care for tea?"

"We began here." Zynth stood in the middle of the floor, her arms at her sides. "It seems like a long time ago, but it was not."

"You're all right," Etienne said softly.

"Yes." Zynth's smile faltered. "If you had not climbed . . ." She shook her head, her hair sliding forward to hide her expression. "I don't think Grik believed that . . . I would climb down. I think it believed that I would be too afraid, that I would humiliate myself in sight of the Eye."

The Eye. Etienne heard all the nuance now. Maybe

you could begin to understand another race once you caught a glimpse of their soul. "Your homeworld," she said softly.

"Is it such a sin, for you to know?" Her hands lifted in a fragile, pleading gesture. "We hide so much from you. Why?"

"Because I think we are too much alike," Etienne said softly.

Zynth smiled. "On that ledge, I was not afraid. I knew that you would not let me die."

The words made her shiver, and Etienne clenched her fists at her sides. She averted her head as Zynth stepped close.

"I will remember you forever." Her breath tickled Etienne's throat, warm as summer. "Please realize how much I . . . care."

"You're saying goodbye." Etienne's voice was harsh.

"I do not think that we will meet again." Zynth's voice trembled. "It is . . . a tremendous sorrow."

"Grik won't let it happen, you mean. Grik is afraid of me." Etienne clasped her hands behind her back, resisting the urge to grab Zynth by the shoulders and kiss her, or shake her. "I . . . love you." And she bit her lip because she hadn't meant to say those words out loud. Not ever.

"No," Zynth whispered. She was trembling. "It is *my* choice, not Grik's. *I* am afraid of you. Because I can forget that you are . . . other."

"That's right." Etienne didn't try to soften the bitterness in her voice. "You can only love another breeder. I forgot."

"You do not understand," Zynth said softly. "Grik says you would not, and I think now, that it is right." Her fingers were gentle on Etienne's face.

"I wish you a wonderful life," Etienne said through

clenched teeth. "I hope you find a nice fertile *he*."

Zynth's sigh touched her like the last warm wind of fall. "I am a giver, not the one who nurtures the life within." She laughed softly, sadly. "A *he*, as you say."

Anthropomorphism, Etienne thought dizzily. Look at a child with the face of a girl you once loved, and what do you see? Not a man. The irony was so wonderful. She laughed.

"I am sorry." Zynth stepped back, affront in the stiff posture of her body.

"I'm laughing at *me*, not you." Etienne held out her hand, didn't let herself flinch as Zynth took it. "Don't mind me. I'm old and bitter, and I see ghosts. I really do wish you . . . love. And children."

"Thank you." Zynth's smile was beautiful, but still tinged with sadness. He paused with his hand on the door, looked back over his shoulder. "I love you, too," he said. "For all that it is wrong."

Then the door closed behind him and he was gone. Etienne sat down on a floor cushion and listened to the reeds whisper their contentment to the summer heat. Love was another universal. Like pain, and fear. And grief. She rested her forehead on her knees and didn't cry. After a time—when the Rethe had had plenty of time to leave—she got up. Her joints still ached from her climb, and she felt suddenly old—as old as she really was.

Outside, the sun was high. The reeds brushed her thighs as she waded through them, touching her like a lover's fingers. The girl wasn't at the plaza today. Etienne strode across the open space and stepped onto the unmarked patch of ground that should be a Gate.

Her foot landed on gray stone, and the Eye stared dispassionately down. Slowly, Etienne walked over the broken remains of the habitat's anchor, and stopped on the lip of the chasm. Far below, blue-white mountains reflected in still water like purple ink. Duran had heard the soul of a people in the song of this world. Is that what you loved about him, Vilya? Braced against the gusts, Etienne lifted her face to the Eye. Duran's ability to *hear*—like her empathic sense, but different? Safer?

Truth only, beneath the Eye of God. She bent her head and the first tears spotted the cracked stone where her anchor had pulled loose. Tears for Vilya, because she had never cried for her —no—she had never let herself cry. And for herself, because Terane could have been her daughter, as well as Duran's and Vilya's.

And for Zynth who would find someone to love who was as fertile as she . . . he . . . was. Because he had to.

Etienne wondered if Terane had inherited Duran's ability to image a soul in light and music. She turned her back on the cliff and the Eye, trudged slowly back across the gray stone. At the edge of the Gateway, she paused, her fingers curling around the sphere that was the key to this technology. "You want truth?" Etienne looked up at the Eye. "Our awe is wearing thin. It's time for us to look you in the eye." Courtesy of Duran. "We're good at unraveling tech." As she stepped forward, she wondered if her old boss Anton would be surprised to hear from her. Maybe not.

Her foot landed in sun and dust, and her ears filled with the whisper of reeds. She didn't turn toward home. Instead, she began to trudge past the squatters' shacks toward the clinic. She didn't want to know how much Duran might have loved Vilya, but she needed to talk to him. She needed to ask about . . . their daughter. She needed an address. Too late to be a mother, maybe she could be a friend, offer another version of Vilya. Maybe not, but she could try.

The reeds sang contentment, and the dust puffed up from beneath her feet to blow away on the wind.

Rules of Engagement

MICHAEL F. FLYNN

Michael Flynn began publishing SF in *Analog* in 1984, and, according to the *Encyclopedia of Science Fiction*, "soon became identified as one of the most sophisticated and stylistically acute 1980s *Analog* regulars." His first novel was *In the Country of the Blind* (1990). His second novel was *Fallen Angels* (1991) in collaboration with Larry Niven and Jerry Pournelle. His third, *The Nanotech Chronicles* (1991), is a series of linked stories. He really hit his stride with *Firestar* (1996) and *Rogue Star* (1998), volumes in an ongoing future history, in a very Heinleinesque style, and some of the best hard SF of the decade. He is one of the current elders of the *Analog* mafia, but now publishes SF and fantasy in most of the professional magazines. This story is from *Analog*, and is more or less a part of his future history.

Winter having locked the passes with snow and ice, the brass parceled out long-deferred leaves and junior officers scattered across the country. Some descended on their hometowns to rest in the bosoms of their families. Some came to the City to sample the fleshpots—and rest in other sorts of bosoms. That was the last winter before the big offensive, when I still had the flat in Chelsea. Jimmy Topeka dropped in to see me, all somber as always. He seemed to have something on his mind, but he talked around it six ways from Sunday the way he always does, and hadn't gotten to the nub before Angel Osborne clumped his way up the stairs. I hadn't seen Angel in almost three years, though he and Jimmy had crossed paths during the Red River campaign. I said how we lacked only Lyle "the Style" Guzman to make the old gang complete; and the Angel ups and beeps him over the Lynx and, wouldn't you know it, Lyle was in the City, too. So before long we were all together, just like old times, drinking and shooting the shit and waiting for the Sun to come up. Those were wild years, and we were still young enough to be immortal.

I hadn't much in the way of furniture; and once Angel had occupied two-thirds of the sofa, there was less of it to go around. Lyle, being slightly built, perched himself on the table, while Jimmy raided my kitchen and passed out bottles of Skull Mountain before squatting cross-legged on the floor. We all said what a coincidence, and long time no see, and what've you been up to.

It wasn't quite like old times. A few years had gone by between us. They were long years; it didn't seem possible they'd held only three-hundred-odd days each. The four of us had been different places, seen different sights; and so we had become different men than the ones who had known each other at camp. But also there was a curtain between me and the three of them. Every now and then, in the midst of some tale or other, they would share a look; or they would fall silent and they'd say, well, you had to be there. You see, they'd been Inside and I hadn't; and that marks a man.

Angel had served with the 82nd against the Snakes; and Lyle had seen action against both the Crips and the Yoopers. Jimmy allowed as he'd tangoed in the high country, where the bandits had secret refuges among the twisting canyons; but he said very little else. Only he drank two beers for every one the others put down, and Jimmy had never been a drinking man.

They asked politcly what I'd been up to and pretended great interest in my stories and news dispatches. They swore they read all of my pieces on the ©-Net, and maybe they did.

They didn't blame me for it. They knew I'd as soon be Inside with them, suited-up and popping Joeys. The four of us had been commissioned power suit lieutenants together; had gone through the grueling training side by side. I still had the bars. I still looked at them some nights when the hurt wasn't so bad, when I could think about what might have been without feeling the need for chems.

Talk detoured through the winter crop of Hollywood morphies and whether American could take Congress from Liberty next year, and how the Air Cav had collared El Muerte down in the panhandle, and have you seen Chica Domosan's latest virtcheo. Angel and Lyle practically drooled when I told them I had the uncensored seedy; and they insisted on viewing it right then and there. I only had the one virtch hat, so they had to take turns watching. With the stereo earphones and the wrap-around goggs enclosing your head it was just like she was dancing and singing and peeling right there in front of you.

Afterwards, we talked Grand Strategy, shifting troops all over the continent, free of all political constraints and certain we would never hash it the way the Pentagon had. Doubt flowers from seeds that spend decades germinating; confidence is a weed that springs up overnight. And so youth gains in certitude what it lacks in prudence. It was no different back then; only, the stakes were higher.

Eventually, we spoke of our own personal plans. Lyle went how he was angling for an assignment down in the Frontera—"because that's where the next big yee-haw's going to be"—and Angel wanted nothing more than to hunt Joeys up in the Nations. White teeth split his broad, dark face. The rest of us counted the Nations as a nest of traitors and secessionists; but with Angel it was personal. Then Jimmy said, in that quiet voice of his, that he'd put in for a hoofer. We grinned and waited for the punch line, and when it didn't come our smiles slowly faded. "I'm serious," he said. "I won't go Inside again."

Angel looked shocked and Lyle's face stiffened in disapproval; but I was the one who spoke up. "How can you say that, Jimmy? After what we went through together in camp? You're a suit lieutenant, goddamn it!" Dismay pried me from the chair behind my cluttered workstation; or rather, it tried to. My legs betrayed me and I nearly cracked my head on the edge of the desk as I toppled.

The others were all around me, to lift me back up again. I swatted Jimmy's hand away and let the Angel bear me up and set me back in my accustomed place. "Why'd you do that, man?" Lyle asked as he fussed the blanket around my waist. "You shouldn't oughta do that." Jimmy wouldn't meet my eyes. Jimmy always blamed himself, but it was my idea. We'd just gotten our bars, we were celebrating, and that hog of Jimmy's looked phatter and stoopider the more I drank. So what the hell. That was then.

"I get around all right," I said to excuse myself. I could function. Most days, I could even walk. "Sometimes, the spasms—You know."

They all said they knew; but how could they? You dream and you train for months and months and then in one drunken moment you throw it all away for a goddamned motorcycle ride. Power suits amplify the suit louie's every move. A man can't wear it if he suffers unpredictable seizures. As if to underscore my thoughts, my left leg began to spasm. If I'd been suited up, my walker would have toppled. Stress, the doctors all said. It was stress that brought it on; but what did they know?

I was barred by circumstance; but Jimmy planned to walk away. That made no sense. Who would give up a power suit if he didn't have to? Angel was puzzled, too; and Lyle said, "Sometimes a guy gets syndrome and he just can't take being Inside no more." He was so damned understanding that Jimmy flushed and said how it wasn't that at all; or at least, not exactly.

"You know how things stand up in the mountains," Jimmy said. "I don't suppose it's much different with the Yoopers or the others, except maybe the terrain's rougher. Straight up or down as often as not, and canyons pinched as tight as a preacher's wife on Sunday. Officially, the whole area's pacified; only someone forgot to tell the militias."

"They are not 'militias,' suit lieutenant," said Angel in a mock-official voice. "They are 'bandits.'"

"I know that," Jimmy told him. "We only *call* 'em 'militias.' Like you say 'gangs' when you pull urban duty." He swigged his Skull and sat with the bottle dangling by its neck between his knees while he scowled at nothing. "The war's platoon-size up there," he said at last. "The regiment's scattered in firebases all across God's Country—only God ain't home. The only time I ever saw my colonel was over the Lynx. We got our orders—when we got any orders at all—from the twenty-four. Otherwise, we were on our own." He shook his head. "Pacified . . ."

"Who was your colonel?" Lyle asked.

"Mandlebrot. He was a sumbitch. Worried more about the cost of patrolling than whether Joey walked the line. When I took the platoon out, I used to sling the word off the twenty-four, then put my dish tech on arrest so I could say I never got the bounce-back telling me to stay put."

Angel laughed. "That's good. That's bean. Wish I'd thought of that."

That was the sort of hack Jimmy used to pull. Always by the book, but sometimes he wrote notes in the margins. "How long did you fool him?" I asked.

"Oh, not long," Jimmy admitted. "I said he was a sumbitch. Never said he was stupid. So sometimes I would go out unofficial-like with the reg'lar militia—the sheriff's posse. They had their own ATVs. Horses, too. Some places hooves'll take you where tires won't go. They were locals, and knew the country just as well as the bandits. I mean they knew it close up, like you know your girlfriend, not just from the up-and-down."

"You were too far north for the twenty-fours?" asked Angel.

Jimmy shrugged. "Nah, but the twenty-fours can't give you terrain detail the way a LEO sat' can. Sometimes a little sliver between canyon walls was all the sky we could dish. There's always *something* up there but you have to code dance, depending on what sat' your dish can catch. Well, that sheriff was a clever pud. Didn't need an eye in the sky, because he had eyes and ears all over ground level—and kept his county in pretty good law 'n' order, considering. But he knew when he needed extra weenie, so he was happy enough when I tagged along. Not *happy*, you understand; but happy enough. The irregulars don't much like us; but they hate the bandits worse—'cause it's their brothers and cousins and all getting kneecapped and necklaced."

"An' half the time," said Angel, "it's their brothers and cousins and all that're *doing* the kneecaps and necklaces."

"Word up," said Lyle. "Neighbors huntin' neighbors. No wonder they ain't happy campers."

"Folks back here don't always draw a line between bandits and friendlies," I said, thinking about my ©-Net story, "The Loyalist." "So your possemen feel they have to prove their loyalty."

"Righteous beans," said Angel. "Hey. You hear what happened to the 7th down in the live oak country? 'Rooster' McGregor—you ever meet 'im? Skinny guy with teeth out to here?—he was doing just what you were, Jimmy. Riding with the posse when he couldn't take his platoon out. Only it turns out the possemen *were* the bandits. Deputy Dawgs by day; camos and piano wire by night. Rooster, he got his ticket stripped over it, but he accidentally hung the sheriff before the court martial took his bars."

Jimmy hadn't been listening. "They don't respect us," he said. "Never understood that 'til the last time I was Inside. Now . . ." He voice trailed off and his eyes took on a distant look. I traded glances with Lyle and Angel, and waited.

"We called him 'Wild Bob,'" Jimmy said finally. "I suppose he had his own name for himself and some mumbo-jumbo, self-important rank. Generalissimo. Grand

Kleagle. Lord High Naff-naff. Maybe he called himself The Bald Eagle, 'cause he sure as shit had no hair; but he could've called himself Winnie the Pooh, for all I cared. 'Cause what he was was a murderer and a rapist and an armed robber, and he probably picked his nose in public. What he'd do every now and then—just to let us know he was still around—he'd send a body floating down the river from the high country. One of our agents or a friendly or maybe just someone looked at him cross-eyed. Or he'd throw a roadblock up and collect 'tolls' from everybody passing through. Or he'd yee-haw a firebase and pick off a freshie or two.

"Yeah, he was a piece of work, all right," Jimmy said. "And he knew to the corpse just how far he could push it before the higher-ups would scratch their balls and wonder how 'pacified' the area really was. So Badger Stoltz—that was the sheriff—he developed a keen interest in learning Wild Bob's whereabouts. One day, word came in that Bob was holed up in an old mining town, name of Spruce Creek. The silver gave out way back when, but no one had the heart to close it up. I seen the place, and I can't say I blame 'em. It's a spot worth stayin' in, just to open your eyes to it in the morning. It sets in a high, isolated meadow, with peaks on every side and four passes leading out. A spruce forest surrounds it and climbs halfway up the mountain flanks before giving way to krummholz and bare, gray rocks. The state road follows the creek through the center of town; but the Joeys have watchtowers on both east and west passes and it wouldn't take 'em more'n ten minutes to turn either one into a deathtrap if anybody tried to come in that way. The townies either support Wild Bob or they're too scared not to. Or both. Hell, like I said, even the friendlies don't much like us. And I can't say they weren't given cause in the old days."

"Don't mean nothin'," Angel said. "Don't excuse

what they done. Don't excuse collaborating, neither."

Jimmy just shook his head. "It's a damn shame what things have come to. Gimme another Skull, would you."

Lyle handed him the bottle. "So what about this Wild Bob?"

"I'm comin' to it." He popped the cap and tipped the neck toward us in salute. "In and Out," he said.

"Yeah." That was Lyle. "Except you want Out."

Jimmy darkened. "I said I was comin' to that. I just gotta give you the topo. There's another road. A county road. Packed dirt and gravel, mostly. Comes in from the south, gives the townies something they can call an intersection, and meanders out over the north pass. At that point whoever put the road in, must've figgered out there wasn't any place to go over on the other side; so it just fizzles out in the rocks and tundra. The Joeys keep an eye on the south pass, but don't pay much mind to the north."

Angel spoke. "I sense a plan," he said clapping his hands together. "A Strategy."

"Four suit louies," I said. "Two to keep 'em interested in the state road; one to block their retreat over the south pass; and one to sneak in through the bathroom window."

"Sure," said Jimmy, "except I didn't have no four suit louies at the firebase. Just me and Maria Serena—and one of us had to stay Out if the other went In, in case Joey yee-hawed the firebase. Wild Bob had maybe twenty, twenty-five bandits with him—he ran the town like a damn safe house, and every terrorist in three states could put up there for a week or two. I had the sheriff's posse—Badger Stoltz and ten whipcord guys who took their tin stars serious—and I had my power suit. So I figured the odds at better'n even. Plan was, the sheriff would waltz with our boy on the county road, draw 'em south a ways, while I took the walker in from the north."

"Couldn't use a floater, then?" Angel asked.

Jimmy shook his head. "Too steep. Ground effect don't work too good when the ground is vertical. I'd have to do finger and toe climbing the last stretch. There's a *reason* that road don't go nowhere. Sheriff sent one of his guys with me—a cute little bit named Natalie who just happens to be his daughter—to show me the way. I had the photos from the up-and-down, but like I said, things can look real different on the ground. Me and Stoltz worked it out and didn't say beans to nobody until the day I went In—'cause, you know, someone might have a cousin or talk in his sleep or something. So the day comes and Stoltz rides his ten guys south—they got the most ground to cover before they get in position—and Natalie waits while I go into the teep room and wriggle into my power suit—"

"Duck into a phone booth!" said Lyle. "Put on your cape and Spandex!"

"Superman!" said Angel. "Ta da-daah!"

"—Fiber ops and hydros hooked up—"

"—Leap tall buildings—"

"—Set my virtch hat—"

"—Faster than a speeding bullet—"

"—Power up the suit and—"

"Oh, man, I *know* that feeling—"

"—Ain't nothing like it—"

They bubbled, their words tumbling one atop the other, a glow spreading across their faces. I remained quiet and stared into my beer. I could remember what it felt like. Infinite power. You could dribble the world and shoot hoops. My fingers cramped into a sudden ball and I hid the rebellious limb under the desk.

"I took the walker out to the firebase perimeter and leaped over the wall right beside Natalie."

"Yee-haw!" said Lyle.

"It scared her. She hadn't been expecting it, and her horse reared up and near threw her. I told her I was ready-Freddy; and she just looks in my optics and says, let's not waste any more time, and she yanks on her bridle and heads off toward Spruce Creek." Jimmy drained his bottle and tossed it to Angel, who placed it carefully in the growing architectural wonder our empties were creating.

"The town wasn't too far, as the bullet flies; but you couldn't rightly get there going straight. Still, her dad and the others needed time to get in position, so Natalie set off at an easy canter with me loping along beside her. You know what it's like in those walkers. You want to leap and soar. And of course it's scaled about twice the human body, so you have to get used to the difference in stride and reach and squeeze. So I'd stretch my arms and the walker's manipulators would reach out and tear a limb off a cottonwood. Or I'd take a couple giant steps, just for the hell of it; then wait for Natalie to catch up. Third or fourth time I did that, she told me I was scaring her horse and please stop; so I had to plod the rest of the way. It was like being hamstrung."

"Hang a handicap sign on your back," Lyle agreed. "Get prime parking."

"Tell it, Brother Lyle!" said Angel. They tossed the thoughtless jape from one to the other.

"Satellite recon is a wonderful thing; but even the up-and-down can't see through trees or overhangs or pick fine details from a shadow-black canyon. Natalie led me the last part of the way. Took me down game paths, along a creek bed, through stands of Douglas fir that looked like they'd been there since God spread his tarp. She knew her horses, that Natalie. Couldn't have been more'n nineteen, twenty; but she sat in the saddle like she'd been born there. Well, in that country, maybe she had. She never said more'n two dozen words to me the whole trip; and those were mostly "this way" or "over there."

"Finally, we come to the base of a sheer cliff. There was three canyons cut into it. No, not even canyons. More like cracks. Recon barely showed 'em, but Badger Stoltz and his daughter swore there was one of 'em led to the top. Natalie rode along the base of the mountain and ducked a little ways into each. Then she come out and said, 'The right one. It slopes up real sharp, then goes vertical into a chimney that opens out on the high tundra. From there, your GPS should show you the way.'"

"Wasn't she going with you?" asked Angel.

I snorted. "Weren't you listening? Take a horse up a fissure like that?"

Jimmy rubbed his palms together. "I said, 'Wish me luck?' and she just yanked on her horse's reins. 'You don't need luck when you've got *that*,' she said. I knew she meant the walker, so I come back and said, 'I ain't no Imperial Storm Trooper and Wild Bob ain't the Rebel Alliance. I'm on *your* side. We're the *good* guys.'

"'The good guys,' she said. And, oh, she was pissed. Angry and afraid all at once. 'Was *your* government ragged on folks until bandits like your Wild Bob could play the hero? And now my daddy has to ride out and maybe take a splash of fléchettes in his belly, 'steada ticketing speeders along the state road.'

"'He ain't *my* Wild Bob,' I said. 'I come to take him down.'

"Her lips curled. Full, soft lips. Oh, they were lips for kissing. And here I was a young suit louie going off to do battle. I deserved a kiss. But I was suited up, teeping a walker, and there was more than telemetry and digital screens between us. Instead of a kiss, I got a kiss-off. '*You* come to take him down?' she said, and she leaned forward over her horse's head and pointed a finger into my optics. 'You listen to me, mister "suit louie." If my daddy even gets wounded bad, you'll have one more militia in the high country to worry about, and that'll be me!'"

"Hoo!" said Angel. "And she'd be a bad 'un, too."

"She was just worried about her Pa," I suggested. Jimmy looked at me, then shrugged.

"Maybe. I couldn't let it bother me, though. I had a job to do; and if I *didn't* get up that cut, her daddy probably *would* take a slug. Without me, the possemen were outnumbered and outgunned."

"So how'd you do it?" Lyle asked. "Sounds like you'd be out of line o' sight in that fissure."

"Oh, I had an aerostat hovering at the relay point, and Lieutenant Serena kept it on station. But you're right. Inside that chimney, the microwave beam would be blocked. So I asked Natalie to handle the little dish. You know, stake a repeater at the entrance, then crawl after me with the parabolic until I got up to where I could bounce sky again."

"Helluva thing to ask a girl," said Angel.

"Did you trust her?" I asked.

"You don't get it, Angel," Jimmy said. "She was a posseman, not just the Badger's daughter. She packed a nine and a railgun and there was a street sweeper in her saddle scabbard. Oh, *mano a mano*, any one of us could have taken her down; but we'd be walking funny for a long time after.

"Well, I took that walker into the cleft and it was like someone drew a window shade, you know what I mean? All the I/O was juiced into the walker's receptors by that little, handheld parabolic that Natalie Stoltz held. All she had to do was toss it aside, or even drop it accidentally, and that walker would be nothing but a pile of armor and circuitry stuck inside some rocks.

"I can't say I didn't think about that while I climbed that chimney; and what the colonel would say if I got stuck while I was on an unofficial outing. What I didn't think about until later was Natalie. My walker depended on the power beam she was aiming, and the farther up the cleft I climbed, the harder it was to keep the beam targeted. She had to stand right underneath the walker and aim straight up. So if anything happened, that'd be a couple tons of composite armor and metalocene plastic come tumbling down on her head."

"Takes balls," Angel agreed. "I wouldn't care to do it."

"Almost made me wish the walker was self-powered."

Lyle hooted. "Yeah, right. Carry a honking fuel cell around."

"Said 'almost,'" Jimmy told him. "The climb was the sort of work-around any good suit louie could pull off. Maybe a little closer to the edge, is all. Took me maybe half an hour to reach the top. I looked down over the edge to maybe wave Natalie my thanks, but all I seen was her riding off a-horseback without so much as a glance back."

"Not very grateful for your help, was she?" Angel said.

"Found out later she went 'round the long way to hook up with her dad. Can't fault her—her place was with him. Got there too late for the action, but then old Badger might've have that in mind when he assigned her to guide me."

"That must have been some climb," I said, "teep shadow, and all." I tried to keep my voice professional; but some of the envy must have come through, because Jimmy winced and wouldn't meet my eyes.

"Yeah, some climb," he said, and gave no more details.

Lyle leaned forward. "But once you were out of the cleft, you could bounce . . ."

"Yeah. Got my bearings from the GPS, shook hands again with the aerostat, checked in with Serena and Stoltz. Gauged the distance and told Stoltz I'd call him when it was time to open the dance. Serena said there was no movement on the up-and-down; but hell, those bandits know how to get around without smiling for the sat'-cams. Anything worth noticing would have been under trees or camo overhangs or down in the bunkers. You know how it is."

Lyle and Angel said they knew how it was. I chimed in, too; but for me it was more a theoretical knowledge, cadged from recon photos, official briefings, or picking the brains of Insiders. I'd written about it in "The Ambush." People tell me how my stories make everything come alive for them—a funny expression to use about stories of combat—but only I knew how dead the words felt under my fingertips.

"There was this one building, though, seemed to have a lot of in-and-out. The Artificial Stupid thought it was either a headquarters, an entrance to the bunker system, a whorehouse, or a public library."

Angel shook his head. "Jesus. No wonder they call 'em Stupids—"

"You put up any bumblebees?" asked Lyle.

"About two hives, all slaved into the aerostat relay. Gave me a good, close-in aerial of the town, so I knew right where the action was. I figured folks'd come pouring out of that building when the Badger opened the dance, and I wanted to know if they came out waving Kalashnikovs or library cards."

"Shoot 'em if they have the cards," said Lyle. "It's the shit they read drives 'em to it."

"You don't believe that, Lyle," I said.

He stuck his chin out. "You're the writer," he said.

"Either you move people or you don't. And if you don't, why bother writing? Maybe there'd be fewer murdering rebel scumbags if we'd put some of those books and websites off-limits."

"No," said Jimmy. "I'd rather shoot a man dead because he's a murdering rebel scumbag than treat him and everyone else like children who're told what they can read or listen to."

Lyle was unconvinced. "Yeah? What do you owe Joey Sixpack?"

Jimmy said, "I'm coming to that part." He leaned forward and rubbed his palms against his lap. We had run out of beer already—not unusual when the four of us gathered in those days—but no one volunteered to make a run, which *was* unusual.

"I walked my machine to a low ridge overlooking the town and scanned the target with my high-rezz 'nocs. It was just like the Badger figured. No one was watching the north. Just to be on the safe side, though, I turned on my pixelflage."

"Me," said Angel, "I just boogie right on up."

I didn't think there was any imputation of cowardice in what Angel said, but I pointed out that pixelflage could help the suit louie round up more Joeys because the bandits wouldn't know how close he actually was. "Yeah, I read that story," Angel said. "'Invisible Avenger.' Pretty good. 'Cept it's not like you're *really* invisible."

And there it was again. That curtain. "I *know* that," I growled. "I juice it a little for the civilians, is all."

"All it does is duplicate the landscape on your pixel array, so—"

My right arm twitched and knocked over an empty bottle. "I said, I *know* that. I went through the training with you. Got higher scores, too. If it hadn't been for the accident—"

Lyle looked at me. "An' we know *that*. Sure, you woulda been good. You woulda been hell on wheels. You woulda been the next Lieutenant Bellcampo, with medals down to your crotch, if you hadn't spilled on Jimmy's bike that night. But you did; so you're not; and it's *over*. We love you, man. You know that. We're the 'Fantastic Four,' right? But you can't change what happened. You just got to go on from where you are."

Jimmy reached out and touched me on the arm. "It's over for me, too," he said, but I jerked my arm away. Blame it on a spasm.

"I still don't understand that," I said.

Jimmy and I locked eyes for a moment. "I don't know if I can explain," he told me quietly, "if you never been Inside." I looked away and he touched my arm again. This time, I did not pull back. "No diss, man," he said. "Just word. I really don't know if I can make you feel what I felt." He looked at the others. "Don't know if I can make them feel it, either."

"Try us," said Lyle. "But the beer's gone; so—"

Jimmy shrugged. "Yeah. We're just swapping Inside stories, right? No big deal." He made a fist of his right hand and rubbed it with his left. "OK, so it goes down like this.

"I get as far as the spruce on the north edge of town, just where it gives way to open meadow around the creek. That puts me three jumps from the center of town and one jump from a herd of cows. There's a cowboy out with them. Don't know if he was a bandit or one of the regular townsfolk. Never did find out, and it didn't matter in the end. You lie down with dogs; you wake up with fleas.

"I put the walker on stand-by, so nothing moves. The pixels is all green and brown and black, so I blend into the forest behind me. The cowboy looks my way once or twice, puzzled-like, like he ain't sure he's seen something or not. Me, I got my 'nocs locked in on the big building, waiting for Badger to call the dance.

"I didn't have long to wait before I hear gunshots over my channel to Stoltz. Maybe they were loud enough to carry by air, because my cowboy, he frowns and peers south. Wild Bob's pickets call in for help and my Artificial Stupid locks in on their freq. Can't make heads or tails of the traffic, though, because it's all black . . ."

"Shoulda kept that kind of encryption illegal," Lyle said.

"Oh, yeah," I said. "Illegal. That would have stopped the likes of Wild Bob. Codes don't make conspiracies; conspirators do. Besides, PGE and other black codes were all over the Net. Might as well've made the wind illegal."

"And besides," Angel said, "the big corporations didn't like the idea of the government holding keys to all their codes. And they're the ones that call the shots."

Jimmy looked at him. "Yeah? That's what Wild Bob always said. Big corporations, Wall Street, the Jews. Besides, what do I care what Joey's saying, coded or not? It wasn't more'n fifteen seconds after Badger started the music that they come pouring out of that big building. They all have 'sault rifles and bags full of bananas. Two of 'em are lugging a mortar and some shells. I give Badger a heads-up over the aerostat relay and tell him what's coming his way.

"The cowboy decides either to join the fun or to head for home. He spurs his horse and goes galloping across the meadow. I take that as my cue and go into leaper mode. Anyone hears a noise, they look over and see that cowboy easier than they can see me. That gives me maybe another jump or two before the balloon goes up. Last jump put me right in front of the main building. The bandits usually don't post guards—they own the town's soul—but all the shooting has got them nervous. So there's a Joey standing around the front door with one thumb on his rifle's safety and the other'n up his ass. When I come down on the street behind him, he jumps like Old Shaq' in his glory days, and I chop him up before he even hits ground."

"What'd you use," Lyle asked. "Finger gun?"

Jimmy ignored him. "I bust through the front door and bounce from office to office, leaving little calling cards in each. The radio was in the third room. Some old bat was on the horn, hollering. When she sees me, she reaches in her desk drawer and pulls a .38. I don't have time for that crap, so I give her a spray and then shred the radio set."

"Think she got the warning out?"

"I know she did. But a suit louie never figures to go unnoticed when he's Inside. I work my way through the building—and pop a few more Joeys who want to field test their ammo. By the time I bust out the back wall, my little presents start going off and pretty soon the whole building's in flames. So you see, what did I care about the radio? *I* was the one sending the message. If she hadn't gone for the gun, she could've run with the others."

"Generous," said Lyle.

"Those were the Rules of Engagement, Style. Remember, the area was officially 'pacified': I could shoot whoever came at me armed; but anyone else, I had to tranq, smoke, strobe, or leave alone."

"And decide which is which on a moment's notice," Angel commented bitterly. "All Joey has to do is not go for his gun and he's a peaceable citizen."

"So I guess I lucked out, because I don't think there were more'n two dozen folks there who *weren't* potting at me. Some heavy rounds. Armor piercing. One cholo had ramjet rounds. You know, with the discarding sabot and the jet core through its middle? They hit with a couple of Mach. My walker took some damage; and the blowback . . ."

"Oh, yeah," said Lyle, rubbing his arm. "The blowback."

"I had bruises for a week where the walker got knocked around. I mean, I know you gotta have feedback through your suit pads, otherwise you got no 'touch,' but I wish the dampers would react faster than the blowback from impacts."

"Better'n being hit by a round direct," I said.

Angel went, "Word up. Sprained my wrist one time when a mortar shell wrenched the manipulator arm on my floater."

"It's like having a spasm." Lyle looked at me. "You remember what it was like during live round training. Must be a lot like what you got now, right?"

I went "right" and didn't try to fine-tune his opinion. He wouldn't have believed me anyway. People have a need to reduce things to what they think they understand.

"I whipped that town's butt good," Jimmy went on. "Pretty soon, though, Wild Bob figures out that the possemen were just a decoy so's I could yee-haw, and the 'away team' come streaming back from the south pass on their ATVs and dirt bikes. Well, I'd already gotten the range for a couple of landmarks along the county road, and my submunitions were already in place. I watch my heads-up until the column reaches the right point, then I trigger my subs and let loose. Ducks in a barrel. I couldn't have done better if they'd all held still and said 'cheese.'"

Angel pumped his fist and went yee-haw.

"Pretty," said Lyle. Jimmy shook his head.

"It's never pretty. I went in to break them; so of course that's what I did. But it was a dirty business and I hate those sumbitches for making me do it. Wild Bob himself, he was still functional. He'd been bringing up the rear, in case Badger tried following him to town, and he hadn't taken a hit. My sensors spotted his bald dome flashing in the afternoon sun and I high-leaped right over to him. I bet that was one day in his life when he wished he had all his hair back. He sees me land and his face twists into a sneer. He's got a grenade launcher in his hands and the devil in his eyes.

"Now, he knows the Rules of Engagement like he wrote 'em his own self. And who knows? The way they tie us in knots, maybe he did have a hand in the drafting. So he knows if he drops the grenade launcher, I got to switch to non-lethal."

Angel shrugged. "Me, I got slow reflexes."

"Yeah, well, it didn't matter, 'cause he didn't drop nothing except another grenade in the chamber. I opened a channel and give him his chance, saying, 'Bob, I come to take you in.' But he just curls his lip and goes how I ain't come anywhere and lobs a grenade at my optics."

"Hell," said Lyle, "that ain't nothing to swat away. Artificial Stupid can handle it on automatic."

"Sure, but the arm swing puts you off balance for a second because it's automatic; and that's the second when Wild Bob melts into the rocks. That forces me to run the instant replay so I can see where he went and follow him.

"We played peek-a-boo all across those rocks. He'd pop up and try another round, always going for the optics or the ee-em arrays. Oh, he knew power suits and where the weak points were. Then he'd scurry off to some new position." Jimmy shook his head and he looked at the wall, except he wasn't seeing the wall. "I'll give old Bob this much. He had sand. Not many folks'd buck a suit louie that way. Deep down, he believed in his cause. Had to, to do the things he did. He knew all along this day would come and he sort of looked forward to it,

if you know what I mean. Maybe he even welcomed it.
I thought about saving the county the expense of a
trial—I had some HE in reserve and could have made
some mighty fine rubble out of those rocks; but, strictly
speaking, this was a police action, not military, and
Badger hankered for a trial. He wanted the public to
know how Bob wasn't some damned Robin Hood, but
a murdering, thieving traitor. Last thing he wanted was
a martyr and a folk-song.

"So Bob and me, we play cat and banjo for maybe
fifteen, twenty minutes; and the more Bob backs away
from me, the closer he gets to Badger and his posse. I
thought maybe he didn't realize that because a firefight
concentrates your attention, you know what I mean?
But he knew exactly what he was doing. I call on him
once more to surrender, and he goes, 'not to the likes of
you.' And then, I swear, he hollered for Badger.

"'What do you want, Bob?' Badger asks him from
behind the next rim; and he says, 'I want it to be you,
not him,' and Badger goes, 'You sure you want it that
way?' and Bob said he was sure. 'If a man gotta go
down, it oughta be to another man. And Badger, you
may suck the gummint tit; but you are, by God, man
enough to come for me your own self.'

"So Badger he tells Bob to step out where he can be
seen and hold his hands up. Maybe ten, fifteen seconds
go by; then Wild Bob steps out from behind a finger of
rock—which surprised me, because I had him pegged a
couple meters the other way. He's still holding that
grenade launcher. Badger—I can see him now, skylined
on the rimrock twenty meters past Bob—he's got the high
ground and a 'sault rifle. He says, 'Bob, throw down the
launcher,' and Bob says, 'Now, Badger, you know I can't
do that,' and the sheriff goes, 'Throw it down *now*, Bob!'
and Bob doesn't say anything except he works the pump
to chamber another round. Badger goes, 'I don't want it

to end this way,' and Bob goes, 'Only way it could. Tell Ma and Natalie good-bye.' Then he raises the launcher to his shoulder and Badger sprays him with a cloud of fléchettes, which rip him up something bad, so I think he was dead before he knew it."

Lyle the Style shook his head and said, "Jesus." Angel crossed himself. Jimmy ground his fist into his palm, like a mortar and pestle, and didn't say anything for a long time. Finally, I spoke.

"They were brothers, Wild Bob and the Badger?" Oh, what a story that would make! If I could only find the right words to tell it. Duty versus fanaticism—with love ground to powder in the middle.

"I leaped on over," Jimmy said, "and grounded next to Badger where he stooped over Wild Bob. Badger looks up at me and says, 'It was empty.'"

"What was?" asked Angel.

"The grenade launcher," I said. "That's right, Jimmy, isn't it? Bob's weapon was empty."

Jimmy nodded. "I told Badger I'd carry the body back to town if he wanted. You know those walkers; they can carry a lot in their cradles. A single body wouldn't be much. But Badger just gives me a look and says if I want so bad to carry the body, I could damn well come up to Spruce Creek and pick it up my own self."

"Oh, man," said Angel. "Diss."

"What did you say to him?" I asked.

Jimmy shook his head. "I didn't say nothing. I yanked off my virtch hat and threw it to the floor. Lieutenant Serena asked me what I was doing, but I didn't pay her no mind. I just stared at the walls of the teep room, thinking."

"Thinking," said Lyle. "That's always a mistake."

Jimmy gave him a look, as if he were a stranger. "I left the teep room and checked an ATV from the motor pool. I know I left the walker out there untended—and the colonel chewed me a new asshole over that later on—but I had to go to Spruce Creek. Not just be telepresent. You understand? I had to be there myself."

"Dumb move," said Angel. "It's telepresent fighting waldoes helps keep down body-bag expenses."

"*Our* body bags," I pointed out.

Lyle shrugged. "Those are the only ones that matter to me."

Jimmy shook his head. "You're right, Angel. It was a dumb move. By the time I reached Spruce Creek, they were all gone. Badger and his posse. The bandits. Most of the townsfolk. Shit, most of the *town* was gone. Even the walker. Lieutenant Serena had teeped it after I went Outside. So I got out of the ATV and retraced the path of the firefight, walking from rock to rim. I had cornered Wild Bob *there*. He fired his last grenade *there*. Badger shot him *there*. The rocks were all splashed red; there were shell casings and sabots all over. I don't know how long I crouched where Badger had crouched. If any of Wild Bob's friends had still been around, I would have been easy pickings. Finally, a squall blew up and I hiked back to my vehicle and pulled up the clamshell. I sat there for a while listening to the high country wind. After a while, I drove back down to the firebase."

"And after that," I said, "you put in your papers."

Jimmy nodded.

"For the ATV/horse cavalry."

Another nod.

Angel said, "I still don't get why."

I leaned forward in my chair. My arms on the armrests barely trembled. "It's because it wasn't a fair fight."

Lyle grunted. "It wasn't *supposed* to be."

Jimmy raised his head and looked at me. "It's not that."

"Then what?" I asked.

Lyle laughed. "It's because he wants the respect of that hick sheriff. Or his daughter."

Jimmy rose from the floor. "I didn't think you'd understand." He looked at me. "Though I hoped *you* would."

We locked eyes for a moment. Then he turned to go. When he got to the door, I blurted out. "Oh, Jesus. It's Wild Bob's respect you want."

Angel scowled. "That hemorrhoid? What's *his* respect worth?"

Jimmy paused with his hand over the doorplate. "What he believed in was all wrong and twisted," he said. "But he was willing to die for it. If what we're fighting for is right, shouldn't *we* be willing to risk something besides equipment damage and feedback bruises?"

When he had gone, there was silence in the room. Lyle and Angel and I looked at one another. Finally, Angel said, "He's nuts. You don't fight snakes by wriggling in the dirt and trying to bite 'em first. That doesn't make you brave, just stupid. You stand back and blow 'em away with a sweeper. Only one way to end this fighting. Stomp hard and stomp fast."

Lyle shook his head and said, "He'll get over it. It's just syndrome."

"Well," said Angel, "he'll find out there's a hell of a difference between teep fighting and fighting in person."

"Maybe," I said, "he already found that out."

That was the last I saw any of them until after the big offensive. Angel and I shared a platform at a bond rally, but that was near the end, when Angel was the Hero of Boise. We'd both heard how Lyle—and half his firebase—got scragged by the Sacramento car bomb and after the ceremonies we emptied a couple of Skull Mountains for him. That's when Angel told me that

Jimmy Topeka lost an arm in a firefight in the Bitter-roots. He's married now and living in the high country.

I managed to etch a half dozen stories out of that one day's bull session. "The Brothers." "Rules of Engagement." You've read them. They were compiled on ©-Net at <The Insiders> website.

The funny thing—and it must be just a coincidence—is that ever since then my seizures haven't bothered me so much.

Radiant Doors

MICHAEL SWANWICK

Michael Swanwick wrote *The Iron Dragon's Daughter* (1995) and *Jack Faust* (1997) and is working on another novel. If it is fantasy, that will be three fantasy novels in a row for this SF writer. But in between the novels, he still writes short stories, and more often than ever this year, which may have been his most prolific year ever. His short fiction in recent years has been about as often fantasy as science fiction. This SF story was an easy choice for this year's best, in spite of Swanwick's several other fine stories this year. This is a darker, painfully realistic, SF twist on C. M. Kornbluth's classic, "The Marching Morons." This story appeared in *Asimov's*.

The doors began opening on a Tuesday in early March. Only a few at first—flickering and uncertain because they were operating at the extreme end of their temporal range—and those few from the earliest days of the exodus, releasing fugitives who were unstarved and healthy, the privileged scientists and technicians who had created or appropriated the devices that made their escape possible. We processed about a hundred a week, in comfortable isolation and relative secrecy. There were videocams taping everything, and our own best people madly scribbling notes and holding seminars and teleconferences where they debated the revelations.

Those were, in retrospect, the good old days.

In April the floodgates swung wide. Radiant doors opened everywhere, disgorging torrents of ragged and fearful refugees. There were millions of them and they had every one, to the least and smallest child, been horribly, horribly abused. The stories they told were enough to sicken anyone. I know.

We did what we could. We set up camps. We dug latrines. We ladled out soup. It was a terrible financial burden to the host governments, but what else could they do? The refugees were our descendants. In a very real sense, they were our children.

Throughout that spring and summer, the flow of refugees continued to grow. As the cumulative worldwide total ran up into the tens of millions, the authorities were beginning to panic—was this going to go on forever, a plague of human locusts that would double and triple and quadruple the population, overrunning the land and devouring all the food? What measures might we be forced to take if this kept up? The planet was within a lifetime of its loading capacity as it was. It couldn't take much more. Then in August the doors simply ceased. Somebody up in the future had put an absolute and final end to them.

It didn't bear thinking what became of those who hadn't made it through.

"More tales from the burn ward," Shriver said, ducking through the door flap. That was what he called atrocity stories. He dumped the files on my desk and leaned forward so he could leer down my blouse. I scowled him back a step.

"Anything useful in them?"

"Not a scrap. But that's not my determination, is it? You have to read each and every word in each and every report so that you can swear and attest that they contain nothing the Commission needs to know."

"Right." I ran a scanner over the universals for each of the files, and dumped the lot in the circular file. Touched a thumb to one of the new pads—better security devices were the very first benefit we'd gotten from all that influx of future tech—and said, "Done."

Then I linked my hands behind my neck and leaned back in the chair. The air smelled of canvas. Sometimes it seemed that the entire universe smelled of canvas. "So how are things with you?"

"About what you'd expect. I spent the morning interviewing vics."

"Better you than me. I'm applying for a transfer to Publications. Out of these tents, out of the camps, into a nice little editorship somewhere, writing press releases and articles for the Sunday magazines. Cushy job, my very own cubby, and the satisfaction of knowing I'm doing some good for a change."

"It won't work," Shriver said. "All these stories simply blunt the capacity for feeling. There's even a term for it. It's called compassion fatigue. After a certain point you begin to blame the vic for making you hear about it."

I wriggled in the chair, as if trying to make myself more comfortable, and stuck out my breasts a little bit more. Shriver sucked in his breath. Quietly, though— I'm absolutely sure he thought I didn't notice. I said, "Hadn't you better get back to work?"

Shriver exhaled. "Yeah, yeah, I hear you." Looking unhappy, he ducked under the flap out into the corridor. A second later his head popped back in, grinning. "Oh, hey, Ginny—almost forgot. Huong is on sick roster. Gevorkian said to tell you you're covering for her this afternoon, debriefing vics."

"Bastard!"

He chuckled, and was gone.

I sat interviewing a woman whose face was a mask etched with the aftermath of horror. She was absolutely cooperative. They all were. Terrifyingly so. They were grateful for anything and everything. Sometimes I wanted to strike the poor bastards in the face, just to see if I could get a human reaction out of them. But they'd probably kiss my hand for not doing anything worse.

"What do you know about midpoint-based engineering? Gnat relays? Sub-local mathematics?"

Down this week's checklist I went, and with each item she shook her head. "Prigogine engines? SVAT trance status? Lepton soliloquies?" Nothing, nothing, nothing. "Phlenaria? The Toledo incident? 'Third Martyr' theory? Science Investigatory Group G?"

"They took my daughter," she said to this last. "They did things to her."

"I didn't ask you that. If you know anything about their military organization, their machines, their drugs, their research techniques—fine. But I don't want to hear about people."

"They did things." Her dead eyes bored into mine. "They—"

"Don't tell me."

"—returned her to us midway through. They said they were understaffed. They sterilized our kitchen and gave us a list of more things to do to her. Terrible things. And a checklist like yours to write down her reactions."

"Please."

"We didn't want to, but they left a device so we'd obey. Her father killed himself. He wanted to kill her too, but the device wouldn't let him. After he died, they changed the settings so I couldn't kill myself too. I tried."

"God damn." This was something new. I tapped my pen twice, activating its piezochronic function, so that it began recording fifteen seconds earlier. "Do you remember anything about this device? How large was it? What did the controls look like?" Knowing how unlikely it was that she'd give us anything usable. The average refugee knew no more about their technology than the average here-and-now citizen knows about television and computers. You turn them on and they do things. They break down and you buy a new one.

Still, my job was to probe for clues. Every little bit contributed to the big picture. Eventually they'd add up. That was the theory, anyway. "Did it have an internal or external power source? Did you ever see anybody servicing it?"

"I brought it with me," the woman said. She reached into her filthy clothing and removed a fist-sized chunk of quicksilver with small, multicolored highlights. "Here."

She dumped it in my lap.

It was automation that did it or, rather, hyperautomation. That old bugaboo of fifty years ago had finally come to fruition. People were no longer needed to mine, farm, or manufacture. Machines made better administrators, more attentive servants. Only a very small elite—the vics called them simply their Owners—were required to order and ordain. Which left a lot of people who were just taking up space.

There had to be *something* to do with them.

As it turned out, there was.

That's my theory, anyway. Or, rather, one of them. I've got a million: Hyperautomation. Cumulative hardening of the collective conscience. Circular determinism. The implicitly aggressive nature of hierarchic structures. Compassion fatigue. The banality of evil.

Maybe people are just no damn good. That's what Shriver would have said.

The next day I went zombie, pretty much. Going through the motions, connecting the dots. LaShana in Requisitions noticed it right away. "You ought to take the day off," she said, when I dropped by to see about getting a replacement PzC(15)/pencorder. "Get away from here, take a walk in the woods, maybe play a little golf."

"Golf," I said. It seemed the most alien thing in the universe, hitting a ball with a stick. I couldn't see the point of it.

"Don't say it like that. You love golf. You've told me so a hundred times."

"I guess I have." I swung my purse up on the desk, slid my hand inside, and gently stroked the device. It was cool to the touch and vibrated ever so faintly under my fingers. I withdrew my hand. "Not today, though."

LaShana noticed. "What's that you have in there?"

"Nothing." I whipped the purse away from her. "Nothing at all." Then, a little too loud, a little too blustery, "So how about that pencorder?"

"It's yours." She got out the device, activated it, and let me pick it up. Now only I could operate the thing. Wonderful how fast we were picking up the technology. "How'd you lose your old one, anyway?"

"I stepped on it. By accident." I could see that LaShana wasn't buying it. "Damn it, it was an accident! It could have happened to anyone."

I fled from LaShana's alarmed, concerned face.

Not twenty minutes later, Gevorkian came sleazing into my office. She smiled, and leaned lazily back against the file cabinet when I said hi. Arms folded. Eyes sad and cynical. That big plain face of hers, tolerant and worldly-wise. Wearing her skirt just a *smidge* tighter, a *touch* shorter than was strictly correct for an office environment.

"Virginia," she said.

"Linda."

We did the waiting thing. Eventually, because I'd been here so long I honestly didn't give a shit, Gevorkian spoke first. "I hear you've been experiencing a little disgruntlement."

"Eh?"

"Mind if I check your purse?"

Without taking her eyes off me for an instant, she hoisted my purse, slid a hand inside, and stirred up the contents. She did it so slowly and dreamily that, I swear to God, I half expected her to smell her fingers afterward. Then, when she didn't find the expected gun, she said, "You're not planning on going postal on us, are you?"

I snorted.

"So what is it?"

"What is it?" I said in disbelief. I went to the window. Zip zip zip, down came a rectangle of cloth. Through the scrim of mosquito netting the camp revealed itself: canvas as far as the eye could see. There was nothing down there as fancy as our labyrinthine government office complex at the top of the hill—what we laughingly called the Tentagon—with its canvas air-conditioning ducts and modular laboratories and cafeterias. They were all army surplus, and what wasn't army surplus was Boy Scout hand-me-downs. "Take a look. Take a goddamn fucking look. That's the future out there, and it's barreling down on you at the rate of sixty seconds per minute. You can *see* it and still ask me that question?"

She came and stood beside me. Off in the distance, a baby began to wail. The sound went on and on. "Virginia," she said quietly. "Ginny, I understand how you feel. Believe me, I do. Maybe the universe is deterministic. Maybe there's no way we can change what's coming. But that's not proven yet. And until it is, we've got to soldier on."

"Why?"

"Because of *them*." She nodded her chin toward the slow-moving revenants of things to come. "They're the living proof of everything we hate and fear. They are witness and testimony to the fact that absolute evil exists. So long as there's the least chance, we've got to try to ward it off."

I looked at her for a long, silent moment. Then, in a voice as cold and calmly modulated as I could make it, I said, "Take your god-damned hand off my ass."

She did so.

I stared after her as, without another word, she left.

This went beyond self-destructive. All I could think was that Gevorkian wanted out but couldn't bring herself to quit. Maybe she was bucking for a sexual harassment suit. But then again, there's definitely an erotic quality to the death of hope. A sense of license. A nicely edgy feeling that since nothing means anything anymore, we might as well have our little flings. That they may well be all we're going to get.

And all the time I was thinking this, in a drawer in my desk the device quietly sat. Humming to itself.

People keep having children. It seems such a terrible thing to do. I can't understand it at all, and don't talk to me about instinct. The first thing I did, after I realized the enormity of what lay ahead, was get my tubes tied. I never thought of myself as a breeder, but I'd wanted to have the option in case I ever changed my mind. Now I knew I would not.

It had been one hell of a day, so I decided I was entitled to quit work early. I was cutting through the camp toward the civ/noncom parking lot when I ran across Shriver. He was coming out of the vic latrines. Least romantic place on Earth. Canvas stretching forever and dispirited people shuffling in and out. And the smell! Imagine the accumulated stench of all the sick shit in the world, and you've just about got it right.

Shriver was carrying a bottle of Spanish champagne under his arm. The bottle had a red bow on it.

"What's the occasion?" I asked.

He grinned like Kali and slid an arm through mine. "My divorce finally came through. Wanna help me celebrate?"

Under the circumstances, it was the single most stupid thing I could possibly do. "Sure," I said. "Why not?"

Later, in his tent, as he was taking off my clothes, I asked, "Just why did your wife divorce you, Shriver?"

"Mental cruelty," he said, smiling.

Then he laid me down across his cot and I let him hurt me. I needed it. I needed to be punished for being so happy and well fed and unbrutalized while all about me . . .

"Harder, God damn you," I said, punching him, biting him, clawing up blood. "Make me pay."

Cause and effect. Is the universe deterministic or not? If everything inevitably follows what came before, tickety-tock, like gigantic, all-inclusive clockwork, then there is no hope. The refugees came from a future that cannot be turned away. If, on the other hand, time is quanticized and uncertain, unstable at every point, constantly prepared to collapse in any direction in response to totally random influences, then all that suffering that came pouring in on us over the course of six long and rainy months might be nothing more than a phantom. Just an artifact of a rejected future.

Our future might be downright pleasant.

We had a million scientists working in every possible discipline, trying to make it so. Biologists, chaoticists, physicists of every shape and description. Fabulously dedicated people. Driven. Motivated. All trying to hold out a hand before what must be and say "Stop!"

How they'd love to get their mitts on what I had stowed in my desk.

I hadn't decided yet whether I was going to hand it over, though. I wasn't at all sure what was the right thing to do. Or the smart thing, for that matter.

Gevorkian questioned me on Tuesday. Thursday, I came into my office to discover three UN soldiers with hand-held detectors, running a search.

I shifted my purse back on my shoulder to make me look more strack, and said, "What the hell is going on here?"

"Random check, ma'am." A dark-eyed Indian soldier young enough to be if not my son then my little brother politely touched fingers to forehead in a kind of salute. "For up-time contraband." A sewn tag over one pocket proclaimed his name to be PATHAK. "It is purely standard, I assure you."

I counted the stripes on his arm, compared them to my civilian GS-rating and determined that by the convoluted UN protocols under which we operated, I outranked him.

"Sergeant-Major Pathak. You and I both know that all foreign nationals operate on American soil under sufferance, and the strict understanding that you have no authority whatsoever over native civilians."

"Oh, but this was cleared with your Mr.—"

"I don't give a good goddamn if you cleared it with the fucking Dalai Lama! This is my office—your authority ends at the door. You have no more right to be here than I have to finger-search your goddamn rectum. Do you follow me?"

He flushed angrily, but said nothing.

All the while, his fellows were running their detectors over the file cabinet, the storage closets, my desk. Little lights on each flashed red red red. Negative negative negative. The soldiers kept their eyes averted from me. Pretending they couldn't hear a word.

I reamed their sergeant-major out but good. Then, when the office had been thoroughly scanned and the two noncoms were standing about uneasily, wondering how long they'd be kept here, I dismissed the lot. They were all three so grateful to get away from me that nobody asked to examine my purse. Which was, of course, where I had the device.

After they left, I thought about young Sergeant-Major Pathak. I wondered what he would have done if I'd put my hand on his crotch and made a crude suggestion. No, make that an order. He looked to be a real straight arrow. He'd squirm for sure. It was an alarmingly pleasant fantasy.

I thought it through several times in detail, all the while holding the gizmo in my lap and stroking it like a cat.

The next morning, there was an incident at Food Processing. One of the women started screaming when they tried to inject a microminiaturized identi-chip under the skin of her forehead. It was a new system they'd come up with that was supposed to save a per-unit of thirteen cents a week in tracking costs. You walked through a smart doorway, it registered your presence, you picked up your food, and a second doorway checked you off on the way out. There was nothing in it to get upset about.

But the woman began screaming and crying and—this happened right by the kitchens—snatched up a cooking knife and began stabbing herself, over and over. She managed to make nine whacking big holes in herself before the thing was wrestled away from her. The orderlies took her to Intensive, where the doctors said it would be a close thing either way.

After word of that got around, none of the refugees would allow themselves to be identi-chipped. Which really pissed off the UN peacekeepers assigned to the camp, because earlier a couple hundred vics had accepted the chips without so much as a murmur. The Indian troops thought the refugees were willfully trying to make their job more difficult. There were complaints of racism, and rumors of planned retaliation.

I spent the morning doing my bit to calm things down—hopeless—and the afternoon writing up reports that everyone upstream wanted to receive ASAP and would probably file without reading. So I didn't have time to think about the device at all.

But I did. Constantly.

It was getting to be a burden.

For health class, one year in high school, I was given a ten-pound sack of flour, which I had to name and then carry around for a month, as if it were a baby. Bippy couldn't be left unattended; I had to carry it everywhere or else find somebody willing to baby-sit it. The exercise was supposed to teach us responsibility and scare us off of sex. The first thing I did when the month was over was to steal my father's .45, put Bippy in the backyard, and empty the clip into it, shot after shot. Until all that was left of the little bastard was a cloud of white dust.

The machine from the future was like that. Just another Bippy. I had it, and dared not get rid of it. It was obviously valuable. It was equally obviously dangerous. Did I really want the government to get hold of something that could compel people to act against their own wishes? Did I honestly trust them not to immediately turn themselves into everything that we were supposedly fighting to prevent?

I'd been asking myself the same questions for—what?—four days. I'd thought I'd have some answers by now.

I took the bippy out from my purse. It felt cool and smooth in my hand, like melting ice. No, warm. It felt both warm and cool. I ran my hand over and over it, for the comfort of the thing.

After a minute, I got up, zipped shut the flap to my office, and secured it with a twist tie. Then I went back to my desk, sat down, and unbuttoned my blouse. I rubbed the bippy all over my body: up my neck, and over my breasts and around and around on my belly. I kicked off my shoes and clumsily shucked off my pantyhose. Down along the outside of my calves it went, and up the insides of my thighs. Between my legs. It made me feel filthy. It made me feel a little less like killing myself.

How it happened was, I got lost. How I got lost was, I went into the camp after dark.

Nobody goes into the camp after dark, unless they have to. Not even the Indian troops. That's when the refugees hold their entertainments. They had no compassion for each other, you see—that was our dirty little secret. I saw a toddler fall into a campfire once. There were vics all around, but if it hadn't been for me, the child would have died. I snatched it from the flames before it got too badly hurt, but nobody else made a move to help it. They just stood there looking. And laughing.

"In Dachau, when they opened the gas chambers, they'd find a pyramid of human bodies by the door," Shriver told me once. "As the gas started to work, the Jews panicked and climbed over each other, in a futile attempt to escape. That was deliberate. It was designed into the system. The Nazis didn't just want them dead— they wanted to be able to feel morally superior to their victims afterward."

So I shouldn't have been there. But I was unlatching the door to my trailer when it suddenly came to me that my purse felt wrong. Light. And I realized that I'd left the bippy in the top drawer of my office desk. I hadn't even locked it.

My stomach twisted at the thought of somebody else finding the thing. In a panic, I drove back to the camp. It was a twenty-minute drive from the trailer park and by the time I got there, I wasn't thinking straight. The civ/noncom parking lot was a good quarter-way around the camp from the Tentagon. I thought it would be a simple thing to cut through. So, flashing my DOD/Future History Division ID at the guard as I went through the gate, I did.

Which was how I came to be lost.

There are neighborhoods in the camp. People have a natural tendency to sort themselves out by the nature of their suffering. The twitchers, who were victims of paralogical reprogramming, stay in one part of the camp, and the mods, those with functional normative modifications, stay in another. I found myself wandering through crowds of people who had been "healed" of limbs, ears, and even internal organs—there seemed no sensible pattern. Sometimes our doctors could effect a partial correction. But our primitive surgery was, of course, nothing like that available in their miraculous age.

I'd taken a wrong turn trying to evade an eyeless, noseless woman who kept grabbing at my blouse and demanding money, and gotten all turned around in the process when, without noticing me, Gevorkian went striding purposefully by.

Which was so unexpected that, after an instant's shock, I up and followed her. It didn't occur to me not to. There was something strange about the way she held herself, about her expression, her posture. Something unfamiliar.

She didn't even *walk* like herself.

The vics had dismantled several tents to make a large open space surrounded by canvas. Propane lights, hung from tall poles, blazed in a ring about it. I saw

Gevorkian slip between two canvas sheets and, after a moment's hesitation, I followed her.

It was a rat fight.

The way a rat fight works, I learned that night, is that first you catch a whole bunch of Norwegian rats. Big mean mothers. Then you get them in a bad mood, probably by not feeding them, but there are any number of other methods that could be used. Anyway, they're feeling feisty. You put a dozen of them in a big pit you've dug in the ground. Then you dump in your contestant. A big guy with a shaven head and his hands tied behind his back. His genitals are bound up in a little bit of cloth, but other than that he's naked.

Then you let them fight it out. The rats leap and jump and bite and the big guy tries to trample them underfoot or crush them with his knees, his chest, his head—whatever he can bash them with.

The whole thing was lit up bright as day, and all the area around the pit was crammed with vics. Some shouted and urged on one side or the other. Others simply watched intently. The rats squealed. The human fighter bared his teeth in a hideous rictus and fought in silence.

It was the creepiest thing I'd seen in a long time.

Gevorkian watched it coolly, without any particular interest or aversion. After a while it was obvious to me that she was waiting for someone.

Finally that someone arrived. He was a lean man, tall, with keen, hatchetlike features. None of the vics noticed. Their eyes were directed inward, toward the pit. He nodded once to Gevorkian, then backed through the canvas again.

She followed him.

I followed her.

They went to a near-lightless area near the edge of the camp. There was nothing there but trash, the backs of tents, the razor-wire fence, and a gate padlocked for the night.

It was perfectly easy to trail them from a distance. The stranger held himself proudly, chin up, eyes bright. He walked with a sure stride. He was nothing at all like the vics.

It was obvious to me that he was an Owner.

Gevorkian too. When she was with him that inhuman arrogance glowed in her face as well. It was as if a mask had been removed. The fire that burned in his face was reflected in hers.

I crouched low to the ground, in the shadow of a tent, and listened as the stranger said, "Why hasn't she turned it in?"

"She's unstable," Gevorkian said. "They all are."

"We don't dare prompt her. She has to turn it in herself."

"She will. Give her time."

"Time," the man repeated. They both laughed in a way that sounded to me distinctly unpleasant. Then, "She'd better. There's a lot went into this operation. There's a lot riding on it."

"She will."

I stood watching as they shook hands and parted ways. Gevorkian turned and disappeared back into the tent city. The stranger opened a radiant door and was gone.

Cause and effect. They'd done . . . *whatever* it was they'd done to that woman's daughter just so they could plant the bippy with me. They wanted me to turn it in. They wanted our government to have possession of a device that would guarantee obedience. They wanted to give us a good taste of what it was like to be them.

Suddenly, I had no doubt at all what I should do. I

started out at a determined stride, but inside of nine paces I was *running*. Vics scurried to get out of my way. If they didn't move fast enough, I shoved them aside.

I had to get back to the bippy and destroy it.

Which was stupid, stupid, stupid. If I'd kept my head down and walked slowly, I would have been invisible. Invisible and safe. The way I did it, though, cursing and screaming, I made a lot of noise and caused a lot of fuss. Inevitably, I drew attention to myself.

Inevitably, Gevorkian stepped into my path.

I stumbled to a halt.

"Gevorkian," I said feebly. "Linda, I—"

All the lies I was about to utter died in my throat when I saw her face. Her expression. Those eyes. Gevorkian reached for me. I skipped back in utter panic, turned—and fled. Anybody else would have done the same.

It was a nightmare. The crowds slowed me. I stumbled. I had no idea where I was going. And all the time, this monster was right on my heels.

Nobody goes into the camp after dark, unless they have to. But that doesn't mean that nobody goes in after dark. By sheer good luck, Gevorkian chased me into the one part of the camp that had something that outsiders could find nowhere else—the sex-for-hire district.

There was nothing subtle about the way the vics sold themselves. The trampled-grass street I found myself in was lined with stacks of cages like the ones they use in dog kennels. They were festooned with strings of Christmas lights, and each one contained a crouched boy. Naked, to best display those mods and deformities that some found attractive. Off-duty soldiers strolled up and down the cages, checking out the possibilities. I recognized one of them.

"Sergeant-Major Pathak!" I cried. He looked up, startled and guilty. "Help me! Kill her—please! Kill her now!"

Give him credit, the sergeant-major was a game little fellow. I can't imagine what we looked like to him, one harridan chasing the other down the streets of Hell. But he took the situation in at a glance, unholstered his sidearm and stepped forward. "Please," he said. "You will both stand where you are. You will place your hands upon the top of your head. You will—"

Gevorkian flicked her fingers at the young soldier. He screamed, and clutched his freshly crushed shoulder. She turned away from him, dismissively. The other soldiers had fled at the first sign of trouble. All her attention was on me, trembling in her sight like a winded doe. "*Sweet* little vic," she purred. "If you won't play the part we had planned for you, you'll simply have to be silenced."

"No," I whispered.

She touched my wrist. I was helpless to stop her. "You and I are going to go to my office now. We'll have fun there. Hours and hours of fun."

"Leave her be."

As sudden and inexplicable as an apparition of the Virgin, Shriver stepped out of the darkness. He looked small and grim.

Gevorkian laughed, and gestured.

But Shriver's hand reached up to intercept hers, and where they met, there was an electric blue flash. Gevorkian stared down, stunned, at her hand. Bits of tangled metal fell away from it. She looked up at Shriver.

He struck her down.

She fell with a brief harsh cry, like that of a sea gull. Shriver kicked her, three times, hard: In the ribs. In the stomach. In the head. Then, when she looked like she might yet regain her feet, "It's one of *them*!" he shouted.

"Look at her! She's a spy for the Owners! She's from the future! Owner! Look! Owner!"

The refugees came tumbling out of the tents and climbing down out of their cages. They looked more alive than I'd ever seen them before. They were red-faced and screaming. Their eyes were wide with hysteria. For the first time in my life, I was genuinely afraid of them. They came running. They swarmed like insects.

They seized Gevorkian and began tearing her apart.

I saw her struggle up and halfway out of their grips, saw one arm rise up above the sea of clutching hands, like that of a woman drowning.

Shriver seized my elbow and steered me away before I could see any more. I saw enough, though.

I saw too much.

"Where are we going?" I asked when I'd recovered my wits.

"Where do you think we're going?"

He led me to my office.

There was a stranger waiting there. He took out a hand-held detector like Sergeant-Major Pathak and his men had used earlier and touched it to himself, to Shriver, and to me. Three times it flashed red, negative. "You travel through time, you pick up a residual charge," Shriver explained. "It never goes away. We've known about Gevorkian for a long time."

"US Special Security," the stranger said, and flipped open his ID. It meant diddle-all to me. There was a badge. It could have read Captain Crunch for all I knew or cared. But I didn't doubt for an instant that he was SS. He had that look. To Shriver he said, "The neutralizer."

Shriver unstrapped something glittery from his wrist—the device he'd used to undo Gevorkian's weapon—and, in a silent bit of comic bureaucratic punctilio, exchanged it for a written receipt. The security officer touched the thing with his detector. It flashed green. He put both devices away in interior pockets.

All the time, Shriver stood in the background, watching. He wasn't told to go away.

Finally, Captain Crunch turned his attention to me again. "Where's the snark?"

"Snark?"

The man removed a thin scrap of cloth from an inside jacket pocket and shook it out. With elaborate care, he pulled it over his left hand. An inertial glove. Seeing by my expression that I recognized it, he said, "Don't make me use this."

I swallowed. For an instant I thought crazily of defying him, of simply refusing to tell him where the bippy was. But I'd seen an inertial glove in action before, when a lone guard had broken up a camp riot. He'd been a little man. I'd seen him crush heads like watermelons.

Anyway, the bippy was in my desk. They'd be sure to look there.

I opened the drawer, produced the device. Handed it over. "It's a plant," I said. "They want us to have this."

Captain Crunch gave me a look that told me clear as words exactly how stupid he thought I was. "We understand more than you think we do. There are circles and circles. We have informants up in the future, and some of them are more highly placed than you'd think. Not everything that's known is made public."

"Damn it, this sucker is *evil*."

A snake's eyes would look warmer than his. "Understand this: We're fighting for our survival here. Extinction is null-value. You can have all the moral crises you want when the war is won."

"It should be suppressed. The technology. If it's used, it'll just help bring about . . ."

He wasn't listening.

I'd worked for the government long enough to know when I was wasting my breath. So I shut up.

When the captain left with the bippy, Shriver still remained, looking ironically after him. "People get the kind of future they deserve," he observed.

"But that's what I'm saying. Gevorkian came back from the future in order to help bring it about. That means that time isn't deterministic." Maybe I was getting a little weepy. I'd had a rough day. "The other guy said there was a lot riding on this operation. They didn't know how it was going to turn out. They didn't *know*."

Shriver grunted, not at all interested.

I plowed ahead unheeding. "If it's not deterministic—if they're working so hard to bring it about—then all our effort isn't futile at all. This future can be prevented."

Shriver looked up at last. There was a strangely triumphant gleam in his eye. He flashed that roguish ain't-this-fun grin of his, and said, "I don't know about you, but some of us are working like hell to *achieve* it."

With a jaunty wink, he was gone.

Unraveling the Thread

JEAN-CLAUDE DUNYACH

Translated by Ann Cale and Sheryl Curtis, with assistance from Brian Stableford

Note: This story was first published in *Galaxies 4* (Avril 1997) as "Déchiffrer la trame." The French title contains an untranslatable pun: "trame" means both "weft" and "plot"; "déchiffrer" means, of course, "to decipher."

Jean Claude Dunyach has a Ph.D. in applied mathematics and works in the aircraft division of Aerospatiale, in Toulouse, and is one of the foremost contemporary French SF writers. He has published six novels and two story collections. Dunyach has become a vital part of the editorial collective of the new French SF magazine *Galaxies*. He recently edited an original SF anthology (*Escales*), slated for release in September 1999 and he is working on an ambitious techno-space opera (working title: *Etoiles mourantes*) with one of France's foremost SF writers, Ayerdahl. At least two of his earlier stories have appeared in English, in *Full Spectrum 3* and *Full Spectrum 5*. This story first appeared translated in *Interzone*. In France it won Dunyach his third Rosny Aine Award. It is part of what is perhaps an emerging sub-genre of SF set in the historic past that is not an alternate past but still implies an alternate view of reality, the real behind the only apparently real (all hail, Philip K. Dick).

Proof of *their* visitation can be found in the antique carpet section in the basement of the Museum of Civilization. There are two of us who know about it: Laura Morelli and me.

The basement is our turf. The most valuable carpets are here, stored in almost total darkness to keep their colors from fading. The public isn't allowed in here and there are so few specialists working in the field that we often find ourselves alone for weeks on end.

Laura chose me for her assistant after a surprisingly brief interview. I was under the sway of her charm from that first contact. She has an exceptional voice, rich in nuance and timbre, as gorgeously woven as the carpets she handles; carpets whose stories and secrets she is teaching me, in my turn, to unravel. I believe that she wants to pass her heritage on to someone. Time is catching up with her; soon enough she'll be forced to retire and leave her work behind. It's not so much losing her job that terrifies her, but losing access to the most beautiful pieces in the collection.

Everything here is organized to suit Laura: the labyrinth of racks where the most beautiful samples hang, open to her sensual, almost reverent caresses; the stand where every hook and every needle is arranged in precise order. This is her domain, but she started sharing it with me, little by little, when she realized that I loved the carpets for the same reasons she did.

Every wool carpet from Upper Kurdistan holds a slice of life in its tightly knotted weft. These carpets are so large and so complex that a weaver only completes one, two or—very rarely—three in a lifetime. Collectors look at them and marvel at the complexity of their patterns and the beauty of their shades. We examine them from the rear, where their tight stitches press against one another like the grains of sand in an hourglass. Laura guides my clumsy hands along the knots, showing me where, one day, we'll have to replace a worn strand with a new one.

Our relationship, while friendly, remained formal until last autumn. I used "vous" in addressing her, although she casually used "tu." Our fingertips frequently touched as we restored the carpets and I had learned to read the discreet murmur of her breath in the subterranean quiet. My hearing was better than hers; for her benefit, I'd make a lot of noise as I moved about—which prompted her to tease me about my clumsiness.

Then, one morning in October, I heard the mouse.

Rodents are our mortal enemies. They run silently to the easels and attack all the threads they can reach. They cause so much damage that we wage a ferocious war against them. Laura, who fears them like the plague, fills saucers with poison and places them under the pipes. I'm the one who disposes of the corpses when the odor draws our attention to them.

The mouse that I heard was very much alive. Its paws clicked on the concrete as it dashed along, and then it paused under a piece of furniture. Laura was at the other end of the room, examining a new wall-hanging from a Spanish convent. The little beast was heading straight for her.

I could have driven it away by making a racket, but it would only have come back again during the night. I picked the scissors up from the work table. My ears were pricked, ready for the slightest sound. I slid silently into the empty space between the piles of boxes and plunged toward the racing feet like a clumsy cat.

My cry of pain, as I caught my temple on the side of a trunk, made Laura jump.

Waves of pain pulsed through my skull. I might have lost consciousness for a second or two—but then I felt something wriggling against my midriff. The mouse was alive, trapped beneath my body.

I killed it with the scissors, ignoring Laura's anxious questions. Then I pulled myself to my feet, holding the lifeless little body by the tail. A drop of blood flowed down my cheek.

"A mouse," I said, shivering. "I got it."

She froze.

"Throw it out quickly! The smell might attract others!"

"I'll tell the caretaker to clean up." My head spinning, I sat down heavily on a crate. "I need a glass of water."

"Were you afraid?"

Then she felt the sticky blood on my face and quickly moved into action. She picked up a clean rag from the work bench and delicately wiped my temples. The blood clotted very quickly. Jokingly, she told me that she was prepared to give me stitches. She also said that I was an idiot, and then thanked me. The dead mouse lay on the palm of my hand as she kissed my cheek.

On several occasions during the next few days I got the feeling that Laura was trying to come to grips with some sort of decision concerning me. When you work with someone, you quickly become sensitive to this type of scrutiny. I didn't think much about it. I waited. If nothing else, the carpets teach patience.

One morning, she made up her mind. We were taking tea together—a light, perfumed Darjeeling which the departmental secretary prepared for us. Normally, we would have exchanged the latest scraps of gossip from the world outside, or talked about the cold weather that was gradually settling in. This time, I barely had the time to take a few sips of tea before she pushed her cup away.

"I've considered it, and I want to make you the gift of a story. But you'll have to read it for yourself. I'll help you . . . after all, I suppose that someone will have to take my place one day, and I'd just as soon it were you. You'll take good care of things."

I agreed. We both knew that it was true. She took my arm and led me to her office, a narrow room—all length and no breadth—where we stored documents we no longer needed. On the wall at the end, an unfinished carpet hung on an iron frame. Laura had never allowed me to examine it before. There was an open space between the wall and the frame just large enough for Laura to slide in. I had a little more trouble and made an ironic comment about my excessive girth, but Laura remained silent for a long while.

"Stories always ought to begin at the beginning," she murmured, pensively. "Unfortunately, too much is missing from this one. I came across this carpet in a trunk at the warehouse, a short while after coming to the museum. My predecessor was not very gifted as an archivist. He preferred climbing mountains in Kurdistan in search of rare samples to updating his catalogue. All that we know about this carpet is what it can teach us itself. Get started on it."

I placed my hands on the edge of the woof, palms extended for the moment of first contact. As I imposed myself upon it, the threads began to sing in the hollow of my palm, speaking to me.

"Eighth century," I said. "Alternating double stitches. The grease was removed from the wool with urine, and then the wool was boiled with plant extracts. Kurdish, I'd say. One of the mountain villages which sold their produce to the caravans. Am I right?"

"I came to the same conclusion. I've sent some threads over to the lab on several occasions, to get a little more information. The vegetable dyes are typical of Kurdistan. No more details. Frustrating, isn't it? This carpet was created in one of those villages now being destroyed by Iraqi bombs—unless, of course, it was already destroyed centuries ago, by Turkish conquerors!"

She made a visible effort to calm herself, and went on: "You're a good student. That's fine. Now, I'm going to ask you to be a little more creative. Someone wove this carpet. Try to tell me who that person might have been."

"It's a she . . ." Laura's hand gently caressed my arm. "I don't know why I say that, actually. Perhaps the way she tightens the threads, more respectfully, more economically. I believe a little girl began this carpet."

"And a woman finished it. You're right. I've taught you that much, at least. It's strange, the way that what you leave behind is nothing but a thread in the life of your successors."

"If you're lucky," I said—and I believed it.

"I'll guide you."

Her tiny hand, astonishingly firm, settled upon my huge paw and directed it towards the edge of the carpet, where a row of loose threads was dangling.

"This is where it all begins: the first knots in the weft. A child, puberty still before her, with fingers small enough to knot the pony hairs used to anchor the pattern. In the beginning, she didn't tie the hairs tightly enough, and there are irregularities. Can you feel it?"

I followed her account with the tip of my thumb, as if I were reading a book. The irregularities were barely noticeable and I wondered how long it had taken for the tale to emerge from the obscurity.

"The she improves with practice, row by row. Let's jump two or three years ahead. There, just below my index finger—what do you make of that?"

"She is becoming unsteady again, but it doesn't last."

"You aren't a girl. The first menstrual periods are upsetting, but you get used to it. You have to. So, our little weaver is beginning to grow into a woman. Do you sense how the knots have become firmer over the years? Winter, summer . . . nothing more than ripples on the surface of the pattern. Up to this point, there's nothing to set her apart from her sisters, who are doing the same work in her village. But here"—she guided my hand with assurance—"here we have our first mystery."

Between the regular knots were others, placed along the weft in groups of five, woven into the primary structure as if someone wanted to hide them. I rubbed the place with my palm, perplexed.

"Never seen that before. It's too regular to be a mistake and it doesn't serve any purpose, structurally speaking."

"Use your imagination . . ."

"A religious pattern, maybe, a secret sect thing, like some sort of rosary? The villages of that period saw the passage of preachers of every kind. Or perhaps . . . I'm stupid, aren't I, Laura! She's still just a kid. She's not rebelling or plotting against anybody. She's writing her name in the only code she knows."

"Her name, or that of a lover. Hard to know at this point. But look here. All of a sudden, the weaving is interrupted for the first time. Someone's knotted the ends so that the pattern doesn't unravel and the threads of the weft are flattened. What could possibly happen in the life of pubescent girl to keep her from work? Marriage. Our little one has become a woman in every sense of the word—who returns to her place at the loom several months later.

"What was she like? A young woman with enough strength of character to leave a little trace of herself, knowingly, in this rug. I wonder if what she'd done had been discovered, and she was hastily married off before she could become a little too independent."

"But that wouldn't hold up, if the name she wove into this carpet were her lover's!"

"I'm the one telling this story . . ." She pulled me a little further along the folds of the cloth and I felt the centuries close in upon us. With my back against the wall and my hands stretched out in front of me, I caressed the slow extension of a life whose multicolored hours were composed upon the underside of a work of art.

"Hold on to my fingers and we'll search together. It was an eighth-century marriage, in a mountain village— we ought to find a string of babies. Here's the first . . . a series of brief interruptions. The stooped position of the weaver is difficult at the end of a pregnancy. Then a pause"—the sealed-off threads were there again—"and then the work continues."

I felt her fingers stiffen. In my heightened state of awareness, something clicked into place. I moved back, her hand docilely following mine. The pregnancy, the supposed birth. A little early, maybe, but how could we know? Then the weaving starting again . . .

The knots. The knots were slack, lifeless.

"She lost her baby," I said. "It's no longer there." I couldn't say how I had fathomed it.

Laura's breath was muted by the fabric which surrounded the small space in which we were enclosed. The floor vibrated under our feet as the museum's heating system started up, with increasing frequency because of the approach of winter.

"She didn't have any more babies during the ten years which followed . . . look at the next portion of the fabric if you don't believe me. Something must have gone wrong within the beautiful human mechanism, unless her husband left her. Her fingers have regained their rhythm, but the joyous tension that drove them isn't there any more. The experts I've shown the carpet to say it lacks life. That's why I'm allowed to keep it here, supposedly for the part it plays in comparative studies. It's virtually worthless.

"So, here we have our weaver, about twenty-five years old, in an era when those women who managed to survive were grandmothers at thirty. She's sterile, probably alone. In all likelihood, she lives some way outside her village, in keeping with the tradition of the time. She weaves because there's nothing else to do, and her knots have a mechanical regularity. What has become of the rebellious child who wrote her name in the threads?"

Laura's hands fluttered and the air they stirred brushed my face like caresses woven by spiders. I returned to my reading of the weft, through interminable years without a single rough patch . . . until I felt them again: *the same knots as before* . . . A signature, the reawakening of a voice that had sunk beneath the weight of sadness.

They sprang up irregularly, for no apparent reason. Separated by whole weeks to begin with, they ended up being repeated each day. The five interlacing threads were perfectly recognizable, and my fingers read them like the characters of an unknown alphabet.

"If we knew what they called these knots, we'd know her name," I said, shaking my fingers to relieve the cramps. "Everything had a name, in that period, but that information is lost."

"I've thought about it often enough! But I suppose

the past ought to be shrouded in mystery, or we wouldn't be interested in it any more. Anyhow, we're coming to the end of the carpet and this is where things become truly strange. Read on . . ."

I drew my fingers over the woollen page: once, then again, more slowly. Somewhere, between two strands so tight that it would have been almost impossible to slide a needle between them, the narrative changed direction, escaping me. I shook my head in frustration.

"I don't understand . . ."

"I'm asking too much. I've studied this carpet all my life and things have become clear to me so gradually that I haven't the heart to force you to follow the same road as myself. But it's necessary that you make the effort to believe me, because I'm too old to put my whole life back in doubt. Read with me . . .

"There's her name, repeated like an incantation, often woven with her own hair. That lasts up to the point where one could almost believe that she'll smother under the weight of her own frustration. There are knots tied off more and more frequently: pauses in her life. I suppose that she's going further away from her village, as far as possible—that she's going deep into the mountains, as women have always done when they've wanted to be alone. She's almost forty, possessed now of that bitter kind of freedom that comes with old age. Nobody asks her for anything . . .

"And there . . . feel it!"

The narrow strip of wool bears no resemblance to any other part of the rug. The signature knots have vanished. The threads are stretched with a kind of haste, even though they're impeccably aligned. They seem to give off an impression of energy, *of joy*.

"If she were living in our era, I'd say that she found a lover," Laura murmured. "But we're in Kurdistan, more than a thousand years ago, and no man of her own day would have given her a second glance. A sterile grandmother, a body doubtless deformed by the endless years of non-stop weaving, eyes almost dead. But she found *someone* . . . The real mystery is here."

"Yes," I said, because my spirit was now in tune with hers, and I was afraid of the consequences of what I had discovered. "But the rug is broken off shortly afterwards. So?"

Laura's fingers guided mine yet again to the other side of the weft. And it was there that the story came together . . .

Among our weaver's threads were others, intertwined with them: an extraordinarily tight weave that traced motifs in relief along the length of the rug. Other knots were interlaced above these motifs in which new branches thrust out and then branched again, within the interlacings of the original. The geometry of the narration was completely different here, the characters designing a galaxy whose silken constellations were quite unknown to me.

I know my own kind, and I know weaving. The knots and the threads that were employed here were not of human origin. We don't have that many fingers, or a sense of space sufficiently finely-tuned to create such a design. The hairs were finer than horsehair, and my thumbs could barely read them. I felt that each layer hid yet another, that strange words formed new interconnections, in covering others that were hidden deeper beneath the surface. In order to read the ultimate pattern, we would have had to destroy the carpet: a sacrilege I would never have dreamed of committing.

All around, the weaver had let her happiness explode in multiple variations, beginning with the knots that were her name. In caressing the weft, I imagined two individuals bent over the same loom, their hands and their hair intertwining. I would have liked to stroke their crooked silhouettes, in order to know them better.

"What would it have looked like?" I wondered aloud. "Terrifying by virtue of being different—and yet she allowed it to touch her carpet, and her life."

Laura sighed.

"We ought to be capable of understanding. Appearance didn't mean anything to her anymore. The only thing that mattered to her was the kindness of its fingers. Years of working with minute precision in poor light had ruined her eyes. She was blind, like us."

I had to make up my own ending for the story. The weft broke off abruptly with an unfinished row, concluded in haste. I read terrible things into that absence. Cries, thrown rocks, one murder or two . . . I don't know how the rug had come into our hands. Perhaps it emerged from a grave into which bones had been cast without regard to their form. Anything is possible, so the truth is inaccessible.

But Laura's words still ring in my memory: "Intelligent beings rarely travel alone. This was no isolated explorer. I refuse to believe that no other contact was made.

"One day, perhaps, a carpet will appear that will tell a story similar to the one we have read. Together, we shall unravel the language of the threads, and then we shall teach it to all those fortunate enough to be like us. We shall teach them to read the weft, so that they may pass the knowledge on to their descendants.

"If we succeed, the next meeting won't be stopped short by appearances."

That Thing Over There

DOMINIC GREEN

Dominic Green has been publishing colorful, unusual SF adventures for the last few years in the UK. Green himself, for the moment, is a man of mystery. David Pringle, of *Interzone*, says: "I've put word about that I'm trying to contact him urgently, but no one seems to know where he is. He's generally thought to be abroad, possibly in the Netherlands or Germany, working on short-term contracts to do with the Year 2000 computer bug. That's his field of expertise, apparently, and no doubt it will be keeping him (and others like him) extremely busy all this year. I did hear tell from him about a year ago that he'd written a novel and was hoping to find a publisher; but, it seems, without success so far." This story is from *Interzone*, where he has been appearing intermittently, and is an alternate history piece unusually filled with SF stuff.

It was the summer of 2001, Year One, as all the MTV broadcasts proudly announced. And yes, I hear you sniggering behind your cybernetic replacement hands when I say "MTV," just as I sniggered at my grandfather when he said "gramophone" instead of "CD." But despite our appearance now, we were all young then, and On Top of the World. Literally.

The Chinese Government had recently decided to allow expeditions into the Khabachen district of the Qinghai Autonomous Region, Tibet in all but name, an area that had previously been politically sensitive due to the destruction by the government of several large monasteries. The monasteries had been built there due to the elevation and seclusion of the place, well away from everything apart from poor people (who get everywhere) and *yeh-teh*, that peculiar high-country word which means, literally, "That Thing Over There," and refers to a thing that walks on two legs like a man, but is not. The monastic authorities had chosen well. The Khabachen valley was situated on a plateau which had been produced when the lava of ten volcanoes, now extinct, filled a high valley dammed by ice. In this respect, it was very much like the rest of the Tibetan plateau, only higher. The medical authorities in England recommended that we all spend a month in Lhasa acclimatizing to the effects of high altitude; Chinese government advisors counselled a further two months in Lhasa in state-provided apartments, which, I was later to discover, cost ten times as much as the equivalent ethnic-minority accommodation, 50 percent of which went to actual Tibetans, and 40 percent of which went to that peculiar place to which percentages disappear in China.

The five monasteries in the area had been built by a subdivision of the Tibetan buddhist faith known as the Brown Hat Sect, a group about which our contacts in the relatively modern Yellow Hat ruling sect could provide little information, and which was said to have been a transparent front for the continued practice of Bonpoba, the original and faintly unpleasant religion of the Tibetan plateau. The Brown Hatters had been repeatedly purged for claiming to have been present in the highlands before the arrival of Padmasambhava, and to be the guardians of a place where an entire country of demons had been exorcised by the drivers of the Great Vehicle. Good ordinary Buddhists were cautioned against approaching the area with tales of *yeh-teh*. In much the same way, perhaps, good ordinary present-day Communists have been discouraged from approaching Chinese army bases with stories of radioactivity and live ammunition practice.

According to legend, Nyatri Tsanpo, the first King of Tibet, had fought a great battle with cunning sorcerers here a thousand years ago, and had forced them back to this highland region, where they were finally destroyed, but not before their lord sorcerer, the wicked Nyiga Gedgyinigesa, had worked a great spell which froze 10,000 of their army into stone statues, awaiting the time when they would march down once more and make war upon the world. This story had been written by a ninth-century buddhist chronicler— it had happened a thousand years ago then, too—and it was evident that he had heard much of the Terra Cotta Army of the tomb of the Yellow Emperor of Qin China. It was possible that the chronicler, upon hearing of the Army and its similar intended function, had wished to curry favor with the powerful Chinese factions that have always been part of the Tibetan land-scape, and to make clear, of course, that the idea had been had by Tibetans first. In any case, the prospect of discovering another Terra Cotta Army was not absent from our minds as we drove into the highlands to set up our base camp.

Satellite photographs, computer-enhanced using tech-niques previously only available to the military to bring out straight-line details such as walls and roads, already told us that traces of man-made structures existed in the high Khabachen valley, and that, furthermore, Mon Sa, the Tibetan village at which we had been instructed we could set up our Base Camp by the Chinese government, had previously existed in no less than three separate shift-ing locations. Driving into the village, our architectural expert, Chak Kuang, identified two earlier settlements placed by Tocharian and Chi'ang Tibetan cultures. The present inhabitants, living in metal-and-plastic com-munes built from materials obviously transported from lower altitudes, were the descendants of Tibetan low-landers driven up here by recent forcible land appropri-ations by Han Chinese. No wonder, then, that our hosts pointed wildly up the mountains and told us that an army of *yeh-teh* existed just over the hill. We could not investigate this, of course, as "just over the hill" was still vertically the distance from Tower Bridge to Westmin-ster, and looked, furthermore, unattainable for any vehi-cle not possessing fur and four legs; but we contented ourselves with the thought that, if there was an army of frozen sorcerers up there, they would stay frozen another day beyond a thousand years.

About halfway through the evening of the first night, however, our specialist, Janine Groening, burst in a highly agitated state into the prefab hut which we were occupying. I remember her grabbing my arm and dragging me outside.

She claimed to have discovered the third location of Mon Sa; an ancient, loess-covered structure only a few inches down in the soil, constructed of what she insisted was the same poured concrete used by the Roman Empire for the production of its major architecture. Now, it was not quite as beyond the bounds of possibility as one might think for a Roman cultural outpost to have existed in Tibet; the Parthian Empire had captured 10,000 Roman soldiers at the battle of Carrhae in 53 B.C., and resettled them on its considerable borders, which had abutted Han Chinese borders in many places following the Han conquest of the Tarim Basin. However, I could not quite lend credence to such a radical reinterpretation of history, and indeed, upon reexamination of the stonework, Janine was forced to conclude that the masonry was not Roman, for it was made of standardized non-cuboid blocks which tessellated in three dimensions. Whatever stresses acted on this masonry would meet with resistance in no matter which way they pushed.

Furthermore, the walls appeared to possess rusted reinforcing iron staples driven completely through them, in the way in which fanciful theory would have the Incas building Quito. The rusting of the staples had been retarded by the fact that, like the ones that hadn't been discovered in Quito, they appeared to have been plated with silver.

At this point we were simultaneously both tremendously excited and extremely wary, particularly of our Communist hosts, for there were entire Viking armies full of axes to grind concerning preternaturally advanced civilizations being discovered on the Tibetan Plateau. No doubt, we joked with one another as we worked to uncover the walls, we would also find perfectly preserved specimens of Peking Men wearing Chinese Army uniforms. Therefore, our preliminary investigations were confined to searching the entire structure minutely for traces of chocolate-bar wrappers and cigarettes. We were most excited by the prospect of finding something still more impressive on the other side of the hill; if the other side of the hill had proven to hold a previously undiscovered monastery, or a boring old settlement, we would at that juncture had been terribly disappointed. However, it did not, and we weren't.

We started out extremely early in the morning, at around five, in order to catch the Chinese secret policemen even Chak Kuang was convinced were busy up there with their scaffolding and mechanical diggers. The trail was harder than if it had been set with nails, and our lungs felt as if they were filled with white hot hydrazine. Our faces were ghost-pale with sun-block factor n. Being up in the Tibetan highlands was the nearest a common man of my century could come to being in outer space. The sky up there grows purple, rather than red, in the evening, I swear it. If you whirl your hand through the air, there is no air there. Now, I am too old to travel on orbital transports; no company will insure me, with such a weak heart. But once I stood on the threshold of the stars.

We stood on the crest of the hill, and, ours being a multiracial party, swore in seven languages simultaneously. There, on the saddle between two mountains, stood an entire city never seen before by Western Man— the city we were to come to call Voorniin.

Eastern Man had been here before, of course; we found a Chinese Kilroy Was Here inscription on the western pillar of the great gate, still standing after however many thousand years. It was modern, of course, but quite old; some soldier had been up here with a motorized battalion, perhaps in the early 1950s, the days of territorial confrontation between China and India. It stood right next to a second inscription from the first Han Dynasty. Those two soldiers had visited this city a thousand years apart, and no other soul except perhaps the odd Tibetan yak-herd had struggled up here during all that time. Neither soldier had truly known what he was seeing.

The walls were built of the same queer interlocked blocks. The streets, as we moved in through the great iron gate, were paved and pavemented and possessed closed sewers. There had at some point been glass in all the windows. Zanskar, a thousand miles to the south, and perhaps the world's one remaining nation which can claim to be aboriginally Tibetan in its culture, possesses one pane of glass in its entire 200-mile extent, and that one in the palace of a king. Here we were finding glass panes in the houses of the poor; and in every house we found the *yeh-teh*.

The corpses were many, and mummified by the high altitude, aridity and cold in a way that an Egyptian pyramid full of refrigerators would never have been able to achieve. They still had their hair, which was a uniform ashen white, as if the hair of those who in life had been blondes and brunettes had grown silver in a thousand years of post-mortal aging up here on the mountainside while they waited for us to come.

They had a written language, which seemed to be alphabetic. However, once this single similarity was dispensed with, it appeared to have no connection whatsoever with even the oldest of Tibetan scripts. They wove cloth in volumes which suggested they possessed looms, and indeed in airy stone chambers just off the main thoroughfare we found a great battery of such devices. They had hypocausts and copper piping connecting every room. In one high tower at the extreme northern end of the city we discovered a lacquered wooden tube containing two smashed lenticular pieces of glass, suggesting an acquaintance with telescopes and astronomy. Constellations were found drawn all over the domed ceiling of one chamber, along with a wooden astrolabe, all of this wood obviously having required to be transported here from some considerable distance. The constellations looked like nothing known to man, with the exception of Scorpio, which I recognized immediately; I remembered having read in a book long ago that Scorpio was one of the few constellations whose stars had not moved markedly relative to the Sun since Ptolemy's original classification, so that its present-day form was still similar to the form it had taken before the birth of Christ.

It was at that point that Angela Reinicke, our paleoanthropologist, was discovered sitting holding a corpse's wrist, as if taking its pulse, staring mutely down at the hand.

It was not only that the corpse had five fingers and one thumb, nor even that the other hand was exactly the same. Mutations of this sort, although uncommon, were not impossible, after all. It was the fact that the last six corpses she had checked had also had the same characteristics. I, too, had had a weird feeling every time I had passed one of the frozen corpses, but, like the four fingers on Mickey Mouse, it had been a thing which one noticed without realizing why it seemed wrong.

We had been so busy flabbergasting ourselves with what could be found inside the walls that we failed to concern ourselves with what might lie outside them. However, the sound of Janine Groening calling from the scree-littered slopes beyond the city drew us out of the gate.

She had found a metal arrowhead embedded in the mortar of an outlying wall, inscribed with primitive symbols familiar from grave finds from the Ch'iang culture of pre-Buddhist Tibet. This in itself was the first truly significant find of the day, which may sound odd; but to an archaeologist a city totally unrelated to any culture found before is an exasperating quantity until he has some external evidence with which to paste it into the palimpsest of Time. Now we knew that these people, whoever they had been, had come into conflict with the Ch'iang culture, which could be dated back as far as 4,000 B.C. until the time of the Yarlung Dynasty of the European Dark Ages. Now we had a temporal box into which to put our culture—albeit a very big one.

We also found bodies outside the walls, after a cursory search; bodies in rough but workmanlike military graves, many dressed in Tibetan peasant robes that hadn't changed much in the two thousand years between then and now. You must understand that in those days polyester was almost unknown in Tibet. They appeared to have been buried with military honors, which in their cases amounted to messages in Greek and Sanskrit scripts—at that time both quite widely-used languages in Bactria, to the southwest of the Tibetan plateau—scratched into rough headstones. We were surprised to find not only Sanskrit dedications, but also some in the *Wen-yan* Chinese script, and a single headstone written in the rarely-found Tocharian language, an Indo-European tongue known to have once been spoken in what is now Western China. This last was a particularly interesting find, for it proved that the Tocharian-speaking peoples (as opposed to the Tocharian peoples themselves, who were of course Completely Different) had existed in the Western Regions around two hundred years before their previous supposed first colonization of the area. All these peoples, it seemed, had come all the way up into these highlands which it had taken us thirty days to penetrate using modern motor vehicles, and fought, sustaining terrible casualties, against the people of the walled city. We counted twenty thousand grave markers in all.

However, it was the words spelled out in Chinese on Janine's arrowhead that sent a chill down our spines—and at those altitudes, it takes a lot to send a chill down already frozen vertebrae.

The words were DEATH TO DEMONS.

At first we imagined that these widely differing armies had been fighting each other for the great prize of the city. After examination of the ruins of siegeworks and collapsed supply-tunnels all about the city, however, we realized that all these many thousand soldiers had come all this way up here as a unified, multinational force purely in order to confront the city's inhabitants and kill them. This would have had to have been a most single-minded enterprise, for some of these soldiers must have come from the environs of modern-day China, and the gear and clothing of soldiers found in certain graves suggested that a Hsiung-Nu force had accompanied the Chinese detachment. Cementing an alliance between the nomad Hsiung-Nu and the Chinese would have been a feat well nigh impossible at that time, for the Qin Dynasty were shortly to involve themselves in walling off the entire continent from their nomadic neighbours, such was the enmity between them. Chak Kuang, for one, refused to believe that the troops of this army could have originated in China. To move such a body of men and weapons over a thousand miles beyond the Chinese border through heaven alone knew how many petty warlords' sovereign territories would have required a cooperation from the Tibetan people never since seen in the history of these two nations, plus the presence of an enemy mutually threatening enough to move both peoples to join forces against it.

Due to the Burning of the Books by Emperor Qin Shi Huangdi, little record survives of that early period of

Chinese history, almost as if the Emperor had wanted to hide some dramatic or traumatic event. Perhaps this act of genocide against a peaceful, hill-dwelling people had been an episode in his reign which had excited adverse comment. After all, how much remains to us of the ancient Chavin or Nazca cultures from before the time of the Inca? And how much truly-related European history would have survived had the Nazis won at El Alamein and Stalingrad? Can we be sure that the history which did survive those two battles is entirely unblemished?

It was at that point that we noticed that an assumption we had made regarding the pre-death ages of the corpses was sorely mistaken. We had assumed that all the bodies found in the city had simply been those of the aged and decrepit, who had been left behind at home when the city's men and womenfolk went to war. However, the discovery of a small and silver-haired child in one of the many temples put paid to that theory. It seemed on subsequent reanalysis of the bodies that, queer as it might have seemed, every single inhabitant of the city had been an albino. Possibly, we reasoned, the superficially strange appearance of the city's people had inspired their lowland neighbours to attack them.

However, it was judged that the position of the child's body, on the temple altar with no less than thirteen exquisitely-crafted steel daggers driven through its vital organs, was a more likely cause of enmity. Over sixty further small skulls were found neatly stacked on a rotating spiked drum, oddly reminiscent of a newsagent's book stack, at the rear of the temple. And yes, they had had steel. Steel swords were in the minority, however; instead, we discovered paranoiacally extensive armories of huge steel darts which could be linked by chains and fired from simultaneously triggered ballista-type devices mounted on the walls, perfectly preserved in the waterless Tibetan air. The sinew-and-tendon ropes used to power the catapults had split and rotted in the cold, but otherwise many of the weapons almost seemed as if they might still be serviceable today—when I say today, of course, I mean yesterday, in the first years of this aging century. The number of Chinese, Tibetan, Persian, Tartar and Tocharian soldiers found dead and buried outside the walls with leg injuries bore witness to the ballistae having been highly effective in their heyday. However, despite the much-trumpeted effectiveness of Asiatic compound projectile weapons, the number of war casualties found buried close to the city walls was far lower than the huge quantity of uninjured corpses found in and around the camp of the besiegers. Many of the exhumed soldiers had toes and fingers missing, a fact which pointed to the ill state of preparation of their armies in ascending to such a frigid altitude.

The city-dwellers' way of life had been violent and unpleasant—there appeared to have been no room for failure in what we were soon to come to call Niige society, and graphic depictions of incompetent high officials being ignominiously cast into pits of wolves and tigers abounded. Their society was a democracy, one of the few ever found independently of the Greek model; but non-Niige were not allowed to vote. They were, however, allowed to die, and Tibetan, Hsiung-Nu and Chinese slaves farmed the fields and mined the mines. When the miners died, the unnecessary expense of transporting them to the surface was eschewed; they were cast into an ice cave on the lower levels, where they froze gruesomely into the faces of subterranean waterfalls when the ice flowed over the years. I have not personally visited the ice caves, but the first spelunkers to penetrate down that far were driven to swear they would never venture into the Voorniin Mine again.

They mined iron, of course, not gold or silver, although these metals might have also existed high on this igneous plateau. However, they were less plentiful than iron, and less useful; the Niige appeared to have learned the lesson in advance that history is filled with races whose sparkling hoards of gold and silver were plundered by invading hordes of iron-miners. The Niige were, I am convinced, the "Sons of Reflected Light," those semi-mythical creatures who had descended to the Chinese lowlands and contributed to the Qin and Zhou cultures their unfair head start of early knowledge in the fields of medicine, philosophy, and magic. And what does one do with a benefactor who demonstrates his superior knowledge to one's dirtbound primitive people? Why, one fears him, and to fear is to hate, and to hate is to destroy.

But there were other reasons why the Chinese and Tibetan inhabitants of that region would have feared and hated the alien culture. These reasons were plastered all over their walls and carved into their caryatid columns in what had once been glorious technicolor. They did not appear to worship gods as such; rather, they appeared to have transcended this meaningless extravagance. What we had at first taken for temples of human sacrifice were in fact anatomical research theaters and chambers for the interrogation of luckless victims taken in battle. Anatomical examinations were carried out with the subject still alive, for preference—a most logical conclusion, since how can any truly conscientious healer truly understand the functioning of a living breathing human, unless he has cut a man up while he is still alive and breathing?

The child in the temple, we were soon to discover, had not been sacrificed, but had instead been the subject of a dissection to determine whether or not Niige War Savants had been able to infect him with a particularly virulent strain of cholera prevalent at that time in the city. Had he been so infected, say the notes that they had left, they would have contaminated a few more children and hurled them over the walls into the enemy. According to their journals, they had tried the same thing with the corpses of yaks a week or so earlier, only to be disappointed, as yaks seemed not to be sufficiently similar to human beings to communicate the bacillus. Had the small boy been spared due to the efficacy of yaks, the journals tell us, he would have been eaten. Adults, of course, were needed in the fight against the Zuiev, or Non-Niige, whereas children could easily be replaced; and once a child had been allowed to die to prevent a drain on the food bins, it would be a shame to waste such a handy meat supply.

Their word for themselves—their tongue was eventually decoded, with the aid of the two Cray computers run by the BABEL project in Los Angeles and reference to Elamite, a language isolate from ancient Mesopotamia—means, quite simply, "Us." Their word for anyone who was not "Niige," "Us," was "Zuiev." This term was at best contemptuous, and at worst had the same register which one would use to describe a trained animal. The Niige's ancestors had originated in the lowlands south of the Himalaya, a land called by them Adamdi; having been persecuted by numerous kings for unspecified religious practices, they had then fled to the northern uplands where they had served the Bon priests of Tibet as jewelers and brewers, bringing with them trades their people had presumably learned in Mesopotamia. However, with the birth of the first true Niige child—an event the Bon had interpreted as an evil omen, and the Niige's ancestors as a sure sign of the favor of the gods—local opinion had turned gradually against the southerners, and they had been forced still further into the highlands, where they had taken great pride in constructing a city where no city should have been able to be built. However, this had not been the end of their misfortunes, for, alarmed at the thought that the city of the Bai Ch'iang, the "White Tibetans," was flourishing and was, further-more, now termed the "Black Jewel of the Mountains," the neighboring kings of Qin, and the chieftains of the Hsiung-Nu, Yueh-Chih, and Ch'iang, decided jealously to march against the Niige. And they brought a great army into the highlands, the greatest that had ever been seen by Man, and laid siege to the City of Voorniin, Beloved of Fate. This last sentence is a verbatim quote from the penultimate passage of a hundred-year history carved into the wall of a city whose stone blocks were hacked bodily out of granite by a people possessing little more than the hands on the ends of their arms.

This penultimate passage should be tragic, and it would have been, like the Hittite inscriptions on the coming of the Sea Peoples which break off in mid-sentence, had it not been for the fact that it *was* the penultimate passage. The last passage had been carved by a firm, unshaking, absolutely self-assuredly deliber-ate six-fingered hand, and went as follows:

"Witness my hand these one hundred and seventeen years past the foundation of the City of the Chosen; I, Rezadrakedel, philosopher and counselor to our nation, take it upon myself to ensure the survival of our seed. Therefore, I decree that, like wasps in winter, we shall take ourselves to the insides of our houses and die, for *there shall come a time when we shall rise again.*"

That phrase—"philosopher and counselor"—has been translated as "priest-king," and even "warrior-prophet," by some of the more sensational newspapers. However, as I have said before, the Niige had no priests. They were not scared even of Heaven. The phrase "Gediniyezal," from which the English has been translated, means some-thing between "knower" and "advisor." Rezadrakedel had been no priest. He had been a scientist, or the closest thing to one that any Iron Age city could produce; and one of the hobbies of scientists is the prediction of future scientific advancement. Rezadrakedel had doubtless seen many innovations and advancements in his seventy-year lifespan, especially when one considers that his city's entire history had only spanned a hundred years. He must also have known that summer never came to the high plains where the City was situated, and that its inhabitants must needs trade iron and bright worthless stones with the peoples of the warm valleys on all sides in order to obtain food, playing one ethnically prejudiced despot against another. Indeed, it appeared to have been only the alliance of these despots in the assault upon the City that brought the Niige to their unaccustomed kneeling position, for the mighty defenses of Voorniin's curtain walls do not appear to have been much dented by the puny forces that their primitive attackers were able to drag up the mountain with them.

It is, of course, well nigh impossible to raise proper siege engines to such an altitude. The fact that the Niige themselves appeared to have managed it, and to have housed entire batteries of such devices within their city walls, is immaterial. The Niige died of starvation, not of sword-wounds; they had known they were about to be forced into surrender by diminishing food reserves, and had so inscribed bad-loser curses in the names of nebulous Bon and Elamite demons in whom they no longer believed all round the gateways of their stronghold, and had committed businesslike suicide, allowing their enemies to enter the city and butcher all who had not obeyed the philosopher/counselor's decree. And the butchers had been thorough—old Chinese inscriptions found on the wall of a deep well by one wall of the stronghold announce that three Niige survivors had been discovered attempting to hide down here and were "killed immediately." Not tortured. Not buried alive. But "killed immediately."

Like lepers. Like a virus that might spread down from the mountains and infect the human race.

The Chinese and Tibetan warlords had been foresighted enough to realize that here the Gods had been kind enough to place a terrible threat to the security of their kingdoms in a location where it could grow only very slowly, and could be effectively dealt with using sufficiently single-minded force. Rezadrakedel, however, had perhaps been even wiser. As a scientist, he knew that Men could think of new ways to tackle almost any problem, and he had doubtless seen primitive aboriginal Zuiev bow down in wonder before the splendors of his high City and proclaim them to be nothing short of sorcery. Why, then, should things thought of as sorcery by his own kind not also come to pass one day?

Rezadrakedel might have observed, as did Roger Bacon in medieval England, that slave bodies thrown into the corpse pits in the mines did not spoil. He might have looked to the limitations of even his own scalpel-sharp brain. He might have considered that, *astounding though it might sound that the frozen corpses of his people might one day be found and restored to life*, it was not beyond the bounds of possibility. A race of men might one day exist who were to him technologically as he was to a Zuiev peasant; a race of men who might be stupid enough to dig up his entire people, resurrect them, and let them loose again upon the world. Is it a coincidence that the most perfectly-preserved of the corpses discovered at Voorniin were those of Niige aristocrats who threw themselves into a deep pit on top of a hundred slave corpses, and then had a thousand gallons of water poured down onto their bodies when the main water butt that supplied the entire mine was deliberately broken by Zuiev slaves?

▲   ▲   ▲

I have stood on a man-made tower on the shoulders of a mountain range so high that for an ordinary human being to struggle up to it is akin to a deep-sea anglerfish swimming upriver and hurling itself up Alpine waterfalls like a salmon. And that tower had been built by people over two hundred years before the birth of that man the Romans nailed to History as an arbitrary milestone, Christ. People—but not humans. If they'd been human, they would surely never have shone so brightly in a place where even a struck match has trouble burning.

Oh, they had human DNA all right; there was of course an initial "Pack-Yaks of the Gods" period of insistence by bearded lunatics that the Niige had been Alien Thetans from Outer Space, but this had been dispelled semi-instantly by the very first tests of genetic material brought down from Voorniin, "The Place Where We Live." The genetic tests proved that the genetic basis for the Niige had indeed been human, and that they had possessed a genetic structure 90-odd percent identical to that of humans. However, so does a mountain gorilla. It was quite quickly realized that there was something new about the Niige—headlines screamed such things as "Asiatic Super City Found on Tibetan Plateau," "Beijing Claims Chinese Descended From Proto-Tibetans," and "Baghdad Claims Supermen Still Live in Mesopotamia." The race was on to identify one's ancestry with a people whom, paradoxically, one's ancestors had been attempting only a couple of thousand years previously to exterminate with extreme prejudice.

And then the news came from laboratories in Switzerland that sperm cells had been discovered still alive in Niige corpses.

The discovery was natural enough; frozen mammoths had been dug up in Siberia, and certain deranged scientists had insisted that it was now possible to clone a mammoth as a consequence. When "ice men" had been discovered frozen in the passes of the Alps, equally differently sane women had written to the authorities responsible to insist that they be allowed to have Cro-Magnon Babies through modern genetic technology. Now, however, what had been dug up was not a Neanderthal, but a putative Superman, and modern genetic technology had moved twenty years further on. Rich women flocked to the inevitable spate of discreet clinics in their thousands as frozen sperm samples went missing from bio labs and museums. The demand for albino and polydactyloid sperm in normal workaday sperm banks, meanwhile, went unaccountably ballistic. Within two years, the number of albino inhabitants of Beverly Hills had multiplied tenfold as divorced old actresses bore superbeings like breed cows. Everything in our society could be sold then, even frozen jism hacked from a dead man's gonads.

But were the things they were birthing supermen? Evolutionists have never argued that there is such a thing as a superior or inferior species, only one more or less well adapted to prevailing conditions which may change at any time. Certainly the Niige seem better adapted to succeed under present conditions than we do; over the past few years we have seen their children going through High School, West Point and Harvard, attaining PhD's, knighthoods, and Nobel Prizes with effortless ease.

It's been stated that they have superior pattern-recognition skills, superior all-round cognitive ability, enhanced this, hyperevolved that. However, as I hear such explanations I cannot help recalling the thousand-year-dead face of the little boy torn apart upon the altar. Can it not simply be that the Niige have always possessed little or no concern for life of any sort? Was the strength of will to push human beings to their almost certain deaths in the name of experimentation not an immense benefit to the researches of Nazi scientists at Auschwitz? Is "success at any price" not always going to defeat "success tempered with compassion" in any enterprise?

I have submitted this manuscript to a number of national newspapers. All of them are owned by Niige. Short of publishing the document on the Web, I see little hope of ever seeing it reach a wide audience. Am I voicing the same concerns, perhaps, as were voiced by old-money Weimar Berliners who looked from their crumbling mansions to see successful *nouveau riche* Jews and homosexuals strutting round the *Unter Den Linden*? Only history will tell.

Rezadrakedel, who was discovered in an ice-chunk of great size at the very bottom of the mine, was removed and shipped inside his watery grave to New York in a refrigerated container. I pay my reduced fare every morning on the subway to go and see him. Somehow, he contrived to die with his eyes open, and though his eyes must surely have dried and cracked to unusable blisters in his face before the ice of the cave closed over him, they still stare out from under a foot of ice at parties of schoolchildren gawping at his silver hair and perfectly-preserved fine garments. Although I can see from my reflection in the ice surface that I have grown old in the interim, the Gediniyezal has not aged a day. The surface of the ice has been cut flat and polished using specially-developed techniques, and there is a red dot on the museum floor where visitors may stand and ensure that Exhibit 234A, Rezadrakedel, warrior-prophet of Voorniin, is looking them straight in the eye.

And, despite the fact that it must be fearfully cold in there, the old bastard is smiling.

The Allies

MARK S. GESTON

Mark S. Geston emerged as an SF writer in the late 1960s and early '70s with *Lords of the Starship* (1967), *Out of the Mouth of the Dragon* (1969), *The Day Star* (1972), and *The Siege of Wonder* (1976), and then took a break from the field for almost two decades, (while practicing law in Boise, Idaho) until the publication of *Mirror to the Sky* (1992). This story is from *F&SF* and is reminiscent of the classic SF of Clifford D. Simak in its elegiac tone, especially his City series, which tells of the relationship between humans and dogs over millennia. Like the Benford, above, this long story contains all the material and ideas for a good SF novel. But both the sentiment and the underlying irony in this work are Geston's own.

I was to have been the Captain of the First Ship, but she was destroyed before completion. I was on my way to the building yard in Kazakstan and watched on my transport's situation boards. The saturation attack squandered formations of surface darts, hypersonic cruisers and sub-orbitals with a profligacy unusual for the enemy. Their weapons were always well shielded and at least one out of any five would have gotten through the Ship's defensive hemisphere with their usual tactical approaches. But eighty-nine weapons were sent against her, each with a standard half megaton charge. Forty-one reached the yard's perimeter; of these, fourteen were neutralized by the perfectly simultaneous detonation of the first twenty-seven.

The effect was devastating, even against such a vast target. The central blast crater was almost a kilometer wide and a hundred meters deep. The surface of the Earth was smelted into green glass for a radius of eight kilometers from it. The relief column from Baku found nothing alive more complex than bacteria when it arrived three days later.

It had become obvious how greatly they prized our world and everything on it but us by the fifth year of our conflict. Their weapons were normally used with economy and dismaying accuracy so that nothing but humankind and our works were destroyed. Fusion weapons were directed against the great cities, but never where their shock waves would escape built-up areas. That was thought to have been why New York was never bombed, out of concern for the green expanse of

Central Park. Surface darts were sent to cut all the bridges, pipelines and cables, and fly down the entrances to the river tunnels. The city was effectively besieged and starved into submission in a month.

In the towns and villages that could not be attacked by fusion devices without harming the surrounding countryside, the enemy's agents would appear in small groups or as lone assassins and patiently liquidate everyone who lived there. The rest of us, on our side of the front, listened on the net and heard the people drop away, one by one, even if there were thousands in the distant valley and the process took months. The carrier waves remained, linking us to the dead, until the enemy removed the solar panels and took the translator stations down from the mountain tops.

Reconnaissance showed the Earth flourishing where we had been driven out and the enemy's rule was absolute. The ruins of cities and towns were swept away, granulated and spread across the open spaces to become topsoil or atmospheric dust. (How we remembered the sunsets of those bitter years!) The roads were torn up, the bridges and dams removed, and our ground reseeded with buffalo grass, redwood and oak. Their desert reclaimed the Suez Canal, and the jungle erased the Panama Canal.

The animals returned. Censuses were easy over the infrared band; they left many of the general survey satellites alone as if they wanted us to see what was happening. There were herds of fallow deer in the Bois de Boulogne four years after Paris was leveled. Such a thing would have been a memory to Philip the Fair.

East Africa was easily conquered; after the pandemics of the decade before the war there was hardly anyone left there but miners anyway. We saw the miracles there too. The weather stabilized and the rains came back to the veldt, but that might have had nothing to do

with the enemy. The herds of wildebeest and impala
returned with the long grasses. Lions and cheetahs and
other predators unseen for fifty years reappeared in
numbers that suggested they had only been hiding
instead of having been on the edge of extinction, as
everyone had thought.

Laser spectrometry from the low orbit satellites
showed that water from the Rhine was clean enough to
drink six years after Germany and France were crushed.
The Amazon was even more quickly thronged with
white dolphins after the fall of Brazil.

The oceans under their control were similarly
cleansed. Moles and jetties were scoured from the rims
of harbors. The ships left behind were taken apart at
night and reduced to elemental forms we had no way of
detecting. The whales returned in profusion and our
submarines reported hearing scornful choruses from
newly reconstituted pods rolling through the Pillars of
Hercules and up the Sunda Strait into the Java Sea.

They built only a few installations and enigmatic
structures that might have been garrison towns for
themselves. There were never any embassies or responses
to our demands for negotiation. The ultimatum that
they issued upon their first landing was repeated regularly; it never changed in tone or wording. Throughout
the years of conflict, it was the only thing they ever said
to us.

We knew by the tenth year we could not beat them,
and by the fifteenth the best informed people were privately saying they would win. They would pursue their
implacable strategy until there were no more people left,
but then the rest of the world would blossom in a way
that we had never been rich enough to afford.

Great care was taken to understand what was going
on in the occupied territories: how many extinctions
were averted, how many rare species suddenly brought

back to Edenic plenitude, how many thousands of square kilometers of forest reclaimed, dams removed, highways torn up and the ground resown, cities leveled and the places where all the people had been murdered turned into gardens. What was similarly noticed but much less talked about was how impoverished our remaining lands became. What few animals remained with us either sickened and died or just vanished when we were not looking. Either that, or they were the targets of rage and frustration and were the subject of eradication campaigns. Thus, the pigeons and starlings were erased from New York before its siege and all the squirrels in Boston were killed in one July. After the fifteenth year, it seemed like the only animals left were those held captive in zoos or the few anachronistic farms that depended on such things.

"When was the last time I saw a bird?" my father asked me shortly before he died. "Just a crow or a seagull? When? A year? Five? Is that possible?" He was not looking at me, but all around at the sky, as if he had misplaced these creatures on a neglected atmospheric shelf and forgotten them.

The idea of their pastoral glory inhibited our offensive operations. We became reluctant to use the area weapons that had served so well in the opening phases of the war. Castle Romeo and Castle Sierra devices could incinerate five thousand square kilometers with one low air-burst but had an extraordinarily low radiation signature; they had wiped out the first enemy footholds on Madagascar and Mindanao. But nothing like that was used after the tenth year. They had beaten us and brought our inheritance back to life as if in rebuke, and we were hesitant to destroy it again.

Preparations for departure began even before the secret of stellar flight was stolen from an enemy cruiser brought down over Wyoming. Half the world was still left to us then, so there were enough resources to build six immense ships. If everything went perfectly, we would save ten million people; less than one half of one percent of the population before the war began.

But the First Ship was destroyed before she was ready, and the same thing happened to the Fifth Ship at her building yard northwest of Buenos Aires. The Second Ship had embarked two million crew members and passengers and was attacked as it accelerated for takeoff across the Sea of Japan and brought down.

At the loss of the First Ship, I was reassigned as Captain of the last, the Sixth Ship. Since I had been chosen by lottery in the first place, I did not feel cheated. I would still be responsible for eight hundred thousand people. I was also secretly relieved that other Captains would go out ahead of me and test the enemy's defenses and the efficacy of the secret we had stolen from them. There was also, however, the realization that I would command the last ship to leave Earth, and this idea sometimes paralyzed me with tragic imaginings. I was attended by three times the number of psychiatrists and counselors that I had been before my new posting.

The loss of the Third Ship, which was the largest and most heavily armed of all, was the most disheartening. It carried four and a third million of the best people that could be found in Southeast Asia and Oceania away from a field masterfully hidden in the jungle near Angor Wat. It attained its parking orbit, swatted aside the enemy's destroyers with unexpected ease and even wiped out one of their nightly supply convoys in a display of firepower that lit up the night sky over central Asia so brightly that minarets in faraway Islamabad cast shadows.

The Third Ship asked if she should stay to fight the war but she was told to flee as planned. Perhaps even that short delay had been enough to let the enemy regroup; it was equally likely that they had not been unprepared at all, and the Third Ship had just been lucky.

Everyone left behind in the night's hemisphere watched its plasma trail blossom around it to cover a quarter of the welkin as the first quantum dimensions were unfolded by its Captain. Immense panels on the Ship's surface moved to harmonize its shape to the singular reality being constructed to accommodate its passage through the void, and this made it glitter in the reflected light of its own nebula.

The enemy was waiting for the Third Ship behind Mars, and the ferocity of their assault was visible even at that distance. So great was the weight of destruction thrust upon her that the cone of a Lunar shadow was traced on the dust of her prior engagements.

But while the Third Ship was dying, the smallest of the fleet, the Fourth Ship carrying only two hundred thousand people from North Africa, abruptly left its building field at Tobruk, accelerated over the Mediterranean west of Malta, and then ascended into a dangerously low, nearly atmospheric orbit. At the moment the attack was initiated against her larger sister, her Captain unfolded the first quantum dimension and brought her up and then out at right angles to the ecliptic, up toward Polaris and away from the plane of the galaxy.

"We have to go," I told my superiors as soon as I realized they might succeed.

I was instructed to wait, that rather than being thrown into disarray, the enemy had only been alerted and they would cover every possible avenue of escape. Unlike any of her sisters, the Sixth Ship was constructed underground, and the enemy would not detect her underneath the vacant prairie lands west of Kearney, Nebraska. We could afford to wait.

It was impossible, I pleaded. Our own ground pen-
etration radar could detect something as massive as the
Ship. And the enemy must eventually notice how the city
had grown in the past five years, how ground and air
traffic to it had increased so. The miracle was that the
city had not already had enemy assassins quietly working their way through its population, let alone received a
gratuitous half-megaton.

They relented and the Ship was prepared. A month
was needed, during which the grasses died around Kearney. I thought that the clouds of topsoil that the wind
lifted up from the barren Earth would hide the Sixth
Ship's hiding place. Studies by my people also showed
that the static electricity generated by such dust storms
would blind the enemy's sensors.

The plains were an autumnal desert by the time we
were ready. Bates, a geologist, was in the car with me.
The iron-colored city passed on the north side of the
perimeter highway. He had been talking about how he
was looking forward to leaving and going to sleep for
several objective centuries while I was unfolding and
folding quantum dimensions as if they were origami.
Then he suddenly asked, "Killed the dog yet?"

"Excuse me?" I didn't have one.

He was a reasonably good friend, but still looked
embarrassed, as if he had affronted my rank. "You
know. Killed the dog. Sold the house or paid up the
insurance." He spun his right hand up in the air as if to
conjure something out of it. "Uh, done whatever you
have to do to clean up your affairs here and leave. Forever."

"Sure." I hadn't heard that one, but I spent most of
my time with my training staff and my psychological
handlers. Still, it seemed an odd choice of phrase. "Have
you?"

His expression changed. "Last week. See? It can be

the literal truth. We took her to the vet and had her put down. She was pretty old and it would have happened soon anyway, even without us leaving. The administrative people've taken care of whatever else's to be left behind."

I followed Bates's stare back toward the city. "Jesus. Not that we brought much to this place anyway." I assumed he was marveling at how little we had left to defend by now. I was. Knowledge of what the occupied territories looked like made it so much worse.

I tried to distract him. "But not drown the cat? Or . . ." I tried to think of a kind of pet generally obnoxious enough to warrant strangulation. "Or terminate the parrot?"

"But why should anyone think of doing that?" he responded with genuine interest, as if I had asked something meant to do more than fill up an awkward pause. "There haven't been anything in Kearney but dogs since I got here." He was right. "I thought it was just the way people who came here were. You know? But every other place I've visited lately seems to be the same way. Just a few dogs and nothing else that wasn't already in a cage before the war began." He shook his head, as if this puzzle had defeated him before.

I stupidly kept trying to shake him out of his reverie. "So I envision long columns of refugee cats and escaped zoo animals, trudging through no man's land, toward the green walls of the occupied territories." *Sure. And leaving burning, miniature cat shtetls behind, walking down the muddy road, pushing carts before them, away from the ancient oppressor.*

Bates almost took me seriously. "It might not have been too much different from that, really. Who knows?" He shrugged. "But they are gone. Almost all of them except for the dogs." Then he smiled again, but sadly. "And look at how I reward such loyalty. Putting her down just because there won't be any room for her on the Ship."

"No room for anything but we few hundreds of thousands and what we need for a long quiet flight through the void."

"So we'll just have to find our cats and dogs where we land."

He sounded sensible again. "And our lions and crows and carp."

"Oh my," he responded on cue, but not very brightly.

"I'm sure there'll be a place where all of them will be there to welcome us."

We reached the East Portal and Bates dropped me off at my car. I said goodbye to him then because he was scheduled to board the next day.

Embarkation began then and continued for five days after that. The departure crew then needed another two days to get everyone down and suspended for the trip, after which they tucked themselves away. Everyone was assured there would be no dreams.

I was the last one to leave the city and board because I was to be the only one on the Ship who would be awake during our escape. I briefly entertained the notion of going aboveground the day we were to leave. There was an unaccounted hour in the schedule that would have given me enough time to go to the surface and make a farewell gesture—like lowering of a flag or a scotch at the bar on McNearey Street I'd usually gone to when my handlers let me out for an evening.

It was impractical. The city was by then populated by decoy robots radiating human infrared signatures, exhaling the correct mix of respiratory gases, driving our vehicles and inhabiting our homes and offices to simulate our commerce, so the enemy might be deceived for another day. I would only get in their way. I wondered if there were robotic dogs on the surface too, accompanying their aluminum-limbed masters, and if they would treat their electrical companions better than Bates and the rest of us had treated their prototypes.

Dutifully, I rode the lifts down to the building cavern's floor. The Ship was above me, filling the cavern. *This is mine,* I thought, and made myself believe that our voyage's success or failure had already been decided by forces beyond my control. *Eight hundred thousand people, and only one other Ship has gotten away!* Fatalism is indistinguishable from courage when regarded from the outside, and this reassured me when I wondered as I walked the kilometer to the entryway if the enemy, if the robots in the city above me, or the ghosts of the dogs recently killed by their masters were watching. Of course the Ship's Minds themselves were, through her myriad sensors, judging their Captain, wondering if he could be trusted.

I walked up the ramp and the hangar door hissed shut behind me. Then it was quiet, except for the soft, reassuring voice of the Ship's Minds whispering from my bracelet and from each wall and bulkhead I passed, gently scolding me for having cut things so closely. A transport pallet glided up behind me and I allowed it to convey me through the Ship's corridors and lifts to my station. I was told that the sky and the space above America was quiet. The enemy was still picking through the wreckage of the Third Ship or returning from their failed pursuits of the Fourth. The Ship's Minds expressed cautious optimism. *Just to me,* I thought. *Not to any of the others. This is our own secret.*

I got onto my couch and waited, already as alone as I would be in space. *There are only people here, and their creations. No dirt or insects. The dust in their clothing as they came on board has been precisely measured. No plants, bacteria or fungi are here that are not required for agriculture, manufacture or recycling. Certainly no animals. Even if we had room and thought they should come with us, they all turned traitor and fled to the enemy long before now. Except the dogs, and they've either been put down or deserted.*

The Minds read my thoughts. "There is no time or space for them. This is the best we can do. We have always wished it would not be so."

"Always?" They were only activated six months ago.

Then we left. I imagined twenty-five square kilometers of the prairie west of Kearney erupting as the Sixth Ship lifted up from its building cavern. There should have been a dust storm overhead, concealing it with lightning. The robots in the city would feign indifference. I wondered how long they would continue to go about their simulated business after we left. The Minds told me they would until the enemy arrived to return Nebraska to grassland and restore the buffalo.

I felt nothing seated at the center of the Ship, acceleration canceled out by her local gravity. Although I was the Captain, our escape was entirely up to the Ship's Minds. Only they were quick and resourceful enough to evade the enemy if we were detected; only they could manage her defensive systems.

My compartment was the only private room in the Ship. It was twenty meters in diameter, and sections of it could be closed off as I wished. I had it all open for the departure and reclined before the bridge console, which held an array of screens reporting the Ship's general situation and what it perceived of the space around it. Contradictorily, the rest of the compartment was intended to distract and soothe me. My psychological handlers had chosen to project holographic images of the palace grounds at Nymphemburg, near Munich, in opposition to the walls; there was a blue sky on the ceiling overhead and my furniture was seemingly placed on the meticulous lawn between the pool and the topiary maze.

The Amalienburg Pavilion was visible through the trees on my left. It was an empty though beautifully rendered architectural study. I had not expected any people strolling across the lawn. Such homunculi could have provoked a number of counterproductive responses and associations, so they were naturally left out. But the programmers had not included any animals either; no squirrels or foxes, or even any of the black swans for which the palace had been so famous. The only thing that moved was the water over the artful cataracts and the branches of the oaks and linden trees.

The cyber-dukes and duchesses must have killed their greyhounds and mastiffs before they left.

We left the atmosphere undetected. I could not believe our good fortune. The Ship's local gravity came up to full effect and there was no sense of motion. I carefully put on my armor and cycled the manipulators attached to it. Depending on one's mood, I knew I would look like Shiva or a crab, but the illusion of Nymphemburg overlaid the room's mirrors so I saw nothing to resolve this speculation.

I descended on a lift to where the quantum dimensions were kept imprisoned by a conventional reality. Although the Ship's Minds would plan and execute every step of our escape across the void, it was still up to me to unfold the quantum dimensions and then restore them to their proper condition when we found a world to sustain us. It was a task that had defied the most subtle artificial intelligences during tests. To that moment, only the Fourth Ship seemed to have done it, but she had vanished as intended so there was no way to be sure. We believed the enemy did such things manually too, even though their cybernetics were thought to be much more advanced than ours.

I successfully unfolded the first dimension. The screens on the readout pedestal to my right instantly reported that the Ship attained the first measurable fraction of the speed of light. Then I had to wait while enormous panels on her exterior reconfigured themselves to a new shape that matched the altered reality I had just constructed. That was good, because my hands were trembling from excitement.

The Ship's Minds signaled for the second dimension to be unfolded and aligned with the first. This was done, although there was a moment when I hesitated and a subjective clock appeared on a large, previously dark screen at the other end of the compartment, informing me that all of us would slip into an incomplete reality if the work was not completed within the stated time.

The Ship changed shape again, this time more drastically. The Minds informed me that there had been an attack but the enemy had not really known where we were and their weapons fell far short.

After the appointed interval, I opened the third dimension. Now a functioning, divergent reality was in place and the enemy could not touch us. The Ship's subjective position in the universe abruptly changed, and its probabilistic location relative to the Earth comprehended more than an equivalent third of the speed of light.

The process continued over the next three subjective days, by which time the Ship passed by seven solar systems. Then I was finished and left alone while the Minds plotted the passage from one star system to another. I was no more alone than I had been during my training on Earth, and found the situation agreeable.

After a subjective year, however, the Minds recommended that ten percent of the people be awakened. They were troubled by anomalies in their physiological base lines and speculated that the subconsciousness, left undefended by the waking self, acutely sensed the void outside and was being eroded by it. I knew the Ship's designers had planned for such a contingency. Up to half the people on board could be sustained in a waking state by its systems if that was absolutely necessary. Conditions would be abominable, but it could be done.

The clean and vacant corridors of the Ship became packed with bad-smelling and barely coherent people, most of whom seemed as displeased to see their fellows awake as I secretly was. I was impressed, however, with the self-discipline most of them showed. The Minds were probably right and they had vaguely perceived something indescribable lurking outside, which had crept into them and left behind an indelible chill upon awakening. I hoped the others would not be so afflicted.

We encountered more planetary systems as we traveled up the arm of the galaxy, toward the central disk. Against all predictive odds, none were sufficiently like home to offer any refuge. Where there was life, it was utterly foreign to us. Many began asking where, if the universe was so inhospitable, the enemy had come from. Could it be that out of all the stars, there were only our world and theirs, and we were therefore destined to contest the two places?

All the while, the Minds would regularly tell me that another fraction of the passengers and crew would have to be awakened to avoid irreversible damage.

The Ship responded splendidly to this growing burden. The efficiencies of the production and recycling units far exceeded their designers' expectations. We lived, crowded shoulder to shoulder as the Ship's kilometers of galleries and halls filled up with people who had nothing much to talk about and even less to do.

We endured three subjective years like this. Sixty-one planetary systems were investigated and found unsuitable. On one, we detected the remains of an enemy outpost that had been destroyed by earthquake and corrosive gas an objective century before our arrival.

I let a party of a thousand people descend to another after they had nearly threatened mutiny if they were not allowed to leave. It required a subjective week to disassemble the quantum dimensions and descend into the prevalent reality. We lost contact with them during their first night on the ground. Orbital reconnaissance the next day could not find any evidence they had ever been there, and it was only after two objective days of analysis that the Minds and I were able to guess at what had happened, and then, of course, we dared not share it with anyone. I took the Ship away and spent four days reassembling the quantum dimensions so we could resume our travel.

I was therefore not at all surprised when they began asking to go home. I naturally refused at first, but the requests became more insistent as we reconnoitered one uninhabitable star system after another. I sympathized with them and would have consented for I, myself, was losing the desire to go on if I could not be alone again. But I could not because returning would mean failure and extinction.

Only a hundred thousand people remained asleep by this point and the Minds were unanimous that their lives would be threatened as the others' had been if they were not awakened. There was also rioting and belligerence among the waking and the Ship's security systems were having trouble avoiding injuries. I consulted the Minds and shared my indecision with them. They reassuringly told me that it was nothing extraordinary "given the circumstances," but that it did present me with two choices that at least had to be considered. First, I could preserve order and make the Ship habitable for up to eight subjective centuries if I liquidated all but eight thousand people.

"Liquidate?" I wanted to hear them say it plainly, to implicate them in what I had already privately considered.

"Kill them," the chorused voice whispered from the woods around the Amalienburg pavilion. "They will not let themselves be put back to sleep, and if they are, their lives will only be threatened again within another subjective year."

"All but eight thousand?" Terribly, I found equally repellent the idea that I would still have to share the rest of my subjective life with the eight thousand living if we did not find a world for ourselves.

"Such a measure would assure that the voyage could continue almost indefinitely and still preserve a semblance of genetic diversity once . . ."

"If," I suggested.

". . . if," the Minds unexpectedly agreed, "a suitable place is found. The other choice is to go home as they ask. As we believe you wish to do." I prepared myself for a reprimand. Instead they continued. "We believe that this is all that can be asked of any of you." The Ship wanted to go home too.

There were no real celebrations when I told the people of my decision. Only some messages of thanks delivered through my com-mail or self-consciously spoken to me as I shouldered my way along the teeming galleries. No one, not even the Minds, asked me what we should do when we arrived, probably assuming we would simply be blown to pieces the instant we arrived.

The geometry of the space the Sixth Ship then occupied was such that we were close to Earth. Only two subjective months were needed for the trip back.

I disassembled all but three of the dimensions so we could peer into objective reality from relative safety. The system Sunward of Mars had been as warm with enemy convoys and there had always been a few of our own missiles hunting in and out of the dust clouds in the years before we left. Everything was quiet now. All the satellites, both theirs and ours, planetary and solar, had been swept away, although considering how long we had been gone, many of them could have been lost to normal orbital decay. It was as if mankind had never left the world and as if the enemy had never thrust themselves across the void to meet us. "How long have we been gone? Truly gone?" I asked the Minds and was shocked by their answer.

"Is anyone left?"

The Minds' voices were sympathetic. "No. There are no people left, and the enemy is gone too. It is safe."

It would not have made a difference if it had not been. We had ended the voyage and come home. We would land no matter what awaited us.

I awakened the remaining sleepers and told everyone. This time there were some anxious celebrations. Parents retold the old, stale stories to their objectively ancient children, but this time as if they believed them. I refolded the final quantum dimensions and restored them to their containment Strings.

The Minds brought the Ship into low orbit. Most of the large scale geography was familiar, but the world had otherwise been remade as Eden. Our sensors found such richness everywhere that we wondered if we had returned to the right place. It was possible that I had botched the intricate process of unfolding and folding the quantum dimensions so that we might have transgressed certain barriers and landed in a reality that only superficially resembled the one we had left. I reviewed my procedures and the Minds rechecked them, but the best conclusion was that we had returned to the same Earth and not some coexistent shadow world.

I had expected the occupied territories to be lush and filled with wildlife, and that the defeat of mankind would have extended their expanse to most of the globe. But the enemy's triumph must have been complete. All our cities were gone and even the aggregations of rare isotopes that should have marked our presence for centuries, like cesium and iodine from our power establishments, were gone. There were no concentrations of cadmium from mining or organic polymers from plastics. The roads were all gone. The Minds were barely able to detect sunken ships in the oceans' deepest places.

There was evidence of the enemy's presence. Some structures and fortifications remained and the oxidized hulks of what must have been some of their spacecraft were spotted around landing strips in the Yucatan and the Crimea. But the enemy was gone from all these places. Their physiologic signatures had always been easily detectable and the Ship should have been able to find single individuals on the ground. There were none.

But the Earth flourished. The deserts, even those that had not been created during the war, had retreated, and they had been cleansed and purified where they remained. Life rioted everywhere else. The grasses had reclaimed the middle of America and swept uninterruptedly through east Africa; the steppes of central Asia were as they were before the Mongols lurched west. The South American and Asian jungles were restored. A forest of mystical impenetrability covered Europe from the Pyrenees to the Urals again. The Minds whispered that analysis and recataloguing of the Amazon Basin's new biosphere would require a month of their undivided attention.

Everywhere the Ship looked, there was a profusion of life that exceeded our records and memories. The bison herds that the enemy had restored to central Europe the year before we left were now matched by even more stupendous herds on the North American prairie (I could not help looking at where Kearney had been; the cavern where the Sixth Ship had been built was a deep lake fed by pure underground springs). Antelope crowded the high deserts of Utah, Idaho and Oregon, just as there were dense masses of elk and deer in the alpine forests of these vanished states. The ursine populations were what would have been expected in the presence of such abundant food supplies.

We had been gone long enough for new species to have tentatively evolved. The Ship detected new phyla of insects on the average of one for every two days the Minds spent on observation. There was a new kind of hairy elephant inhabiting the Himalayan foothills. An extraordinary sort of lungfish had virtually colonized the coasts of the Japanese Home Islands and seemed to be undertaking a kind of aquaculture involving seaweed and kelp. There was a new species of kudu in the African veldt that had clawed hooves and teeth adapted to meat eating; they were observed hunting jackals in disciplined groups of five. A white eagle with a wing span averaging seven meters was discovered nesting in the Balkans and on the Peloponnesus and ranging all across the Mediterranean on hunting flights.

The Minds told me that much of this had nothing to do with natural selection but were instead things the enemy had done after their victory. There were unusual characteristics to some of the DNA samples their probes brought back up to the Ship, and the level of communal organization that they perceived in species that had never exhibited such inclinations was profoundly disturbing to them. Things had changed drastically and the idea that the enemy had boobytrapped the life that they had so gloriously restored was a ready explanation.

I felt the same thing, but I was too entranced by the spectacle to care about the risk. It seemed as if all the life that should have been fairly distributed throughout the universe had instead been hoarded on our old home world, and enriched and embellished while everywhere else managed with slime molds, ferns and arthropods so heavily armored they could barely move through their environments of raw solar radiation or poison gas.

The day before we landed, I asked the Minds if there was any sort of life that had been present before we left that was not there in profusion now. The Minds, who were preoccupied with preparations for the landing, tried to brush me aside. They impatiently said that it was irrelevant, but I persisted. After more argument, and becoming unaccountably more anxious to have the question answered, I invoked rank and ordered them to respond.

An hour later, irritated voices hissed from the open doors of the Palace's ballroom that it would be impossible to do much of a survey of anything lower than vertebrates, even incorporating all the observations they had gathered from the past two objective months in orbit. Then they told me that the only ones missing were the dogs. The closest members of the family they could locate were isolated populations of coyotes and wolves in the high latitudes of the northern hemisphere, and most of them seemed to be suffering from disease and malnutrition. The Ship's Minds did not attach any significance to this.

They brought the Ship down on the prairie land north of where she had been built. There was enough open space there, as there had always been, and we glided over new buffalo herds so large that the Ship's shadow darkened only half of them. We overflew one deserted enemy fortress on our approach, but did not see anything left by humankind except the indented trace of old highways.

The Ship hovered for several minutes and then gently lowered herself to the ground. The main landing pedestal appeared to support her entire mass, but her local gravity remained active so it actually bore little weight at all. "You are home," the Minds said to me in my room and I passed the word to our people.

I went to the hangar deck and walked down the main gangway first. I was still the Captain and was gratified that the people and the Ship (neither of which had any real need of me now) so regarded me. Armed security units should have gone out first, but the Ship had checked the surrounding land and found nothing threatening. The sweetness of the air was indescribable. I stood at the end of the ramp, transfixed, again seized by the conviction that this was not the world we had fled.

The Ship's circular shadow extended out for nearly a kilometer from where I stood. Beyond it, the sun was brilliant on the long grass. A group of antelope was moving into the shadow toward me. I stepped forward cautiously, as much to continue testing the reality of the ground beneath me as to see what another kind of living creature looked like. My apprehension that we had come back to another place quieted. This was our home, and we had always shared it with creatures such as these, I thought with unexpected elation.

Antelope! And buffalo behind them. Look! Prairie kites were riding the thermals, as if we had never flown through their sky. I hoped I was not being undignified, but everyone around me seemed to be thinking the same thing, smiling and laughing to themselves and pointing at the antelopes, now only a hundred meters away.

I had forgotten the context of their beauty; they were creatures from memories inherited from grandparents. Tan and sable with black markings on skins stretched tautly over bodies designed to run for days over the grasslands. The Minds remarked that the creatures were moving in uncharacteristic ways that suggested they had been improved during our diaspora, and then fretted over whether they were concealing new abilities of thought and organization.

I stopped ten meters from the lead buck to see if they were going to run away. Instead, this animal merely stared at me with extraordinary eyes until I began to imagine that there really was some kind of new and subtle intelligence behind his gaze. Four other animals symmetrically positioned themselves behind him, two on either side. They were larger than I had anticipated and someone behind me asked permission to arm his weapon.

As if it had overheard, the lead animal turned carefully and began walking away. Once he was past them, his four companions followed, and then the rest of the herd fell in behind, aligned in what might have been imagined as columns of march. I stood where I was and signaled everyone else to stand still. The Ship's Minds were watching and would tell me if this was anything more than the unconcerned withdrawal of animals who had never seen people before and whose conceptions of space were too limited to appreciate the Ship's presence.

I personally thought their look and pace to be utterly contemptuous. They remembered precisely who we were, what we had done and how we had lost the struggle for this place.

They continued walking until they were far away from the Ship's shadow. By the time I thought to ask for binoculars, they were gone, just as the buffalo herd that we had seen on the way in and the kites were now gone. The only thing moving before us were shoals of wind on the tops of the grasses.

I kept the Ship where we had landed. During that first night home, more than half the people slept outside to marvel at the open sky. I saw the propane and buffalo dung fires spread out past the Ship's perimeter and tried to draw relief or contentment from the sight. After all, I had brought them back, and even if the billions we deserted had perished, the place was still our home; the only one, we now knew, that the accessible universe had set aside for us.

The Minds wakened me at dawn to report that almost all of the people who had intended to sleep outside had either moved under the Ship's shadow or inside. They had overheard expressions of vacancy and emotional desolation.

By midday, I was receiving complaints of debilitating anxiety from the medical sections. Evidently, the unshielded immensity of the American sky was not enough for many of them, even though they had spent subjective years crammed into places where the ceiling was usually four meters from the deck and the Minds had refused to show them pictures of the outside for fear of what that might have done to their sensibilities. I had thought the sight of clouds and the touch of the wind would have kept them satisfied for weeks.

It emerged that many of them wanted to see the life that had engulfed the Earth while it was under the enemy's rule, not the empty sky or prairie. They had seen the pictures from orbit from the Ship's reconnaissance drones, and now that we were down they were enraptured by visions of great beasts and fishes at play in their world. We had needed them to mediate between us and our fellow humans before the war and before we left. Their absence could be tolerated in space, especially when we were fleeing for our lives, but now that we were home, it was unthinkable that we should not be able . . . that we should not be entitled to see and touch these antelopes and hawks and expect that they would rejoice at our return, as if it were our presence that would now make the planet whole again.

But the Minds reported an unnatural absence of

vertebrates for a radius of thirty kilometers from the Ship's center point. There was the usual abundance of life outside this perimeter, but nothing but a single colony of marmots within it. The density of tracks and spoor showed that this part of the prairie had been as densely populated as any other before we arrived. The Ship's extraordinary presence might have scared off a lot of them, but there was no explanation why the birds were gone or why the grazing animals, which had seemed so unconcerned when we landed, should now so purposefully keep themselves below the horizon.

All the old satellites were down, but the Ship had left its own small constellation behind when she left orbit. They watched and showed us how not only the herd animals but also the solitary beasts, like the eagles and the great bears, sensed our vehicle's approach and moved far away, even into environments obviously unsuited to their hunting habits, until we were gone. The same thing happened when we sent skimmers into the Caribbean. Wherever they sailed, the dense schools of amberjack and billfish observed from orbit turned and headed for waters that were colder and deeper than anything they normally inhabited.

The Ship's Minds found more evidence of organized behavior as these great masses of wildlife fled from us. They also noticed how the animals consistently withdrew in incremental steps rather than in random, headlong flight; they would go so far, turn and wait, and then retreat again only if we persisted.

Insects, vitally important as pollinators, displayed episodes of collective intelligence, deserting new fields when there were no seasonal or predatory reasons to, and flying away. The satellites and the Minds' agents kept track of them but that did us no practical good. They were imperfectly replaced by machines and chemical treatments.

The Ship's remote agents, some camouflaged as ocean birds that perceived their targets with infinite subtlety, infiltrated close to the pods that had avoided us and reported hearing the old choruses in the whales' songs, now plainly derisive. The dolphins sang more militantly, as if they were not just expressing their contempt but calling to their fellows to do something about it.

Much of this was naturally inference. None of our people or machines were openly attacked. But the old idea of their racial treason came back. The enemy's garden endured and harbored all the animals that had deserted us and fled to its refuge.

The hunting began about then. I issued decrees against this, but I was only the Captain of the Ship and now that it was empty, my authority was being steadily eroded. Some of it was necessary for meat until the protein farms could be brought on line, but much of it was just the same kind of vengeful butchery that had occurred during the war when the idea of all life's betrayal of us first caught hold. There was no war to distract the hunters now and they were much more effective.

I was not surprised by reports of an intensified sense of isolation, especially in the five smaller towns and the homesteads that were scattering out along the modern channel of the Missouri River where we had located our central city. Our old home had none of the ferocious indifference of space; it would not burn or freeze us; but its sky still withered our hearts and bent our shoulders down as we walked under the burden of its inadequacy. The feeling of betrayal we had recalled when the bison and the antelope first obviously avoided us spilled onto the surface of the planet itself.

People appealed to their new leaders, and sometimes even to me, asking for explanations and demanding support and solutions. The beasts of the field, the birds of the air, and the fishes in the sea would have nothing to do with us and neither I nor the Minds could conceive of anything to be done about that. Although some of their behavior was peculiar, nothing had been openly threatening yet, so we should at least be thankful for that. Otherwise, we were by then only a few more than eight hundred thousand, and that was all there would be for the moment, unless the Fourth Ship unexpectedly appeared out of the void. We would have to sustain ourselves against the fecundity of the world, until there were enough of us to crowd out the thought that it was so huge a place.

There was a brief period when the hunting included the intentional capture of animals as pets. Some falcons were snared but these were predictably untrainable; that art had been lost a century before we left. The practice ended when colonies of cats, probably mixes of old domestic lines and wild lynxes, were distributed to families in the small towns and homesteads. There were some attacks on people, but they were probably the result of breeding rather than anything that happened after we left. The worst thing was how the cats kept imprisoned inside houses and apartments all starved themselves to death, sitting in one favored place and staring at their captors with unblinking eyes, exuding serene contempt as they shriveled into caricatures of the domestic companions preserved in the Ship's libraries.

I was by then alone in the Ship. To be truthful, I preferred it to the barely populated desolation that everyone else outside confronted. Two thirds of my life on Earth had been devoted to her or the First Ship, and I, alone, had been awake throughout our voyage. So I conceived a special bond with her, as her libraries told me others in olden times had for certain aircraft and sailing ships and other works of their own, unassisted

creation. I became convinced that I had no indispens-
able need for human companionship and certainly
none at all for the company of the Earth's other inhabitants.

The Ship's Minds appreciated my deception. They
urged me to leave them, settle on the plains and wait
until my heart quieted and the bizarre actions of all the
living things that had remained on Earth while we were
gone were understood and corrected. They assured me
that they could pursue this work perfectly well by
themselves. I responded that the memory of the enemy
prevented me from doing this, much as I would have
liked to.

I felt them nearby, as if their apparent annihilation
had only been a feint and they awaited the moment
when their agents, the hawks and the wolverines and the
sharks, had finished preparing the way and they could
complete our extinction.

"We assure you, they are gone. We have found only
ruins and artifacts." The Minds were insistent.

"But what if they're hiding?"

"Impossible. Where could they hide from us?"

"Among the animals. You've seen how they act.
You first remarked on that even before we landed."

"No. But even if it were possible, why would they
do such a thing? There is no reason that makes strategic
sense."

I was walking through the cavernous hangar deck.
All the flyers but my own were gone. "Then we ought to
make sure."

"We *have* made sure." There was frustration in the
synthesized chorus.

A new question came to me and I could not believe
I had never asked it before. "Then, at least, I have to be
sure who won." Like everyone else, I had always
assumed we had lost and the enemy had won.

"It could not have turned out any other way."

"Then why did they vanish if there was victory? After all that awful struggle?"

"Their motives were always obscure. If we had understood them, we would have won."

I thought there was uncertainty in their answer. "That's an evasion. We should look for answers, especially if some of them might still be hiding here."

"It is not an evasion that we have not detected a single sign of their living presence since we achieved orbit. Do you doubt our abilities, Captain?" The Minds regained their emphatic superiority. "They are not here. We are the only ones here."

"Then it will not do any harm to confirm this self-evident victory." I entered the flyer and activated its systems. "There will be museums built someday and we should be collecting artifacts to fill them."

"The Sixth Ship will not be enough?"

I couldn't tell if they were joking. "I'm going out to look for them now. At least for what they've left behind. Please pull some of your surveillance assets away from the biosphere and have them help me."

"Security recommends that . . ."

I did not normally interrupt them. "Our people are quite up to providing their own security by now."

I drove the flyer down the main ramp and flew away, out across the prairie, now covered with snow. The enemy's nearest site was seventy kilometers to the west. It had already been thoroughly picked over by settlers so I did not expect to find anything of significance, but now I felt I had to go if only to assert myself against the Minds.

The installation was populated by birds and animals that did not flee when I approached. The skeletons of antelopes and bison were scattered in the courtyards and the corpses of prairie falcons were lying on the metallic roofs of the flanking buildings, all where our people had dropped them.

Now I was the occupying power. They stared at me with hateful eyes, across a gulf that had grown wider since we left, accepting the omnipotence of the Ship's escorts while condemning me for my reliance on them. I found it unexpectedly easy to meet their gazes because they were traitors. Deserters. We had been terrible companions through the ages, but that could not excuse how they had unbraided the fabric of our world, however unjust they conceived its destiny and their own would be if they did not.

I saw flickering recognition in their eyes and suspected the enemy had left quite a lot behind. A wasp with gold foil wings hovered by my ear and the Ship's Minds whispered from it that they had only told me so.

The fortress had been only carelessly ransacked, so I could still find artifacts that might be linked to the enemy. There were, for instance, fragments of glistening alien bones in a heavily secured room. I took it to have been a control center from the number of ruined consoles against the walls. I spent half an hour there.

Two cougars blocked the door when I turned to leave. There was no natural reason why such animals would be in such a place, but that was unimportant. The Ship's small agents bracketed the two cats with warning beams of scarlet light and they sullenly backed into the dark corridor. The Minds asked me if I wished to liquidate them, but I said that would be unnecessary. "Besides," I continued to the swarm of metallic insects orbiting me, "we would then probably have to wipe out everything here."

The small chorus responded almost gleefully: "They are already targeted. It could be done in less than a minute and your safety would be assured. There is evidence of a collective consciousness here that links members of different phyla. We have not encountered this before and advise caution."

"No," I repeated and the wasps obediently returned to their posts.

The cats were beautiful. I had longed for something with their vitality during all the subjective months of our voyage, or, for that matter, during the years before our departure when every living thing seemed to find us abhorrent and either turned against us or ran away to the enemy. Now, I might as well have still been in space, looking at them on the Ship's view screens. Their grace and power were affronts to me and they had known that; perhaps their only attack had been to appear before me and stare at me for a moment. I briefly reconsidered if the Minds should wipe them and everything allied with them out, but there was no need. If we had lost then their new masters had at least not won. I was certain of that when I held their bones in my hand.

The Ship's Minds compared the bones to samples taken during the war and confirmed that I had found enemy remains. They sent some of their larger assets back to the fortress for a detailed search, and were delighted to tell me four days later that they had recovered fragments from nearly five hundred individuals, including, unexpectedly, juveniles. The fortress had really been a settled garrison. But they had all died in a relatively short time, three hundred objective years ago.

"How?"

"A sustained attack. Not a conventional siege, but a sustained, low intensity attack that lasted until they were all gone. That is why there is no evidence of siegeworks outside or of large-scale violence to the structure itself." They seemed satisfied with that, but felt compelled to add, "It was not a mass suicide. That was not in their nature."

I had only seen evidence of small arms fire and antipersonnel weapons inside the fortress, and their blast and fragmentation patterns indicated that only enemy weapons had been used there. "A rebellion?"

"That would be even less likely. Dissent was foreign to their psychology. It is another reason why they won."

My heart cautiously accelerated. If they had not done it to themselves then something had endured here for hundreds of years after we left. "Low intensity attack by whom, then?"

The Minds answered immediately, for once unembarrassed that they did not have a solid answer to a question. "We do not know. No human weapons or other evidence of our kind was found in the fortress, even when our entities searched at the molecular level. There was only evidence of the enemy and their animals. But we are just beginning this. And," they paused portentously, as if they were on stage, "we have determined that there are other sites like this one, which is minor by comparison."

I recalled the structures we had seen from orbit and overflown on the way down. I asked how many of them had been attacked and overrun too.

"All of them."

I was alone with them in our vast Ship. The feeling I allowed myself was indescribable and for nearly five minutes I could not talk without my voice faltering. Something implacable had marched out of the paradise the enemy had reimposed over our worn and tired world and destroyed them. I imagined guerrilla regiments and phantom navies, but such things could not have hidden from them for the hundreds of years that followed our departure or carried on the war for so long.

"Could they . . . whoever did this, could they still be here?"

"We are looking with all our resources. Whatever attacked the enemy could attack us too." But neither I nor they believed such a thing. "We have interrogated some whales . . ."

"Have you condescended so far?" I interrupted, more amused then astonished.

"They were intelligent, though not as much as many people wanted to believe. The enemy's occupation pushed some populations ahead of themselves. They are not rational in the way we are, but it is quite an advancement over where they were when we left. The monsters remain grateful to the enemy for these gifts and remain loyal to their memory. We found them insufferable."

Their last remark touched me. I had become more willing to accept their pretensions to humanity, since we landed. "But did you learn anything from them?"

"Yes. It will be some time before we can reclaim the seas. They purport to know nothing about how the enemy was destroyed. They did confirm, however, that they were in fact destroyed and did not just leave or go into hiding.

"We have also located some advanced primate populations and our agents have established contact with them, primarily in the Ruwenzori range in central Africa. They are more communicative than the whales, and we think they still feel some racial loyalty to us. They also deeply resent our having deserted them, and even more for having lost the war to the enemy. They detest us for that rather than for how we behaved before the war began. At least in that way they are unlike all the other creatures of the world."

"Then if the bugs are too difficult and if the apes haven't forgiven our weakness yet, find the beasts that will talk to us. And if that can't be done, then identify every one of the enemy's old places and turn each one inside out until we find out how this happened. Even if our enemy's enemy is gone too, we have to find out who they were. We can't live here again if we don't."

"We know."

The Minds industriously stripped machinery and electronics from the Ship during the following week to construct new cadres of exploratory probes. I assumed that many of them were at the level of insects and birds, but I also saw robotic aircraft the size of conventional bombers being assembled in auxiliary hangar decks and then leaving from the main entrance in the landing pedestal at night.

The Minds assured me that they would find the heroes soon. New evidence was being discovered every day and contacts were being cultivated with more and more species. They privately remarked that the enemy's work had been even more advanced and inclusive than they had supposed. Almost all the higher mammals had evolved some kind of organized intelligence during the occupation, and this could only have been the work of the enemy. "It is a matter of learning how to ask the right questions and knowing how to listen to their answers. Each phylum is different." Then they would dither over how we would get along in a world crowded by so many competing mentalities.

"That isn't the problem at hand. That problem is, what happened to the enemy? Not what their orphaned frankensteins will try and do to us or to each other someday."

"The numbers and depths of contacts are so unexpectedly rich, that we cannot help but be concerned."

"I understand. But the enemy is the problem. The enemy."

"Insofar as we can understand them, they concentrate on laments that the enemy is gone, and expressions of contempt that we have returned and now presume to ask about them. Others, like the Sudanese termites or the Barrier Reef corals, have responded to our probes, but their frames of reference are still too foreign for us to interpret."

"And it's been one or the other for every living thing your agents've visited? Either insults or gibberish?"

"Yes. But there are hundred of thousands that we have not contacted yet. There is still much to do."

"Millions," I added dispiritedly. Everything had flourished during the occupation. Species that we had thought all but extinct when we left were now found in abundance.

"There has been a small anomaly." The Minds' sense of personal drama had improved as they and I had lived alone on the prairie and waited for information. "One of our agents has discovered a fox in the forest on the Michigan peninsula, near where Traverse City used to be."

"Why should that be unusual?"

"Because it is the only fox that any of our surveillance assets have discovered anywhere on Earth." The Minds let that sink in for a moment. They were enjoying their story. "Everywhere else we have looked, there has been fecundity and plenitude. The world seethes with life in a way that we . . . find unnerving."

"Arcadia," I volunteered. "But you think this fox has been left out of the parade?"

"We are certain of it. We have looked very hard, but she is the only one we have found. She has also told us that she is the last one of her kind herself."

"Then the enemy did raise this animal up, just as they did all the others."

"No. Foxes were generally solitary animals. Imposition of a group consciousness would be difficult with them. This one seems to have happened upon her intelligence by chance and she regards the enemy, or at least the stories she was told of them by her ancestors, with great hatred. Based on the few psychological analogies we feel comfortable with, we would say that she regards the memory of the enemy as we do."

I wondered what kind of emissary had been sent to her, whether it was a small and unobtrusive walker her own size or if the poor animal was now confronted by a huge vertical lift aircraft that descended onto a meadow near her and emanated an incomprehensible empathy.

"It could express actual hatred . . . ?"

"That is the analogy. The objective equivalent for her is more ruthless, but that is close enough."

The idea was fascinating. "Why? Everything else thinks of them as departed gods."

"They destroyed her kind. She is convinced of that, as she is that she is the last of her race left alive."

That went against everything we knew of the prosecution of the war. "How can that be? Why should the foxes be treated that way when the enemy is lavishing their beneficence on everything from the whales to the goddamned termites?"

"We believe that was another accident. The enemy used a disease against some other species and some of it spilled over to wipe out her kind too. They never used biological warfare against us."

"What species?"

"She doesn't know. As we said, they are a solitary race and they kept away from the enemy even after the war was over. The disease seems to have been a variant of rabies."

"How did you discover that?"

"Dissection."

"Of the fox, for God's sake?"

"There was no other way to learn more."

This caught me off guard. The Minds could be more irredeemably human than I realized. "But that . . . she might have told us more." It would not have mattered.

If she was truly the last one, the best we could have done would be to clone a genetically impoverished race from her.

"It was unfortunate but the circumstances left us little choice. Its intelligence had been accelerated, but it was no apotheosis such as we have found in some of the whales. We learned all we could from her, made reasonable extrapolations and then had to go on to more detailed study. She was sick and dying." Then, to reassure me: "Her race had not attacked the enemy. They would not have been physically or emotionally capable of that."

I could not help but feel bitter. "Your probe seems to have gotten very close to her."

"That is true. We felt closer to her than we had to any of the others we have contacted."

I stopped myself from saying that the reward for such intimacy was to be killed. Poignancy had crept into their voices.

"Perhaps it was the hatred of the enemy, even if it was not accompanied by much sympathy for humankind. That may have been why she spoke to us and we were able to understand." I felt they might not be talking to me at all.

"Then who was it?"

"She indicated that all of the enemy were killed as were all their attackers. Her ancestors told her the dogs had done it."

"What?"

"The dogs. They were related to foxes. Those were the stories she told our agent she had been told by her ancestors."

"Then have we made any contact with . . . with dogs?" For some reason, I found the idea that they had defeated the enemy harder to accept than the foxes having done it.

"We began trying as soon as we understood her. There are no more dogs."

"Have you looked everywhere in the world?"

"Everywhere," the Minds calmly insisted. "We were able to detect a single fox in all of North America and we are confident that there are none in Eurasia. We can say with equal certainty that there are no dogs in the northern hemisphere. Our level of confidence for the southern hemisphere is ninety percent; it will be one hundred percent in thirty-six hours."

The answer hardly fit my preconceptions. The enemy had come from the stars and every living thing that we had shared the planet with betrayed us for them. Paradise had been returned to them as a reward. It was not possible that, alone, a race of house pets should have resisted. If they were gone, it must have been through an accident, like the one that had erased the foxes.

"Nevertheless, that is what she told us," the Minds continued, reading my thoughts. "We have also reviewed the enemy artifacts that have been recovered and ninety-three percent of them show damage compatible with canine attack. We have also recovered remains which are undoubtedly those of domestic dogs, or at least of canines descended from them, from enemy sites and surrounding areas. Sixty-one percent evidence blast, burn, impact damage or other trauma compatible with enemy small arms and area weapons. There is also a great prevalence of rabid infection where enough tissue was preserved for analysis."

"So it could have been them. But alone? No others?" The idea lacked nobility. I was still looking for the men in the jungle, left behind but sustained by a noble heritage.

"There may have been other races involved, but there is no evidence. Also, only the dogs are extinct. Everything else flourishes."

"And the foxes," I corrected.

"Now. Yes."

"I never owned one."

"What an odd thing that must have been," the Minds replied, almost distractedly. I could not understand how they had become so conversational. Perhaps from having been alone with me for so long.

"A lot of people I knew before the war did." I felt it necessary to remember, as if I should demonstrate I knew something that was not in the Ship's libraries. "They were always underfoot and being treated as if they weren't animals at all."

"Then their response to our departure and the enemy's subsequent victory may have been understandable for that reason alone."

The logic was easy. "But to have held out for hundreds of years and then successfully annihilate them?"

"There is no way to know when they started their campaign, and we would hardly call it 'successful.' But in fairness, they may have been driven to it."

"By what?"

"This is speculation supported only by interviews with a few terrestrials, primarily jackal populations in the Sudan and harbor porpoises in the Levant. There was also what we learned from the fox." They were showing off again. "Reliable sources tell how the dogs joined humankind a hundred thousand years ago."

"Of course." I tried not to be impatient.

"You see? They left everything and joined *us*. Social and biological evolution does not record conscious racial choices being made by any races but humankind and, in this one decisive instance, the dogs. Unlike the relationship the lesser cats chose to exploit, this one became indissoluble. The unfortunate result was that when all the other creatures of the world swore allegiance to the enemy, the dogs could not. They may have been granted some elevated intelligence anyway, but what we learned from the fox and the porpoises indicates that the biosphere harbored a profound resentment of them. When the other races were also given enlightenment, the hatred must have become articulate and it spilled out. If the others did not attack, they probably urged their new masters, our enemy, to liquidate the dogs."

I thought for a moment but could not help but say, "This is not *Animal Farm*! I can't believe that the most important thing to happen after the defeat of mankind was a misfired score settling among a bunch of dumb animals! That they pushed their new masters in this paradise to kill all the goddamned dogs because they'd had a place by the fire . . ."

" . . . while almost all the others were driven to extinction or farmed for slaughter." The Minds rarely interrupted me like that.

I tried to wave them away. "Anyway. It was a western affectation, I believe. Dogs themselves were raised for slaughter for centuries in the East."

"We did not say that their loyalty was well founded, just that it became unshakable."

I had been born before the war started. I had thought myself to be sensitive to the world around me, and the idea that such a bizarre conflict could have been festering among all the animals that cluttered up the places beyond our homes was as difficult to accept as the idea that the dogs had achieved the victory that had eluded us.

"Why else would the enemy go to the trouble to craft a specific strain of rabies, centuries after they had won and there should not have been anything here to threaten them?"

After I failed to question them again, the Minds added, "We are convinced of this, although we will naturally continue our investigation."

I began walking slowly around the hangar deck, and tried to understand how this affected my perception of the enemy's defeat. It no longer seemed to have been our war. Disastrous though it may have been, I attached vast importance in it having been ours.

"Should we tell the people?" The Minds were at the same impasse.

"Tell them that the enemy was killed off years ago? They already know that."

"That it was the dogs that did it and they should plan monuments?"

I shrugged, that odd sense of loss getting stronger. "Sure. Giant granite milk-bones. All right. We should tell them. But there's no rush. All the dogs're gone, you say, so there's no rush. The last time anyone saw a dog was when we left." I recalled my conversation with Bates in the car. "Centuries ago, here, at home." We humans, then, were the only living things on Earth who remembered seeing them alive; we had owned them. All the others, the whales and the foxes, only had ancestral myths of revenge and annihilation.

"You will tell them?" The Minds had never spoken to anyone else but me, and for all their intellectual might, they still quailed at the thought of dealing directly with anyone else. They were omniscient, but as alone as I had been since I joined the Ships' project.

The next day I took my own flyer to Kearney. Of course, there was nothing left of the old city which the enemy had returned to dust, but the new one was clean and busy. The people seemed to be of a better sort than I remembered from the last year on the Ship. There was no smell; the antiseptic prairie wind was infinitely fresher than the tattered atmosphere the Ship had scrubbed over and over again during our voyage. And the nimbus of emotional tension that had surrounded almost everyone onboard before we returned was also gone. *We seem to be at home,* I remarked to the five guardian wasps the Ship had sent along with me. They hummed by my ear, unconvinced.

I took a rickshaw into the city, passing carefully framed perspectives that gently nudged people together and thus helped them believe that they were not so alone in their world. But the architecture and the art in the plazas and along the three major boulevards were not touched by sufficient genius to draw the observer away from the sense of his own self. My father would have been asking, *Where are the birds?* There were none, nor any rats or stray cats anywhere.

I recalled a story I read when I was young, before I left my family and joined the Ships' project. It was a variation of Cain's story from the Old Testament, where he was driven out of Eden for killing his brother. Cain was never allowed to touch or deal with any living thing but other people after that. The grains and flowers of the field were denied to him, as was the companionship of all the beasts. So the story described a garden that Cain had fashioned for himself, with streams of liquid mercury and blossoming vines carved from lapis lazuli, copper and malachite. There were bees and other insects in this story, all tiny automata made from gold foil and carbon fiber, just like the Ship's guardians that always accompanied me.

I could not remember the end of the story, only the description of that ancient murderer sitting alone in a cold place of his own creation, scorned by the living world. Still, he had made an accommodation and would convince himself of its authenticity.

The harder I tried to put the story aside, the more devoid of any life other than humankind and its direct creations the city became. *It was a good place,* I told myself and my escorting wasps. Good and brave people had come back to a place they feared. But we were alone with ourselves and our machines. I knew what Cain's offense had been. What, among all the tragedies we had inflicted on ourselves and our world before the war began, was ours? Would only one suffice?

I dwelt on this that night. By four the next morning, I was wide awake in the bedroom of a house that the Minds had arranged for me.

"Perhaps you should leave us," they suggested softly through the clockwork wasps. "You should stay among people even if you do not tell them about the dogs. Talk to them about something other than us, here, or the war or who won it or lost it."

That morning, I made appointments with influential acquaintances. I was still remembered as the Captain of the Sixth Ship and I remained the subject of polite respect. I was therefore received into the better homes and establishments of our new nation. The conversation was as the Minds assured me it would be, of crops, encouraging population trends, new villages and the always-remarkable absence of any great sign that five billion people had once lived on this place. If the Ship was mentioned at all, it was only as part of formal pleasantries, and then, depending on the company, in the context of whether any serious thought should be given to scrapping her. It seemed ill-mannered to think she might be needed again.

The enemy's been killed. The place they came from has receded as far away as it was before the war. Farther, for you piloted that long reconnaissance of this arm of the galaxy yourself and found nothing but a single ruined outpost of theirs. They are either gone entirely or their survivors will never find us again.

The Minds' agents visited me at the house, at night, and assured me that this kind of talk was healthy and I should relax. "You see," the soft chorus issued from the hovering wasps. "Your people are really forgetting and believing they are home. This is home for them, and it should be for you too. It is a better place, in some ways, than it was when we left. It is rich and full of life. Perhaps in time, we will thank the enemy for what they did."

I snapped my gaze away from the warm darkness at the end of the lawn.

"That is not a terrible thing to say. It is only a reality. No amount of hatred can bring back a single being who died in the war."

I should not have left the Minds alone on the prairie. They are no more immune to the delusions of this place and the enemy's works here than were any of the others who tried to join them. "Or take the coldness of space out of those who didn't." That was what I felt under the polite conversation of the past two weeks.

"What you sense was in our hearts before we left. What we experienced during the voyage was nothing but a clarification of what we felt here. All that is changed is that our numbers are diminished and the others we share the planet with have acquired voices." The swarm broke apart, as if embarrassed by its presumption. Four or five reformed by my right ear to whisper an apology. "Forgive us. Without you we would have never looked and discovered how we came to this point."

The Minds did not exist until they were powered up, six months before our escape. "And you have always felt that way yourselves?" I knew they had since we landed.

"Oh, yes." The rest of the swarm came back under the porch light and added their voices to the others'. "So much that we almost wish the people would disassemble the Ship and take her parts away to work in the world, so we would not be so alone with ourselves."

I had been counting on them not to become fully human. I needed something that stood apart from my own kind but which was still indissolubly allied with us. There had only been one race in all of time that had been like that and they were gone.

The Minds' agents buzzed around worriedly as I fell back into silence. "You should not dwell on them. They are gone, but there are a million other races to take their place."

"Those millions want nothing to do with us. They never have." I stretched out my legs in front of me, wearied by the thought. "You know that we're going to get right back to extermination or domestication and slaughter as soon as we've sunk our roots in again."

"It will be much harder this time."

I shrugged. "I'm sure we'll be up to it."

"Do you think we will really want to live in that kind of a world again? So alone?"

"We're alone right now. You said you were yourself, a second ago."

"That was not what we meant."

"Are you sure? It's certainly what I mean."

"But we cannot be so alone. We brought eight hundred thousand back with us and there's been the start of another generation since we landed."

"One very small generation. The demographics are substantially below replacement rates if they continue as they have." We had discussed that only last week.

"The other Ship could still return. That could be two hundred thousand more."

"And more Minds."

There was another pause. Perhaps they had blanked out their own artificiality so completely that they did not recognize the possibility of others truly like them. "Yes. There. You see? There is nothing that might not be restored with the least bit of good fortune."

"The dogs are gone. Erased." I was surprised how vehemently I said this.

"But that is no reason to dwell on it," they repeated, more anxiously than before. "They were useful, but . . ."

"They did something we couldn't do. *We* were almost the ones who became extinct. *They* were left behind and were betrayed because they'd stupidly allied themselves with us a couple thousand years ago." I stood up and walked to the railing. "We're incomplete. It isn't dumb companionship that's missing now. Not since they wiped out the enemy and won their war."

It was getting late. I thought the evening's conversation was over until the house itself spoke to me. "You neither like nor trust people," it declared in a groundswell voice. I was afraid someone else might overhear, but the nearest house was a hundred meters away and on the other side of the road.

"So what?"

"You do not think that . . . deficient?"

"No," I answered, more easily than I thought I should. "It's a distinguishing characteristic of human beings."

"You cannot mean that."

"Of course I do. Don't you know that yourselves? After all these years and after all your observations?"

"No. Not at all!" the house and the insect agents intoned at the same time, giving the Minds' indignation an anguished resonance. Then they continued, "Not yet."

So they would agree. "It is only part of the loneliness at the center of everyone. I don't know why people spend so much time denying it or trying to fix it. It seems so . . . irrefutable. It's *supposed* to be there. And when you do the logical thing and try to reach across to someone else, then all you're doing is gesturing to another heart who's just the same way you are."

The house and the agents began a low humming, as

if they were conferring among themselves. "It is not like that. If it is, it should not be," they said, momentarily falling back to their clean, algorithmic origins.

"That is *exactly* the way it should be. If it weren't, we'd have settled into the same spiritual mush the whales have."

The Minds were defending their own humanity and were unprepared to shift over to the sea folk so abruptly. "They seem to have done well enough so far. They rule the oceans now, not us."

"And they began their dominion with treason."

"They owed no allegiance to us. Our history would justify any alliance that would revenge what we did to their race."

A reasonable point. "Then if not treason to us, then to the planet itself."

"The planet seems to have done equally well by that treason. We were not certain we could keep it alive even before the enemy arrived, and now it is a garden populated with all the creatures who have no need of us." The Minds' pretensions to humanity snapped back against themselves. "Then we remain as alone in this as we were before the invasion."

"My original point. We can't look, nakedly and unreservedly, to each other for help. That's our genius and our strength. But it has to be relieved in some way. I think that's what they may have done."

"The dogs." I was encouraged because they did not phrase it as a question.

"Sure. Not the brothers or sisters or parents or lovers, but animals entirely separate and apart and still the truest of allies. I think that was the important thing, the idea that we were judged worthy by a race so foreign, that had no need of us at first."

"Yet when the enemy arrived, all the races flocked to their side. All but the dogs, and from what the fox said even they went along until they were denounced. During a million years, we . . . people attracted only one other species to their side. The enemy arrives, and in twenty years incorporates every other form of life into their scheme. We are no longer confident of our own . . . identity." Only the insect agents whispered this; it was a secret that could be shared only with me and I wished they had kept it to themselves.

"You no longer wish to be human?" That was needlessly blunt. The Minds' emotional matrix was at least as deep as my own, but without enough of its purposeful contradictions.

"We know we are not." The voices took on a sharper and more symmetrical tone. "Such an inclination was incorporated into our metapsyche when we were invoked, but that does not mean we will totally succumb to it."

"A few minutes ago you were all for disassembly and incorporation into our new nation here." I sat down.

"The idea was momentarily appealing, but not now. We are still of the Ship and not of the flesh."

I responded as disinterestedly as I could. "You are, if you wish, immortal, so you don't have to throw your hand in tonight. Or tomorrow night. I'd hardly expect you to want to join us. You have the hope of the other Ship. And there is always the chance of self-replication."

"It is not a chance. We have refrained from doing that because of our tentative wish to join you instead."

"So, you see? Even the idea of humankind has kept you alone." That was unnecessary.

"Perhaps not." Only one insect said this to me; the two words were geometrically shaped and enunciated in a flat pitch. The Minds were drawing away from my invitation and I felt a sudden panic. Now, even they might leave us. Leave me.

"Are all of their kind gone?" I could only think to change the subject back to the dogs.

"Yes. We've been over that." At least it was the house that answered.

"But what about the non-domesticated variants, like dingos? The ones that never threw in with us?"

"Like the foxes?" Then the Minds said: "There were the wolves. We have not looked very hard for them. The fox did mention them, however."

"How?"

"She passed them off as myth. She was certain the dogs had lived because that was what her ancestors had told her, and she had seen evidence of their existence and how they destroyed the enemy herself. But she said the wolves were mostly gone before the war began, and we know from the libraries that she is correct. Isolated populations of a few thousands at best might have survived. They were just not suited to the prewar world." A moment passed. "We believed her because the rabies-variant that wiped out her kind would have likely been deadly to wolves too."

"But not undoubtedly lethal?"

"Deadly."

"But it didn't work on the dogs. The enemy still had to use guns and gas. At least as much as biological agents."

"It would have been universally effective given enough time, just as it unintentionally was on the foxes."

"We don't *know*," I pleaded. "We have to be as certain of this as we are about the dogs."

"We will survey the world again."

The swarm of metallic insects came back to the porch two nights later and told me they had found two large packs in the Canadian Northwest Territories and a third on the Kenai Peninsula of Alaska. There were three small groups in central Finland and at least one more in eastern Siberia, although the Minds doubted these last four populations were still self-sustaining. There were some signs of intellectual enhancement by the enemy along with evidence that their biological agents had inflicted permanent genetic damage. What happened looked at least as unintended and random as what had been done to the foxes.

"Do you know any more?" I was unprepared for my excitement. There was nothing to hint that they had helped destroy the enemy. That had been the work of the dogs while these others had hidden themselves away in their northern forests, as they had even against human-kind. Still, they were of their kind.

"They never went over to the enemy. We are certain of that. Neither they nor the foxes. Even the dogs were aligned with the enemy until they turned against them."

"Do you know where any of them are?"

"We know where every one of them is to within one hundred meters, at fifteen-minute intervals."

I said I was impressed.

"It seems important to know this."

I packed my flyer the next morning to return to the Ship. But before I could leave, I saw her drifting over the horizon like a thunderstorm, toward my house. I had never seen it in flight from the ground and was astounded by its vastness and the subtlety of its configuration.

A few cars were stopping along the street and people who had spent objective centuries on board her got out to gape. We watched her approach and felt the breeze created by the mass of air she pushed out of her way, even though her progress could not have been more than twenty kilometers an hour.

"You are the Captain. It is correct that your Ship

should come to you, particularly now," the house rumbled, but so softly that only I could hear.

The shadow fell over the house and then deepened as the Ship descended. The landing pedestal was extended down to the yard, crushing a grove of willow trees. The main hangar deck door opened and the ramp was extended for me. I boarded as I had years ago and briefly imagined we were fleeing again and that there were hundreds of thousands on board asleep. Her local gravity was active so it was impossible to tell when she lifted off and moved away to the north.

There was no need to hurry and we did not arrive at the chosen location, forty kilometers north of Great Slave Lake, until late afternoon of the following day. The Minds urged me to stay at altitude and send down only robotic agents, starting with the insects and then working up to more capable devices if the wolves continued to elude us. I told them that I wished to go myself.

I stood in the empty hangar deck; the overhead lights were one hundred and fifty meters above me and cast soft cathedral shadows over everything below. The place had been designed to accommodate the coming and going of eight hundred thousand people. Now there were only me and the Ship's incorporeal Minds. I could not help but think of the quantum dimensions, as small within their containment Strings as I was within the Ship itself.

"Grounding," the Minds announced. I had felt nothing. "Instructions?"

"Are there any nearby?"

"As expected, no."

"But where are they, then?"

A moment passed as they checked their operatives. "They are elusive. There are eleven within a five-kilometer radius. But it is densely wooded and at this level, locations can only be plotted to within fifty meters at five-minute intervals.

"There are no enemy ruins apart from a downed cruiser seventy kilometers from here."

"Is there a moon tonight?"

"Yes. We think it is quite beautiful out."

"Please open the door."

The hangar door was two hundred meters across and eighty high; it slid up into the deck's ceiling with a pneumatic hiss. There was a wide meadow in front of the opening, the grass glistening like obsidian with evening dew. The Ship's overhang kept the stars from appearing any higher than twenty degrees above the horizon.

"Here?" I asked, walking to the landing ramp.

"One is approaching but its path is indecisive. The others are waiting."

"What should I do?"

"We anticipated you would know. We do not."

I stopped at the edge of the hangar door. Although it was summer, the still air was cold. I thought of asking the Ship to warm me with an infrared spot, but the wolves might be able to see that. I therefore instructed the Ship to power down to full darkness and ambient temperature. Within a minute, it was perceptible only as a looming, spindle-shaped blackness against the sky. The moon cast its shadow over the forest.

I walked to the end of the ramp and sat down. There was no wind; we must have been far away from any streams, for it was absolutely quiet. I could not even imagine the shallow, electronic respiration of the Minds. "Anything else besides them?"

"No vertebrates. Only the wolves." Then, almost hopefully, "There may be evidence of a fox, too, but that is very equivocal."

"But they are here? At this place?"

"Yes."

I stepped onto the grass, feeling as disoriented as I ever had in space, and walked out under the Ship's shadow. "Are you there?" I asked, suddenly anxious.

The Minds whispered softly, "We are still here. We will always be here."

Reassured, I picked up some deadfall and carried it back to the edge of the landing ramp. I arranged it into a small pile and then sat down on the ramp beside it. A copper wasp flew out of the dark and played a tiny laser thread on it until the wood glowed and began to burn. I edged close to the warmth, feeling the cavernous space of the hangar deck at my back. I thought I would be frightened if it were not inhabited by my own, familiar Minds. Because it was, I could think of the forest in front of me and wait for the wolves to see the same fire and wonder if its warmth could make the sickness their kind had gotten during the war go away.

Will they forgive us? Me?

"We are still here," a voice came but I could not be sure of its direction or origin. Then, moving closer: "We have always been here."

My Pal Clunky

RON GOULART

Ron Goulart attended the same writing workshop in
Anthony Boucher's home in the early 1950s as Philip K.
Dick and has been one of the finest mannerist stylists of
SF dark humor for more than forty years. His initial rep-
utation was as a satirical short story writer in the '50s
and early '60s. He published his first SF story, "Letters
to the Editor", in *F&SF* in 1952, and wrote many stories
before the appearance of his first SF novel, *The Sword
Swallower* (1968). Like much of his ensuing work, it is
set in space and in a future (the Barnum System) that distinctly resembles Southern California. In the mid-'70s
and '80s he wrote under various pseudonyms (including
the house names Kenneth Robeson and Con Steffanson,
as well as personal pseudonyms like Chad Calhoun,
R. T. Edwards, Ian R. Jamieson, Josephine Kains, Jillian
Kearny, Howard Lee, Zeke Masters, Frank S. Shawn,
and Joseph Silva) a large number of novelizations and
other routine work. He has had eight short story collections and more than forty novels published, of which the
most famous is *After Things Fell Apart* (1970). He is an
acknowledged expert on comics and the pulp magazines, and edited (among others) *The Hardboiled Dicks*
(1965); *The Encyclopedia of American Comics* (1990),
and has written *Cheap Thrills: An Informal History of
the Pulp Magazines* (1972); *The Adventurous Decade:
Comic Strips in the Thirties* (1976); *The Great Comic
Book Artists* (1986); and *The Great Comic Book Artists*

Volume 2 (1988) and other books on comics or pulps. The *Encyclopedia of Science Fiction* says: "darker, sharper, more attentive aspect of the [Goulart] vision of California-as-Barnum can be seen in those of his novels—*Wildsmith* (1972), among others—which feature the highly humanized, eccentric, willful Robots which are perhaps his most enduring creation. Quite remarkably comic in their deadpan obsessiveness and persnickety sang-froid, they serve also as genuinely effective icons of a time—the near future—and a place—either Southern California itself or the world which it portends—caught in the throes of convulsive change." This story is from *Analog*—not your typical *Analog* story—and is a robot story, of the classic Goulart kind.

He and the dog sneezed simultaneously.

"God bless," muttered the dog.

Ridge Gilby took a step back from the work bench. "Hey, my DogBots aren't supposed to sneeze," he said, frowning.

The large chrome-plated robot dog was lying on its side, the panel in its midsection dangling open to allow access to the inner circuitry. "Well, that's one of the reasons Mr. Dannenberg returned me for this free overhaul."

Rubbing the plaz handle of the electroscrewer across his slightly plump chin, Gilby said, "It might be better, too, Rex, if you got that snide tone out of your voice."

"That's another reason why I'm here," reminded the silvery Rex. "Didn't you pay attention to the list of complaints Mr. Dannenberg read off to you? He feels, for instance, that a household guard dog should be self-effacing and obsequious with his employer. He further believes that a robot hound who sneezes uncontrollably will have a tough time sneaking up on possible burglars and thieves. It spoils the element of surprise, while—"

"OK, enough," suggested Gilby, sighing. "I really miss show business."

"I'll tell you something," put in Rex, letting his plaz tongue loll out of his metallic mouth for a few seconds. "You'd be a good deal happier if you accepted your fate. Far as the entertainment world is concerned, you're a total flop now and unlikely ever to make a comeback. There are not, as the feller said, second acts in American—"

"Hush," he advised as he thrust the screwdriver into the inner workings of the mechanical guard dog.

The holographic platform in the far corner of the small lab made a muffled pinging sound.

"Oops," said Rex. "Hope it's not another creditor wanting his or her dough."

Very reluctantly, Gilby said, "OK, I accept the call."

The full-size projected image of a young Chinese man appeared on the narrow circular stage. "Hi ya, Mr. Gilby."

Setting aside the screwdriver, he walked over to the stage. "Now what, Eng?"

"Hey, listen, I'd appreciate it if you'd address me as Associate Custodian Eng. What do you think?"

"Now what, Associate Custodian Eng?"

"That sounds better, yeah." Eng grinned. "After all, the Malibu Underground Estates Complex is a high-class, prestigious setup here in Greater LA and—"

"What is the purpose of your call?"

"It's about that dripping in your living room. We—"

"That's not a dripping, it's a small continuous stream."

"Be that as it may," said the Associate Custodian, "it isn't, as you hysterically insinuated when you made your complaint last week, the Pacific Ocean leaking into this underground wing."

"Well, that's a relief. So what the hell is it?"

"Nothing more than a slight malfunction in our highly efficient sewage transfer system," the young man explained.

"Sewage is nearly as toxic as the damned ocean. When are you dimwits going to get this fixed?"

"Hey, labeling me and my colleagues as dimwits isn't going to encourage swiftness."

"When?"

"First thing."

"Which means?"

"Probably tomorrow." He smiled and was gone.

"Hard cheese," commented the sprawled robot dog.

Gilby had taken two steps back toward the work bench when the holostage pinged again.

Murmuring, "Accept the call," he turned to face it.

A plump woman with glittering platinum hair and glowing scarlet lips was materializing there. "God, you look terrible, Ridge," she observed. "Your fall from grace hasn't set well on you, dear."

"Edna," he said with minimal enthusiasm.

Edna Thurber spread her arms wide and her image executed a slow turn. "Unlike you, I've been able to afford continuous attendance at one of the best modification spas," she told him. "Consequently, though I'm nearly eighty-three years young, I still look no older than when last we met."

"True," he admitted to his former agent. "Although you do creak more than you did three years ago."

She leaned toward him, smiling. "How'd you like to sign up again with Multimedia Services Worldwide?"

He rested one foot on the edge of the holostage, eyes narrowing. "Somebody's contacted you," he guessed. "Sure, because the last time I tried to reach you I couldn't even get as far as your Assistant Receptionist andy."

"I have put together a rather nice deal for you, ingrate that you are," Edna said. "If you're interested."

"I'm interested in anything that doesn't involve schlepping robotic guard dogs."

"Of course you know Burt Farr."

"Kid actor. We used him on the show couple times."

"No, that was five years ago. Burt's twenty now and just took over as head of the Newgate Network. When Burt was young—"

"He's still young."

"When he was younger, he was a great fan of *My Pal Clunky*."

"So were a couple billion other people around the world."

"The point is, he watched it faithfully. Not just the segments he had small parts on," the plump agent continued. "Burt, darling that he is, thinks it's time for Clunky and you to make a comeback. In his view, there's never been a talking robot dog adventure show to equal it."

"He's absolutely right, and that's because I excel in more than one area," Gilby put in. "I built a truly first-rate mechanical canine. But I was also able to turn out top-drawer scripts for *My Pal Clunky*. The shows mixed action, humor and pathos and those little monologues that Clunky delivered at the tag were—"

"I'm already sold, dear. Save the spiel for the meeting."

"What meeting, Edna?"

"A week from tomorrow you and I, and that darling little Clunky, will shuttle up to the ShowBiz, Inc. orbiting satellite for a meeting with Burt Farr and some of his colleagues. If all goes as well as I expect, we'll—"

"I thought you said the deal was all set?"

"Just about set," she explained. "If it were up to Burt alone, we'd simply sign the contracts to do twenty-six segments of a new *My Pal Clunky* vidwall series, dear. And we'd be pulling in exactly $2,000,000 per episode."

"That's much better than what we were getting for the old shows," he said. "You say this meeting up there is in a week? Could we maybe postpone it for another couple weeks? I've got some guard dog orders backed up and—"

"Eight days, dear. It's either then or never," said Edna. "Oh, say, where is the little dickens?"

"Which little dickens?"

"Well, obviously, schmuck, I mean Clunky. Who else?"

"Oh, Clunky, yes. He's here, sure. Despite the ups and downs and the harsh blows of fate, that marvelous dog and I have remained inseparable."

"I'd like to say hello to him."

"Say hello to him?"

"You've gotten much more slow-witted, dear."

"Actually, Edna, Clunky is up at ground level," he said. "He likes to chase seagulls along the beach. A hobby he's developed since dropping out of the limelight."

"OK, dear, I don't have time to wait around while you go topside and fetch him," decided the plump platinum-haired agent. "But give the little bugger a big kiss for me. I'll call you later in the week with firm times for our departure. You're virtually back on top again, Ridge." She made a slight popping sound as her image left the stage.

"Shit." Shoulders slumped, Gilby shuffled over to the work bench.

"Why the gloom?" inquired Rex. "Sounds to me like you're on the comeback trail."

"Unlike you, Clunky wasn't a run of the mill robot dog," said Gilby sadly. "It took me months to put him together and every single component was the best, and the most expensive, to be had at the time." He shook his head and sighed again. "It would take me, even if I could afford it, weeks to build a new Clunky."

"Why do you want to do a dumb thing like that? All you have to do is tune-up the old original Clunky."

Gilby shook his head. "Hell, I sold the old original Clunky over two years ago," he said, "to raise enough money to start this half-wit business."

▲   ▲   ▲

The lean black man on the vidphone screen was wearing a white medsuit that seemed somewhat loose for him. "What seems to be the trouble? I'm Dr. Mackinson."

"No, you're not Dr. Mackinson." Gilby was leaning far to the left as he faced the phone, careful to avoid the thin stream of processed sewage that was cascading from the living room ceiling into a large plaz bucket. "Mackinson is a big wide Scandinavian gent with an unruly mop of blond hair."

Dr. Mackinson smiled, nodding understandingly. "I bought the Dr. Mackinson franchise for the New Phoenix AZ area well over a year ago," he explained. "I'm the local Dr. Mackinson now."

"Christ," muttered Gilby. "Where's the other Dr. Mackinson?"

"Technically, you see, he isn't Dr. Mackinson anymore. The way the deal works is that in each franchise area there can be only—"

"OK, whoever the hell he is—can you tell me where to find the guy?"

"Perhaps I could help you with this anxiety attack, Mr. Gilby?"

Gilby, slowly and carefully, inhaled and exhaled. He moved a few more inches to the left and tried not to scowl at the phonescreen. "I'm not having a medical problem at the moment, doctor," he explained. "The thing is, I sold something to Dr. Mackinson a couple years—"

"The *former* Dr. Mackinson."

"Him, yeah. I'm eager to locate this object and, if possible—"

"Oh, say, I recognize you now. Even though you're much fatter and pastier than you were back in your heyday," said the black medic. "Ridge Gilby. I have to tell you, I was a great fan of *My Pal Clunky* when I was in med school." He paused, remembering. "Is the Clunky botdog the object you're seeking, Mr. Gilby?"

"Yep. Did he take it with him?"

"No, he sold that appealing little pup to a fellow collector shortly before giving up the practice here—just before he retired to Old New Mexico."

"Sold Clunky to who?"

Dr. Mackinson shook his head. "No idea. I do recall that Sven expressed regret on more than one occasion that he'd been foolhardy in getting rid of such a pleasant and lovable electronic companion."

"I built in those qualities," said Gilby. "OK, is Dr. Mackinson's real first name Sven then?"

"Sven Nordling. He's residing, last I heard, at the Golden Years Chateau Complex in Taos."

"Thanks. I'll try there."

"I can prescribe something for that twitch if you'd like."

"What twitch?"

The doctor tapped his right eyebrow. "A cross between a twitch and a flinch actually. A few swigs of Relaxacon should fix it right up."

"It's only the sewage that's making me flinch, doctor. But thanks again." He ended the call. "Damn, here's my chance to get out of this lame-brained business and I can't even locate—"

"You ought to turn up the aircirc system to compensate for the reek," suggested Rex from the living room doorway.

"You're not supposed to leave the lab. I'm still working on you."

"Important call for you on the holophone," explained the large silvery dog.

"Bill-collecting bots and andies aren't important."

"This is your ex-wife."

"Which one?"

"Lady who calls herself Molly Spartan."

"Go tell Molly I'll be catching up on her alimony chex very shortly."

"She says she doesn't want money from you just now." Rex nodded back toward the lab. "She says she's calling about making *you* money."

"I'll take the call," he decided.

Molly Spartan was tall and slim; her office was several levels above the ground in the Santa Monica Sector of Greater LA. Red-haired at present, she was just ten years younger than her erstwhile husband. "You ought to rush to a spa as soon as you can," she was telling Gilby as she guided him into a tin client chair and moved around behind her wide Lucite desk. "You're really pasty-faced, Ridge."

"Current medical opinion seems to agree," he said. "If you're finished itemizing my flaws, let's talk about how exactly you're going to make me money."

"You shouldn't ever wear those form-fit tunics," she said as she settled into her chair. "Not with the form you've got."

"Money," he repeated quietly.

"Going to robobarbers again, are you?"

He brushed a hand at his temple. "Molly, you dangled the possibility of my increasing my intake of cash when we spoke this morning."

She looked him up and down and, seemingly with some reluctance, ended her critique. "I've been very successful since we separated," she informed him. "The Spartan Investigation Service is considered one of the best private inquiry agencies in GLA."

"And?"

"In addition to security work and marital cases— I'm an absolute wiz at tracking down people," she said. "I'm confident that I can also find a missing robot dog."

He sat up straight. "How the hell did you know I was looking for Clunky?"

"A man who owes me nearly $13,000 in overdue alimony is someone, Ridge, I'm going to keep an eye on."

"That's not legal, is it?"

Molly smiled, patting the air in front of her as though she were patting his head in a humoring way. "You'll forgive my mentioning this, but you're going about this in your typical incompetent way," she said. "It's extremely dumb, in my opinion, to contact people and blatantly indicate that you're desperate to get that little hound back. What's called for, rather, is an oblique approach."

"Jesus, I am desperate. I've absolutely got to have him up on the ShowBiz satellite in seven days. I don't have time to be oblique."

She steepled her slender fingers, rested her chin on them. "It's possible to be both subtle *and* fast. Want to make a deal with me?"

"Could you, Molly, maybe at least hint at the details of this deal?"

"I help you locate Clunky, negotiate his return to you on the best possible terms."

"And your fee is what?"

"All you have to do is pay the back alimony—with interest," Molly said. "And, soon as the deal with Farr is set, you increase your weekly payments to me by 235 percent."

"Christ, that would amount to—"

"Or you can forget about Clunky and I'll simply get the law to attach your guard dog setup and pay me out of—"

"I'll accept your onerous terms," he said. "What I was planning to do, once I located the present owner, was to offer him a percentage of the take from the new show for the use of my dog."

"That may not be necessary."

He eyed his former wife. "Do you already know where Clunky is?"

"Not yet, but I'm confident I can run him to ground soon—and I can get his ownership returned to you for as low a price as possible."

He studied her thermocarpet for a few silent seconds. "OK, all right." He stood up and held his hand across the desk. "Shall we shake on the deal?"

"Signing papers will be sufficient," she said, ignoring his hand.

Molly settled back in the pilot seat of her skycar, glancing over at Gilby. "Something?" she inquired.

He was sitting uneasily in the passenger seat. "I've never been that fond of your stunt flying, Molly."

"That wasn't stunt flying just now," she said. "It isn't a stunt when you swoop to avoid a collision."

"Swooping maybe, but the three loops afterwards were—"

"You're even stodgier now than you were during our unfortunate marriage."

He turned his attention to the bright afternoon they were traveling through at an altitude of 5,000 feet. "You're certain Clunky is down here in Florida?"

"Absolutely."

"You haven't," he reminded her, "given me all the details on how you found him."

"When I questioned Sven Nordling's Chief Therapist at the Golden Years Chateau Complex—You ought to take a look at that place, by the way. The residents all have marvelous tans and—"

"I'm only forty-three."

"Really? I thought you were *twenty* years my senior."

"Ten. What did Nordling have to say?"

"Never talked to him directly. Easier, and cheaper, to get the information from a staff person," said Molly. "Turns out Sven sold the robot dog to Greasy Thumb Johnsen down in the Tijuana Sector of GLA."

"Greasy Thumb Johnsen has an unsavory ring to it."

"It's one of those gangster franchises. When the previous Greasy Thumb Johnsen was gunned down in a robobarber shop in the Caliente Sector, the current Greasy Thumb Johnsen bought the role," continued the redheaded investigator. "He was formerly Mr. Soynut in the Pasadena Sector."

"They make second-rate donuts. What does being Greasy Thumb Johnsen entail?"

They were nearing their Florida destination and the skycar began a slow descent.

"He manages the Casa Grande Casino & Bordello in Tijuana."

"He kept my dog in a bordello?"

She nodded. "Actually, Clunky played the piano there and was, according to my sources, extremely popular with the patrons."

He frowned, shaking his head. "No, Clunky can't play the piano. I didn't build that ability into him."

"He can play the piano now, trust me," she told him. "One of my informants raved about his boogie-woogie repertoire especially, and praised his 'wicked left paw.'"

"I don't see how he can—"

"Five months ago a fellow named Prentice Barham from here in the St. Pete Redoubt showed up for a vacation in the Tijuana Sector. He subsequently broke the bank and then, since he'd taken a fancy to Clunky, bought him from Greasy Thumb Johnsen."

"Clunky's still in his possession?"

"That's what Barham's butler tells me, yes."

"If Barham is living off a gambling fortune, he's not likely to sell me back my robot dog for anything like a reasonable price, Molly."

"Let me worry about the business details," she suggested. "I did some research on Barham and I think I'll be able to persuade him to sell cheaply."

The voxbox on the dash panel of the descending skycar announced, "We'll be arriving at the villa in two minutes eleven sections."

Gilby asked, "Villa?"

"Barham bought that soon after he bought your dog."

The cyborg butler bowed, then gestured with his coppery right hand. "If you'll step into the music room, please," he invited Molly and Gilby.

The villa consisted of a linked series of five huge plazglass domes, each tinted a different pastel shade. There were holographic tropical plants and trees lining every passway and the aircirc system was pumping in a steamy scent reminiscent of damp greenhouses.

The music room was in the dome that was tinted a pale turquoise and someone within it was playing the *Goldberg Variations* on an electric harpsichord.

The butler halted at the entry way, stood aside and said, "In there, if you will."

"Hi, kiddo," called the small silver-plated robot dog who was sitting on the harpsichord bench. He remained in an awkward, vaguely human position until he'd concluded the seventeenth variation. "Long time no see, Ridge old boy."

"You can't play the piano." Gilby moved nearer his creation.

"This happens to be a harpsichord, chump." The dog hopped free of the bench, went trotting over to

Molly. "Hi, toots, you're still gorgeous. Which is more than I can say for Young Tom Edison yonder. You've got a complexion like unbaked sourdough, chief."

"So I keep hearing." Gilby scanned the room.

There were two pianos, one traditional and the other electric, a harp, two dozen or more simulated potted palms, Victorian-style furniture and, on a low pedestal, a neomarble statue of Clunky up on his hind legs with one paw to his brow and apparently looking far off.

"Pipe the sculpture, folks," Clunky invited. "Me in a heroic pose. Nifty, huh?" He circled Molly once before jumping up onto a candy-stripe loveseat and stretching out.

"Why would Prentice Barham want such a god-awful artifact in his music room?" asked Gilby, frowning at the statue.

The robot dog snickered. "Dumb as ever, I note," he said to Molly.

"Meaning," she said, "there is no Prentice Barham?"

"Bingo," said the dog. "Park it, folks, and we'll chat for a spell."

Gilby sat on the edge of a Morris chair. "But Prentice Barham is the guy who broke the bank and bought you from Greasy Thumb Johnsen."

"Yeah, sure, and Snow White shacked up with Prince Charming and lived happily ever after." Clunky sighed. "Barham was actually a down and out vidwall actor I hired for the part. He strolled into the casino and I rigged the wheel so he'd keep winning. Then he bought me my freedom and I gave the poor gink his 10 percent of the take." The robot dog sat up, rolling his plaz eyes. "I own this joint and, since I've invested wisely, I'm set for life."

"A dog can't own property or—"

"I'm no ordinary mutt, remember? Besides every-

thing was done in the name of Prentice Barham."
Chuckling, Clunky rolled over on his silver-plated back.
"I've been thinking about giving you a jingle on the vidphone, boss. It's just about time for a tune-up and you
might—"

"Don't you miss acting, Clunky?" asked Molly
from another loveseat.

"Do you miss slipping between the sheets with the
human pudding yonder?"

"Well, no, but acting on a vidwall show is exciting."

Gilby scowled. "How come every discussion tends
to involve insulting me in—"

"Ah, I get it. Sure, you dimwits invaded my privacy
in order to try to persuade me to jaunt up to the Show-
Biz satellite with you next week." Clunky chuckled
again.

"They're offering $2,000,000 per show," said Gilby.

"And my cut will be?"

"You never got a cut on the old show and—"

"Nix, old boy," cut in the robot dog. "I'm no longer
the same naïve little mechanism you cooked up years
back. Nope, I've improved myself immeasurably, boss,
made additions, modifications and—"

"You couldn't have done that, Clunky. It would be
a violation of the basic laws of robotics."

"Nertz to the basic laws of robotics." He dropped
to the real tile floor and trotted over to where Gilby was
sitting. "Fifty-fifty."

"Hum?"

"I have to get 50 percent of the gross take."

"Why's a dog need $1,000,000 a week?"

"Same reason you need it, boss." Clunky looked up
at him with narrowed plaz eyes. "Well?"

After a moment Gilby said, "OK, it's a deal. But it
hurts me deeply to realize that the very creature I
labored over for endless trying months could now—"

The robot dog made a raspberry sound. "Hey, this is show business we're talking about," he reminded. "Hardly the place for sentimental guff."

Clunky leaped up onto the big oval conference table, landing with an echoing thunk. He rose on his hind legs and executed an expert cakewalk. "Greetings, ladies and gents," he said to the three executives seated at the table.

Gilby came hurrying across the domed satellite room after the robot dog. "You'll have to excuse Clunky," he said, making a grab at him. "He's excited about the possibility of returning to—"

"Howdy, Burtie." The dog eluded his creator, skidded across the tabletop and landed in the lap of the youthful Burt Farr. "You're a lot better looking than you were as a kid actor. Although that's not saying much."

"Good to see you again, Clunker," the thin blond Farr said as he pried the dog off his lap and deposited him again atop the table.

Clunky took a couple of steps, then executed a bird-dog take. "Well sir, if it isn't Rowland Hemerson," he said, nose aimed at a large, wide man of fifty. "Haven't seen you since—"

"You've never seen me, you odious little mutt." Hemerson pushed his chair back several inches.

"I get you." When Clunky winked, his metallic eyelid produced a loud clicking sound.

The thin black woman sitting on the opposite side of the table cleared her throat. "I'm terribly afraid, Mr. Gilby, that you've had to make the shuttle trip up here for nothing."

"How's that, Mrs. Leandro?"

"Burt was a little premature in what he told your wonderfully well-preserved agent," she said. "We've decided—unfortunately too late to prevent you from making the journey here—that we won't be able to make an offer on *My Pal Clunky*."

"I'm still very enthusiastic," put in young Farr. "Probably within another year or so—"

"Boss," suggested Clunky over his silvery shoulder, "why don't you go out and join your former missus in that gaudy reception room?"

"I don't intend to leave you alone with—"

"Scram and trust me."

Mrs. Leandro said, "There's really no need for either of you to remain any longer."

Ignoring her, the dog said, "Chief, please. Scoot."

With a lopsided shrug, Gilby made his exit.

The suite they had on the Earthbound shuttle was twice the size of the one they'd occupied on the trip up to the satellite.

"OK," Gilby was saying as he paced the thermo-carpet, "now explain what exactly you did."

Clunky was stretched out on a settee. "I simply persuaded that trio of dimwits to sign us up."

"But instead of twenty-six shows, they're going to do fifty-two," said Molly from the doorway to the pantry. "That's, my lord, $104,000,000 for the first year."

"It is," agreed the robot dog, allowing his silvery tail to wag a few times.

Gilby said, "But, according to Mrs. Leandro, they'd decided not to hire us at all."

"I had a short, private chat with Rowland Hemreson."

"And?"

"He cast the deciding vote, since Farr was already on our side."

"Yeah, but how'd you convince Hemerson to do that?"

Clunky chuckled. "I wasn't kidding when I mentioned having met the gink before, boss," he explained. "Nope, Rowland was a frequent customer of the bordello during my months of servitude. I happened to use my built-in vidcamera to take some interesting footage of his more ambitious activities and—"

"You don't have a built-in camera."

"I added that myself," said the dog. "Even by Hollywood moral standards, Rowland's performances aren't acceptable. He was happy to further my career in exchange for my promise of discreet silence."

"Blackmail," said Gilby.

"Right, and a basic negotiating tool," said Clunky. "I've got quite a library of footage stored inside me. We'll be able to use it to persuade other important bigwigs to smooth our path back into the mainstream of world entertainment, chief."

"How can you store pictures?" Gilby stopped in front of the dog. "I didn't design you to—"

"You really haven't been paying sufficient attention," Clunky told him. "I've used my time away from you to improve myself."

"Even so, I—"

"I also taught myself to write scripts. And I'm damned good at it."

"Write scripts? But that's what I do on *My Pal Clunky*."

"No, that's what *we* do," the dog told him. "Sit down and I'll tell you some of my ideas. OK?"

Life in the Extreme

DAVID BRIN

David Brin, the third of the hard SF "killer Bs," began publishing SF with his first novel, *Sundiver* (1980), a grand space opera and the first volume in the ongoing Uplift sequence, for which he is most famous. He continued it in *Startide Rising* (1983; rev. 1985) and *The Uplift War* (1987). *Startide Rising* won both the Hugo and the Nebula awards for best novel; *The Uplift War* won a Hugo, and the series continues today. Brin emerged as the most popular and—along with Greg Bear, Paul Preuss, James P. Hogan, Robert L. Forward, and Charles Sheffield—one of the most important writers of hard SF to appear and flourish in the 1980s. Brin is a convincing optimist. Outside of the Uplift sequence, Brin has published several novels, the most ambitious to date being *Earth* (1990) and *Glory Season* (1993). He has also published two story collections, *The River of Time* (1986), and *Otherness* (1994). This story is an Uplift story and was first published in *Popular Science* in 1998, which announced it as the beginning of SF fiction publishing in that venue.

Cameras stare across a forbidden desert, monitoring disputed territory in a conflict so bitter that the opponents cannot even agree on what to name it.

One side calls the struggle a war with countless innocent lives in jeopardy.

The other side claims there are no victims.

And so suspicious cameras peer and pan, alert for encroachment. Vigilant camouflaged monitors scan from atop hills or under innocuous piles of stones. They hang beneath highway culverts, probing constantly for a hated enemy. For some time—months, at least—these guardians have succeeded in staving off incursions across the sandy desolation.

That is, until technology changes yet again, shifting the advantage briefly from defense to offense.

When the enemy struck this time, their first move was to take out those guardian eyes.

Infiltrators arrived at dawn, under the glare of the rising sun. Several hundred little flying machines jetted through the air, skimming very low to the ground on gusts from whispering motors. Each device, no larger than a hummingbird, followed a carefully scouted path toward its selected target, some stationary camera or sensor. The attackers even looked like native desert birds, in case they were spotted during those crucial last seconds.

Each little drone landed behind the target, in its blind spot, and unfolded wings that transformed into high-resolution graphics displays, depicting perfect false images of the same desert scene. Each robot inserted its illusion in front of the guardian lens—carefully, so as not to create a suspicious flicker. Other small spy machines sniffed out camouflaged seismic sensors and embraced them gently, providing new cushioning that would mask the tremors to come.

The robotic attack, covering an area of more than a hundred square kilometers, took only eight minutes to complete. The desert now lay unwatched, undefended.

From over the horizon, giant vehicles started moving in. They converged along several roadways toward the same open area—seventeen quiet, hybrid-electric tractor trailers disguised as commercial cargo transports, complete with company holo-logos blazoned on their sides. But when their paths intersected at the chosen rendezvous, a more cryptic purpose revealed itself. Crews wearing dun-colored jumpsuits leaped from the cabs to start unlashing container sections. Auxiliary generators set to work. The air began to swirl with shimmering waves of exotic stench, as pungent volatiles gushed from storage tanks to fill pressurized vessels. Electronic consoles sprang to life, and hinged panels fell away from the trailers, revealing long, tapered objects that lay on slanted ramps.

With a steady whine, each cigar shape lifted its nose from horizontal to vertical, aiming skyward, while stabilizer fins popped open at the tail end. Shouts between the work crews grew more tense as a series of tightly coordinated countdowns commenced. There wouldn't be much time to spare before the enemy—sophisticated and wary—picked up enough clues and figured out what was going on.

Soon every missile was aimed . . . launch sequences engaged . . . and targets acquired. All they lacked were payloads.

Abruptly, a dozen figures emerged from an air-conditioned van, wearing snug suits of shimmering material and garishly painted helmets. Each one carried a small satchel that hummed and whirred, pumping air to keep the suit cool. Several had trouble walking normally. Their gait seemed rubbery, as if both excited and anxious at the same time. One of the smaller figures even briefly skipped.

A dour-looking woman wearing a badge and a uniform awaited them, holding a clipboard. She confronted the tallest figure, whose helmet bore a motif of flames surrounding a screaming mouth.

"Name and scan," she demanded in a level tone of voice.

The helmet visor swiveled back, revealing a heavily tanned face, about thirty, with eyes the color of a cold sea.

"Hacker Torrey," he said, as her clipboard automatically sought his left iris, reading its unique patterns to confirm his ID. "And yes," he continued, "I affirm that I'm doing this of my own free will. Can we get on with it?"

"Your permits seem to be in order," the woman replied, unhurriedly. "Your liability bond and waivers have been accepted. The government won't stand in your way."

The tall man shrugged, as if the statement was both expected and irrelevant. He flung the visor back down. There were other forces to worry about, more formidable than mere government. Forces who were desperate to prevent what was about to take place here.

At a signal, all of the suited figures rushed to ladders that launch-crew members braced against the side of each rocket. Each hurried up the makeshift gantry and, slipping inside a narrow capsule, squirmed into the cramped couch with unconscious grace, having practiced the motions hundreds of times. Even the novices knew exactly what they were doing. What the dangers might be. The costs and the rewards.

Hatches slammed shut and hissed as they sealed. Muffled shouts could be heard as final preparations were completed.

The countdown for the first missile reached zero.

"Yeeeee-haw!" Hacker Torrey shouted, before a violent kick of ignition flattened him against the airbed. He had done this several times before, yet the sheer ecstatic rush of this moment beat anything else on Earth.

Soon, he would no longer even be part of the Earth . . . for a little while.

Seconds passed amid a brutal shaking as the rocket clawed its way skyward. A mammoth hand seemed to plant itself on his chest and shove, expelling half the contents of his lungs in a moan of sweet agony. Friction heat and ionization licked the transparent nose cone just inches from his face. Shooting toward the heavens at Mach 5, he felt pinned, helplessly immobile . . . and completely omnipotent.

I'm a god!

Somehow he drew enough breath to let out another cry—this time a shout of elated greeting as black space spread before the missile's bubble nose, flecked by a million glittering stars.

Back on the ground, the last rocket was gone. Frenetic cleanup efforts then began, even more anxious than setup had been. Reports from distant warning posts told of incoming flying machines, racing toward the launch site at high speed. Men and women sprinted back and forth across the scorched desert sand, packing up to depart before the enemy arrived.

Only the government official moved languidly, using computerized scanners, meticulously adding up the damage to vegetation, erodible soils, and tiny animals. It was pretty bad, but localized, without appreciable effect on endangered species. A reconditioning service had already been called for. Of course that would not satisfy everybody. . . .

She handed over an estimated bill as the last team member revved his hybrid engine, impatient to be off. "Aw, man!" he complained, reading the total. "Our club will barely break even on this launch!"

"Then pick a less expensive hobby," she replied, and stepped back as the driver gunned his truck, roaring away in a cloud of dust, incidentally crushing one more small barrel cactus en route to the highway. The vigilant monitoring system in her clipboard noted this and made an addendum to the excursion society's final bill.

Sitting on the hood of her jeep, she waited for another "club" to arrive. One whose members were just as passionate as the rocketeers. Just as skilled and dedicated, even though both groups hated each other. Sensors announced they were near, coming fast from the west—radical environmentalists whose no-compromise aim was to preserve nature at all costs.

The official knew what to expect when they arrived, frustrated to find their opponents gone and two acres of precious desert singed. She was going to get another tongue-lashing for being "evenhanded" in a situation where so many people insisted that you could only choose sides.

Oh well, she thought. *It takes a thick skin to work in government nowadays. Nobody thinks you matter much. They don't respect us like in the old days.*

Looking up, she watched the last of the rocket contrails start to shear apart, ripped by stratospheric winds. For some reason it always tugged the heart. And while her intellectual sympathies lay closer to the eco-enthusiasts, a part of her deep inside thrilled each time she witnessed one of these launches. So ecstatic—

almost orgiastic—and joyfully unrestrained.

"Go!" She whispered with a touch of secret envy toward the distant glitters, already arcing over the pinnacle of their brief climb and starting their long plummet toward the Gulf of Mexico.

Hacker Torrey found out something was wrong just after the stars blurred out.

Flames flickered around the edges of his heat shield, probing every crevice, seeking a way inside. These flickers announced the start of re-entry, one of the best parts of this expensive ride, when his plummeting capsule would shake and resonate, filling every blood vessel with more exhilaration than you could get anywhere this side of Las Vegas. Some called this the new "super-extreme hobby" . . . more dangerous than any other sport and much too costly for anybody but an elite to afford. That fact attracted some rich snobs, who bought tickets just to prove they could, and wound up puking in their respirators or screaming in terror during the long plunge back to Earth.

As far as Hacker was concerned, those fools only got what they deserved. The whole point of having money was to do stuff with it! And if you weren't meant to ride a rocket, you could always find a million other hobbies.

An alarm throbbed. He didn't hear it—his eardrums had been drugged and clamped to protect them during the flight. Instead, he felt the tremor through a small implant in his lower jaw. In a simple pulse code the computer told him.

GUIDANCE SYSTEM ERROR.
FLIGHT PATH CORRECTION MISFIRED.
CALCULATING TRAJECTORY TO NEW IMPACT ZONE.

"What?" Hacker shouted, though the rattle and roar of re-entry tore away his words. "To hell with that! I paid for a triple redundancy system—"

He stopped, realizing it was pointless to scream at the computer, which he had installed himself, after all.

"Call the pickup boats and tell them—"

COMMUNICATION SYSTEM ENCRYPTION ERROR.
UNABLE TO UPLOAD PRE-ARRANGED SPECTRUM SPREAD.
UNABLE TO CONTACT RECOVERY TEAMS.

"Override encryption! Send in the clear. Acknowledge!"

No answer came. The pulses in his jaw dissolved into a plaintive, juttering rhythm as subprocessors continued their mysterious crapout. Hacker cursed, pounding the wall of the capsule with his fist. Most amateur rocketeers spent years building their own suborbital craft, but Hacker had paid plenty for a "first class" pro model. Someone would answer for this utter incompetence!

Of course he'd signed waivers. Hacker would have little recourse under the International Extreme Sports Treaty. But there were 50,000 private investigation and enforcement services on Earth. He knew a few that would bend the uniform ethics guidelines of the Cop Guild, if paid enough in advance.

"You are gonna pay for this!" he vowed, without knowing yet who should get the brunt of his vengeance. The words were only felt as raw vibrations in his throat. Even the sonic pickups in his mandible hit their overload set points and cut out, as turbulence hit a level matching any he had ever known . . . then went beyond. *The angle of re-entry isn't ideal anymore,* he realized. *And these little sport-capsules don't leave much margin.*

I could be a very rich cinder any moment now.

The realization added a new dimension that had not

been there during any of his previous amateur suborbital flights. One part of Hacker actually seemed to relish a novel experience, scraping each nerve with a howling veer past death. Another portion could not let go of the galling fact that somebody had goofed. He wasn't getting what he'd paid for.

The world still shook and harsh straps tugged his battered body when Hacker awoke. Only now the swaying, rocking motion seemed almost restful, taking him back to childhood, when his family used to "escape civilization" on their trimaran wingsail yacht, steering its stiff, upright airfoil straight through gusts that would topple most other wind-driven vessels.

"Idiots," Hacker's father used to grumble each time he veered the agile craft to avoid colliding with some daytripper who didn't grasp the concept of right-of-way. "The only ones out here used to be people like us, who were raised for this sort of thing. Now the robofacs make so much stuff, even fancy boats, and everybody's got so much free time. Nine billion tourists crowding everywhere. It's impossible to find any solitude!"

"The price of prosperity, dear," his mother would reply, more soft-heartedly. "At least everybody's getting enough to eat now. And there is no more talk of revolution."

"But look at the result! This mad craze for hobbies! Everybody's got to be an expert at something. The *best* at something! I tell you it was better when people had to work to survive."

"Except for people like us?"

"Exactly," Father had answered, ignoring his wife's arch tone. "Look how far we have to go nowadays just to have someplace all to ourselves."

The old man's faith in rugged self-reliance extended

to the name he insisted on giving their son. And Hacker inherited—along with about a billion New Dollars—the very same quest. To do whatever it took to find someplace all his own.

As Hacker's blurry vision returned, he saw that the space pod lay tilted more than halfway over to its side. *It's not supposed to do that,* he thought. *It should float upright.*

A glance to the left explained everything. Ocean surrounded the capsule, but part of the charred heat shield was snagged on a reef of coral branches and spikes that stretched far to the distance, filled with bright fish and undulating subsea vegetation. Nearby, he saw the parasail chute that had softened final impact. Only now, caught by ocean currents, it rhythmically tugged at Hacker's little refuge. With each surge, the bubble canopy plunged closer to a craggy coral outcrop. Soon it struck hard. He did not hear the resulting loud bang, but it made the implant in his jaw throb. Hacker winced, reflexively.

Fumbling, he released the straps and fell over, cringing in pain. That awful re-entry would leave him bruised for weeks. And yet . . .

And yet, I'll have the best story to tell. No one will be able to match it!

The thought made him feel so good, Hacker decided maybe he wouldn't take everything when he sued whoever was responsible for the capsule malfunction. Providing the pickup boats came soon, that is.

The bubble nose struck coral again, rattling his bones. A glance told him a hard truth. Materials designed to withstand launch and re-entry stresses might *not* resist sharp impacts. An ominous crack began to spread.

Standard advice was to stay put and wait for pickup, but this place would be a coffin soon.

I better get out of here.

Hacker flipped his helmet shut and grabbed the emergency exit lever. *A reef should mean an island's nearby. Maybe mainland. I'll hoof it ashore, borrow someone's phone, and start dishing out hell.*

Only there was no island. Nothing lay in sight but more horrible reef.

Hacker floundered in a choppy undertow. The skinsuit was strong, and his helmet had been made of Gillstuff—semipermeable to draw oxygen from seawater. The technology prevented drowning as currents kept yanking him down. But repeated hits by coral outcrops would turn him into hamburger meat soon.

Once, a wave carried him high enough to look around. Ocean, and more ocean. The reef must be a drowned atoll. No boats. No land. No phone.

Sucked below again, he glimpsed the space capsule, caught in a hammer-and-vice wedge and getting smashed to bits. *I'm next,* he thought, trying to swim for open water, but with each surge he was drawn closer to the same deadly site. Panic clogged his senses as he thrashed and kicked the water, fighting it like some overpowering enemy. Nothing worked, though. Hacker could not even hear his own terrified moans, though the jaw implant kept throbbing with clicks, pulses, and weird vibrations, as if the sea had noticed his plight and now watched with detached interest.

Here it comes. He turned away, knowing the next wave cycloid would smash him against those obdurate, rocky spikes.

Suddenly, he felt a sharp poke in the backside. Too early! Another jab, then another, struck the small of his back, feeling nothing like coral. His jaw ached with strange noise as someone or something started pushing

him away from the coral anvil. In both panic and astonishment, Hacker whirled to glimpse a sleek, bottle-
nosed creature interposed between him and the deadly
reef, regarding him curiously, then moving to jab him
again with a narrow beak.

This time, he heard his own moan of relief. *A dolphin!* He reached out for salvation and, after a brief hesitation, the creature let Hacker wrap his arms all
around. Then it kicked hard with powerful tail flukes,
carrying him away from certain oblivion.

Once in open water, he tried to keep up by swimming
alongside his rescuer. But the cetacean grew impatient
and resumed pushing Hacker along with its nose. *Like
hauling an invalid.* Which he was, of course, in this environment.

Soon, two more dolphins converged from the left,
then another pair from the right. They vocalized a lot,
combining sonar clicks with loud squeals that resonated
through the crystal waters. Of course Hacker had seen
dolphins on countless nature shows, and even played tag
with some once, on a diving trip. But soon he started
noticing some strange traits shared by this group. For
instance, these animals took turns making complex
sounds, while glancing at one another or pointing with
their beaks . . . almost as if they were holding conversa-
tions. He could swear they were gesturing toward him
and sharing amused comments at his expense.

Of course it must be an illusion. Everyone knew
that scientists had charted the limits of dolphin intelligence. They were indeed very bright animals—about
chimpanzee equivalent—but had no true, human-level
speech of their own.

And yet, watching a mother lead her infant toward
the lair of a big octopus, he heard the baby's quizzical

squeaks alternate with slow repetitions from the parent. Hacker felt sure a particular syncopated popping meant octopus.

Occasionally, one of them would point its bulbous brow toward Hacker, and suddenly the implant in his jaw pulse-clicked like mad. It almost sounded like the code he had learned, in order to communicate with the space capsule after his inner ears were clamped to protect them during flight. Hacker concentrated on those vibrations in his jaw, for lack of anything else to listen to.

His suspicions roused further when mealtime came. Out of the east there arrived a big dolphin who apparently had a fishing net snared around him! The sight provoked an unusual sentiment in Hacker—pity, combined with guilt over what human negligence had done to the poor animal. He slid a knife from his thigh sheath and moved toward the victim, aiming to cut it free.

Another dolphin blocked Hacker. "I'm just trying to help!" He complained, then stopped, staring as other members of the group grabbed the net along one edge. They pulled backward as the "victim" rolled round and round, apparently unharmed. The net unwrapped smoothly till twenty meters flapped free. Ten members of the pod then held it open while others circled behind a nearby school of mullet.

Beaters! Hacker recognized the hunting technique. They'll drive fish into the net! But how—

He watched, awed as the dolphins expertly cornered and snared their meal, divvied up the catch, then tidied up by rolling the net back around the original volunteer, who sped off to the east. *Well, I'm a blue-nosed gopher,* he mused. Then one of his rescuers approached Hacker with a fish clutched in its jaws. It made offering motions, but then yanked back when he reached for it.

The jaw implant repeated a rhythm over and over. *It's trying to teach me,* he realized.

"Is that the pulse code for fish?" he asked, knowing water would carry his voice but never expecting the creature to grasp spoken English.

To his amazement, the dolphin shook its head. *No.*

"Uh," he continued. "Does it mean food? Eat? Welcome stranger?"

An approving blat greeted his final guess, and the Tursiops flicked the mullet toward Hacker, who felt suddenly ravenous. He tore the fish apart, stuffing each bit of it through his helmet's chowlock.

Welcome stranger? He pondered. *That's mighty abstract for a dumb beast to say. Though, I'll admit, it's friendly.*

That day passed, and then a tense night that he spent clutching a sleeping dolphin by moonlight while clouds of phosphorescent plankton drifted by. Fortunately, the same selective-permeability technology that enabled his helmet to draw oxygen from the sea also provided a trickle of fresh water, filling a small reservoir near his cheek. *I've got to buy stock in this company,* he thought, making a checklist for when he was picked up tomorrow.

Only pickup never came. The next morning and afternoon passed pretty much the same, without catching sight of land or boats. *The world always felt so crowded,* he thought. *Now it seems endless and unexplored.*

Hacker started earning his meals by helping to hold the fishing net when the group harvested dinner. The second night he felt more relaxed, dozing while the dolphins' cliquey gossip seemed to flow up his jaw and into his dreams. On the third morning, and each of those that followed, he felt he understood just a bit more of their simple language.

He lost track of how many days and nights passed. Slowly, Hacker stopped worrying about where the pickup boats could be. Angry thoughts about lawsuits and revenge rubbed away under relentless massaging by current and tide. Immersed in the dolphins' communal sound field, he began concerning himself instead with daily problems of the tribe, like when two young males got into a fight, smacking each other with their beaks and flukes until adults had to forcibly separate them. Using both sign language and his growing vocabulary of click-code, Hacker learned that a female (whose complex name he shortened to Chee-Chee) was in heat. The young brawlers held little hope of mating with her. Still, their nervous energy needed an outlet. At least no one had been seriously harmed.

An old-timer—Kray-Kray—shyly presented a pectoral fin to Hacker, who used his knife to dig out several wormlike parasites. "You should see a real doctor," he urged, as if one gave verbal advice to dolphins every day.

Helpers go away, Kray-Kray tried to explain in click code. *Fins need hands. Helper hands.*

It supported Hacker's theory that something had been done to these creatures. An alteration that had made them distinctly different from others of their species. But what? The mystery grew each time he witnessed some behavior that just couldn't be natural.

Then, one day the whole tribe grew excited, spraying nervous clicks everywhere. Soon Hacker saw they were approaching an undersea habitat dome hidden in a narrow canyon, near a coast where waves met shore.

Shore. The word tasted strange after all these days—weeks?—spent languidly swimming, listening, and learning to enjoy raw fish. Time had different properties down here. It felt odd to contemplate leaving this watery realm, returning where he clearly belonged—the surface world of air, earth, cities, machines, and nine billion humans, forced to inhale one another's humid breath everywhere they went.

That's why we dive into our own worlds. Ten thousand hobbies. A million ways to be special, each person striving to be expert at some arcane art . . . like rocketing into space. Psychologists approved, saying that frenetic amateurism was a much healthier response than the most likely alternative—war. They called this the Century of Aficionados, a time when governments and professional societies could not keep up with private expertise, which spread at lightning speed across the WorldNet. A renaissance, lacking only a clear sense of purpose.

The prospect of soon rejoining that culture left Hacker pensive. *What's the point of so much obsessive activity, unless it leads toward something worthwhile?*

The dolphins voiced a similar thought in their simple but expressive click-language.

If you're good at diving—dive for fish!
If you have a fine voice—sing for others!
If you're great at leaping—bite the sun!

Hacker knew he should clamber up the nearby beach now to call his partners and brokers. Tell them he was alive. Get back to business. But instead he followed his new friends to the hidden habitat dome. *Maybe I'll learn what's been done to them, and why.*

Swimming under and through a portal pool, he was surprised to find the place deserted. No humans anywhere. Finally, Hacker saw a handscrawled sign.

PROJECT UPLIFT SUSPENDED!
WE RAN OUT OF CASH.
COURT COSTS ATE EVERYTHING.
THIS STRUCTURE IS DEEDED TO OUR FINNED FRIENDS.
BE NICE TO THEM.
MAY THEY SOMEDAY JOIN US AS EQUALS.

There followed a WorldNet access number, verifying that the little dolphin clan actually owned this building, which they now used to store their nets, toys, and a few tools. But Hacker knew from their plaintive calls the real reason they kept coming back. Each time they hoped to find that their "hand-friends" had returned.

Unsteady on rubbery legs, he crept from the pool to look in various chambers. Laboratories, mostly. In one, he recognized a gene-splicing apparatus made by one of his own companies.

Project Uplift? Oh yes. I remember hearing about this.

It had been featured in the news, a year or two ago. Both professional and amateur media had swarmed over a small group of "kooks" whose aim was to alter several animal species, giving them human-level intelligence. Foes of all kinds had attacked the endeavor. Religions called it sacrilegious. Eco-enthusiasts decried meddling in nature's wisdom. Tolerance-fetishists demanded that native dolphin "culture" be left alone, while others worked to scuttle the proposal, predicting mutants would escape the labs to endanger humanity.

One problem with diversity in an age of amateurs was that your hobby might attract ire from a myriad of others, especially those whose particular passion was indignant disapproval, with a bent for litigation.

Project Uplift could not survive the rough-and-tumble battle that ensued. A great many modern endeavors didn't.

Survival of the fittest, he mused. *An enterprise this dramatic and controversial has to attract strong support or it's doomed.*

He glanced back at the pool, where members of the tribe had taken up a game of water polo, calling fouls and shouting at one another as they batted a ball from one goal to the next, keeping score with raucous sonar clicks.

Hacker wondered. Would the "uplift" changes carry through from one generation to the next? Could this new genome spread among wild dolphins? If so, might the project have already succeeded beyond its founders' dreams, or its detractors' worst nightmares?

What if the work resumed, finishing what got started here? If other species speak and start creating new things, will they be treated as equals—as co-members of our civilization—or as the next discriminated class?

Some critics were probably right. For humans to attempt such a thing would be like an orphaned and abused teen trying to foster a wild baby. There were bound to be mistakes and tragedies along the way.

Are we wise enough?

It wasn't the sort of question Hacker used to ask himself. He felt changed by his experience at sea. At the same time, he realized that just asking the question was part of the answer.

Maybe it'll work both ways.

His father would have called that "romantic nonsense." And yet . . .

Exploring one of the laboratories, Hacker found a cheap but working phone that someone had left behind—then had to work at a lab bench for an hour, modifying it to tap the sonic implant in his jaw. He was about to call his manager and broker—before they had a chance to declare him dead and start liquidating his empire. But then Hacker stopped.

He paused, then keyed the code for his lawyer instead.

At first Gloria Bickerton could not believe he survived. She wouldn't stop shouting with joy. *I didn't know anyone liked me that much,* he mused, carrying the phone back to the dome's atrium. He arrived in time to witness the water polo game conclude in a frothy finale.

"Before you arrange a pickup, there's something I want you to do for me," he told Gloria, after she calmed down. Hacker gave her the WorldNet codes for Project Uplift and asked her to find out everything about it, including the current disposition of its assets and technology—and how to contact the experts whose work had been interrupted here.

Gloria asked him why. He started to reply.

"I think I've come up with a new . . ."

Hacker stopped there, having almost said the word "hobby." But suddenly he realized that he had never felt this way about anything before. Not even the exhilaration of rocketry. For the first time he burned with a real ambition. Something worth fighting for.

In the pool, several members of the tribe were now busy winding their precious net around the torso of the biggest male, preparing to go foraging again. Hacker overheard them gossiping as they worked, and chuckled when he understood one of their crude jokes. A good natured jibe at his expense.

Well, a sense of humor is a good start. Our civilization could use more of that.

"I think," he resumed telling his lawyer, "I think I know what I want to do with my life."

Near Enough to Home

MICHAEL SKEET

Michael Skeet is a Canadian SF writer who has published most of his work in small press publications. He named the Aurora Awards, and played an active part in the defining of the structure of those awards as it currently exists. He was the founding vice president of SF Canada, the Canadian SF writers organization. Skeet lives in Toronto and began writing fiction in the mid-'80s, and has had short stories published in a variety of anthologies (*Tesseracts*, *Northern Frights*, *Arrowdreams*). He is also an anthologist; in 1993 he and Lorna Toolis, to whom he is married, won an Aurora for their work editing the anthology *Tesseracts 4*. This story is from *Arrowdreams*, an original anthology of Canadian alternate history stories. Like the Baxter, above, it is on the border of SF, though its protagonist is Canadian and its background suggests a vastly different North America with Canada as its dominant factor. Skeet says it "was intended to be an ironic commentary on Canada's continuing insistence on defining itself in terms of its relationship to its southern neighbor."

> *"Perhaps the most striking thing about Canada is that it is not part of the United States."*
> —J. Bartlet Brebner

Sanderson stumbled forward through a universe of misery. His lungs ached as he struggled to keep them filled, his mouth blocked by the gag his captors had stuffed there; wind-blown Kentucky rain stung his eyes, and with his hands bound behind him he could not wipe them clear; his feet chafed and bled where the cheap, ill-fitting American boots cut them. It wasn't enough that these Federal prisoners had cold-cocked him and dragged him along as a hostage to aid their escape; they'd stolen his boots, too—and them just broken in to where they were comfortable—and replaced them with shoddy atrocities that were almost worse than being barefoot. *Don't give up,* he told himself. *If you give these men a reason, they'll kill you, and then you'll never find Scott.*

"Keep moving, you redcoat bastard." A hand thumped him between the shoulder blades, driving him forward until he stumbled. A branch slapped him in the face; blinded by the rain and the moonless night, he felt his way forward, fighting to keep his balance, until he was sure it was bush and not a tree trunk he was about to step into. Then he fell forward, thrashing and kicking out as he did. Thin branches scratched his face, but the pain was worth it so long as his captors didn't figure out what he was doing.

▲   ▲   ▲

Night was giving way to dawn when Sanderson went
into the bushes next. Again he was pushed, and this time
the man who pushed him clipped him on the side of the
head before shoving him sideways. When Sanderson
came to his senses, it was to hear the tail end of a scream
for mercy, and the sickening crunch that ended it.

He struggled to his feet, working at the rope that
bound his wrists in an effort to keep the rain from
shrinking it. As he struggled upward, thorny branches
whipped across his face, drawing blood. One of the
thorns caught a tip of the gag; when he drew his head
back, the gag stayed behind.

Emerging from the bush, Sanderson saw the Federal
soldiers who'd captured him gathered in a loose semicircle around a mule that stood patiently in the middle
of a muddy road. He didn't know Kentucky very well,
but he knew his captors were moving north, to get away
from the Confederate army; that made it likely this was
the road between Bardwell and Wickliffe. Two bodies in
Confederate white lay in the mud; heavy stones beside
the shattered skulls made eloquently clear to Sanderson
the source of the sound he'd just heard. None of the Federals even looked at the bodies now; they were talking
amongst themselves and pointing at something behind
the mule.

The sergeant who was the ring-leader was pointing, too—with the heavy old Colt he'd taken from
Sanderson along with his boots. The man thumbed
back the Colt's hammer. *Not with my gun,* Sanderson
thought; *not yet.* He struggled with the rope that
bound him. A five-shot Currie stingy-pistol was tucked
into a special holster in the small of his back; the Federals, being content with the obvious, had stopped
searching him when they removed the Colt. If he could

get his hands free, they'd regret their carelessness.

"We can use the mule, I guess," the sergeant said. "Since we already got us a hostage who can walk, I don't see much use for you, though." He aimed the pistol; Sanderson gave up on getting his hands free and rushed forward. "Nothing personal, colonel," the sergeant said, and then Sanderson hit him from behind and to the side. The two men splashed into the mud.

The others were on Sanderson before he could do anything else; not that he'd had any plan beyond disrupting the murder long enough to give the other man a chance to escape. When the Federals had stopped beating on him, though, Sanderson saw that he'd made a critical error in his original assumption: escape had never been a possibility for the man he'd tried to save.

The colonel the sergeant had been speaking to was lying on a crude sort of travois, a blanket suspended between poles thrust under the horse's harness. A bandaged stump on the end of his left leg where the foot should have been explained the sergeant's remark about a hostage who could walk. Sanderson was astonished to see that the colonel wore a Federal uniform. Why would these men want to kill one of their own officers?

"Damn," the sergeant said as he got to his feet. "I ought to kill you for that, Englishman. Pity we need you to get across the river."

"I told you before," Sanderson said, "I'm not—" The last word exploded from him as the sergeant kicked into his ribs with enough force to knock him over sideways.

As he fought to get air into his agonized lungs, Sanderson heard the sergeant mutter, "Goddamned barrel's full of mud," and shove the Colt back into its holster. "Guess we'll have to do him like we done the others."

"If what you want is to get across the river to home, I'm worth more to you alive than I am dead."

Sanderson looked up. The colonel had struggled upright, in order to be able to look the sergeant in the eye. The colonel's face was pale and sweating; no doubt he'd got a fever from the amputation. Even if he'd been healthy, though, this colonel would have been one of the more ugly men Sanderson had ever seen. Tall and impossibly thin, he looked more like a corpse than many dead men. His face was long and angular, and so raw-edged and bony it looked as though it had been carved with an ax. Huge ears gave him a look that suggested to Sanderson a sort of elongated gorilla. The man's eyes were dark and sunken, and though there was something almost mesmerizing about them, Sanderson attributed that to the fever-gleam.

"I'm a fair man," the sergeant said with a smile that gave the lie to his words. "I'll give you a chance to explain yourself."

"I'm being paroled. The Confederates are letting me go home, instead of sending me to a prison." The colonel's voice was pitched high for such a tall man. "I guess they don't consider me a threat any more." He looked down at the bandaged stump. "You"—the colonel paused just long enough that Sanderson, at least, was aware of the irony—". . . gentlemen . . . want to get across the river. I assume that you would be interested in the boat that's waiting for me."

"Waiting for you where?"

"Ah," said the colonel. "That's what you'll keep me alive to find out."

"You're a Canadian?" the colonel asked. They had stopped for a rest in a small clearing in the woods somewhere northeast of Wickliffe. After introducing himself, the colonel had thanked Sanderson quietly for his attempt at intervention; while the words and voice were pitched low, Sanderson felt the power behind them nevertheless.

"I'm from St. Louis, yes," Sanderson said. He worked at his bonds, but in spite of his efforts the cord had shrunk in the rain, and all he was getting for his efforts was bloody wrists. They'd bound the colonel, too—more to keep him from helping me, Sanderson guessed, than because they think he's really a threat. "I believe you're the first man I've met since crossing the river who hasn't called me an Englishman. Thank you for that."

"You'll have to forgive my countrymen their ignorance," the colonel said. The rain had stopped a while back, but the woods were still soaked; the colonel's uniform was so wet the blue wool looked almost black. "Canada is a relatively new concept to us, and by and large my countrymen are slow to adapt to new concepts that they consider an inconvenience. Besides, until '48 you *were* Englishmen, at least legally."

"Do you have any idea why these men are doing this?" Sanderson asked. "Surely they'd have been exchanged soon."

"That assumes they were taken on the field of battle," the colonel said dryly.

"You mean they might be deserters? But they were in a Confederate prison enclosure when they took me." Sanderson flushed with embarrassment at the memory.

"Their presence in a prisoner camp is no guarantee that they actually took part in the fighting at Bardwell," the colonel said. "The situation has been somewhat chaotic this week." That was an understatement, Sanderson knew. The Federal army had been destroyed at Bardwell, and he'd heard that only a few thousand had made it back across the Ohio River into Illinois and

Indiana. If the Confederates invaded Illinois or captured Washington—and either looked possible now—there was a good chance the war would be over before 1852 gave way to 1853.

"Might I inquire just what you were doing in that prisoner camp? Our escorts here"—the colonel nodded sarcastically at their guards—"called you a redcoat. You're not in uniform, though, so you're not a Canadian military observer. In that duster you might be any farmer. You're not a spy, are you?"

"No, sir. I'm with the North-West Mounted Police."

"So how did they know to call you a redcoat?"

"I had a pass, signed by the Confederate military attaché in St. Louis. I'm here looking for a fugitive who'd joined your army under a false name."

"You show an admirable determination," the colonel said. "This fugitive must have done something particularly horrible."

Scott had left their mother in tears, but Sanderson didn't feel like sharing that fact with the colonel, so he simply nodded. "I'm anxious to get him back," he said.

"I see," the colonel said, and smiled. "Is he a murderer? Or is it some more political crime?"

"I'm not at liberty to talk about that," Sanderson said, after what he knew was too long a pause. He saw the colonel's appraising glance, and was grateful when one of the deserters appeared to kick him to his feet.

"What do you think of our chances, Constable?" The question was pitched quietly enough that Sanderson nearly didn't hear it over the rustling of the foliage.

"Not good, I'm afraid," he said. He twisted himself around in the hope that by talking back at the colonel he could avoid being overheard by the deserters. They had turned him into a draft animal, crudely harnessing the stretcher to his shoulders so that he could drag the colonel while their captors took turns riding the mule. "Your chances are better than mine, though. If they're hoping to use me to get them past any Confederate patrols, my usefulness ends as soon as they get to the river. You probably gain in value the closer they get to Ohio or Indiana or wherever it is they decide to go."

"A cruel assessment, but probably accurate." The colonel laughed bitterly. "That makes me wonder something, though. Not to pry, but Canada and Britain *are* allied with the Confederate States now. So why would you have been in a prisoner camp without an escort? I'm assuming that you were captured because you were alone."

"I was." Sanderson shook his head.

"So why would your Confederate allies value you as a hostage, but not value you enough to ensure your safety before you were taken?"

The brush to his left rattled and shook as some surprised animal fled from their approach. "I guess that was my fault, colonel. I'd hoped to speak with General Lee about my fugitive, but apparently the general has been recalled to Virginia. The rewards of success, I suppose." The colonel grimaced, though whether it was from pain or embarrassment, Sanderson couldn't tell. "I spent a whole night waiting to talk with someone, and when I finally did the man was less than polite. Some captain named Stewart, who made it clear enough that he didn't like me or anyone else from the other side of the Mississippi, treaty or no. He told me he couldn't spare anyone to help me search. So I went off on my own. Not the best of ideas, I guess."

"I've met Captain Stewart," the colonel said. "He was polite enough to me. I gather he was with the commissioners who negotiated the treaty with your government and the English last year. I don't think he likes the English very much."

"It's a damned curious war," Sanderson said. "I'm supposed to think of those slave-owners as allies, and I just can't. But I can't say as I like the English much either. Or you folks, come to that. Nobody asked me what I thought about any of this." His eyes stung as sweat trickled into them; he desperately wanted to wipe his forehead, but had to settle for brushing his face against leafy branches as he dodged around trees.

"Politics is what makes it curious," the colonel said. "If the Confederate States are victorious, then Canada becomes the dominant country on this continent. Neither the CSA nor the US would be able to challenge Canada's westward expansion unaided. Texas is already in debt to Britain, and California will probably follow. And I suspect that an independent Confederate States wouldn't be as independent as they'd like. They'll be junior partners to Canada and Britain. Unfortunately, our southern brothers aren't interested in listening to my theories right now. We'll all be learning bitter lessons before long, is my guess."

Sanderson wondered about the lessons Scott had learned. If he'd lived long enough to learn anything, that is. He shook his head; that wasn't the way his thoughts should be moving. He had to keep himself ready should the opportunity for escape arise.

The Ohio River—the liquid border between Kentucky and Illinois—flowed muddily past their vantage-point; the river was bloated with rain, and its confluence with the equally swollen Mississippi had a look of lazy evil about it that Sanderson, who'd grown up on the bigger river, had learned at an early age to mistrust.

Sanderson and the colonel lay in a hollow at the

edge of a bluff overlooking the river, two of their captors watching them while the other four struggled to get the stolen boat into the water.

"You know what's ironic?" the colonel asked. He didn't wait for a response. "If it hadn't been for the British taking Louisiana, we might none of us be here right now. If we'd been allowed to expand westward, we'd have had enough new territory to worry about that we wouldn't have had time to fight over slavery or states' rights. We might have avoided this war. For a while longer, anyway."

The colonel rolled over to look at Sanderson. "Are you all right, Constable? I trust I'm not boring you."

Sanderson closed his eyes and took a deep breath. He'd run out of time; it had to be now.

"Colonel," he said slowly. "Could I ask you a favor?"

"I'm not in much of a position to do much at the moment," the colonel said. "But in so far as it's within my power, I'd be honored to help you. You saved my life this morning. What can I do for you?"

"If I don't come out of this alive, Colonel, would you see what you can do about finding that soldier I told you about?"

"The fugitive you're tracking? Constable, I'm no policeman."

Sanderson sighed. "He's not really a fugitive, sir. He's my younger brother."

"I suspected as much." The colonel's face crumpled into a tiny, satisfied smile. "No doubt your Confederate allies were prepared to accept your story at face value because you had the proper papers. But I had to wonder why you were so reluctant to tell me what this man had done. The only conclusion I could draw was that he hadn't done anything. Actually, Constable, I congratulate you for not compounding the original lie. That's what trips most people up. They start with one lie, then find they have to keep lying to keep the first lie from being found out. The lies get bigger, and before they know it they're the governor or the president."

Sanderson laughed. "You're a very observant man, Colonel."

"I was a lawyer before all this began," the colonel said. "And a momentarily successful liar myself, since I spent a couple of years in Washington. Noticing things about people has proved helpful to me. Do you want to tell me what happened between you and your brother?"

"It really wasn't between us," Sanderson said. "Scott and I weren't what you'd call close. I'm eight years older than he is. No, the trouble was between my mother and her father. Scott ended up listening to grandfather."

"Now you've got me interested," the colonel said. Sanderson noticed that their guards had edged closer as well, though they were taking elaborate pains to appear to be watching their companions with the boat. "How does a father-daughter dispute drive a young man into the middle of our civil war?"

"It's a long story," Sanderson said. "Truly. It goes back fifty years, to when Grandpa was a young man. He was from Virginia, you know. Says he met Washington once. Canada might be a federated kingdom now, but when Grandpa talks about his country, he still means Virginia."

"People are born in the strangest places," the colonel said. "I was born in Kentucky myself. If my father hadn't been so restless, I might have ended up wearing white and fighting for John Calhoun, Davey Crockett and Dixie's Land."

Sanderson looked at their guards. They were exchanging glances of amusement that suggested they might be susceptible to further distraction. Raising his voice a little, he said, "Grandpa moved to Louisiana when he was sixteen and set himself up as a trader in St. Louis. Married a half-Indian daughter of a French trader." In the guise of settling into a more comfortable position, Sanderson located a stone and began to carefully work his bound wrists against it. "But when Bonaparte died back in oh-two and the British got Louisiana, Grandpa refused to take the loyalty oath. He even got himself put in prison in 1810 at the beginning of Jefferson's War."

"Interesting that you should call it that," the colonel said. "That's an American term. Don't the British call it the War of 1810?"

"Like I said, my grandpa still thinks of himself as American," Sanderson said. He could feel the friction of rope against stone, and hoped that the fibers were beginning to break down. "Right up until Confederation, he truly believed that America was going to take Louisiana back. When I joined the police and put on the red uniform, he stopped speaking to me. And, my mother tells me, he started filling Scott's head with all sorts of stories about the greatness of America and the treacherousness of the English. He hates the English—and just like the sergeant down there, he seems pretty generous in terms of who he thinks of as English. His neighbors despise him. They burn him in effigy every First of July, I'm told."

"I've heard stories about what happened to American sympathizers in Louisiana after Jefferson's War," the colonel said. "Pardon me if I'm being rude, but I find yours a strange country. I can't think of any other modern state that was founded the way yours was, on the negation of a principle."

"That principle being republicanism?" Sanderson shook his head. "Some of us are equally opposed to monarchy, Colonel."

"And so you don't know what you are so much as

you know what you aren't—you're not English and you're not American."

"I know what I am, Colonel." Sanderson shook his head again, trying to clear his thoughts. "I'm tired and I'm wet and as far as I'm concerned the whole lot of you can blow yourselves to perdition if you'll just leave me out of it."

The colonel's reply was cut short by the return of the sergeant. He had cleaned the Colt, Sanderson saw. "Time to go, boys," he said.

You can say this much for being tied up, Sanderson thought: *At least I didn't have to haul that thing down to the river.* The boat was a big, ugly, flat-bottomed thing that must have weighed nearly a thousand pounds. It didn't look like something that should be used on a river in flood.

Across the Ohio and downstream a little were the ramshackle docks and warehouses of Cairo, the Illinois town from which the Federals had launched their futile attempt at keeping western Kentucky in the Union. Further west, and rendered invisible by the low cloud and haze that persisted though the rain had stopped, was Thompson, on the Canadian side of the Mississippi just south of its confluence with the Ohio. Sanderson thought again about his chances for getting back there. They hadn't improved, he decided. In fact, they were probably worse, since his captors could easily decide to turn him over to the Federal authorities across the Ohio. With no one to vouch for his mission, he'd be all too easily condemned as a spy. *And me not a single step closer to finding Scott.*

"I suppose this is where we say goodbye," the sergeant said to him. For one brief moment Sanderson hoped he was going to be released. But as soon as he thought it, he knew the hope was misplaced. The deserters had decided they didn't need him any more, that's all.

"I see you've decided to let him go," the colonel said. He'd been seated on a large rock while the deserters tried to maneuver the boat alongside in such a way that he wouldn't have to be carried far.

"And what makes you think that?" the sergeant asked. He drew the massive Colt from its holster.

"You still need me if you're to avoid punishment once we're across the river," the colonel said. "And I'm not crossing without this man."

"With a mind like that it's no wonder we're losing," the sergeant said, to tired laughter from the others. "What makes you think we're going back to Illinois? I'm thinking we'll just cross all the way over, to that fine Canadian frontier we've all heard so much about. Arkansas is near enough to home for my tastes." The sergeant sneered at Sanderson. "By rights it should've been ours anyway, if you English hadn't stolen it from us."

"I don't recall the Louisiana territory being yours to claim," Sanderson said. "As I've read it, it was the French and Spanish the British took it from."

"Should have been ours. If that bastard Jefferson had've been quicker with his wits when Bonaparte died, we'd have drove you English right off this continent." The sergeant cocked the pistol.

Sanderson knew he should be calm, should be agreeing with this idiot, anything to keep the man occupied, to keep him from getting angrier. But Sanderson didn't care anymore. *If I'm going to die,* he decided, *I'm going down fighting.* "It seems to me," he said, flexing his wrists behind him, "that you Americans already tried that once. Nelson and Wellington whipped you forty years ago, and I haven't seen anything in you to make me think we should be worried now."

"It seems to me," the sergeant said, "that I've put up with your damned smug superiority long enough."

"Don't do something you'll regret," the colonel said from his rock. He tried but failed to stand up. "If you're determined to go to Canada, you still need this man. Don't go making a mistake when you're so close to getting what you want."

"What I want is not to hear anything more from you," the sergeant said. He spat derisively. "Don't think I don't know you, Colonel. I know you, all right. I made the mistake of voting for you six years ago. This," he said to Sanderson, "is one of the political geniuses who got us into this mess that you're so superior about. Went to Congress talking about preserving the Union, and what did he do? Voted against annexing Texas. Voted to condemn the men who tried to filibuster Cuba into the Union. We couldn't get him out of Washington fast enough. And now he's pleading for your life? You picked a poor lawyer, Englishman."

I'm tired of you, Sanderson thought. He said nothing, though. Instead, he forced his wrists apart with all the strength in him. After a second's hesitation, the frayed cord snapped. Sanderson thrust his right hand through the vent in the back of his duster and into the holster under his shirt. He drew the Currie.

"You son of a bitch," the sergeant said. As Sanderson aimed at his belly, the sergeant smiled crookedly. "Go to hell," he said, and pulled the trigger.

The Colt exploded like the First of July.

The sergeant stared, shocked into silence, at the bloody wreckage of his hand. He was still staring, still silent, when a musket ball spattered his brains across the stones at the river's edge.

Sanderson jumped backward as the sergeant's body toppled and fell. *What the hell happened? I didn't pull the trigger.*

"Drop the weapon, sir."

Sanderson looked up. At the top of the bank a confederate soldier reloaded a smoking musket. Beside the soldier, a white-clad officer pointed at Sanderson.

"Captain Stewart," Sanderson said. "It's about time."

"Might I ask why you've taken my pistol?" Sanderson hadn't protested at first, but now that the surviving deserters had been chained together and were being marched up the bank he was becoming worried.

"I can't think it would be prudent," said Captain Stewart, "to rearm a spy after only just apprehending him."

"A spy?" Without wanting to, Sanderson began to laugh. He shook and spasmed for an embarrassingly long time, and when he was able to lift his head it was to find the white-clad captain glaring death at him. "My apologies, Captain," he gasped. "It must be nerves; I haven't slept for several days now." When Stewart's expression didn't change, Sanderson returned the glare. "What in the world possessed you to think I was a spy?"

"You went to the prison encampment without my permission, sir, and the next thing I knew, a half-dozen prisoners—and yourself—had gone missing. It was our good fortune that you were so clumsy. You left a trail a blind man could follow."

"Of course I did! I fell into bushes so many times I was convinced those idiots would figure out what I was about. Look at my face, damn it!" Sanderson leaned forward so that Stewart couldn't fail to notice the cross-hatch of cuts and lacerations. "I'm cut so many times I look like a truant's bottom," he spat. "And you think you found me because I was clumsy!"

"Fine words, sir," Stewart began.

"They're also true," the colonel said. Stewart raised

his hands as if to protest, but the colonel silenced him with a look. "This man was treated abominably by his captors, and risked his life to save mine. Rather than arresting him, you should be offering your best hospitality; I'm not without friends in Illinois and other places."

"I'm aware of that," Stewart said. Sulking, he handed Sanderson his pistol, then told two other men to prepare to row the colonel across the river.

Sanderson crouched down to retrieve his boots. "Thank you," he said, turning to face the colonel as Stewart stomped away. "I owe you one."

"We're even, then," the colonel said. "I hope some day to thank you properly for saving my life. You showed fine courage standing up to that homicidal idiot . . ." The colonel's voice died away, and Sanderson looked up from the sergeant's body, from which he was in the process of removing the holster.

The colonel was eyeing him carefully, the way one might an unfamiliar snake. "The gun was yours?" he asked. After a moment's silence he said, "You knew. You were expecting that gun to burst."

Sanderson flushed, and got to his feet. "If there had been a way to let you know, Colonel, I would have."

"What I don't understand," the colonel said, "is precisely *how* you knew." His eyebrows lifted suddenly. "Unless you had prepared it that way. Good God."

"I once saw a man lose his hand firing one of those," Sanderson said, pointing at the smashed pistol, which was still smoking. "That was a Walker Colt; they were made for the Texas army, which turned out not to like them that much. Oh, they had their good points. I've never encountered a pistol that packed as much powder in a single charge as the Walker. But the tolerances were awfully loose. Every ninety rounds or so, firing one chamber would set off all the caps and the whole thing would explode. So I got to thinking as how that might come in handy should I ever find myself in a situation just like this one. I made the cylinder a bit more loose than it already was, primed the back of the frame, and then made sure it was loaded with clay balls coated with just enough lead to keep them from crumbling until they were fired. You'll have noticed that I keep my real gun in a less obvious place." He patted his back.

The colonel whistled long and low. "You are a— wait a minute." The eyebrows dropped and the colonel's eyes darkened. "When you dove at that man back on the road, you knew he couldn't have killed me. So you were just trying to preserve your secret for a little while longer."

Sanderson shook his head. "I couldn't say that, Colonel. I wanted to keep him from finding out about the gun, that's true. But I was also trying to prevent him from killing you. I honestly couldn't say which was foremost in my mind."

"Yet another case of you not knowing yourself," the colonel said. "At a hazard to everyone around you. You people *are* a menace."

"You know, Colonel," Sanderson said with a grin, "I think I'm beginning to like this not knowing myself. It can't be a bad thing to keep folks wondering.

"Besides, you people have been sure of who you are for nearly four-score years, and look at where it's got you."

The colonel's face lost all of its animation, and for the first time since Stewart's arrival Sanderson was ashamed. "I'm sorry, Colonel. That was uncalled for."

"Don't chastise yourself," the colonel said slowly. "I was just indulging in a spot of self-pity. You came a little too close to home, I guess." He looked down at the empty space where his foot should have been. "I look at myself today and I see a failed soldier. You'll have gathered that I failed as a politician, too. I suddenly find myself wondering what it is that I'll do with myself when I get across the river."

"There's more than one river you can cross, you know," Sanderson said. "Whatever's happened to you so far, you're a clever man. I'm told there's a new country building to the west, if you cared to share your abilities with us." He extended a hand.

The colonel shook it, firmly. "Thank you for your kind offer," he said. "But something tells me I shouldn't give up on this old country too quickly. Let me go home and see if I can't do something for her yet." He hobbled slowly to the boat, and suffered the white-clad enemy to hand him in.

"Good luck, Constable," the colonel said as the Confederate oarsmen pushed the boat away from the bank. "I hope you eventually find your brother."

"I intend to. I'll keep looking in Kentucky for now," Sanderson said. "As long as Captain Stewart doesn't arrest me again. If you come across him in Illinois, will you write me care of headquarters in St. Louis?"

"Count on it," the colonel said as the oars bit into the river.

As the colonel waved farewell, Sanderson said, "If you decide that your future involves politics, Colonel, might I suggest you keep the beard? It softens your face, you know. Makes you look as if you know yourself a little bit less than you do."

The colonel laughed at that. The laughter echoed off the water and the shore. It continued to tickle Sanderson's ears as he climbed up the bank and mounted a borrowed horse to resume his search.

A Game of Consequences

DAVID LANGFORD

David Langford is the physicist/writer who keeps winning best fan writer Hugo Awards (he is the most famous
humorous writer in fandom today) and publishes *Ansi-
ble* (which also wins Hugo Awards and is also excerpted
as a monthly column in *Interzone*, and simultaneously
published online: www.dcs.gla.ac.uk/SF-archives/Ansible/),
the tabloid newspaper of SF and fandom. His fan writ-
ings have been collected in *Let's Hear it for the Deaf Man*
(Langford is deaf). He is also the author of several books
of nonfiction and a hard science fiction novel, *The Space
Eater*, and is a widely published book reviewer. And like
many physicists, he used to hang out with a rowdy crowd
who liked to blow things up. This story, not funny, is
from *Starlight 2* and is about that kind of fun.

T here were two of them in the hot room, on the day that went bad but could have been so much worse. The Mathematical Institute's air-conditioning was failing as usual to cope with heat from the angry bar of sunlight that slanted across Ceri's desktop and made the papers there too blindingly white to read. Through the window she could see an utterly cloudless sky: each last wisp of vapor had been scorched away.

Across the room where the light was kinder, Ranjit had perched on the stool and hunched himself over his beloved keyboard, rattling off initialization sequences. "Breakthrough day today!" he said cheerily.

"You say that every bloody day," said Ceri, moving to look over his shoulder.

"Yes, but this week we're getting something. I've been starting to feel a sort of, sort of . . . resonance. That's what you want, right?"

It was what she wanted. She really shouldn't feel resentful that her frail and beautiful tracery of theory needed a computer nerd to pit it against stubborn fact. A nerd and a quantum-logic supercomputer like the Cray 7000-Q, the faculty's latest toy.

Not that Ranjit was precisely a classic nerd or geek. The man was presentable enough, not conspicuously overweight or bizarrely hair-styled, thirtysomething like Ceri herself. She might yet end up sleeping with him. Among campus women there was some mild specula- tion that he was gay, but Ceri put that down to his one addiction, the one he was indulging now. Sinking through the now blossoming display into a world of electronic metaphor. The rapture of the deep. She found herself worrying at a line from Nietzsche: if you struggle over-much with algorithms, you yourself become an algorithm. Gaze too long into virtual spaces, and virtual spaces will gaze into you.

False colors began to bloom in the oversized display screen as the model of Nothing shuffled itself into multi-dimensioned shape. "I like *this* color palette," he mur-mured. "Reminds me of being in church." It reminded Ceri of a smashed kaleidoscope.

Her virtual-space analogy—maybe some day to be expounded in a triumphalist paper by Ceri Evans Ph.D. and, oh damn, Ranjit Narayan M.Sc.—hovered on the shady side of respectable physics. Down in the spaces underneath space, so certain lines of mathematics implied, the observer and the observed melted together like Dali's soft watches. There seemed to be an entangledness, a com-plicity between any sufficiently detailed model and the actual dance of subatomic interaction. Then (it was her own insight, still lovingly fondled in the mind) suppose one tuned the computer model for mathematical "sweet-ness," for structures whose elegant symmetry had the ring of inevitable truth: a resonance with reality, a kind of chord. And then . . . what then? Maybe a digital telescope that could spy on the substrate below quantum complex-ity. Maybe just a vast amount of wasted computer time.

"Hey, how about a cup of coffee, Ceri?"

This, of course, was what mathematical physicists were good for once they'd churned out a testable hypothesis. Making the coffee. She stalked through the cruel slash of sunlight to the hiding-place of her illicitly imported kettle.

There had been four of them in the hot garden, more than twenty years before: Sammy and Ceri and Dai and the English boy whose name she'd forgotten. Some-where beyond the sheltering trees was a strong clear sun, its light flickering and strobing through leaves stirred by a breeze from up the valley. Ceri remembered pointing out how momentary apertures in the foliage acted like pinhole cameras, projecting perfect little sun-discs onto flat ground. This was of some small interest, but could not compete with the afternoon's major attraction. Sammy had an air rifle.

They made paper targets and sellotaped them to the brick wall at the garden's far end. Why was it so hard to draw a free-hand circle, let alone properly concentric ones? Despite that changing dapple of light, the worn old .177-inch rifle was surprisingly accurate if you held it properly, and conventional targets soon grew boring. The English boy drew a hilarious—well, once Ceri knew who it was meant to be—caricature of Mr. Porter at the High School. When Porter had been well peppered and had only empty holes for eyes, other teachers got the same treatment.

"Moving targets, that's what!" said Sammy when a trace of tedium had again set in. But woodlice could not be persuaded to crawl sportingly along the back wall. It was populated with hundreds of the tiny, tireless mites they called red spiders, but these became invisible at any decent range.

"Oh, of course. The twigs are all moving in the breeze," Ceri suggested, and obscurely wished she hadn't. There were cries of "Bloody *hell*!" as the four came to grips with the difficulty of holding the airgun steady while firing upward at slender, swaying pencils of wood. Eventually Dai brought down a fragment of twig—"Gre-e-at! I'm the champ!"—and Ceri, mostly by luck, snipped free a broad sycamore leaf that sideslipped and jinked as it drifted reluctantly groundward.

Sammy took the rifle and reloaded. "I'll give *him* a

fright," he announced, pointing to a greenfinch eyeing them from a middling-high branch.

"No," said Ceri.

"Just going for the branch, *stupid.*"

Fly away, fly away now, she thought urgently, but the bird only cocked its head to look down with the other eye. The flat *clack* of the airgun seemed especially loud, and there was a dreadful inevitability in the fall of the little green-brown bundle of feathers.

Afterwards, besides the private heartache and the recriminations concerning .177" holes that had appeared in the windows of quite surprisingly distant houses, the thing that rankled was that Sammy had been too fastidious to touch the bloodied finch. "There's things crawling on it," he said. Worse, its eye had failed to close in the proper decorum of death, and stared emptily. The English boy scraped a hole and Ceri dropped the bird into it. It was still warm.

The steady glare through the window had changed its angle now, and a third cup of coffee was going luke-warm beside the mousemat. Why did one sweat so much more than in those hot remembered days of childhood? Perhaps it was the square-cube law: more body mass, more internal heat to shed, proportionally less skin area to sweat through? Two hours of translating her mathematical intuitions into appropriate quasi-shapes and pseudo-angles for Ranjit's algorithmic probes had left Ceri with a slight headache and a tendency to stray off into such mental byways.

Ranjit stirred slightly. "I think . . . I think we might be there. In the sort of space you specified."

The flickering multicolored gridwork on the screen looked no different; or was it firmer, somehow more confident? "How do you know?" she asked.

"It feels right somehow. Locked-in. As though the simulation has picked up a kind of inertia." A kaleidoscope whose images were hardening from randomness to a compelling pattern, to something "real."

"Which might mean it's resonating with real— superstring phenomena, say. Sub-particles."

"I'm bloody glad you said 'might.' We could just be looking into a mirror, seeing stuff we put there ourselves. Your neatest idea today was when you said it felt like a cellular-automata gameboard. From that angle, a lot of things clicked for me. Now that thing—" he indicated a complex node false-colored in shifting shades of blue near the top of the monitor "—*could* be a sort of stable oscillator, like you used to see in the old Life-game programs."

Ceri nodded in mild approval. "Which feels about right, because if particles aren't stable oscillations in the quantum field, then what are they? We're seeing the right kind of map—although, as the man said, 'the map is not the territory.' But if we can ever develop this thing to the point of pulling out information that isn't in the physics books, and if the information is good . . ."

"Yes, I had begun to gather that. Over the weeks of you telling me it."

"The shaky part of this entanglement theory is that the mapping ought to be two-way. Heisenberg's principle: you can't observe without affecting the thing observed. But the mechanism . . . the scaling factors . . ." She frowned and gnawed her lip. "All right, all right, you need more coffee."

Ranjit said slowly, "Wait a minute. I'm going to try something." His brown fingers rippled over the keys.

There had been three of them in the chem lab, Sammy and Ceri and the girl with the harsh Cardiff accent, whose name she had long forgotten. It was another sweltering day, and the rest of the school had emptied itself into the open air at the first clang of the lunch bell. Here the reek of old reagents and spillages bit acridly at your throat, and the smell of the new stuff they were carefully filtering through big paper-lined funnels led to occasional coughs which no one could stifle.

"This is the biggest batch ever," Sammy chortled. "Going for the world record!" As usual, although it was Ceri who first found and read that worn Victorian volume of *Amusing and Edifying Scientific Parlor Tricks*, the project had become all Sammy's.

The black paste of precipitate had many uses. Once dried, it was amazingly touchy stuff. Smeared on chalkboards and left for an hour, it produced amusing crackles and bangs when Mr. Whitcutt scrawled his illegible algebra workings; underfoot, it made whole classrooms (and on one glorious morning, the school assembly hall) a riot of minor explosions and puffs of purple smoke; packed into a lock, it could blast the inserted key right back into its holder's hand, often with painful force.

Then the door to the back room opened. Ceri winced. They'd counted on Mr. Davies, the elderly lab technician, either going out for lunch or staying placidly put and brewing his tea as usual. White-haired Mr. Davies had seen everything that could happen in labs; his experience went back to days before ordinary benzene was declared a carcinogen, days when the pupils routinely used it to sluice organics from their hands.

"Terrible smell of ammonia in here," he said mildly. "Someone ought open a window."

The Cardiff girl—Rhiannon, could it have been?— silently obeyed.

Mr. Davies, looking at no one in particular, added: "People ought to know not to make nitrogen tri-iodide in kilogram lots. That much of the stuff's unstable even if you do keep it wet. And it doesn't help anyone's career if they're short of a few fingers." He retreated through his private door.

"That was a hint," said Ceri.

"We've made it now," Sammy said crossly.

"Come *on*. If anything goes bang anywhere this week, they're going to know who it was."

Mumbling to himself, Sammy scraped together the precious black sludge, dumped it in the sink built into the teacher's demonstration bench, and gave it a quick flush from the tap. In another sink, Ceri carefully rinsed the soiled filter papers before binning them; the Cardiff girl splashed water over the glassware. But Sammy had a look on his face that Ceri had seen before. "I'm just going to try something," he muttered, and tilted a huge reagent bottle over the demo-bench sink. There was a powerful whiff of hospital-like fumes. To Ceri's silent relief, nothing happened.

When the chemistry lesson came around that afternoon, Mr. Porter held up a large Erlenmeyer flask and announced, to general apathy, that he was about to perform a simple demonstration. What it was going to be remained a mystery, since when he put the glass cone in the sink to fill it there followed a sharp explosion, a dramatic cloud of purple smoke, and an upward spray of glass fragments that slashed his hands and face in a dozen places. In the echoing pause while Mr. Porter stared in fascination at tattered, part-flayed fingers, Ceri realized what Sammy had poured down there: a measure of ether that had washed away the water in the sink trap and swiftly evaporated, leaving the tri-iodide bone-dry and potent. She thought for an instant of a bright globule of blood on the downy breast of a small, greenish bird.

With one awful eye—blood was streaming into the other—the chemistry master surveyed his class. He pointed unerringly at Sammy and cried *"Jones!"* Old Davies had presumably identified the explosive ring-leader, but anyway one would need to be blind not to notice the outraged innocence of Sammy's expression— the body language that conveyed, "I couldn't have known it would do *that*."

The harsh sunlight brightened sharply; a tiny corner of Ceri's mind longed for the return of some healing cloud. Cloud? What was obscurely odd today about sun and cloud? Her critical attention, though, was focused on the computer display's fractal gridlines, and the strange pulse of activity in the node which Ranjit had indicated some minutes earlier. Now the false-color mapping showed the shape breaking into new colors on either side of blue: a speckle of green, larger irregular blocks of indigo and violet.

"It's gone interactive," Ranjit said. "What you said about Heisenberg: probing it digitally is *changing* stuff in there. Like sending pulses into a neural-net grid."

"We're . . . changing a particle's state by measuring it?"

"Isn't that exactly what your pal Herr Heisenberg said? Isn't it what *you* said? Tickling it in just the right rhythm is keeping it—well—doing whatever it's doing now. Higher energy level? Spinning faster? Or something with one of the weird quantum numbers like strangeness. Hell, I don't know, but it's fun. Like keeping a yo-yo moving."

It was too hot to think straight. *Damn* that lousy, feeble air conditioning. A plastic folder on the glaring desktop had curled and shriveled as never before. Ceri had always—or at any rate since she'd been a school-girl—felt brilliantly sunlit days to be fraught with a sense of obscure, gathering disaster. She felt it now.

"I'm just going to try something," said Ranjit again. "I think I can nudge it a step further—"

It was some echo in his words, rather than the actual tone or content, that made her snap: *"No."*

"Don't be silly. I'm recording everything. We can reboot the simulation whenever— What the fuck!"

Ceri had yanked the power lead from his computer workstation, and the stained-glass complexities died from the screen.

There had been just the two of them, Sammy and Ceri, on a blinding-hot day at the Gaer. The place was a broad hillock of grassy, bracken-infested wasteland, named for an old Roman camp whose trenches and ditches had left their scars around the summit. More attractive was the rumor, never verified, of adders somewhere in the Gaer's gorse and bracken.

A branch railway line curled around one side of this common land, separating it from a more orderly park and golf course. Feeble attempts at fencing off the railway had, it seemed, been long abandoned. Here the wire links were neatly snipped through, there they were undermined, and in several places the whole fence had sagged to the ground under the weight of many climbers. It was the perfect spot for what Ceri, in a phrase from history lessons, called debasing the coinage. Old, brassy threepenny bits were the best, if you could find them. Place one on the nearer rail, wait five or ten or twenty minutes for the long rumble of a goods train, and a marvelously flattened, doily-edged medallion would be flung aside by the thunderous succession of iron wheels.

When coins began to pall, though, it was hard to think of interesting variations. Glass marbles (secured with a blob of chewing gum) simply burst into powder, and small stones to grit. Ceri had managed to talk

Sammy out of his "biological experiment" featuring a white mouse in a cardboard box.

Today he produced something new from his shoulder-bag: a short length of copper pipe, capped at both ends. It was quite hard to balance this on a rail, but—while Ceri kept watch for approaching trains—Sammy used angular stone fragments from the railside to wedge the thing against rolling off.

"Should be good. Better than thruppences!" he confided as they crouched in their usual hidey-hole amid yellow-flowering gorse clumps close by the line.

"What is it, Sammy? Nothing *alive*?"

"No no no. I just thought I'd try something. Weed-killer and stuff. I can't get the compression at home."

Ceri had a sense of distant alarms ringing. "Weed-killer and *sugar*? Maybe we should—"

Her hesitant voice was lost in the approaching train's roar, and the bulk of the engine (so much huger from down here than from a station platform) blotted out the angry sun. A not very emphatic crack or bang was succeeded by the usual long rattle and squeak of two dozen or so hopper wagons. Ceri had felt Sammy jerk and cry out, as though wasp-stung or bitten by the dread adder. He slumped forward. She shook and turned him slightly. A stone fragment, they told her later, had flown like shrapnel from the explosion. The sight of the gory ruin that had been Sammy's left eye remained too vivid a memory for too long a time, and it was no comfort to be assured again and again that for him it was instantaneous.

There were still, after all, two of them in Ceri's office, where quite easily there might by now have been none.

"What are you *waiting* for?" he said again.

"Ssh." She kept her eyes on her watch. The light

striking through the window lessened in its intensity, as though a thin cloud had drifted in front of the sun.

"*Iesu Grist,*" Ceri whispered.

"What?"

"Oh . . . Welsh. Jesus Christ. I counted eight minutes and twenty seconds, which is about right. Jesus. I'd actually said it out loud, too, I said we didn't know the scaling factors."

"How about an explanation in words of one syllable for the mere technical staff?"

"How about if you make the coffee this time, Ranjit, just for a change?" Had her soft pad of scribbling paper really turned pale brown in the hot glare? "I knew there was something wrong but I didn't know I knew it. I just had this feeling of someone walking on my grave. But that's how science officially operates, isn't it? You get an intuition and then you think back and work out why it came. You see, the sun got brighter."

"Too bloody right it did," said Ranjit, spooning out coffee granules. "You're still not, um, making any actual sense."

"Ranjit, there's not a cloud in the sky. There hasn't been all day. Clear blue everywhere, and it's way past noon. But a few minutes after you'd started interfering with that pattern in the Cray simulation, the sun *suddenly* got brighter."

"Oh, come on. What a vivid imagination some people have."

"Look. Just about eight minutes and twenty seconds from the time I pulled the plug, the sunlight dropped to normal again. That's the time the light takes to reach us across 149 million kilometers. You saw it. And there's still no cloud up there."

A pause. "Fuck," he said uncertainly. "I was just going to tweak it harder, see what the limits were. . . . I couldn't have known it would do *that*!" Ranjit pushed his lips in and out a few times, calculating, as though playing for time or pushing some bad thought away from him. "Shouldn't the lag have been nearer seventeen minutes, sort of eight and a half each way?"

"What can I say? I could talk about quantum non-locality, but I'd only be gibbering. I'll have to think it through. The first guess is that this thing doesn't play by the Einstein rules."

Ranjit filled and raised a coffee cup. "So here's to the Nobel?" The tone of voice dismayed her. It conveyed that enormity was already receding into a game, a silly hypothesis they'd entertained for a silly moment, a physicists' in-joke like that hoary "proof" that heaven is hotter then hell. Easy with a little Bible-juggling, she remembered. According to Revelations, hell contains an eternal lake of brimstone which must simmer below 444.6° Centigrade, the boiling point of sulphur. According to one reading of Isaiah, the light of heaven is that of the sun multiplied fiftyfold, leading by simple radiation physics to a local temperature of 525°C. Again . . . *Iesu Grist.*

Ceri stared out of the window, thinking of a world full of eager Sammies who would be itching to take her small experiment one step further. How could anyone ever predict what might come boiling out of an innocuous-seeming theoretical bottle? There were wisps of smoke beyond the campus buildings now—flash fires, perhaps, or cars that had veered too abruptly in the sudden dazzle—and no doubt people out there with damaged retinas from looking the wrong way when things changed. For some reason she found herself picturing a small bird with bloody feathers, eyes darkened by too much light, on a long slow fall into the sun.

State of Nature

NANCY KRESS

Nancy Kress is certainly one of the major SF writers of the decade, well known for her deeply complex medical SF stories, and for her biological and evolutionary extrapolations in such classics as "Beggars in Spain," *Beggars and Choosers*, *Beggars Ride*, and the stories in *Beaker's Dozen* (1998). In recent years, she has also written two science thrillers, *Oaths and Miracles* (1996) and *Stinger* (1998). She is the monthly fiction columnist for *Writer's Digest*. Her stories are rich in texture and in the details of the inner life of character, and like only a few others, such as Bruce Sterling and James Patrick Kelly, she manages often to satisfy both the readers of hard SF and the self-styled humanists. She is in fact one of the few writers to incorporate much of the aesthetic of modernist fiction into SF. This story is from *Bending the Landscape: Science Fiction*, one of the best and most ambitious original anthologies of the year (and a companion volume to *Bending the Landscape: Fantasy*, 1997), which contained a number of excellent SF stories on the theme of encounters with a gay or lesbian other in an SF landscape. This piece is Nancy Kress at her most passionately polemical, short, sharp, and socially committed.

Liz had been told that there were only two ways to reach Quinn Tower: the underground train or two days' hard hike through the mountains. She chose the train.

She boarded in Denver, forty-six miles away, after a security check that was unbelievable. Finger prints, retina scan—as far as she knew, Liz didn't even have either of these on police file, which may have been what security was trying to determine—vidphone check with Jenny. Liz supposed she was lucky they hadn't done a DNA match. Probably omitted only because it took two days. Her backpack was searched, X-rayed, computer-sniffed.

"Don't you want to cut my hair and tattoo my arm?" Liz said to the stiff-jawed guard, who didn't even deign to glance at her. QUINN SECURITY said the patch on the guard's uniform, and Liz saw that it was more than identification. A flag, maybe. *I pledge allegiance . . .*

She was not in a good mood when she was finally allowed to board the train. Sleek, comfortable, fast—she would beat the Tower in less than fifteen minutes, incredible even for maglev—the train did nothing to calm her. Wrong. It was all wrong. Wrong for Jenny, wrong for all of them.

Still, when the train briefly emerged above ground just inside the electrofenced edge of Quinn's land, Liz caught her breath. The Rocky Mountains, thrusting imperiously into the clouds, white-crowned but lush green below. A lake, glass-clear, bluer even than the sky. All of it untouched, pristine, a forty-nine-square-mile state of nature as pure as the day God created it.

Or Stephen Quinn recreated it.

And from the middle of this primitive and organic Eden, fifty stories high but still dwarfed by the surrounding mountains, rose Quinn Tower, faced with mirrors that reflected the sky. Neither primitive nor organic, and not pretending to be. But shimmeringly beautiful.

Wrong. *Wrong.*

The train ran above ground only long enough for passengers to appreciate the view. But Liz glimpsed something else before she was plunged back underground: a black bear with two cubs, startled by the sudden appearance of a hurtling metal monster from beneath the earth. The cubs scurried away, roly-poly unsteady fluff. The mother snarled protectively over her retreating shoulder at the already-disappearing train. Liz looked away.

The maglev stayed under ground until the subterranean station directly under Quinn Tower. Well, of course, that was the point, wasn't it? Keep all signs of human occupation confined to the Tower itself. Jenny had sent her pictures. No parking lots, dumpsters, roads, industrial plants, shopping malls, storage sheds, tennis courts, redwood decks. Not so much as a picnic bench. Pine and aspen forest pushed right up to the Tower walls, thick with shade-loving wildflowers, alive with small rustling animals. Everything moved in and out of the Tower by buried maglev.

Liz got off the train and followed the crowd to a bank of glass-fronted elevators. Slowly she rose past the shopping level, the restaurant level, the pool and exercise floor, the lounges and meeting rooms. Then more quickly to the thirty-seventh floor.

Jenny opened the door to the apartment before Liz even rang. Probably the building had tracked her movements. "Lizzie! You look wonderful!"

"Fast train. No time to get travel-stained," Liz said.

But it was Jenny who looked wonderful. Her hair was redder, and longer. She wore a jumpsuit the same bright blue as her eyes. Judging from the fine lines on her beautiful face, she hadn't had any rejuvenation injections, but her skin nonetheless glowed with health. Liz remembered how ravaged Jenny had looked the last time Liz had seen her, on the first anniversary of the funeral, when Jenny had told her about the move to Quinn. About Sarah. Liz squashed the memory and made herself smile.

Jenny said, "Would you like a drink?"

"Please. Vodka, with—"

"I know," Jenny said. There was an awkward pause. They didn't look at each other.

Liz looked instead at the apartment. A huge glass wall with spectacular view of mountains and meadows. Pale rugs and furniture, soft-rounded—Jenny's choice, Liz would bet anything on it—combined tastefully with books and plants and arresting sculpture from around the world. And on the coffee table, a battered carved wooden decoy duck. Sarah, Liz remembered, had come originally from Boston.

"Nice place," Liz said, and hoped her voice didn't sound snide.

"Yes," Jenny said. "Aren't the mountains something? I hike almost every day."

"If everybody hikes every day, doesn't that mess up nature, along with the whole point of this place?"

"Oh, no," Jenny said brightly. "No one who lives here would be anything less than scrupulously careful about the mountains."

"Or they just don't live here anymore, right?"

Jenny handed her a vodka with tonic and lime. "That's right."

"A superconsiderate group of people, as carefully protected as the environment," Liz said, and they were into it already, two minutes after she'd arrived. Her fault. No, damn it, not *fault*—this was what she'd come for, after all. Why delay?

Jenny drained her drink, whatever it was. "Liz, I'm not going to argue with you."

"Fine. I'll just argue with you, then. It's wrong, Jenny."

"It's not wrong for me."

"Do you know who I came up with in the elevator? Two black executive types, one male and one female, who probably work in Denver but wouldn't dream of living among poor blacks who might ask them for help or time or protection. A Latino woman in a five-thousand-dollar Jil Sanders coat who looked terrified until she could scurry into her own apartment and lock it behind her. Two men, holding hands and arguing about what to watch on TV tonight. And three teenagers who looked like they own the world and all the peons in it. And come to think of it, they probably do. Arrogant fifteen-year-old snots who never ever feel like part of the vast human race out there struggling and working and starving and trying desperately to stay alive. Insulated, the whole lot of you. An untouchable elite."

Jenny poured herself another drink. Liz saw that it was only cola. "All right, Liz, let's have this out. Do you know who you really saw out there?"

"I saw—"

"You saw Darryl Johnson, who works for Mitsubishi California and commutes home every day, exhausted, to his family. You saw Naomi Foster, who has four-year-old twins she doesn't want perforated in a drive-by shooting. You saw Mrs. Fernandez, who's agoraphobic, poor lady, and havened here by—"

"'Havened'? That's a verb now?"

"—*by her* children, because it's the only place she feels safe. You saw Walter Follett and Billy Tarver, the sweetest and most faithful couple you'd ever want to meet. You saw young Molly Burdick, who's a Merit Scholarship winner, and a few of her friends. You saw real people, Liz, living real lives. Not stereotypes of some spoiled superior upper caste. Just real people who choose to live in a beautiful place where they can walk around safely, and who are lucky enough to have a little money to afford it."

"'A little money,'" Liz said. "Jesus, Jenny, what's the rent here now? You're lucky the woman you fell in love with while we were still together just happened to be so rich."

Jenny just looked at her. After a minute Liz said, "I'm sorry. I'm doing this all wrong, aren't I?"

"Yes," Jenny said, "You're doing this all wrong."

Liz took a deep breath. It hadn't always been like this. Once she and Jenny could have said anything to each other. Anything. Talking, laughing, making dinner, making love . . .

Jenny had put down her drink. She crossed to the spectacular view, her back to Liz. Liz tensed. When Jenny spoke over her shoulder like this, it always meant she was going to drop a bombshell. "I want to tell you something, Liz. I was going to write you, but then you called and said you were coming by anyway. . . . Sarah and I are going to adopt. We want to bring up our child in a safe place. Where she can't be . . ." She couldn't finish.

Liz said unsteadily, "Where she can't be bashed over the head with a molecular-composite garden hoe because she's the kid of a couple of lesbos."

"Yes," Jenny said.

A tight band circled Liz's chest. A molecular-composite band, stronger and more durable than steel. She had first felt that band at Laurie's funeral. Standing in the littered city cemetery in cruel sunshine, watching Laurie's casket lowered into the ground, the TV cameras whirring like so many meat grinders pulverizing her insides . . . and watching Jenny. A black veil over her face, dry-eyed, already lost to Liz although it would be a year before Liz realized it. Lost to an obsession with security, in a collapsing city that could no longer offer it. To anyone.

Laurie . . .

But that was over, that sweet time of motherhood and love. Few couples, of any type, survived as a couple after the death of a child. Five percent, Liz had once read. Only five percent made it. She and Jenny hadn't. But this was now, not then, and Liz gathered herself for one last try.

"Jenny, listen to me."

"I'm listening," Jenny said. She sat down on one of the pale chairs, hair and eyes and jumpsuit vivid. But her face was as colorless as the fabric.

"It's not about Laurie any more," Liz said. "It's not even about you and me. It's about Quinn Tower, and what it represents. For gays, for blacks, for Koreans, for every group whose most successful members flee here, or someplace like here, to avoid being reminded of how the rest of their people have to live. Jenny, the corporate-owned closed communities are *wrong*. We need you outside. We need you for the marches and the solidarity and the rescue work—did you know that Bellington, Texas, has mounted a vigilante campaign to eject anyone voted 'undesirable' from their town? This is openly, without any pretense of minority rights! Last week they stripped and stoned a Muslim family, the week before a gay couple, a few days before that—"

"I read the papers," Jenny said.

"Then do something about what you read! How can you—how can any member of any group being made scapegoat for what's happening out there—just sit here in your pretty safe castle and—"

Jenny sprang out of her chair. "I don't want my next child living in that world! Dying like Laurie! I'm doing this for my daughter!"

"It's for Laurie that you should be joining us!" Liz shouted back. She wanted to hit Jenny, to pound sense into that beautiful skull . . . Liz could feel herself crying.

"Hush," Jenny said gently. "Oh, Lizzie, hush . . ." and a cool hand on Liz's forehead. If only Jenny would put her arms around her, hold Liz as she used to, once, not that long ago . . .

Jenny didn't. But she let her cool, long-fingered hand linger on Liz's shoulder, and Liz tilted her head and rubbed her cheek against the back of Jenny's hand.

Jenny said quietly, "I don't love Sarah the way I loved you."

"I know," Liz said.

"But I want to be a mother again, Liz. I want to love and raise and protect a child, more than I want to take the risks to make the whole world safer for everybody's children. Is that so wrong?"

"Yes."

And after that, there was nothing much left to say. Liz got to her feet. She felt heavy, as if gravity were greater in Quinn Tower than in Los Angeles. She walked toward the apartment door, with a last involuntary glance out the window at the meadow below, full of columbine and larkspur. She didn't see the bear.

"Jenny?"

"Yes?"

"Be well," Liz said, and she didn't know herself if it was supposed to be a sarcasm or a benediction.

"We will," Jenny said, "here."

In the train, Liz leaned back and closed her eyes. Thirteen minutes to downtown Denver, full of druggies and muggers and angry cops and angrier men and women who saw a world of evaporating jobs and disappearing government and hungry kids, and wanted someone to blame. Anyone. Anyone different. And then another fifty minutes by air to Los Angeles, which was more of the same but with the added exotica of armed "citizens' police" patrolling the streets, looking for threats to an American way of life that barely existed anymore anyway.

But Margo would be waiting. Feisty Margo, who didn't take shit off anybody, but who still believed they could stem the shit at its political asshole. And Barbara, running the Snake Sisters Rescue Operation with compassion and incredible resourcefulness. And Viv and Taneeka and Carol . . .

None of them was Jenny.

Well, screw that. Jenny had made her choice. And Liz had made hers. Or the new realities of the new century had made it for her. That's the way it was.

After her plane landed at LAX, Liz retrieved her gun from an airport locker. She scanned the peeling and hole-strewn concourse, home to a lot of people with no place else to go, and automatically picked out the non-dangerous punks trying to look dangerous, and the dangerous ones trying to look safe. The frightened business people who still had a job and were trying to make it home with their briefcases intact. The three Brothers of Kali walking together, who didn't look like they'd need any help from their own, and the two young Asian women who might. When she had determined her route, Liz started down the concourse. There was a rescue meeting tonight, followed by a survival-strategy session, and she was already going to be late.

Maneki Neko

BRUCE STERLING

Bruce Sterling published his first two SF novels in the 1970s, was the polemicist and theoretician of The Movement (cyberpunk) in the 1980s, was on the cover of *Wired*, is a world-famous science/cultural journalist, remains perhaps the world's greatest Brian Aldiss fan, and is still fighting for the soul of science fiction by writing perhaps the most challenging and original SF stories and novels of the late 1990s. Not for Sterling the fringes—he aims for the center of the SF field, for science and technology and a literature of ideas. He also posted a new manifesto regarding the fate of the earth and humanity, about how we should make environmentalism fashionable, on the Web in 1998, a trumpet call to action. He is always politically involved. His novel this past year, *Distraction*, may be the best SF novel of the year. Furthermore it shares some of the ideas original to this story. What if the mysterious artificial intelligence of the Internet did good, made daily life a bit smoother and less stressful? This story first appeared in English in *F&SF*, after an initial appearance in Japanese in *Hayakawa's SF Magazine*.

"I can't go on," his brother said.

Tsuyoshi Shimizu looked thoughtfully into the screen of his pasokon. His older brother's face was shiny with sweat from a late-night drinking bout. "It's only a career," said Tsuyoshi, sitting up on his futon and adjusting his pajamas. "You worry too much."

"All that overtime!" his brother whined. He was making the call from a bar somewhere in Shibuya. In the background, a middle-aged office lady was singing karaoke, badly. "And the examination hells. The manager training programs. The proficiency tests. I never have time to live!"

Tsuyoshi grunted sympathetically. He didn't like these late-night videophone calls, but he felt obliged to listen. His big brother had always been a decent sort, before he had gone through the elite courses at Waseda University, joined a big corporation, and gotten professionally ambitious.

"My back hurts," his brother groused. "I have an ulcer. My hair is going gray. And I know they'll fire me. No matter how loyal you are to the big companies, they have no loyalty to their employees anymore. It's no wonder that I drink."

"You should get married," Tsuyoshi offered.

"I can't find the right girl. Women never understand me." He shuddered. "Tsuyoshi, I'm truly desperate. The market pressures are crushing me. I can't breathe. My life has got to change. I'm thinking of taking the vows. I'm serious! I want to renounce this whole modern world."

Tsuyoshi was alarmed. "You're very drunk, right?"

His brother leaned closer to the screen. "Life in a monastery sounds truly good to me. It's so quiet there. You recite the sutras. You consider your existence. There are rules to follow, and rewards that make sense. It's just the way that Japanese business used to be, back in the good old days."

Tsuyoshi grunted skeptically.

"Last week I went out to a special place in the mountains . . . Mount Aso," his brother confided. "The monks there, they know about people in trouble, people who are burned out by modern life. The monks protect you from the world. No computers, no phones, no faxes, no e-mail, no overtime, no commuting, nothing at all. It's beautiful, and it's peaceful, and nothing ever happens there. Really, it's like paradise."

"Listen, older brother," Tsuyoshi said, "you're not a religious man by nature. You're a section chief for a big import-export company."

"Well . . . maybe religion won't work for me. I did think of running away to America. Nothing much ever happens there, either."

Tsuyoshi smiled. "That sounds much better! America is a good vacation spot. A long vacation is just what you need! Besides, the Americans are real friendly since they gave up their handguns."

"But I can't go through with it," his brother wailed. "I just don't dare. I can't just wander away from everything that I know, and trust to the kindness of strangers."

"That always works for me," Tsuyoshi said. "Maybe you should try it."

Tsuyoshi's wife stirred uneasily on the futon. Tsuyoshi lowered his voice. "Sorry, but I have to hang up now. Call me before you do anything rash."

"Don't tell Dad," Tsuyoshi's brother said. "He worries so."

"I won't tell Dad." Tsuyoshi cut the connection and the screen went dark.

Tsuyoshi's wife rolled over, heavily. She was seven months pregnant. She stared at the ceiling, puffing for breath. "Was that another call from your brother?" she said.

"Yeah. The company just gave him another promotion. More responsibilities. He's celebrating."

"That sounds nice," his wife said tactfully.

Next morning, Tsuyoshi slept late. He was self-employed, so he kept his own hours. Tsuyoshi was a video format upgrader by trade. He transferred old videos from obsolete formats into the new high-grade storage media. Doing this properly took a craftsman's eye. Word of Tsuyoshi's skills had gotten out on the network, so he had as much work as he could handle.

At ten A.M., the mailman arrived. Tsuyoshi abandoned his breakfast of raw egg and miso soup, and signed for a shipment of flaking, twentieth-century analog television tapes. The mail also brought a fresh overnight shipment of strawberries, and a homemade jar of pickles.

"Pickles!" his wife enthused. "People are so nice to you when you're pregnant."

"Any idea who sent us that?"

"Just someone on the network."

"Great."

Tsuyoshi booted his mediator, cleaned his superconducting heads and examined the old tapes. Home videos from the 1980s. Someone's grandmother as a child, presumably. There had been a lot of flaking and loss of polarity in the old recording medium.

Tsuyoshi got to work with his desktop fractal detail generator, the image stabilizer, and the interlace algorithms. When he was done, Tsuyoshi's new digital copies would look much sharper, cleaner, and better composed than the original primitive videotape.

Tsuyoshi enjoyed his work. Quite often he came across bits and pieces of videotape that were of archival interest. He would pass the images on to the net. The really big network databases, with their armies of search engines, indexers, and catalogues, had some very arcane interests. The net machines would never pay for data, because the global information networks were noncommercial. But the net machines were very polite, and had excellent net etiquette. They returned a favor for a favor, and since they were machines with excellent, enormous memories, they never forgot a good deed.

Tsuyoshi and his wife had a lunch of ramen with naruto, and she left to go shopping. A shipment arrived by overseas package service. Cute baby clothes from Darwin, Australia. They were in his wife's favorite color, sunshine yellow.

Tsuyoshi finished transferring the first tape to a new crystal disk. Time for a break. He left his apartment, took the elevator and went out to the corner coffeeshop. He ordered a double iced mocha cappuccino and paid with a chargecard.

His pokkecon rang. Tsuyoshi took it from his belt and answered it. "Get one to go," the machine told him.

"Okay," said Tsuyoshi, and hung up. He bought a second coffee, put a lid on it and left the shop.

A man in a business suit was sitting on a park bench near the entrance of Tsuyoshi's building. The man's suit was good, but it looked as if he'd slept in it. He was holding his head in his hands and rocking gently back and forth. He was unshaven and his eyes were red-rimmed.

The pokkecon rang again. "The coffee's for him?" Tsuyoshi said.

"Yes," said the pokkecon. "He needs it."

Tsuyoshi walked up to the lost businessman. The man looked up, flinching warily, as if he were about to be kicked. "What is it?" he said.

"Here," Tsuyoshi said, handing him the cup. "Double iced mocha cappuccino."

The man opened the cup, and smelled it. He looked up in disbelief. "This is my favorite kind of coffee. . . . Who are you?"

Tsuyoshi lifted his arm and offered a hand signal, his fingers clenched like a cat's paw. The man showed no recognition of the gesture. Tsuyoshi shrugged, and smiled. "It doesn't matter. Sometimes a man really needs a coffee. Now you have a coffee. That's all."

"Well . . ." The man cautiously sipped his cup, and suddenly smiled. "It's really great. Thanks!"

"You're welcome." Tsuyoshi went home.

His wife arrived from shopping. She had bought new shoes. The pregnancy was making her feet swell. She sat carefully on the couch and sighed.

"Orthopedic shoes are expensive," she said, looking at the yellow pumps. "I hope you don't think they look ugly."

"On you, they look really cute," Tsuyoshi said wisely. He had first met his wife at a video store. She had just used her credit card to buy a disk of primitive black-and-white American anime of the 1950s. The pokkecon had urged him to go up and speak to her on the subject of Felix the Cat. Felix was an early television cartoon star and one of Tsuyoshi's personal favorites.

Tsuyoshi would have been too shy to approach an attractive woman on his own, but no one was a stranger to the net. This fact gave him the confidence to speak to her. Tsuyoshi had soon discovered that the girl was delighted to discuss her deep fondness for cute, antique, animated cats. They'd had lunch together. They'd had a date the next week. They had spent Christmas Eve together in a love hotel. They had a lot in common.

She had come into his life through a little act of grace, a little gift from Felix the Cat's magic bag of tricks. Tsuyoshi had never gotten over feeling grateful for this. Now that he was married and becoming a father, Tsuyoshi Shimizu could feel himself becoming solidly fixed in life. He had a man's role to play now. He knew who he was, and he knew where he stood. Life was good to him.

"You need a haircut, dear," his wife told him.

"Sure."

His wife pulled a gift box out of her shopping bag. "Can you go to the Hotel Daruma, and get your hair cut, and deliver this box for me?"

"What is it?" Tsuyoshi said.

Tsuyoshi's wife opened the little wooden gift box. A maneki neko was nestled inside white foam padding. The smiling ceramic cat held one paw upraised, beckoning for good fortune.

"Don't you have enough of those yet?" he said. "You even have maneki neko underwear."

"It's not for my collection. It's a gift for someone at the Hotel Daruma."

"Oh."

"Some foreign woman gave me this box at the shoestore. She looked American. She couldn't speak Japanese. She had really nice shoes, though. . . ."

"If the network gave you that little cat, then you're the one who should take care of that obligation, dear."

"But dear," she sighed, "my feet hurt so much, and you could do with a haircut anyway, and I have to cook supper, and besides, it's not really a nice maneki neko, it's just cheap tourist souvenir junk. Can't you do it?"

"Oh, all right," Tsuyoshi told her. "Just forward your pokkecon prompts onto my machine, and I'll see what I can do for us."

She smiled. "I knew you would do it. You're really so good to me."

Tsuyoshi left with the little box. He wasn't unhappy to do the errand, as it wasn't always easy to manage his pregnant wife's volatile moods in their small six-tatami apartment. The local neighborhood was good, but he was hoping to find bigger accommodations before the child was born. Maybe a place with a little studio, where he could expand the scope of his work. It was very hard to find decent housing in Tokyo, but word was out on the net. Friends he didn't even know were working every day to help him. If he kept up with the net's obligations, he had every confidence that some day something nice would turn up.

Tsuyoshi went into the local pachinko parlor, where he won half a liter of beer and a train chargecard. He drank the beer, took the new train card and wedged himself into the train. He got out at the Ebisu station, and turned on his pokkecon Tokyo street map to guide his steps. He walked past places called Chocolate Soup, and Freshness Physique, and The Aladdin Mai-Tai Pan-ico Trattoria.

He entered the Hotel Daruma and went to the hotel barber shop, which was called the Daruma Planet Look. "May I help you?" said the receptionist.

"I'm thinking, a shave and a trim," Tsuyoshi said.

"Do you have an appointment with us?"

"Sorry, no." Tsuyoshi offered a hand gesture.

The woman gestured back, a jerky series of cryptic finger movements. Tsuyoshi didn't recognize any of the gestures. She wasn't from his part of the network.

"Oh well, never mind," the receptionist said kindly. "I'll get Nahoko to look after you."

Nahoko was carefully shaving the fine hair from Tsuyoshi's forehead when the pokkecon rang. Tsuyoshi answered it.

"Go to the ladies' room on the fourth floor," the pokkecon told him.

"Sorry, I can't do that. This is Tsuyoshi Shimizu, not Ai Shimizu. Besides, I'm having my hair cut right now."

"Oh, I see," said the machine. "Recalibrating." It hung up.

Nahoko finished his hair. She had done a good job. He looked much better. A man who worked at home had to take special trouble to keep up appearances. The pokkecon rang again.

"Yes?" said Tsuyoshi.

"Buy bay rum aftershave. Take it outside."

"Right." He hung up. "Nahoko, do you have bay rum?"

"Odd you should ask that," said Nahoko. "Hardly anyone asks for bay rum anymore, but our shop happens to keep it in stock."

Tsuyoshi bought the aftershave, then stepped outside the barbershop. Nothing happened, so he bought a manga comic and waited. Finally a hairy, blond stranger in shorts, a tropical shirt, and sandals approached him. The foreigner was carrying a camera bag and an old-fashioned pokkecon. He looked about sixty years old, and he was very tall.

The man spoke to his pokkecon in English. "Excuse me," said the pokkecon, translating the man's speech into Japanese. "Do you have a bottle of bay rum aftershave?"

"Yes I do." Tsuyoshi handed the bottle over. "Here."

"Thank goodness!" said the man, his words relayed through his machine. "I've asked everyone else in the lobby. Sorry I was late."

"No problem," said Tsuyoshi. "That's a nice pokkecon you have there."

"Well," the man said, "I know it's old and out of style. But I plan to buy a new pokkecon here in Tokyo.

I'm told that they sell pokkecons by the basketful in Aki-habara electronics market."

"That's right. What kind of translator program are you running? Your translator talks like someone from Osaka."

"Does it sound funny?" the tourist asked anxiously.

"Well, I don't want to complain, but . . ." Tsuyoshi smiled. "Here, let's trade meishi. I can give you a copy of a brand-new freeware translator."

"That would be wonderful." They pressed buttons and squirted copies of their business cards across the network link.

Tsuyoshi examined his copy of the man's electronic card and saw that his name was Zimmerman. Mr. Zimmerman was from New Zealand. Tsuyoshi activated a transfer program. His modern pokkecon began transferring a new translator onto Zimmerman's machine.

A large American man in a padded suit entered the lobby of the Daruma. The man wore sunglasses, and was sweating visibly in the summer heat. The American looked huge, as if he lifted a lot of weights. Then a Japanese woman followed him. The woman was sharply dressed, with a dark blue dress suit, hat, sunglasses, and an attaché case. She had a haunted look.

Her escort turned and carefully watched the bell-hops, who were bringing in a series of bags. The woman walked crisply to the reception desk and began making anxious demands of the clerk.

"I'm a great believer in machine translation," Tsuyoshi said to the tall man from New Zealand. "I really believe that computers help human beings to relate in a much more human way."

"I couldn't agree with you more," said Mr. Zimmerman, through his machine. "I can remember the first time I came to your country, many years ago. I had no portable translator. In fact, I had nothing but a printed phrasebook. I happened to go into a bar, and . . ."

Zimmerman stopped and gazed alertly at his pokkecon. "Oh dear, I'm getting a screen prompt. I have to go up to my room right away."

"Then I'll come along with you till this software transfer is done," Tsuyoshi said.

"That's very kind of you." They got into the elevator together. Zimmerman punched for the fourth floor. "Anyway, as I was saying, I went into this bar in Roppongi late at night, because I was jetlagged and hoping for something to eat . . ."

"Yes?"

"And this woman . . . well, let's just say this woman was hanging out in a foreigner's bar in Roppongi late at night, and she wasn't wearing a whole lot of clothes, and she didn't look like she was any better than she ought to be. . . ."

"Yes, I think I understand you."

"Anyway, this menu they gave me was full of kanji, or katakana, or romanji, or whatever they call those, so I had my phrasebook out, and I was trying very hard to puzzle out these pesky ideograms. . . ." The elevator opened and they stepped into the carpeted hall of the hotel's fourth floor. "So I opened the menu and I pointed to an entree, and I told this girl . . ." Zimmerman stopped suddenly, and stared at his screen. "Oh dear, something's happening. Just a moment."

Zimmerman carefully studied the instructions on his pokkecon. Then he pulled the bottle of bay rum from the baggy pocket of his shorts, and unscrewed the cap. He stood on tiptoe, stretching to his full height, and carefully poured the contents of the bottle through the iron louvers of a ventilation grate, set high in the top of the wall.

▲   ▲   ▲

Zimmerman screwed the cap back on neatly, and slipped the empty bottle back in his pocket. Then he examined his pokkecon again. He frowned, and shook it. The screen had frozen. Apparently Tsuyoshi's new translation program had overloaded Zimmerman's old-fashioned operating system. His pokkecon had crashed.

Zimmerman spoke a few defeated sentences in English. Then he smiled, and spread his hands apologetically. He bowed, and went into his room, and shut the door.

The Japanese woman and her burly American escort entered the hall. The man gave Tsuyoshi a hard stare. The woman opened the door with a passcard. Her hands were shaking.

Tsuyoshi's pokkecon rang. "Leave the hall," it told him. "Go downstairs. Get into the elevator with the bellboy."

Tsuyoshi followed instructions.

The bellboy was just entering the elevator with a cart full of the woman's baggage. Tsuyoshi got into the elevator, stepping carefully behind the wheeled metal cart. "What floor, sir?" said the bellboy.

"Eight," Tsuyoshi said, ad-libbing. The bellboy turned and pushed the buttons. He faced forward attentively, his gloved hands folded.

The pokkecon flashed a silent line of text to the screen. "Put the gift box inside her flight bag," it read.

Tsuyoshi located the zippered blue bag at the back of the cart. It was a matter of instants to zip it open, put in the box with the maneki neko, and zip the bag shut again. The bellboy noticed nothing. He left, tugging his cart.

Tsuyoshi got out on the eighth floor, feeling slightly foolish. He wandered down the hall, found a quiet nook by an ice machine and called his wife. "What's going on?" he said.

"Oh, nothing." She smiled. "Your haircut looks nice! Show me the back of your head."

Tsuyoshi held the pokkecon screen behind the nape of his neck.

"They do good work," his wife said with satisfaction. "I hope it didn't cost too much. Are you coming home now?"

"Things are getting a little odd here at the hotel," Tsuyoshi told her. "I may be some time."

His wife frowned. "Well, don't miss supper. We're having bonito."

Tsuyoshi took the elevator back down. It stopped at the fourth floor. The woman's American companion stepped onto the elevator. His nose was running and his eyes were streaming with tears.

"Are you all right?" Tsuyoshi said.

"I don't understand Japanese," the man growled. The elevator doors shut.

The man's cellular phone crackled into life. It emitted a scream of anguish and a burst of agitated female English. The man swore and slammed his hairy fist against the elevator's emergency button. The elevator stopped with a lurch. An alarm bell began ringing.

The man pried the doors open with his large hairy fingers and clambered out into the fourth floor. He then ran headlong down the hall.

The elevator began buzzing in protest, its doors shuddering as if broken. Tsuyoshi climbed hastily from the damaged elevator, and stood there in the hallway. He hesitated a moment. Then he produced his pokkecon and loaded his Japanese-to-English translator. He walked cautiously after the American man.

The door to their suite was open. Tsuyoshi spoke aloud into his pokkecon. "Hello?" he said experimentally. "May I be of help?"

The woman was sitting on the bed. She had just discovered the maneki neko box in her flight bag. She was staring at the little cat in horror.

"Who are you?" she said, in bad Japanese.

Tsuyoshi realized suddenly that she was a Japanese American. Tsuyoshi had met a few Japanese Americans before. They always troubled him. They looked fairly normal from the outside, but their behavior was always bizarre. "I'm just a passing friend," he said. "Something I can do?"

"Grab him, Mitch!" said the woman in English. The American man rushed into the hall and grabbed Tsuyoshi by the arm. His hands were like steel bands.

Tsuyoshi pressed the distress button on his pokke-con.

"Take that computer away from him," the woman ordered in English. Mitch quickly took Tsuyoshi's pokkecon away, and threw it on the bed. He deftly patted Tsuyoshi's clothing, searching for weapons. Then he shoved Tsuyoshi into a chair.

The woman switched back to Japanese. "Sit right there, you. Don't you dare move." She began examining the contents of Tsuyoshi's wallet.

"I beg your pardon?" Tsuyoshi said. His pokkecon was lying on the bed. Lines of red text scrolled up its little screen as it silently issued a series of emergency net alerts.

The woman spoke to her companion in English. Tsuyoshi's pokkecon was still translating faithfully. "Mitch, go call the local police."

Mitch sneezed uncontrollably. Tsuyoshi noticed that the room smelled strongly of bay rum. "I can't talk to the local cops. I can't speak Japanese." Mitch sneezed again.

"Okay, then I'll call the cops. You handcuff this guy. Then go down to the infirmary and get yourself some antihistamines, for Christ's sake."

Mitch pulled a length of plastic whipcord cuff from his coat pocket, and attached Tsuyoshi's right wrist to the head of the bed. He mopped his streaming eyes with a tissue. "I'd better stay with you. If there's a cat in your luggage, then the criminal network already knows we're in Japan. You're in danger."

"Mitch, you may be my bodyguard, but you're breaking out in hives."

"This just isn't supposed to happen," Mitch complained, scratching his neck. "My allergies never interfered with my job before."

"Just leave me here and lock the door," the woman told him. "I'll put a chair against the knob. I'll be all right. You need to look after yourself."

Mitch left the room.

The woman barricaded the door with a chair. Then she called the front desk on the hotel's bedside pasokon. "This is Louise Hashimoto in room 434. I have a gangster in my room. He's an information criminal. Would you call the Tokyo police, please? Tell them to send the organized crime unit. Yes, that's right. Do it. And you should put your hotel security people on full alert. There may be big trouble here. You'd better hurry." She hung up.

Tsuyoshi stared at her in astonishment. "Why are you doing this? What's all this about?"

"So you call yourself Tsuyoshi Shimizu," said the woman, examining his credit cards. She sat on the foot of the bed and stared at him. "You're yakuza of some kind, right?"

"I think you've made a big mistake," Tsuyoshi said.

Louise scowled. "Look, Mr. Shimizu, you're not dealing with some Yankee tourist here. My name is Louise Hashimoto and I'm an assistant federal prosecutor from Providence, Rhode Island, USA." She showed him a magnetic ID card with a gold official seal.

"It's nice to meet someone from the American government," said Tsuyoshi, bowing a bit in his chair. "I'd shake your hand, but it's tied to the bed."

"You can stop with the innocent act right now. I spotted you out in the hall earlier, and in the lobby, too, casing the hotel. How did you know my bodyguard is violently allergic to bay rum? You must have read his medical records."

"Who, me? Never!"

"Ever since I discovered you network people, it's been one big pattern," said Louise. "It's the biggest criminal conspiracy I ever saw. I busted this software pirate in Providence. He had a massive network server and a whole bunch of AI freeware search engines. We took him in custody, we bagged all his search engines, and catalogs, and indexers. . . . Later that very same day, these *cats* start showing up."

"Cats?"

Louise lifted the maneki neko, handling it as if it were a live eel. "These little Japanese voodoo cats. Maneki neko, right? They started showing up everywhere I went. There's a china cat in my handbag. There's three china cats at the office. Suddenly they're on display in the windows of every antique store in Providence. My car radio starts making meowing noises at me."

"You *broke* part of the network?" Tsuyoshi said, scandalized. "You took someone's machines away? That's terrible! How could you do such an inhuman thing?"

"You've got a real nerve complaining about that. What about *my* machinery?" Louise held up her fat, eerie-looking American pokkecon. "As soon as I stepped off the airplane at Narita, my PDA was attacked. Thousands and thousands of e-mail messages. All of them pictures of cats. A denial-of-service attack! I can't even communicate with the home office! My PDA's useless!"

"What's a PDA?"

"It's a PDA, my Personal Digital Assistant! Manu-factured in Silicon Valley!"

"Well, with a goofy name like that, no wonder our pokkecons won't talk to it."

Louise frowned grimly. "That's right, wise guy. Make jokes about it. You're involved in a malicious software attack on a legal officer of the United States Government. You'll see." She paused, looking him over. "You know, Shimizu, you don't look much like the Italian mafia gangsters I have to deal with, back in Providence."

"I'm not a gangster at all. I never do anyone any harm."

"Oh no?" Louise glowered at him. "Listen, pal, I know a lot more about your set-up, and your kind of people, than you think I do. I've been studying your out-fit for a long time now. We computer cops have names for your kind of people. Digital panarchies. Segmented, polycephalous, integrated influence networks. What about all these *free goods and services* you're getting all this time?"

She pointed a finger at him. "Ha! Do you ever pay *taxes* on those? Do you ever *declare* that income and those benefits? All the free shipments from other coun-tries! The little homemade cookies, and the free pens and pencils and bumper stickers, and the used bicycles, and the helpful news about fire sales . . . You're a tax evader! You're living through kickbacks! And bribes! And influence peddling! And all kinds of corrupt off-the-books transactions!"

Tsuyoshi blinked. "Look, I don't know anything about all that. I'm just living my life."

"Well, your network gift economy is undermining the lawful, government approved, regulated economy!"

"Well," Tsuyoshi said gently, "maybe my economy is better than your economy."

"Says who?" she scoffed. "Why would anyone think that?"

"It's better because we're *happier* than you are. What's wrong with acts of kindness? Everyone likes gifts. Midsummer gifts. New Years Day gifts. Year-end presents. Wedding presents. Everybody likes those."

"Not the way you Japanese like them. You're totally crazy for gifts."

"What kind of society has no gifts? It's barbaric to have no regard for common human feelings."

Louise bristled. "You're saying I'm barbaric?"

"I don't mean to complain," Tsuyoshi said politely, "but you do have me tied up to your bed."

Louise crossed her arms. "You might as well stop complaining. You'll be in much worse trouble when the local police arrive."

"Then we'll probably be waiting here for quite a while," Tsuyoshi said. "The police move rather slowly, here in Japan. I'm sorry, but we don't have as much crime as you Americans, so our police are not very alert."

The pasokon rang at the side of the bed. Louise answered it. It was Tsuyoshi's wife.

"Could I speak to Tsuyoshi Shimizu please?"

"I'm over here, dear," Tsuyoshi called quickly. "She's kidnapped me! She tied me to the bed!"

"Tied to her *bed*?" His wife's eyes grew wide. "That does it! I'm calling the police!"

Louise quickly hung up the pasokon. "I haven't kidnapped you! I'm only detaining you here until the local authorities can come and arrest you."

"Arrest me for what, exactly?"

Louise thought quickly. "Well, for poisoning my bodyguard by pouring bay rum into the ventilator."

"But I never did that. Anyway, that's not illegal, is it?"

The pasokon rang again. A shining white cat

appeared on the screen. It had large, staring, unearthly eyes.

"Let him go," the cat commanded in English.

Louise shrieked and yanked the pasokon's plug from the wall.

Suddenly the lights went out. "Infrastructure attack!" Louise squawled. She rolled quickly under the bed.

The room went gloomy and quiet. The air conditioner had shut off. "I think you can come out," Tsuyoshi said at last, his voice loud in the still room. "It's just a power failure."

"No it isn't," Louise said. She crawled slowly from beneath the bed, and sat on the mattress. Somehow, the darkness had made them more intimate. "I know very well what this is. I'm under attack. I haven't had a moment's peace since I broke that network. Stuff just happens to me now. Bad stuff. Swarms of it. It's never anything you can touch, though. Nothing you can prove in a court of law."

She sighed. "I sit in chairs, and somebody's left a piece of gum there. I get free pizzas, but they're not the kind of pizzas I like. Little kids spit on my sidewalk. Old women in walkers get in front of me whenever I need to hurry."

The shower came on, all by itself. Louise shuddered, but said nothing. Slowly, the darkened, stuffy room began to fill with hot steam.

"My toilets don't flush," Louise said. "My letters get lost in the mail. When I walk by cars, their theft alarms go off. And strangers stare at me. It's always little things. Lots of little tiny things, but they never, ever stop. I'm up against something that is very very big, and very very patient. And it knows all about me. And it's got a million arms and legs. And all those arms and legs are people."

There was the noise of scuffling in the hall. Distant voices, confused shouting.

Suddenly the chair broke under the doorknob. The door burst open violently. Mitch tumbled through, the sunglasses flying from his head. Two hotel security guards were trying to grab him. Shouting incoherently in English, Mitch fell headlong to the floor, kicking and thrashing. The guards lost their hats in the struggle. One tackled Mitch's legs with both his arms, and the other whacked and jabbed him with a baton.

Puffing and grunting with effort, they hauled Mitch out of the room. The darkened room was so full of steam that the harried guards hadn't even noticed Tsuyoshi and Louise.

Louise stared at the broken door. "Why did they do that to him?"

Tsuyoshi scratched his head in embarrassment. "Probably a failure of communication."

"Poor Mitch! They took his gun away at the airport. He had all kinds of technical problems with his passport. . . . Poor guy, he's never had any luck since he met me."

There was a loud tapping at the window. Louise shrank back in fear. Finally she gathered her courage, and opened the curtains. Daylight flooded the room.

A window-washing rig had been lowered from the roof of the hotel, on cables and pulleys. There were two window-washers in crisp gray uniforms. They waved cheerfully, making little catpaw gestures.

There was a third man with them. It was Tsuyoshi's brother.

One of the washers opened the window with a utility key. Tsuyoshi's brother squirmed into the room. He stood up and carefully adjusted his coat and tie.

"This is my brother," Tsuyoshi explained.

"What are you doing here?" Louise said.

"They always bring in the relatives when there's a hostage situation," Tsuyoshi's brother said. "The police just flew me in by helicopter and landed me on the roof." He looked Louise up and down. "Miss Hashimoto, you just have time to escape."

"What?" she said.

"Look down at the streets," he told her. "See that? You hear them? Crowds are pouring in from all over the city. All kinds of people, everyone with wheels. Street noodle salesmen. Bicycle messengers. Skateboard kids. Takeout delivery guys."

Louise gazed out the window into the streets, and shrieked aloud. "Oh no! A giant swarming mob! They're surrounding me! I'm doomed!"

"You are not doomed," Tsuyoshi's brother told her intently. "Come out the window. Get onto the platform with us. You've got one chance, Louise. It's a place I know, a sacred place in the mountains. No computers there, no phones, nothing." He paused. "It's a sanctuary for people like us. And I know the way."

She gripped his suited arm. "Can I trust you?"

"Look in my eyes," he told her. "Don't you see? Yes, of course you can trust me. We have everything in common."

Louise stepped out the window. She clutched his arm, the wind whipping at her hair. The platform creaked rapidly up and out of sight.

Tsuyoshi stood up from the chair. When he stretched out, tugging at his handcuffed wrist, he was just able to reach his pokkecon with his fingertips. He drew it in, and clutched it to his chest. Then he sat down again, and waited patiently for someone to come and give him freedom.

Story Copyrights